Mafia Angel

The Mancinelli Brotherhood

Sabine Barclay

Nov 2023

Natalie,

Are you ready
to fall in love?

Happy reading,
Sabine Barclay
SB

OLIVERHEBERBOOKS

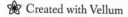 Created with Vellum

We sin as devils do. We love as angels do.

Find me writing Historical Romance as Celeste Barclay.

Happy reading,
Sabine

Subscribe to Sabine's Newsletter

Subscribe to Sabine's bimonthly newsletter to receive exclusive insider perks.

Have you read *The Syndicate Wars*? This FREE origin story novella is available to all new subscribers to Sabine's monthly newsletter. Subscribe on her website.
www.sabinebarclay.com

The Mancinelli Brotherhood

Mafia Heir

Mafia Sinner

Mafia Beauty

Mafia Angel

Mafia Redeemer

Mafia Star

Do you also enjoy steamy Historical Romance? Discover Sabine's books written as Celeste Barclay.

Chapter One

Gabriele

"What the fuck? This is some fucking bullshit."

I don't flinch when I slam my fist down on the wood conference table, even though it smarts. I'm tempted to throw the papers across the room, but my outburst is enough. Throwing them just looks like a temper tantrum. Though the idea of stomping my feet while screaming is appealing. That's not a very Mafioso thing to do.

And that's the motherfucking problem. I'm fucking *Cosa Nostra*.

"Gabriele."

I know that tone from Uncle Salvatore. It's the only warning I'll get to get my temper under control. He's right, of course. But why the fuck should that matter? He's not the one looking at prison time. At least, his whole damned future isn't on the line this time. Who the fuck is the woman? She hasn't said a fucking word since we arrived, but neither Uncle Salvatore nor Uncle Massimo are keeping anything from her. She's fucking hot as hell. Like I'm only not having a tantrum because I don't want to humiliate myself in front of the hottest woman I've ever seen. She's my kind of hot. Pretty, but doesn't realize just how pretty. She's not a Barbie doll. Her clothes are understated, but professional. My guess is high-end for women's suits. I wouldn't know. My tailor only does men's clothes.

Fuck me. Stop staring. Uncle Salvatore expects me to respond. I can't if my tongue is longing to be in her pussy.

"I'm sorry, Uncle Sal. But this is bullshit."

Salvatore Mancinelli isn't my biological uncle or even one by marriage, and for most of my life, he's wished he didn't even know me. His actual nephew, Carmine, is my best friend and has been for twenty years. We're like self-selected fraternal twins. We're both only children, so he became a member of my family as much as I became a member of his. But that friendship has tested my loyalty beyond anything I could have imagined when I was ten and moved here from Sicily. That said, as many times as I've considered strangling Carmine, there's nothing I wouldn't do for him. Which means there's nothing I wouldn't do for his family. Especially Uncle Salvatore. He's our don.

It's Uncle Salvatore's younger brother who speaks next. It's like having two fathers disappointed in you at the same time. I can't wait to call my own father. At least my parents are back in Palermo. I brace myself for whatever Uncle Massimo has to say.

"It may be bullshit. But it is what it is for now. They've released you on bail, so we move forward."

"Yeah, a five-million-dollar bail, and I've had to hand over my passports."

So much for dual citizenship.

Uncle Massimo, with his scowling perpetual optimism, keeps going.

"It could be worse. You've been through the arraignment, and we know the charges. The prosecution hasn't released this in discovery, so I shouldn't be showing you this privileged information but I am. I shouldn't even have it yet."

I'm charged with two felonies: First, detonation of a destructive device of explosives with intent or that causes death, mayhem, or great bodily injury to another, and second, extortion or criminal threats done for the benefit of a street gang.

A motherfucking street gang? Motherfucking please.

"Gabe, you might as well be screaming your thoughts. We can hear them. Like I said, you know I shouldn't have shown these reports to you. There's witness information that I could get disbarred for disclosing."

Uncle Massimo is our *consigliere*, which means he's Uncle Salvatore's chief advisor. He's also our *Cosa Nostra* branch's lawyer for our— more unsavory —endeavors. Uncle Salvatore's wife, Sylvia, is our attorney for our aboveboard business. I'm somewhere in the middle. One look at me, and it's obvious I'm not some yuppie attorney. Even if I do have an Ivy League education for undergrad and law school. No one believes I'm Aunt Sylvia's second chair, so I help her behind the scenes. When I need to make an appearance as a fully admitted-to-the-bar attorney, it's often beside Uncle Massimo.

"And that's why, for now at least, no one but the four of us needs to know what they're charging me with. I have no intention of being my own counsel, but I can help with my own defense. Uncle Massi, you already know the case and what's involved."

Who the fuck is the woman? We don't do outsiders. All will be revealed in time. I know my uncles, but it makes me want to twitch. Uncle Salvatore shakes his head.

"That's not possible. That's exactly what they expect. That's why we've brought in outside counsel."

Uncle Salvatore turns to the woman at the end of the table. I already figured she was an attorney and one who will handle this case. She's hot, and I'd fuck her given half a chance. But when it comes to my life and a stint in prison, I trust no one I don't know. I've never seen her before in my life. I'd remember.

"Gabriele Scotto, this is Sinead O'Malley. She will represent you."

I can tell Uncle Salvatore and Uncle Massimo are bracing themselves. I place my palms flat on the arms of my chair when all I want to do is curl them into fists until my knuckles are white. That's too much of a tell.

"It's nice to meet you, Ms. O'Malley."

It was until I heard her last name. My gaze darts to Uncle Salvatore. My face shows none of my thoughts now. They're locked up tighter than a virgin in a whorehouse.

"Mr. Scotto, I understand your frustration and your wish to assist in your own defense. I advise against that. I have no interest in this going to mistrial or you being remanded back into custody. Neither helps my reputation, and neither gets you closer to being free."

Her fucking reputation? That was a jab if ever there was one. Like she's doing me some fucking favor. How many zeros are at the end of the check she'll be getting?

"I'll make sure neither your reputation nor your bank account suffer, Ms. O'Malley."

"Mr. Mancinelli has already put me on retainer. That's not what concerns me."

Sinead. Why the fuck does she have to be Irish? And not like just Irish on St. Patty's Day. With a name like that, it's recent. Her family hasn't been here more than two or three generations.

"Is it your ties to the O'Rourkes that should concern me?"

I'm not pussyfooting through the daisies. I know Uncle Salvatore and Uncle Massimo have vetted her. I'm certain now that Carmine already knows about this, even though I haven't had time to tell him. He'll have done her background check. But I want to know for myself. I want to see her when I ask these questions.

"I'm an O'Malley, not an O'Rourke. I'm not connected to the mob. Do you believe I wish to die? If I were part of a mob family and sold out to help a Mafia family, I would die. If I betray you by taking anything back to the mob, I will die. I'm not interested in either. I have a vacation in the Caribbean coming up. I intend to enjoy it. Breathing is a requirement for that."

She stands as though she might leave if I get within one more inch of insulting her. Her blue eyes shoot shards of ice. The only people who have the same color eyes are the Kutsenkos. That gives me pause. Is she Russian bratva? Definitely not. If she were, she wouldn't be within a mile of this office. There's no way they would let any of their women near us alone, even for a business meeting. She's pulled her black hair back into a bun at her nape, and it accentuates her face. Modest. Practical. Asking for me to take it down, fist my hand in it, and devour her.

"What are your qualifications?"

I have a right to know.

"Mount Holyoke College for undergrad, and Yale for law school."

Impressive academic pedigree. A Seven Sisters and an Ivy League.

"How long have you been practicing?"

"A lot longer than you. Seven years."

My brow furrows. Seven years?

5

"Were you in the same class as Laura Doyle?"

There's half a breath's hesitation. Why?

"I was in the same class as Laura Kutsenko."

So, she knows Laura married the leader of the bratva. How close were they? How close are they?

"Believe it or not, Mr. Scotto, before this morning, I never imagined I would get involved with organized crime. Laura and I haven't spoken to one another in nearly two years. Not since a fundraiser for the Bar Association, where I met her husband. She practices civil law. I practice criminal law. So far, our paths have yet to meet. As you know, since you went to Yale Law School too, there are nearly two hundred people in each class. She and I were not close. We didn't run in the same group."

"Why not?"

I watch every mannerism, every blink, every moment she refrains from snapping at me. If this wasn't about keeping my ass off the list for execution, I'd call this flirting.

"Because I knew from the start that I wanted to practice criminal law, and she knew from the start that she wanted to specialize in corporate law. I don't mean to offend you, Mr. Scotto or Mr. Mancinelli, but corporate law could put me in a coma. Those courses were the most boring they forced me to take."

"Have you seen a dead body in person?"

She doesn't even blink.

"Plenty. I've gone to the city coroner more often that I can count. I've been to crime scenes. And I've already seen the photos of what you allegedly did. Gruesome."

She beat me to the punch. She's seen the photos in the stack of papers I saw only minutes before my uncle introduced us. They are gruesome. It looks like something I could do. But it wasn't my handiwork that time. Someone made it look like it was me, though.

"How many acquittals have you had?"

"I handle anywhere from fifty to a hundred-and-five cases a year, Mr. Scotto. I have a ninety-eight percent acquittal rate. Like I said, I'm not looking to damage my reputation."

"So, you're doing this for you. It's about you, not your client."

I cross my arms as I sit back in the chair. She's still standing, and it makes me look like a smug asshole. Just what I want. My shirt strains over my arms and shoulders. I'd rolled the sleeves halfway up my forearm, and I know the muscles flex. I don't see fear, arousal, disinterest, or arrogance. I see nothing but confidence. A bit disappointing about not seeing the arousal. The table is still shielding any of them from seeing my hard on.

We stare at one another until Uncle Salvatore rolls his eyes. I don't see him. I just know him. Uncle Massimo gathers the papers I left on the table.

"When do we start planning my defense, Ms. O'Malley?"

"You might be starting now. I'm already halfway done."

I watch as she gathers her coat and bag. Both are practical but well made. They suit her. I'm not ready for her to leave.

"Do you think I did it?"

That makes all three of them freeze. Her gaze is unwavering.

"Does it matter? I'm not the jury."

"Care to share how you're keeping me off death row?"

"With a solid defense." She glances at her watch. "I need to be in Foley Square next. I have another appointment. Good day, gentlemen."

I glance at my uncles and cock any eyebrow. They smirk. Now it's my turn to want to roll my eyes. They're closer to the door. They chirp at the same time.

"Goodbye, Ms. O'Malley."

She glances at them before turning her focus back to me.

She's confused about why they just walked out since she's headed out, too. They can guess what's going to happen, and as much as I've entertained them already, they have other things to do besides watching the ensuing battle of wills.

"Ms. O'Malley, how many high-profile clients have you represented? I don't mean this to be snide at all. I'm asking for a reason, and it's not about your ability to defend me."

She's taken aback by my softer tone. It's not patronizing. At least, I hope not. I stand, glad my trousers hide what she does to me, then I walk to her end of the table. She meets me in the middle.

"Several."

"Were any of them accused of what I am?"

"I've handled several murder cases."

"High-profile murder cases?"

I've never heard of her or seen her on the news.

"You think I haven't had cases like yours because you haven't heard of me or seen me on the news."

"I hope your mind reading skills work as well with the jurors as they do me."

I crack my first smile, and I see it. That tiny flash of interest. The one I was sure was there before she forced it out of her expression. This is the most inopportune time to want a woman. Pursuing anything would be a monumental conflict of interest. I step a little closer. She's tall, probably five-feet-nine. But I'm six-feet-four. I also weigh two-hundred-and-forty pounds with nine percent body fat. I'm large, lean, and usually intimidating. I don't want that right now. Not when I tower over her and must weigh eighty pounds more than her.

"I understand you're testing me, Mr. Scotto. I won't hold that against you given the circumstances."

"Gabriele, please."

"Sinead."

She concedes begrudgingly.

"I'm not testing you now. When my uncles approached you, did you know it was to represent me?"

"Uncles?"

"Sorta. Our family tree is complicated. You'll need to understand it, but not today. Did you know who you were going to defend?"

"I knew it was someone in your organization who has a senior position. I got the impression my client was part of Mr. Mancinelli's family. Both Mr. Mancinellis."

"Why did you take this case?"

"Part of it is because it'll be high-profile. I suspect you detect lies easily, so I won't bother with them. At least, not directed to you. But I like a challenge. Cases are puzzles. All the pieces are there. Sometimes they fall on the floor or get left in the box. But if I look, I can find them. Then I arrange them and put them together."

"You like watching the picture grow without being the one to paint it."

Her brow furrows for a moment.

"Yeah. Is that how you see it?"

"Yeah. Sinead, we have to talk about something practical but more important than my defense."

"What's more important than your defense?"

"Your safety." I pull out a chair for her. "Please sit."

I wait until she does, then I pull out a chair for me. Her right eye narrows a sliver. I have manners. I just didn't use them earlier. I sat when she stood. Normally, I wouldn't. I would be on my feet when a woman stands, and I don't sit until she has. I don't see these types of Italian traditions as archaic. If they've lasted this long, why change them?

"Now that you're associated with my family— not just me and my case —but with the *Cosa Nostra*, you're in danger.

Did Uncle Sal or Uncle Massi explain that? Did they warn you?"

"They never admitted that you're Mafia. But they didn't have to. They said there were risks involved, but that's a given with a crime— with a syndicate."

"Crime family? I'm not offended, and neither would anyone in my family. That's the least of the things we've been called. You are working for the Mafia as a criminal defense attorney on a felony case. Reporters and bloggers and nosey assholes will follow you. *Everywhere.* That's annoying, but you can get a protective order against them if they make you feel unsafe. But there's an entire world who doesn't give a shit about a restraining order. You couldn't serve them if you wanted to. And you sure as hell can't enforce it."

"I know all of this."

"Maybe on a theoretical level. But not in application. This is more complicated than you could imagine. Yes, I tested you because I need the best defense I can get. But I also want you to understand just what's happening here. Once the public and press link your name with mine, there's no going back. There's no undoing the ties to the Cosa Nostra. Even if we never see each other again, everyone will always know you as the attorney who represented a Mafioso. It will keep you from getting clients, even if it boosts your firm's reputation. It'll put your entire career under scrutiny until the day you retire. But the thing that worries me the most is your safety. Being near my family is a risk. That's a given. Being near me when someone is clearly framing me means you're in as much danger as I am."

She absorbs everything I'm saying. I can tell she's considering every layer I reveal. She's moving those puzzle pieces, and I'm giving her time to find all the corner and side pieces. I haven't even begun to give her the center pieces to put together.

"Do you not want me to represent you?"

I offer her a smile that's genuine. There's no smugness or arrogance. It's not provocative or patronizing. I think an author would describe it as soft.

"I want you to represent me. You impress me, and my intuition is the only thing that has kept me alive more times than I can count. I trust it. It says you'll be excellent at this. I wish Uncle Massi could represent me simply because it keeps anyone outside the family from getting sucked in. I don't know why they approached you, but I trust both men with everything I have— including my life. They wouldn't have hired you if you weren't excellent."

We're going around in circles. I need to get to the point, but I don't want to. I want to keep talking to her. She said she's going on a vacation soon, but she's already suntanned. It's the permanent kind, but she doesn't have olive skin like I do. I just go from dark to darker in summer. She's not fair, but it's more of a sun-kissed, peaches and cream. With the black hair and blue eyes, she's entranced me.

"I'm glad we've agreed to that much."

"It's the next part that I don't think you'll agree to. Sinead, if you represent me, you must have a safety detail at all times."

"Okay."

"That's it?"

"Is it someone in a dark car parked outside my place? Someone who follows me to work, the store, the gym, and stands outside the restroom door?"

I grit my teeth. She's not making light of this. She's genuinely asking. I'm not controlling in anything outside of work. But I want to demand she goes nowhere ever without me at her side. It's utterly unreasonable. It's fucking batshit bonkers.

"You don't want me to go to the store or the gym. You don't

want me to go anywhere where I might need a public restroom."

"I want you safe. I don't want anything to happen to you because of me."

"I suppose hiring private security isn't an option."

"No. We'll provide it for you. Does anyone know you came here?"

She shakes her head, then looks down at her watch.

"Shit. I'm so late. I'm going to be held in contempt. I have to go, Gabriele. Can we talk about this later?"

"Yes."

I stand and roll down my sleeves. I grab my suit coat from where it's hanging over the back of the chair I originally sat in. We leave the office where we met in the building Mancinelli Developers owns. We next to never come here. It's only when we need a respectable place to meet people. There are other companies that rent suites here, so the building doesn't stand empty.

"Did you drive?"

Sinead looks up at me as we get in the elevator.

"No. I don't have time to find parking in Midtown or near Foley Square. I took the subway."

"I won't tell you not to take the subway, but you need two guards with you if you do."

"Two?"

"It's always crowded. You need the eyes watching what's going on. And if something happens, you need one guy to deal with whoever or whatever threatened you and the other to get you to safety. I have a car waiting outside. The driver will be one of your guards, but he can't do it today. I'll take you to the courthouse, but I can't go inside with you. No one can see you with me right now. Not until I set your safety detail. But I will wait outside until you're done. Then I'll take you wherever else you need to go today."

She looks at the button panel, then the floor. She looks at the door and the ceiling. She looks everywhere but at me. I'm unprepared for what she says when she turns toward me.

"Who's going to protect you?"

Chapter Two

Sinead

From me.

I want to pounce. Gabriele is beyond hot. I don't even have words for it. It's not just his face and body. It's the sex appeal he exudes. I know most women wouldn't see it that way. Good. But he's the type I'd let take down my hair, fist it, and devour me. The type I'd say "yes, sir" to. Most women would call him intimidating. I'd call him whatever the fuck he wants as long as he's naked, and we're fucking.

Get your fucking self together. He's your client.

"From you?"

He grins as he stares down at me. Huh? Oh, I just asked a question.

"Do you need protecting from me? I get the feeling you're pretty fierce."

I smile back. He was joking. But my brow furrows. That wasn't what I meant at all.

"If I'm in as much danger as you say, then doesn't that just add to yours? I mean, if someone might go after me, then they'd be going after you, too. Someone obviously has ill intentions toward you to begin with. Add me as a target and us having to meet and that makes you even more tempting prey."

When he turns to face me, I see just how enormous he is. We stood in front of each other for just a moment before he pulled out my chair, then we were walking side-by-side. He's a fucking giant.

"No one is going to approach me. That's why whoever is trying to frame me did it like this. They did it behind my back rather than confront me. They know they wouldn't win. They need to—"

He snaps his mouth shut. I wait for him to pick something else to say, but he doesn't. I can guess.

"They need to live long enough to do their job."

"Is it just me?"

"Just you what?"

"Whose mind you can read. It's disconcerting. Only my best friend can guess what I'm thinking, and that's because we've known each other for twenty years."

"I watch people for tells. I can usually guess from those. But you've had none you didn't intentionally want me to see. I just know."

"Intuition?"

"Maybe. I can already tell we think alike. You say what I would say."

"Uncanny."

I hope he can't tell everything I'm thinking. Like how I want to run my hands all over him, taste him, and have him fuck me. Hmmm. Then again, if we think the same way, is he thinking that about me? I doubt it. Men like him don't go for women like me. I don't work out as often as I should, and he looks like he lives at the gym. They don't go for women who'd rather read or watch TV than go out. He doesn't know me, but I've seen him in the newspapers. He goes to the hottest night clubs and has the hottest women on his arm. And I doubt he's into the same stuff as I am when I have sex.

"Sinead?"

"Yes?"

"Lost in thought? Worried about me?"

He flashes that grin again. My panties are soaked. Will this elevator never reach the ground?

"Yes. I'm already so late. I was thinking how much my fine will be."

"That's my fault. I will cover your fine."

"I don't need—"

"I can tell you don't need me to. That's not the point. I caused the problem. It's my responsibility to solve it."

He looks guilty. Like he's embarrassed and is remorseful. It's not pretend. Or if it is, he's the most manipulative fucker alive. Given what I can guess he does for a living, maybe it really is the latter.

"I'll be taking you wherever you need to go after you're done with court. Tell me what the judge fines you, and you'll have it by morning."

"Seriously, though. If you're protecting me and you think I should have other people assigned to me, who makes sure you're safe?"

"My family."

That's a definitive answer that tells me not to push. Fine. I get the hint. At least I changed the subject away from me. The elevator finally stops. That was the longest ride down from the twentieth floor ever. How did no one else get on? He waits for me to step out, then angles himself, so he's slightly ahead of me. His right shoulder's a little in front of my left one, as though he could shift in one step and block me. I glance up at him and

17

notice he's looking around. His eyes dart down to me before he continues to sweep the surrounding area. When we get to the door, he stops for a moment. I spot a black sedan outside, pulled up to the curb directly across from the doors. A man steps out and walks around to the passenger side. He opens the door and stands beside it.

Now, Gabriele opens the door. He doesn't want us waiting outside. His pace is brisk, but I easily keep up. Once we're past the building's shadow, he steps to his left enough for me to move past him with the next step. Now he's protecting my back. It must mean he's confident his driver can protect me from the front. When we get to the car, he steps close enough that I'm sandwiched between him and the door frame. I duck in and slide over. I hear him say the courthouse before he sits, and the driver closes the door. There's privacy glass, and it's up. When his hand rests between us, all I can think of is it slipping up my skirt. All the things we could do. I cannot fuck my client. It's the height of misconduct and unethical. Besides, this is completely one-sided.

We ride in silence for two blocks before he looks at me again. His tone tells me I can argue if I want, but it would be pointless. Actually, his tone tells me not to argue at all.

"You will always know the name and face of the men assigned to you. I'll make sure you get a photo of them with hair and eye color and height. If they aren't the men assigned to you that day, you go nowhere with them. I'm serious. If the rotation changes, someone from my family or I will tell you. Never get into a car without your guard checking it first. Sometimes your guard will be your driver. Sometimes the man will only guard you. Never get out of a car before the driver or guard opens the door. Rap on the window when you're ready. They won't open the door before then. If you have even a moment's doubt, call me or text me."

He holds out his hand. I realize he wants my phone.

GPS: 914-555-8585

Westchester? GPS? He shoots me a text, so I get his number.

"Gabriele Porfirio Scotto."

I look up from my phone screen and tilt my head. I've never heard that name before. Then again, maybe it's common in Italy and not in America. There are Sineads all over Ireland, but the only one in America that I've heard of is Sinead O'Connor. And she was from Ireland.

"If you can believe it, I was a small baby when I was born. I was on time, but only seven-pounds, three-ounces. But according to my mom, I hit and kicked like a martial artist. Porfirio means 'he who crushes.'"

"An angelic crusher?"

He laughs, and it goes straight to my pussy. I clench, but I ache. His hand could be up my skirt in two seconds if he wanted to. But again, men like him aren't into women like me.

"Something like that. Apparently, I was an easy delivery and came out with chubby, red cheeks and already smiling. Gabriele hadn't been on their list, but they said I looked like a cherub."

He blinks a few times, and I can tell it surprises him he shared that with me. I doubt many people know that. It feels special that he told me.

"It fits."

I mumble it, but I'm certain he heard it.

"Maybe, but it definitely wasn't a middle name I loved when I moved here in fourth grade."

He did hear me.

"Kids can be little shits to each other."

"It didn't help that I didn't stay small for long. I was tall for my age by the time I was five. At ten, I was the same height as some fourteen-year-olds I knew. I was athletic too, but that made it worse. No one believed I should compete in my age group, and none of the older kids wanted an elementary school kid on their teams."

This conversation is keeping the ride from being boring, but I feel like I should share something about myself before it becomes one-sided. I don't want him to regret sharing.

"I was the opposite. I was an eight-pounds, eleven-ounce baby, but I seemed to stop gaining weight when I was four months old. I kept getting taller, but I didn't gain weight. I was skinny until I was twelve and grew like eight inches that year. I was taller than all the other girls at five-feet-two. Then I had another growth spurt at fourteen, almost fifteen, and got to my current height. How tall are you?"

"Six-feet-four-and-three-quarters."

He is a giant.

"You?"

"Five-nine-and-a-half."

I'm taller than average. If I were thinner, I would have been the perfect height to model. Not that I have the looks for it. But I'm in that ambiguous area of not being regular size or plus size. Some of my clothes are regulars, and some are plus size. Most don't fit well except for my suits. I get them altered. I guess my adult weight caught up. Heavy baby, heavy woman. But I'm good with it. I'm comfortable in my body. It took years to get there, but I'm happy that I don't worry about it anymore.

"That's a good height."

"For what? I don't play basketball or volleyball."

His eyes dart to my lips. I can't help it. The tip of my tongue peeks out and swipes across them. His gaze meets mine, but it's shuttered. For once, I truly don't know what he's thinking. Does he regret looking at my mouth like that? Regret me realizing he was? Am I totally making it all up in my mind?

"When will my security detail start? I get you coming along today because someone might have seen me leaving your family's office. But no one knows I'm working for you. I'm not the attorney on record yet."

"It starts today. I'll be outside your place until midnight. Either Vinny or Luigi will relieve me until you leave for work. I'll be in the car tomorrow, but someone else will escort you to and from whatever office or courtroom you're in."

"I have plans tonight."

I wince.

"A date?"

Was there something in his tone?

"Yes."

"Are you involved with someone?"

"No. We've only been out twice before. He was going to pick me up."

"Then I follow you. Where are you going?"

"Constantine's for dinner, then Spotlight after."

"Good thing my family owns both."

"What?"

"Lorenzo Mancinelli owns both of them. We're like cousins. Sort of. But not by blood or marriage. Remember how I said our family tree is complicated?"

"Yeah."

"Uncle Salvatore is the oldest, then Uncle Massimo. They have a sister who is my best friend's mother. Uncle Massimo has four children, and Lorenzo is one of them. Our families go back generations and probably were related at some point. But my best friend and I were inseparable until he married. You read the arrest report, right?"

"Yes. Just before you arrived."

"My best friend's wife owns the bakery where they arrested me. I was her guard that day. I'm so close to my best friend that we each had a bedroom at each other's house. So, the Mancinellis are like my family. Everyone calls the adults uncle or aunt."

He shakes his head for a second.

"The adults. That's sounds ridiculous when I say it out loud, but that's just the way we've always thought of them."

There's that smile again. His grin is flashy and sexy. But his smile seems rarer and softer. But I can't consider that anymore because we've just pulled up to the courthouse. The driver is opening my door after I tap the window.

"Go ahead. Pauly will take you inside. I can see you the entire way, but no one will see you with me. Text me when you're ready to leave. I will be outside the courtroom door. Keep walking and get on the elevator to the parking garage. Don't acknowledge me. The town car will wait for us. Walk around to the far side but wait for me to open the door. I'll take you wherever you want."

"Home. I have that date to get ready for."

Which I wish I didn't. I shouldn't feel embarrassed, but I do. I don't have time to think about it anymore because Pauly's waiting, and I'm gathering my stuff. I look back as I slide out.

"Thank you. I'll text when I need you."

Chapter Three

Gabriele

When she needs me. Fucking hell. I wish she needed me to get her off as much as I want her to get me off. I cannot stop thinking about having sex with her. I wasn't this bad when I was in college. But there is something I can't get past. When she licked her lips, I thought I was about to lick them for her. My palm itched to slide up her thigh until I could make her wet. But that's not even remotely a possibility. Right now, she's my lawyer. Either I have to wait until the trial is over, which could be months, or I could be in prison, so that definitely makes it impossible.

If it were just physical attraction, I would go to my club and fuck someone until she's out of my system. I don't do random women. I belong to a club for particular tastes. There's actually only one woman I scene with these days. I never imagined the fucking arrangement I have now. I definitely didn't know she was a swinger when we connected— no pun intended —the first time. I definitely didn't expect her husband to like to watch. I don't care if voyeurs do. Whatever gets their rocks off. The only conditions I have are I'm always masked and never naked. My tats are too distinct, and no one needs to see my face. Since I'm the one giving the commands, it works just fine. Her husband joins sometimes, but our swords never cross. We stay at opposite ends.

But I'm not in the mood for that at all. I only want Sinead. Though I wouldn't mind having her restrained, bent over the back of a couch, with my hand spanking her tits and ass. What I want is more time to talk to her. Our back-and-forth intrigued me. I like that she didn't back down from me, and we do think a lot alike. I felt the same way about civil law classes. I took them because I had no choice, but I prefer criminal law. Aunt Sylvia and Uncle Massimo handle more corporate stuff. Uncle Massimo does criminal law too as needed, but now that's my specialty.

I'm interested in how she's assembling the puzzle of my defense and want to know more, so I can avoid life in prison. Uncle Massimo was right. I shouldn't have seen the court documents, but there was no way he would keep them from me. Not as a practicing lawyer who understands them, nor as a family member. It's not the first time he's revealed stuff like that. And he has come dangerously close to qualifying to be disbarred.

Who the hell is the guy Sinead's going out with? Carmine would know. I pull out my phone and hit his contact. I look out the tinted window as I wait.

"What's up?"

"Hey. When did you find out about Sinead?"

"Last night. Why? Are you the one she's representing?"

"Yes."

"But Uncle Massi was there for the arraignment. I figured they were hiring her for someone outside the family."

He means for a Made Man or even an associate. Made Men

are Italians, mostly Sicilians, in our branch. It's sorta hereditary but not guaranteed. An associate is the equivalent for a non-Italian. They're down a rung, though.

"It's me. It's for the sake of appearances, and so no one can claim a conflict of interest. And she's good. I can tell."

"Doesn't hurt that I can tell she's exactly who you'd be into."

"Yeah, well, my dick and my mind can disagree all day. I don't need life without the possibility of parole or death row."

"You know New York doesn't have the death penalty."

I can picture his expression. His "you're making a big deal out of nothing" face.

"Lucky me. The point is, if Uncle Massi can't represent me, I have a good feeling about her. I want to ensure my trust won't be misplaced. What do you know about her beyond Mount Holyoke and Yale?"

"She's from Rhode Island. Her mom died of cancer when she was thirteen, and her dad has early onset dementia. She brought him to a memory care facility on East 65th."

"Isn't that one of the best in the city?"

"Definitely. And it's not cheap either, but she has her dad on the wait list for one in Hudson County."

"Jersey? Why move him? And how do you know?"

"I hacked her email. She wants him to have more fresh air and time outside. I guess he was an avid fisherman and hiker."

"She must be doing well if she can afford that. Did she have college or law school loans?"

"Yes, to both. They're affording it from the sale of her parents' home, pensions, private retirement funds, and his VA benefits. She got hired by Timmons, Kelsey, and Schmidt right out of law school. She interned with them and impressed them. She's frugal to the point of painful, but she isn't cheap."

"I can tell the not cheap part. Her clothes are impeccable. They have to be custom."

"From what I can tell, she shops at outlet stores with steep discounts, then gets them altered. She has a tailor in the Bronx."

"The Bronx?"

That I don't like. It's not like there's crime happening every minute of every day on every corner. But there are some really rough parts. It's the perfect place for someone to grab her.

"I know that tone. You won't like where she lives any better."

"Don't tell me she lives in the Bronx."

"Worse. Staten Island."

There's disgust in Carmine's voice. I'm concerned about the Bronx for Sinead's sake, but I have nothing against Staten Island. Neither does Carmine really. Neither of us gives a shit that much about Staten Island, but it's the butt of every joke that isn't about Jersey.

"I'm taking her home after work. Get this. She's having dinner at Constantine's, then going to Spotlight."

"Girls' night?"

"Date."

"Ouch. But don't worry. He's a douche."

"Why?"

"He's some hedge fund asshole that her friend set her up with. She's gone out with him to be polite, but it won't last."

"How'd you get all that?"

"She's an Apple user. It was easy to put spyware on her phone. That's why I've been telling you and the others to go Android for years. Only Maria and I have the sense to get phones no one can hack remotely. Anyway, Sinead's told her friend Andrea that she did what Andrea asked and now she's done. She plans to tell him after their date. She feels obligated to go on this third one."

"Have they fucked?"

"Simmer down, tiger."

Okay. Maybe that came out a little harsher than I intended. And maybe Carmine's laughing his ass off at me, even if I can't hear him.

"Have they?"

"No. They've been to dinner twice. They saw a movie the second time. There are street cameras close enough to catch the front of her building. He never went inside with her, and she didn't let him kiss her. She pulled away then laughed it off as though it was an accident. It looked like she said something to pass it off and to give her a reason to go straight inside."

"Is there anything else that makes him a db or just his job?"

"He goes to the Hamptons all the fucking time, but always stays at someone's place. He couch surfs mansions. He only goes when there's a party or event to attend as his host's guest. He likes his watches. He's blown close to a hundred grand on them using several credit cards and his trust fund."

"Anything else?"

"Just one more."

"What, Car? Spit it out."

"He lives in your building."

"What the fuck?"

"Yeah. He's on the fifth floor."

I live in a luxury condo building in Hudson Yards. It's a new construction since the area is being gentrified. It's near Hell's Kitchen and wasn't nearly as nice as it is now. I own the entire top floor. I have the largest penthouse and rent the other three. I have a private elevator into mine, and the elevator for the other three requires biometrics. The only way into my apartment that's out of my control would be landing on the roof and repelling down to my windows, which are High-Rise Impact hurricane ones. They're not entirely burglarproof, but I'll know someone's there before they can get through it. Only my place has them. The fifth floor ain't shabby though. I know because I own the building.

"How long's he been there?"

"Like two years."

I don't know all the tenants' names since there are condos people own. I have property managers for that, and some people sublet. With a private elevator, I rarely see people since I use an entrance off the street. I prefer it that way.

"That's it?"

He hesitates. I know my friend. I wait him out.

"This might be a good thing."

"Carmine, spit it out."

"She belongs to Cries and Whispers."

That I didn't expect. Not even remotely. It's the BDSM club I belong to. I'm certain I've never seen her there. I would remember. But then again, plenty of members disguise their identities. I'm not sure how I feel knowing I've likely seen or been near guys— people, I shouldn't assume —she's fucked. It does, however, make the image of tying her up, bending her over a sofa with nipple clamps, while I fuck her and spank her way more vivid.

"Good to know. I'll make sure we don't go at the same time."

"Ha!"

Carmine's barks a laugh.

"She's my attorney, and you know my arrangement."

"It's not like you're exclusive with that woman. You're not the one married. You could scene with anyone if you wanted to."

"Does she have a Dom?"

I really don't like that thought.

"Not that I can tell. She's had an insane caseload lately. It's been like three months since she's been. But she was a regular before that. Same two guys, though. She doesn't do randoms either."

"How far back did you scroll her texts?"

"Eighteen months."

"Didn't you sleep?"

"No."

"Ew."

"I'm married, and my wife's hot."

I knew from his tone he meant any time he wasn't investigating Sinead, he was doing whatever he does with his wife. They're blissful together. He's more like the kid I knew when I moved here. His bitterness has evaporated, and he gets along with everyone besides just his cousin Maria and me. That wasn't the case from the day we met.

"That's her personal life. Any clients I should worry about? Any colleagues?"

"No. She's represented about sixty people accused of murder. She's gotten half of them dismissed on technicalities."

"Were they guilty?"

"No. That's why she found the technicalities. Cops who didn't look hard enough for someone else, contaminated evidence, coerced statements. She's convincing as hell in and out of the courtroom. She handles mostly felonies, but she does some misdemeanors. As for the handful of guilty clients she couldn't get off, she pled them down. They all got reduced charges and reduced sentencing."

"How has she had that many innocent clients?"

"Because our legal system is shit."

No greater truth has ever been said. If it worked the way it should, everyone in my family— even some of the women —

would be in prison. But greased palms go a long way and making sure the right evidence shows up— or disappears — helps. The only reason we couldn't make my charges go away is some fucknut with a police scanner heard the radio when the police arrested me. He had a drone, so he saw the five cop cars and them taking me out in handcuffs. Luckily, what he didn't see were the ten men who slipped into the bakery through the backdoor. Carmine was there first. I can only imagine what traffic laws he broke to get from the Upper Eastside to Harlem. He made the twenty-minute drive in ten. I stalled until I saw his car. He lost his ever-loving mind with the cops for touching even one thing in his wife's bakery and scaring her. She was more unfazed by it than he was. But then again she grew up with Venetian Mafia on her dad's side and Sicilian Mafia on her mom's.

"And her guilty clients that were convicted. Why'd she lose?"

"Because there was no way to win. The evidence was too clear. She even had a couple confess before lawyering up. She's gotten a few first and second degree murders dropped to manslaughter."

That's a pretty big jump from first degree murder to third. They had to have been manslaughter in the first degree convictions in New York. It's the same as voluntary manslaughter. I'm lucky they didn't throw those charges at me. 'Explosive devices with intent which caused bodily harm' implies malice and aforethought. Premeditation. First degree murder. Second degree is acting without premeditation but with a depraved indifference to human life. That would be pretty damn hard to disprove if I did, in fact, set the bombs that killed those people. Pleading down to manslaughter means there was no premeditation or aforethought. More like a crime of passion. Good thing I paid attention to that first week of law school.

"Gabe?"

"I'm here. Just thinking I'm lucky they didn't add any counts of murder to the charges."

"Because they know it's bullshit. They don't have solid evidence to convict you of the explosives, let alone evidence to prove murder. They want you to be guilty so they can get the good press for putting away a *Cosa Nostra* member. If Sinead's as good as she looks on paper, you'll be free by the end of the week."

"It's Thursday."

"I know. She's gotta be filing motions today and tomorrow."

"Submitting motions on a Friday doesn't bring good luck."

"Eh. The judge wants it done and not looming over them for Monday."

"Always the optimist."

Carmine snorts.

"Keep me posted. Fina and I are meeting Matteo and Maria for dinner."

"Double date. How quaint."

"*Fanculo.*" Fuck off.

I wish I was fucking. Good Lord. Fucking one track mind.

"*Ciao.*"

We hang up, and I look out the window until Pauly drops the privacy glass to tell me Santino is pulling up to take him to Uncle Massimo's place. He and Auntie Nicoletta are going to Luca and Olivia's to help set up the nursery. I stay in the back where it's easier to see until Sinead texts me to say she's almost done. I move to the driver's seat and pull into the underground garage. I take the elevator up to her floor. Immediately, flash bulbs go off and mics are stuck in front of me.

"Mr. Scotto, in which prison are you spending life without parole?"

What the fuck?

I don't look at any of them, instead searching for Sinead. She has a swarm of reporters around her, too. She's looking toward the elevator, and I see her relief when she spots me. I say nothing, just walking straight off the elevator and making other people move for me. No one wants me bulldozing through them. I don't have to tell Sinead to say nothing, either. We turn back to the elevator, and now all the reporters hurry to get in front of us. There's a glass case next to the window, and I can see her expression. She's as stoic as I am. When three reporters try to step in with us, she stands in front of me.

"Come any closer to my client, and I will file a claim of intrusion. You are physically invading my client's private affairs. He is not a public figure. Further, I will file claims of menacing in the third degree for myself. I am in reasonable fear of you inflicting bodily harm. Touch me with that mic, and I'll file a claim for assault. Back up."

The three reporters step away, but it doesn't stop them from shoving their mics toward us. Sinead crosses her arms. I wish I could see her face because the three assholes take a few more steps back.

"Ms. O'Malley, when did the Mancinelli crime family hire you?"

"Mr. Scotto, do you expect to go to prison?"

"Ms. O'Malley—"

"Mr. Scotto—"

Blessedly, the doors close, and we're in silence. Sinead doesn't move, standing guard for when the doors open again. There will be reporters there to meet us. I'm certain.

"You handled that well. Thank you."

She looks back over her shoulder as I speak.

"I know you know not to speak, but I'm new to their three-ring circus. They need to know I don't cower. If they do anything to cross any professional ethics as a reporter, I'll shut their shit down. I can't stop them from following you and asking questions. I can't stop them from taking photos and trying to mob you. But I can make them understand I won't put up with them accosting you like that."

She exhales as she faces forward. Her body remains tense and on guard. I can't blame her.

"What I said earlier still applies. Stay beside me, closer to the parked cars. Walk around to the far side of ours. I have to look inside. While I do, stand behind me."

She nods as the elevator chimes. The doors open and flash bulbs go off. She shifts so we can step off at the same time. The reporters give us more space this go around while we walk to the car in silence. I'm quick to look in the front and back of the vehicle. The privacy glass is down as she gets in. I shut the door and climb into the driver's seat. Neither of us says anything until we're on the street.

"I didn't leak it, Gabriele."

"I didn't think you had."

"Then how'd they know?"

"Either someone saw you entering or leaving the Mancinelli Developers' building, or they saw you getting out of a Mancinelli-owned town car. My arrest and arraignment aren't a secret. I'm the only person facing trial, so they put two and two together and got us."

Us. I like that idea.

"This is why you want me to have bodyguards."

"Yes."

"Are they going to follow me even at night? Like when I go out?"

"Probably not. Where are we headed?"

"My place." She winces. "Great Kills, Staten Island."

It's a nice neighborhood. Not a great name all things considered. She gives me the address, and I plug it into the

GPS. I figured we were headed there, so I set off in that direction. I watch her through the rearview mirror as she pulls out her phone, which I now hear vibrate. She unlocks the screen and must be reading a text. Her shoulders droop as she tilts her head back and closes her eyes.

"That was Josh. Tonight's going to blow."

Chapter Four

Sinead

I really don't want to see Josh. I'm just not in the mood to deal with him after court today, which didn't go as well as I would have liked for one of my clients. Now that I'm sitting in the back of a town car, I just want to close my eyes and ignore the rest of the world. But that's not possible.

"Do you have to go on the date tonight?"

There's something in Gabriele's tone that's different from right before I got in the car. It's back to being untrusting of me.

"No. I'm going to reschedule. I know it's last minute, but I'm just not in the mood for it."

As I rest against the seatback, I realize I need to go back to my office because I have to prep for a meeting. It's not how I want to spend my Friday because the client is an ass.

"Actually, Gabriele, could you drop me off at my office, please? I have some stuff I need to work on for a client meeting tomorrow morning. I just want it done, so I don't have to think about it once I get home."

"Sure."

It's terse, but I'm still not sure why.

"I'm going to be there for a few hours. I don't want you to have to sit around, waiting with nothing to do."

He looks at me in the review mirror, and I can tell he's contemplating arguing with me, but we barely know each other. He relents and nods.

"I'll drop you off and text one of our guys to be here. He'll drive you home."

"That's still someone waiting with nothing to do."

"That's what we pay our drivers to do."

Now it's my turn to contemplate arguing. But I know I won't win, and I don't want to start a conflict when we've only known each other a few hours. That won't set our relationship on the right path.

"Thank you."

It's only twenty minutes later, and we're at my office. Gabriele pulls into the parking structure and agrees to walk me to my office.

"There are still plenty of people here, Gabriele. I'm safe. I'll be over there." I point. "In my office."

"Text me before you get on the elevator. I'll make sure the driver is waiting for you outside the front door. Don't leave the building without him."

He pulls out his phone and holds up a photo of him and two other guys.

"The one in the center is Afonso. He'll be here. Don't go with anyone else. If they say they work for the Mancinellis, don't believe them. Call me immediately. I'll have my phone nearby."

"Thank you. I appreciate it."

I do, but it's overkill. Better to have the guard and not need him than to need him and not have him. That's what I keep telling myself as I head into my office. It's almost three hours later before I'm ready to leave. I finished one task and found another. It happens a lot. I'm so ready to take off these heels.

I have trial prep with a man charged with embezzlement. From what I've seen of the evidence the prosecution has already gathered, the man is guilty as the day is long. But everyone's entitled to a rigorous defense and all the rights the U.S. Constitution bestows. At least, that's my mantra many a day when I have guilty-as-sin clients. We're going to trial next week, and it's going to take pulling a fluffle of rabbits out of my hat to get him off. I'm hoping the prosecution will come through with a plea deal, but I'm not holding my breath. He defrauded elderly people who depend on Social Security to get by. I'm fairly certain he's paying his legal fees with his ill-gotten gains. He came to us just before the feds seized his accounts. He paid a massive amount— a medium-sized fortune —to retain us.

Gabriele's case is still in discovery, so it's evidence and deposition gathering. I have a meeting with him tomorrow morning to review what we already have. My hope is the prosecution cannot gather enough evidence to go past the preliminary hearing. The burden of proof is on them, not me. If it goes to trial, I can still file a motion to dismiss.

I know the Assistant DA trying the case, and he's a fucking asshole. I know because I dated him in law school. We went out for seven months, and he was a douche after the first three. It was like he got me on the hook, then did a one-eighty. He was a good fuck and good to study with. Beyond that, he was pompous, socially inept, and a mama's boy. Can we still say that? He truly was. He talked to the woman at least once, if not twice a day, and she still picked out clothes for him. That was a nugget I didn't discover until I broke up with him, but it explained *so* much.

In the afternoon, we have a pre-trial conference with the prosecution. I'm going to advise Gabriele against attending, but I know he'll insist. I can only imagine what he's going to think when he meets Tyler. He won't say a word, but I'm certain he'll think plenty. I just need to get through today.

"Sinead?"

I look up as Ashley, my administrative assistant, knocks on my open door.

"Hey. Mr. Cohenour is here. I took him to the conference room and am about to get him a cappuccino. I mentioned I'd have to run across the street to get that. All he said was 'great.'"

She rolls her eyes, but she'll do it and return with a smile. She's in college and one of the most hardworking people I've ever met. If she stays local for law school, the senior partners have already offered her an internship along with her regular job as my admin assistant. I don't know how she'd juggle all that, but if anyone can, it's her.

"Thanks, Ash. Let me gather my things."

I make my way to the conference room with a stack of folders, girding my loins for this meeting. I've never had a cavity, but I have to imagine getting one filled would be better than this. I take a deep breath, grit my teeth, exhale, slap a smile on my face, and push the conference room door open.

"Good morning, Mr. Cohenour."

"Morning, Ms. O'Malley. What're we doing to get these charges dropped today?"

Try not being guilty.

"I could file a motion for dismissal, but it's unlikely the judge will decide in our favor. As your attorney, Mr. Cohenour, I strongly advise you to consider taking any offer the prosecution makes. You may get a reduction in sentencing if you make a plea bargain."

"No."

He slams his hand on the table. This isn't the first outburst I've ignored, but if he tries this in front of the bench, it will get him held in contempt. That's something I've told him before. The judges at his arraignment and at his preliminary hearing fined him when he did the same thing in the courtroom.

"Mr. Cohenour, the preponderance of evidence is not on our side. They have two audio recordings and three videos of you admitting you committed your crimes to an undercover FBI agent. You boasted about it in thinly veiled texts. Your warehouse's security cameras and agents' body cameras captured you threatening them and their families during your arrest. You left a paper trail ten miles long since you wrote everything in your notebook. Forensics has already identified your prints and confirmed they are the only ones on your notebook and that the handwriting matches yours. We can take this to trial, and you will lose. I'm good, but I can't undo what you did to sabotage your own defense. Embezzlement of over a million dollars is grand larceny— a Class B felony —in the state of New York and comes with a mandatory sentence of one to three years. You could face eight-and-a-third to twenty-five years. Which do you prefer? Three or twenty-five?"

"Bah. It won't come to that."

I rein in my temper.

"It will."

"No, it won't. I want immunity."

What the ever-loving fuck?

"It's far too late for that. And you'd have to offer the FBI something in exchange."

"I know about your client Gabriele Scotto. I know he's guilty."

"Do not say another word. I can't defend you or Mr. Scotto if you testify for the prosecution or reveal information that could harm another client."

"That thug—"

"Enough."

My voice is strident as I gather my paperwork.

"You will stop, or I will walk out. We will not discuss this further until I'm able to remove myself from Mr. Scotto's case."

"But if I don't tell you what I know, then how will you make my plea agreement to the prosecution?"

"I didn't say you wouldn't tell me. I said not to do it while I represent you and Mr. Scotto."

There's a throbbing pain behind my left eye. Anything Cohenour tells me would likely come out during discovery for Gabriele's case, but talk about a fucking conflict of interest. The prosecution for Gabriele's case would go to town if I was privy to their witness's statement before them, and I still represented Gabriele. The shitstorm would start with Cohenour's case and roll over. The Assistant DA for this case isn't Tyler. It's a woman with an itchy trigger finger for filing motions that swamp defense teams. Judges hate her, but she always has the law on her side, so there's little they can do. She's a pain in the ass, but she's good. We've gone up against each other several times, and our score is tied.

The last thing I want to do is step down from Gabriele's case, but I can't walk out on this one since we're going to trial next week. And even if I heard this asshole's claims after stepping down from Gabriele's case, it's not like I could pass that along to Gabriele's new attorney. It would violate Cohenour's attorney-client privileges. This is a fucktastrophe about to happen.

Fuck me. Fuck me. Fuck me.

I can't send him to talk to the prosecution not knowing

40

what he'll tell them and without a lawyer. Let me see if I can probe enough to know if this is even a thing or if he's bullshitting.

"Mr. Cohenour, if you've been aware of Mr. Scotto's alleged illegal activities, why are you now stepping forward?"

"Because it didn't matter until now. I don't want them coming after my family or me."

"If that's the case, that still begs the question: why are you now stepping forward? You contradict yourself if protecting your family is your main concern. Don't you fear testifying will endanger them?"

Does someone in Gabriele's family already know Cohenour might have evidence against him? Is that why he fears for his family? It seems more like this about himself than anyone else.

"I don't want to go to prison. I have too much to lose if I do."

"You've lost everything. Your assets are frozen. Your wife filed for divorce. Your investors all pulled out."

"And I can get it back with an immunity deal."

This is already pointless. We're going to go around in circles.

"Did you gain this information during the committal of a crime?"

"Ah— no."

That was way too much hesitation.

"Was it while planning to commit a crime?"

"No."

"Do you have this information firsthand?"

This pause stretches.

"If this is hearsay, Mr. Cohenour, it's unlikely to do you much good. You may aid in an investigation, but I can't promise immunity if you don't have firsthand knowledge."

"I do. I do."

Now he's trying too hard again. All my Spidey senses are tingling.

"How did you gain this information?"

"That goon—"

"No. Do not tell me what you believe is the relevant information. Tell me how you got it."

"I heard from a guy who belongs to a different— uh —organization that Mr. Scotto was probably looking to get back at some Polish mobsters."

"Probably? That's what you have? A probably?"

"I trust this guy who told me."

"Who is it? How would he know?"

"Um— I— I —can't say."

"Why not? Whoever it is will get dragged in for questioning. There's no way you'll get around telling the DA if you want them to believe you. So, who?"

He visibly swallows.

"Do you intend to perjure yourself to get this deal? Do you realize that if they prove your statement to be a lie under oath, you will face a Class D felony with three to seven years in prison? It's up to five years for federal perjury if anything escalates to that. You will only add to your sentence. Let me try to negotiate the minimum sentencing for grand larceny. You could be home in a year."

"How about no prison and just house arrest?"

I try not to sigh.

"I can present that, but it would be foolish to believe that's a likelihood. Are we in agreement that you will not perjure yourself and will not request immunity?"

"Yeah."

"Let's move forward in a way that's beneficial to you and your case."

I put the files down and sit across from him. We spend the next two hours going through all the evidence for the umpteenth time. When I escape back to my office, I shoot off an email to the DA's office stating we're amenable to hearing a plea agreement offer. As I sit back in my chair, my elbow on my armrest, my hand over my eyes, I'm resisting the urge to throw something. I generally don't have violent reactions to things that annoy me. But I don't want off Gabriele's case even though I temporarily considered it. I want to represent him and make sure he's exonerated of all this bullshit. But Cohenour proved people are likely to come out of the woodwork to take down a Mancinelli member.

Who the fuck will be next?

Chapter Five

Gabriele

This weekend was a pain in the ass, but fruitful. We have a garage in Queens where we handle our less than savory activities. It's a place where we take people who need encouragement to talk. The shy types. We give them a little moral support and get them to tell us what we need to know. The best I could tell Sinead was that I was on a rotation to help the family. I might have made it sound more like I had bodyguard duty, but it wasn't entirely untrue. I rotated with Lorenzo and Matteo.

For years, I was the Mancinellis' top enforcer. Because of my close friendship to Carmine and his position as resident persona non grata, I existed in limbo. Usually, an enforcer is toward the bottom of our hierarchy below associates which are below Made Men. But Uncle Salvatore elevated me to higher than a regular Made Man but lower than a *capo*. With things now resolved between Carmine and the family, Uncle Salvatore promoted him and me to *capo*. That didn't unteach me all that I learned over years of practice. I'm still the best at coercing information. But I'm only human, and I need a break every few hours. I might have played D1 baseball, but even my shoulders get tired swinging a tire iron or metal pipe.

We picked up a mid-level player in another lesser syndicate. One of our guys heard him shooting off his mouth at a casino in Jersey while he was drunk. He didn't come out and say it, but our guy understood the man suggested his boss knew something about my case. I got curious. Can you blame me? Apparently, this shit stain's boss, some guy named Art Cohenour, thinks he can plead down some grand larceny case by going state's witness against me. I don't know who the fuck Cohenour is or what he thinks he knows, but I needed to know.

The asshat we picked up held out longer than I thought, but it all came spilling out after I took out his left kneecap. Then it became a matter of beating him to revive him when he passed out. I suppose a bucket of water might have brought him around, but cracking his ribs was much more effective. He told Lorenzo that his boss is going to claim he heard about what I did from some idiot in the Polish mafia.

Fucking hell. When are people going to understand the difference? The Mafia— with a capital M —are Italians, and more often than not Sicilians. He was talking about the Polish Mob, fucking unoriginal name as you can get. We are not fucking interchangeable with these peon syndicates. The Russians are bratva, the Latin Americans are cartel, the Irish are the original mob— because that's about as organized as they get —and we are the Mafia. Not hard, fucknuts.

We discovered there's no real Polish syndicate member. Cohenour picked some guy he didn't like who backed out of some investment and is going to say this unsuspecting patsy told him about me. He'll vanish conveniently when the cops are ready to interview him. Cohenour plans to implicate me in that, too. He believes telling the cops that he knows what I allegedly did will make him valuable. It's about to make him dead if the Polish find out he's sucking them in. I'd make him dead, but there's one teensy-tiny speed bump to that.

He's Sinead's fucking client. Carmine looked up the public records to find out what Cohenour's facing, and the documents list Sinead's name right beside his as his counsel. I can't touch him. It's bad enough I can't take him out. It's going to be a disaster when Sinead finds out Uncle Salvatore contacted Bartlomiej Nowakowski, the Polish Mob's boss. I can't confess to knowing a crime is about to happen, but if she learns I had anything to do with it after the fact, she'll never trust me.

"How was your weekend?"

I'm trying to make nice since I have to at least trust her not to let me wind up in jail for life with no possibility of parole.

"Boring but restful. Thanks for dropping me off here Thursday evening. I got even more done than I expected, so I really had no work to even think about over the weekend. That's a pleasant change. How about you?"

"You know. Hanging out with Lorenzo and Marco. Same old same old."

I grin because what else can I do? But I get serious when I glance at my watch. We only have an hour-and-a-half to review the evidence we have so far. Then we're breaking for lunch before my pre-trial conference. I shift our attention to work and keeping me out of prison.

"Where do we stand on things?"

"The case still feels flimsy. The DA must have something they're planning because they wouldn't bring this to trial if they didn't believe they could win. This is high profile, so they won't want to fall on their faces. But I'm not seeing anything that really locks down any claim that you're guilty."

"We both know they don't have to have concrete evidence

to get a guilty decision. All they have to prove is motive, means, and opportunity. They're going to say my motive is a rivalry or revenge. They're going to say I had the means because I can get to explosives and coerce people into doing things. They'll finally claim opportunity because it happened at night. All they have to do is keep hammering that home with even an ounce of support, and people will buy it."

"That's why we need something that's absolute. Something that's irrefutable against them. It won't be hard to prove your known affiliation with the Mancinellis. Your family is pretty fucking squeaky clean for what you're into, but it's not a secret who you are. There's just never enough to make any charges stick. The DA wants to change that."

"There might be someone."

Her eyebrows shoot up with that comment, but she's trying for nonchalant when she responds.

"Oh?"

"Yeah. Someone you know. Sinead, I spoke to someone over the weekend who said your client Art Cohenour could be involved. He's going to claim he heard about my guilt from some guy in the Polish Mob. There is no guy, but he wants to get off the charges he faces."

She sits back for a moment and bites the left corner of her bottom lip. The things I'd like to do while I nibble on it.

"I know. That's who I met with last week."

"He told you that was his plan?"

"You know I can't get into more than that. Suffice it to say, I convinced him that trying it would be the height of stupidity."

"He's going to get himself killed, claiming someone in the Polish Mob is feeding him secrets. They will find out."

I won't say that we told them. I'm curious how she's going to play this. Discovering one of her clients intends to testify against me raised all my suspicions against her. I may want to fuck her into next week, but that doesn't mean we're friends going out for a beer.

"I think I convinced him without having to scare him."

"I hope you're right."

I can hope it, but I don't think that's the case. We switch subjects and examine the evidence we've collected on our side along with what the prosecution has already turned over.

"You know all the people on the witness list. Is there anyone on here you think would convince the jury of your alleged guilt?"

"There are a few who'd love to see me sentenced to life, but none of them know enough to put me away. They would have to perjure themselves."

"Do you think any of them would?"

"Probably most of them."

"Is there anyone at the top of the list?"

"I'd say your client still tops it. I'm not convinced you've dissuaded him from going through with his plan."

"He wanted to go state's witness for immunity from his charges. That won't happen."

"Then a reduction in sentencing."

"Maybe."

I can tell she doesn't want to talk about her client more, so I don't press. I'll do my own digging and get Carmine to help me if I need it. I can't think of what Cohenour looks like or who this guy is, but I predict it's going to be nothing but a shit storm.

"At best, the evidence against you is circumstantial. There's no evidence directly linking you to the scene, and there's no evidence at the location that proves you were there the day or night it happened. The most damning thing they have is that you met with the construction foreman and the building inspector the day before. They'll say you did something nefarious to them to get access to the building, or that you coerced them into helping you."

"They buy materials from my hardware stores. That's where I met them. The foreman was placing an order for lumber. The inspector was getting stuff for his garden. It was coincidental we were all there at the same time. I was only at that store because my manager had the flu. My stores generally run themselves. I only go in for payroll, which wasn't until the following week."

"But security footage shows you talking to them."

"By the register. If I were plotting something, would I do it where any customer could overhear?"

"I know that. You know that. The prosecution knows that. But can they convince a jury otherwise? Possibly. The upside is we have the email your manager sent and the time-off request. Since she sent it the night before, and there's no email or phone record you contacted either man, we should be able to poke holes in that argument. What the prosecution is really going to hammer home— forgive the pun —is that you have all the necessary supplies for the explosives right in your store. You have easy access to it all."

"If I was using a fertilizer bomb. These were demolition bombs that require nitroglycerines and explosives. Those aren't things I stock."

"But Salvatore owns a construction company that has access to them. The prosecution will argue you used those."

"They'll argue that I got the supplies from my hardware stores, then they'll say I got them from Mancinelli Developers' warehouses. It can't be both."

"I know Tyler. He'll use the store video to say you conspired with the other men. He'll insinuate that you consid-ered the supplies from your store, maybe even tested them.

Then you decided to use the construction company's more powerful explosives."

"We run security at the warehouse around the clock, so no one can steal from us. I haven't been there in months."

"Since he's arguing this is premeditated, he may suggest you stockpiled them until the right time. Or that someone abetted your crime and got them for you."

"This grows more ridiculous by the moment, Sinead."

"You know that. I know that. The prosecution knows that. But if they can convince the jury, then it's completely logical to at least some of them. After that, it'll be up to those jurors to convince anyone on the fence."

"That's a lot of ifs that have to line up."

"Tyler is persuasive."

"You sound like you know that from more than just the courtroom."

"I dated him most of my second year of law school."

That's a gut punch. I didn't expect the idea of meeting a past boyfriend to bother me so much. Meeting someone she's fucked at Cries and Whispers would be unpleasant, but that would just be about sex. Most of a school year implies an emotional connection.

"Gabriele, that was years ago. I ended it."

Was I that transparent? Does she know it's because I want her? Or does she think I'm doubting her professionalism? It's the former, but I hope she thinks it's the latter.

"What else could they have against me?"

I push on. I don't want to linger over this.

"You employ more than one former gang member. They're going to say you exploited and extorted them to place the bomb."

"Hiring men who have been jumped out and repaid their

debt to society doesn't mean they're willing to commit crimes again."

"And we have them on our side. They've all become model citizens, and their parole officers have nothing negative to say against them. They've all been on the stand before, so they know what to expect during cross examination. I'm not worried about that, so they'll need minimal coaching. My hope is it won't get that far. I'll take it whether it's voluntary or involuntary for the DA's office. I think there's enough lack of evidence to get this dismissed during the pretrial conference. I'm just not convinced we should play that hand yet."

"You mean a motion for dismissal?"

"Yeah. Let's not rush that until we're sure it'll be granted."

We spend another thirty minutes reviewing photos and security footage. I'm feeling more confident than I when I walked in.

We continue to work through lunch, her admin assistant grabbing us Chinese food from around the corner. We discuss all the situations that could arise during the conference. She's pushing me not to go, which is what I would tell a client. The only reason I might attend is because I'm a lawyer, too.

"Gabriele, the judge probably won't allow you into the conference."

"Then I'll wait outside."

I infuse authority into my voice. We both know I'll get what I want simply because she has no way to stop me.

"No. The reporters are bound to harass you."

"Will you protect me?"

I smile at her wolfishly.

"I've already proven I can."

Her smirk is sexy as hell.

"We should get going."

We walk out together, and I lead her to one of our SUVs. I

think that surprises her. It's one of the biggest on the road, seating seven and still having enough trunk space for us to store gear and seven high-powered rifles. It's Giuseppe today, so he opens the door. Once we're underway, I can tell she wants silence. I don't know how, but it's just a sense. She's looking out the window, but I can tell she's not taking in the sights. She's considering all her options during the upcoming conference. We've been driving for ten minutes before she turns to me.

"Gabriele, I don't think we're ready to file a two-ten-twenty after all, but if we can, I will."

"If you file a Motion to Dismiss or Reduce Indictment, which are you going for?"

I'm very familiar with the New York Section 210.20 of the Criminal Procedures. I've filed that motion more times than I can count since I became an attorney. It's a criminal motion that's gotten most Mancinelli Mafia men off the hook. Except, in my case, there's no witness to intimidate or bribe. It works so much better when there is.

"The dismissal. Nothing less. I won't back down if this gets forced into trial. But I know we'd both rather if not get that far."

It's not long before we show up at the courthouse. There are no buzzards circling outside, but I don't know what to expect when we get inside. We make it through security without issue, and we're on our way up to the third floor. It's quiet here too. Maybe, just maybe, we can get through this without there being a spectacle.

"Sinead."

I watch a tall, sandy-haired guy approaching us as Sinead turns around. He's definitely good looking. I can see how she would be attracted to him, but he looks like a smug dick. He's got a muscular build a lot like the other guys in my family. Thank God the Mancinellis treat me like family because I'd be screwed every which way from Sunday if I was doing this alone.

I recognize this guy. He was the Assistant DA during my first trial where I was the lead attorney. He's good, but he's pompous. I'm glad Sinead knows him even though I want to crush his head against the wall. I'm certain she can use that to her advantage. The level of possessiveness I feel is completely irrational and unjustified.

"Hello, Tyler. This is my client, Mr. Scotto."

I extend my hand. He glances at it for a second before he takes it. When we release each other, I half expect him to pull out a bottle of hand sanitizer since he looks like he just stuck his hand in shit.

"Good afternoon, Mr. Yaeger."

"Mr. Scotto. Good to see you again."

"I doubt that. The last time we saw each other, my client walked free. Then again, maybe you're hoping to lock me up and throw away the key to even our record."

Sinead looks back and forth between us. She's markedly uncomfortable. Neither he nor I are adversarial as we talking. I'm just holding up my end of the conversation, but Sinead gets to the point.

"You know each other?"

I answer first.

"Not well. Tyler was opposing counsel during my first trial. It's been about a year since we've crossed paths."

Tyler interjects as his eyes now bore into me.

"Are you representing yourself?"

"You know I'm not."

"Clients rarely attend these meetings. Are you sitting second chair on your own defense?"

"I could."

I don't want to engage further, so I remain quiet. Sinead is likely to chew me a new one when we're alone. I honestly didn't put two-and-two together when she said her ex-boyfriend was Tyler, which meant an Assistant DA. I haven't forgotten him; I just wasn't thinking about him earlier. At least not as opposing counsel. I need to pull my head out of my ass. I follow Sinead into the office with Tyler and his paralegal bringing up the rear.

"Mr. Scotto, I didn't expect you to join us."

"Good afternoon, Your Honor. I realize it's unusual for me to be here, so I will be an observer."

I take a seat off to the side near Sinead, but not directly in front of the judge.

"Very well. Mr. Yaeger, do you have anything to offer the defense?"

"No, Your Honor. The nature of these crimes is heinous and does not warrant a plea offer."

"What say you, Ms. O'Malley?"

"That's fine. We aren't interested in a plea agreement since my client is innocent."

"As brief as this meeting could be, counselors, where are we with discovery? The prosecution already presented sufficient evidence to necessitate a preliminary trial. Are we ready to move forward?"

I watch Sinead watch Tyler. Neither of them says anything, so Sinead cocks an eyebrow. Tyler remains silent.

"Mr. Yaeger, the burden of proof is on you, not me. You have provided no further evidence than you did to Mr. Mancinelli— Massimo Mancinelli —at the beginning of discovery. If this is all you have, then I'll be moving to dismiss."

"Which Judge Hutchens will deny since we have motive, means, and opportunity."

"Excuse me, Mr. Yaeger. I hadn't realized we switched places. Do not speak on my behalf."

The woman is glowering at Tyler, and I'm trying not to be the one smirking now. He looks like he almost forgot the older woman was there. He looks appropriately chagrined.

"I apologize, Your Honor. Ms. O'Malley, we have more than what we've sent you."

"Were you planning to share that?"

"Yes. Of course."

"Did I miss the memo? I haven't seen any emails from you or your paralegal. Do you have the witness list at least?"

"Yes."

I watch him pull papers from his briefcase. I can't tell from where I'm sitting if it's just the witness list or more, but I can see the staple. It looks like four or five pages. Sinead scans through each page, then flips back to the beginning. She runs her finger down the page before glancing up.

"I assume this is my copy."

"Yes."

When the paralegal speaks up and confirms Sinead's statement, she reaches into her bag and pulls out a pen and highlighter. She marks up the document and turns it toward Tyler.

"Set up a time for me to interview each highlighted name."

"Oh, please."

Tyler mutters under his breath, but Sinead doesn't flinch. She continues to bore her gaze into him until he nods.

"Camille will set them up and confirm the time."

"I've underlined the items you listed but have not shared with us. Have those to me by the end of the day."

I watch Judge Hutchens to see whether she appreciates Sinead's assertiveness or whether she sees it as rudeness. Her expression is completely neutral, but she's studying them both intently. She hasn't interrupted, so I'm going with she's fine with Sinead's disposition. I think it's hot.

"And do you have your witness and evidence list?"

56

Tyler adopts a smug mien, and I can practically see Sinead's eyes wanting to roll. She twists and points to something Camille has in her lap.

"It's right there. I sent it over Thursday evening."

She reaches into her bag and pulls out an additional copy, which she hands the judge. She compiled a list of four character witnesses who are respected community members and not Italian-Americans. She has the foreman and building inspector on her list. They didn't appear on the prosecution's list, which shocked the hell out of me. There's video evidence that gives me an alibi at the time of the bombing. I was Serafina's bodyguard while she and Carmine had dinner with her sister and brother-in-law. There're street camera images of me getting out of the limo and holding the door open for the women. There's building footage of me entering and exiting, and footage from inside, showing me standing off to a corner. All of it has time stamps that show I didn't leave and come back.

The owner of the site, relatives of the deceased gang members, and witnesses from the neighborhood are all on the prosecution's list. It doesn't surprise me to see the family members of the UBN— United Blood Nation —affiliated gang members on there. Except neither man who died ever worked for me. At least not on the record. The reformed gang members I employ come from the Bronx into Queens to work. It's not convenient, but I work with a transition program for young men and women.

The people I employ are all under the age of twenty-three. The gangs coerced them to join, and later the state incarcerated them. Now, they have left the gangs to start new lives. Getting them out of the Bronx for at least eight hours a day reduces the chances for recidivism. I didn't have a choice about being born into a generations old Mafia family, and I can never leave.

That's why I help people get out of their situation. I get where they're at.

I watch Sinead jot down something in a notebook she pulled from her bag. I can see her circle it, but she holds it in a way that neither Tyler nor Camille can see her notes. She angles it so I can see. The name shocks the shit out of me. Maybe Cohenour wasn't all talk. Maybe there were some hints of truth to what he said.

It doesn't take long to finish the conference since Tyler offered no agreements, and we wouldn't have taken any. Judge Hutchens, Sinead, and Tyler are discussing further discovery and projected trial dates. Part of me would be happy for it to never come, while another part of me just wants it over. I hate limbo.

Chapter Six

Sinead

"Gabriele, their witness list is filling out, but they still don't have anyone who can definitively link you to the crime. After I interview the witnesses I want to see, I may have grounds for the motion, but it's going to be a hard sell. My gut says I need to wait to use that card."

When we got back into the SUV, I showed him my notes on the papers Camille handed me, then I showed him the name I wrote in my notebook. I didn't expect to see a name I suspect is connected to the Polish Mob. It was a security guard where the bombing happened. It made me think of a name I heard a while back. Someone important in the Polish Mob; I just don't know how.

Gabriele's expression went blank when I looked at him. He cautioned me that the Polish Mob might send someone to Cohenour's trial if he persists in spreading rumors about them. To him, it was clear someone tipped off the Polish Mob about the rumors. It makes me wonder if it was Salvatore or Massimo. I don't think it was Gabriele.

His tone hardens compared to when we started talking about next steps in the car. It makes me uneasy.

"I agree. But I don't want you interviewing Jacek Nowakowski alone. He's Bartlomiej Nowakowski's younger brother. Bartlomiej is strategic and likes to keep his friends close and enemies closer. Right now, we're friends. But Jacek lashes out then thinks. He won't threaten you in front of anyone, but he will make sure you have a second, third, and fourth shadow to intimidate you. I know I can't go with you to his interview. You have to let Uncle Massimo be there. Jacek'll behave with our *consigliere* there. Him or Luca."

Gabriele's terrifying me now, but I force my voice to remain calm.

"Why Luca?"

"He's our underboss. Uncle Salvatore won't go because it'll appear like we're issuing the threat. Luca isn't an attorney, but you can state he's part of your team for that day. As our *consigliere*, it would be preferable for Uncle Massi to go. He's an attorney, and his position is just as respected as Luca's. He's also known Jacek his entire life. The man's uncles on his mother's side used to do work for us. They wanted nothing to do with the old bratva *pakhan*. They paid us good money for our protection."

I furrow my brow. I don't know who these people are. But it sounds like the Mancinellis have been extorting them for years. I can't believe Gabriele just admitted that. All of this confirms I've stepped into a world I know nothing about.

"Maksim Kutsenko is the current bratva leader. He's ruthless and pretty much every stereotype of a Soviet hitman in movies. However, he's night and day different from Vladislav Lushak, his predecessor. That man was what they make psychological thrillers about. He had enough psychotic tendencies to have the next DSM— that book psychologists and psychiatrists use that describes mental illnesses —written about him. The DSM-6 Lushak Edition. He was fucking insane. Certifiably, lock him up and throw away the keys, Hannibal Lecter fucking warped and twisted."

"Doesn't that set the wrong tone arriving with muscle at my back?"

"Not when you're dealing with these types of men. Sinead, I do not doubt you can hold your own intellectually with any of them. You'll run circles around them. But they will see you, and they will think they can eat you for dinner. I need them to understand you are untouchable. If you weren't my attorney, I would be the one to go with you. People know what my position was for years. Very few cross me when it comes to targeting anyone I protect."

"I wish you could go with me. I don't know Luca, and I barely met Massimo."

"Luca has a jagged scar on his face. It's obvious it was a gnarly wound that had to be stitched up. Not only does it lend an air of danger to him— as his wife would say—" He rolls his eyes. "—It's obvious that it's old, and anyone who survived that isn't a weak-ass bitch, for lack of a better way to put it."

"Well, good. I wouldn't want a weak-ass bitch guarding me."

I nod at him, and I'm pretty sure he tempered his language for my sake. He's not saying anything I hadn't already suspected, but I appreciate him saying it. Yes, it's obvious. But I like that he's taking the time to explain it rather than issuing a unilateral order or expecting me to obey simply because he said so. I don't expect him to justify everything. Some things I'm certain I will have to accept purely because he said so. For now, it's nice.

"Make sure he comes to your office for the interview. Do not meet him somewhere. Luca or Uncle Massi will say the same. Do not give him any opportunity to think he has home court advantage or that you'll jump at his command. But don't let him act as if him coming to you is doing you a favor. The moment he thinks that, he'll believe you owe him. He's complicated in a simplistic way. He's a narcissistic sadist. That's simple to see and understand. He's sometimes illogical, so that can make him complicated and unpredictable. Do not speak to him alone, Sinead. I'm serious."

"I get it. I know you're not trying to freak me out. But you've made your point."

"I'll be in the car outside your office during the meeting. I want you to wear an earpiece. In case anything goes wrong, I want to hear you. You'll be on the same frequency as Luca or Uncle Massi."

"You can't record the meeting."

"I'm not going to. But I am going to be certain you and whoever goes with you survive."

Would this guy attack me in an office building with at least fifty other people? Is he truly that deranged? From the way Gabriele's talking, he is. I need to consider my line of questioning carefully.

We're pulling up to my office, and Gabriele's already told me he has to go to one of his stores to check some water damage from the storm we had over the weekend. I really don't want to say goodbye. I know I have work to do, but I want more time with him. Something about him just has me wanting to trail after him like a puppy. Or is it a bitch in heat? I don't know much about him beyond what I need to for this case, but I want to. It's the opposite of what a sane woman would want. He's shared things with me, and he's warned me for the sake of my protection. But I still get the impression he doesn't trust me. I want to trust him since he's looking out for me.

"Thanks for the ride."

"Afonso will be here. Remember, don't leave the building without him."

"I know. Thanks."

There's that edge again in his voice. The way he goes from cordial to disdainful. Is it that, though? No. That's not it. Closed off. That's better. I don't think he looks down at me, but he's only letting me in as far as he's willing to. I'm realizing he has control of all our conversations.

I drove to the office this morning since I was running late. I know I could have had one of the Mancinelli drivers take me, but I'm not used to having people around me all the time. I enjoy being able to blast my music. Giuseppe followed me this morning, and now Afonso will have the evening shift. Somewhere between me getting to the office and Gabriele and me leaving for the meeting, Giuseppe wound up with an SUV. I'm trying to just go with it all and not ask unnecessary questions. But part of me wants to ask all the unnecessary questions since there is so much I know I can't ask.

Once Gabriele leaves me just inside the office suite door, I head to my office. I review what I have for the Cohenour case since that trial begins the day after tomorrow. My client knowing about Gabriele's case came out of nowhere. I thought he was making shit up about the Polish Mob. He accepted my pushback about committing perjury. Now I'm wondering if there's another connection to the Polish Mob that I'm missing for Cohenour? Did someone overhear him then go to Jacek? Nothing during discovery for that case leads me to think there is. Jacek is involved in this somehow. This coincidence can't be a coincidence.

I pull out some paperwork and find a phone number.

"Mr. Cohenour, this is Sinead O'Malley."

I don't enjoy making phone calls if I can avoid them, but I can't do this via email.

"Hello, Ms. O'Malley. Is everything all right for the trial to start?"

I hear the anxiousness. His voice is less strident than usual. Hopefully, he shows up with a little of that humility.

"I have some questions before we go into trial based on what you told me the other day."

"Okay."

The hesitation. Fuck me if he sounds like that on the stand. This isn't humility. It's fear, but he's insisting he wants to testify. It's his right, but it's yet another thing I've been strenuously urging him *not* do.

"I need you to come into the office, please."

He agrees, and thirty minutes later, he walks in. I lead him to the conference room and jump straight in.

"The story you planned to concoct. Why the Polish Mob?"

"What do you mean?"

"I know your story was going to be that someone in the Polish Mob told you about Mr. Scotto's alleged illegal activities. Why did you pick the Polish Mob?"

"Because— uh —I know they have connections to the Mafia. The guy who heads it is friends with Salvatore Mancinelli, I guess. That's what I've heard. I figured it would be plausible that they'd do him a solid by covering for him."

More contradictions.

"But you made it sound like this person you were going to claim was your source would speak up because they wanted Gabriele to be found guilty. It can't be both."

"Yeah, it can. Bartlomiej and Jacek Nowakowski get along with Salvatore out of necessity and would help him out if he asked. But neither of them like Gabriele because he's been the one to enforce some of Salvatore's wishes. Since those brothers don't like him, neither do members of their organization. Any of them would be happy to narc on him."

"Aren't you worried that implicating anyone in the Polish Mob in Mr. Scotto's case could be dangerous for you? If word gets around you said a Polish Mobster knows what Mr. Scotto did, do you think Bartlomiej will turn a blind eye? Not with you drawing attention to them. What happened to wanting to protect your family?"

"Um. Hmm. He knows it's just business."

For fuck's sake. None of this makes sense. He's fucking all over the place.

"Does he, though? Have you told him about your plan? If pressed for a name, do you have one to give? One that belongs to a person the cops can question?"

"Uh, no."

"If NYPD can't find your supposed source, they won't give up. They'll just dig deeper and stir up more complications. That's not what anyone needs. So, was there any truth in what you said?"

Hesitation. My fucking word. He still needs so much coaching. He's like a deer in the headlights kind of hesitant, not a measured and thoughtful hesitant.

"Someone in the Polish Mob knows something. I don't know any names or details. I just overheard a few guys in a parking lot at the casino in Atlantic City."

"Did you tell anyone what you overheard?"

His face flushes. Why can't his story be consistent? It's making me think he knows something; he just hasn't figured out how to use it. It's making him jump all over the place.

"I got a bit tipsy at the roulette table, and I might have said something about knowing the person who's going to take down the mobster to a guy who works for me. We met up there because the place has the best buffet."

Why fucking me? I've had other trying clients, and he's hardly the worst. But everything about him irritates me. And this started well before I met Gabriele. But discussing anything that connects him to Gabriele sets me on edge.

"Do you intend to speak to either brother before the Assistant DA interviews you for this?"

"Uh, no."

"You're just going to let someone find out about this lead of yours and tell the Polish Mob, meanwhile, praying for the best? You'll be safer in prison."

"I can't play my hand."

"There is no hand to play. Once the prosecution interviews you, they *will* get this information, and they *will* send out cops to pick up anyone else you name. The prosecution *will not* settle with just your hearsay testimony. They *will* want the firsthand account. Two things *will* happen if you don't make that connection for them. Actually, three things. One, they won't offer you immunity. Two, they won't call you as a witness. Three, the defense attorney will impeach you. If you're the prosecution's witness, I will have to step down from Mr. Scotto's case. I can't represent Mr. Scotto and question you during his trial since I already have prior knowledge about you. If you perjure yourself or an attorney can poke holes enough to impeach you after I'm forced to walk away from Mr. Scotto's case, I won't be pleased."

I raise an eyebrow and narrow my eyes at the same time. It's the look I mastered in high school when I used to babysit three sisters who were monsters to each other. It would make them stop dead in their tracks, and it's doing the same to Cohenour.

"So, what do I do, Ms. O'Malley?"

"You can tell the ADA that you know someone who could

be an informant for them. You could even see if the prosecution will consider a minimum sentence in exchange for your cooperation. But you're already weakening your defense by insisting upon taking the stand. If you also testify during Mr. Scotto's trial, you risk adding to your sentence with the crime of perjury."

"All right. I won't ask for immunity, but I will tell the police that there's a possible informant."

"Good."

I pull out my phone and tap my contacts before I show Cohenour a phone number.

"This is the lead detective for Mr. Scotto's case. Call him now from your phone."

I don't trust him at all to make the call on his own. I want the phone record that he placed the call with his attorney present, but not under duress. I don't want him claiming someone intimidated him into making the call. Who knows who he'd name. I watch him dial before putting the phone to his ear.

"Speaker."

He taps the button while it rings.

"Detective Morris."

"Hello, Detective. My name is Arthur Cohenour. I'm calling because I have information about the Scotto case that my attorney is advising me to share."

"Hello, Mr. Cohenour. Who is your attorney?"

"Sinead O'Malley."

I can imagine what Philip Morris— yes, his parents really gave him the same name as a tobacco company —must be thinking right now. He and I do not get along. At all. Ever. I've impeached him on the stand six times. Yes, I have kept count. He's a clean cop and a good one. I have ears like a dog when I listen to testimonies and compare them to depositions. I snag

67

even the slightest thing I can make look like an inconsistency. It's gotten six clients off.

"Ms. O'Malley, I assume you're present."

"I'm here, Detective Morris."

I can practically hear him grimacing and grinding his teeth. It's his usual reaction to me.

"Mr. Cohenour, what would you like to tell me?"

"I heard some men discussing Gabriele Scotto and the bombing, and they seemed to know he did it."

"When did you hear this?"

"Two days after the bombing."

"Where were you?"

"At the Grand Toucan in Atlantic City."

"Were you intoxicated?"

Not surprising that's one of the first questions. If my client hadn't told me he heard this before going inside, I would have dismissed it as him probably being drunk as a fucking skunk.

"No. I heard them in the parking garage before I went inside."

"They were just standing around talking about it?"

"They didn't know I was sitting in my car with the window open, smoking a cigar. It's a good luck thing. Their voices carried as they walked past."

"What exactly did you hear?"

"One of them said Scotto was finally going down. The other said it was about time and that it serves him right for being so sloppy."

"That isn't enough to substantiate they know anything first-hand. They could have heard about it on the news."

"Like I said, it was two days after it happened. It was the day before the NYPD arrested him."

That's suspect. But if that's all he heard, none of us can be sure these men actually knew anything about the bombing.

They could just be repeating gossip they heard through their associates who have dirty cops working for them. There's any number of ways a syndicate could already know the NYPD was looking at Gabriele for this.

"Mr. Cohenour, you and Ms. O'Malley need to come down to the station to file a report. Ms. O'Malley, I assume this call means you intend to remain Mr. Cohenour's attorney for this case and will no longer represent Mr. Scotto?"

"That is no longer guaranteed. Mr. Cohenour begins his own trial the day after tomorrow."

I shoot my client a look that tells him not to question me. I'm going to call Diane, the ADA on this case. I'll see if she's willing to negotiate anything to plea down the charges or convince her to recommend the minimum sentence. If she says she'll consider him testifying against Gabriele as a reason to go easier on Cohenour, then I have to step down from Gabriele's case. If she says there's nothing she will do, then I remain on this case for the duration of the grand larceny trial. But someone else at my firm will handle his involvement in Gabriele's case. I'm not walking away from Gabriele. So far, Cohenour hasn't said anything I wouldn't learn through discovery. Nothing is privileged.

"Meet me at the station at nine tomorrow morning."

I speak up.

"Detective, that won't work. We will meet you there at one."

I'm assuming my client can make it. He better make sure he can. I need more time to sort out getting someone to replace me.

"Very well. Only for you, Ms. O'Malley."

Detective Morris sounds about as enthusiastic as a man about to get castrated. After they hang up, I explain the new situation to my client— that I may need to find someone else to represent him if he testifies against Gabriele. I also tell him I will confirm who will join him at the precinct station in the afternoon. Either someone else from my firm or me. As soon as he leaves, I make my way to one of the managing partners and rap on his door.

"Come in."

I open it partway and lean my head in.

"Jason, is this a good time to discuss something that's come up that involves two cases?"

"Yes. What's going on?"

He moves some papers aside, and I take a seat across from his desk.

"I'm going to trial in two days for the Art Cohenour grand larceny case. He informed me on Thursday that he'd heard incriminating information about Gabriele Scotto. I'm now caught between the two. Cohenour wanted to negotiate immunity from his current charges if he cooperates. I've told him it's highly unlikely, but we might convince Diane to suggest the minimum sentence. I was just on the phone with him and Detective Morris."

"And if you represent him for this, you can't represent Scotto. You'd have to hide what you know came from Cohenour to protect his privilege rights while compromising Scotto's right to a proper defense."

"Exactly."

"And I suppose you have a solution that you want me to agree to."

"Yes."

"Has anyone ever told you that you're incredibly blunt for an attorney?"

"Of course."

I grin at him, and he smiles back. He's right. I can be subtle any time I want, but right now, I want this resolved to my advantage. I won't beat around the bushes, and I don't need to maneuver Jason.

"Let me guess. You'll continue as Cohenour's attorney for his current case because it's too close to trial for someone else to take it. But you want someone else to represent him for any involvement he has with the Scotto case. Have you heard anything that would give the prosecution grounds for a mistrial?"

"I don't believe so. He told me he'd overheard some members of the Polish Mob talking about Mr. Scotto. His story's fluctuated a bit between what he originally suggested happened to this. Right now, he claims he was in his car, smoking a cigar, at the Grand Toucan. The men said something to the effect that Mr. Scotto deserves a conviction, and he shouldn't have been careless. He hasn't named either man, but he clearly recognized them if he knows they're Polish Mob. When he first told me, it sounded like he was going to stray from this and fabricate a story good enough for him to think it was worth the immunity. I warned him that doing that— doing this —would put him in the Mob's crosshairs. I haven't asked him how he's connected to them. That said, the prosecution witness list for the Scotto case has a known member of the Polish Mob on there because he was the security guard that night. I believe the key to what the Polish Mob does or doesn't know is Jacek Nowakowski."

"Who?"

"He's the mob boss's younger brother. His reputation precedes him. He's apparently conniving and vindictive. Maybe he knows something and mentioned it to the two men, or the two men overheard something. Then, either way, Cohenour heard it, too. Maybe Nowakowski is the person who shifted blame to Mr. Scotto. I won't know until I can interview him. I want to see what he has to say before I let the ADA know because we risk the ADA finding out and trying to recruit him to their side. He is not a man who'd side with the state unless he can get something out of them. He's fine risking being in contempt, so I'm certain questioning him will only benefit us."

"But what if he gives damning information that proves your client's guilt? What if he testifies in order to get something out of the NYPD or even the DA's office?"

"There's nothing to get other than lies since Mr. Scotto is innocent."

Jason watches me for a long moment, and it tempts me to shift nervously. Can he tell I'm attracted to Gabriele? Nothing's happened between Gabriele and me, but I want it to. If I'm lucky, it will. I know it should wait until after the trial, but fuck, he's the hottest man I've ever seen.

"Very well. Who do you recommend take over Cohenour?"

"Marcy. She can't stand me. There won't be any questions of impropriety, suggesting she might share anything with me to benefit Mr. Scotto. She'd spit on me if I was drowning."

"Really? Why the animosity?"

"She's been here two years longer than I have, but I made junior partner before her. She's certain it was nepotism because of my relationship with Marta. She thinks the managing partners are playing favorites."

I keep my tone neutral and my expression blank. I need to establish there wouldn't be any cause for the partners or the DA's office to claim we shared information inappropriately. I also don't want to come across as trashing her.

"She may not like me, but she's got the patience for Cohenour, and she's one of the best we have."

That's all true and most of the reason I suggested her.

"Very well. Let me have her join us."

I watch him dial her extension and ask her to come in. I

turn when she knocks on the door. She glances skeptically at me, and I shoot Jason a look that says *see*. She sits next to me.

"Marcy, Sinead's client, Art Cohenour, may be a prosecution witness for the Gabriele Scotto case. If that happens, Sinead can't represent both men. She will continue on as Art's lawyer for his case since it's going to trial this week. But she's recommended you represent him while he serves as a witness. If he serves as a witness."

She looks point blank at me.

"Why not give me the Scotto case?"

I knew that was coming. This is a make or break a career case. It would get her name and face in front of a lot of people. She'd likely get a raise here or get poached by an even better firm. I also saw her practically salivating over Gabriele when she walked past the conference room four times during our meeting. She didn't need to go past it at all. Yet another thing to add to the tally of why she doesn't like me. Fuck her. I don't give a shit.

"Because the Mancinellis requested her personally."

That makes me whip my head around to look at Jason.

"They did?"

"Yes. Massimo and Salvatore Mancinelli conducted an exhaustive search for an attorney, and they not only chose our firm, but you specifically. They are very convincing."

Oh, God. Did they threaten the firm? Clearly, Marcy thinks the same.

"Just how convincing were they?"

"Convincing to the tune of four times the regular retainer and three times the regular hourly rate."

Holy fucking shit! The regular retainer for a junior partner is fifteen-thousand-dollars, so they paid sixty thousand. My hourly rate is five hundred, so they're paying fifteen hundred.

This could wind up costing them more than a quarter of a million dollars. That's insane.

"Fine."

I come out of my fog and realize Marcy just agreed to take over for me with Cohenour.

"His case shouldn't run longer than a week, two tops. I'll pass along everything once it's done. I'll brief you, so you're up to speed on whatever his legal status becomes."

"Thank you."

She hardly sounds grateful. Whatever. It'll be easy shit for her since all she'll have to do is make sure he says nothing that could wind up with him on trial for something new. She won't be defending him in court. The ADA will coach him if he has to testify.

We leave Jason's office, and all I want to do is lock my office door until it's time to go home. But I can't. I head into my office and start making calls to cops who like me. I have connections in narcotics, homicide, violent crimes, gang squad, and forensic investigations. I have to leave the arson and explosions unit alone for right now. But I'm going to see what I can learn about the Polish Mob. I want all their known associates along with everything to do with the Nowakowski brothers.

Three hours later, and my head is spinning. The Nowakowskis may not lead a major syndicate, but they sure as fuck want to. I found out they're trying to increase their influence in New York and New Jersey, so it made sense that they could be involved in Gabriele's case. I got a lead on a restaurant the brothers frequent almost nightly. Apparently, there's a back room that's not well sound proofed. It's next to the women's restroom.

Since none of them use that, they don't realize that almost everything they say is clear as day in there.

My connection in the gang squad lives three subway stops from me. We see each other all the time. She's been good to me plenty of times. She's a real sweetheart, but I would put my money on her any day in a street fight. She has no fucks to give with anyone who causes trouble.

She said I'd learn something; she just couldn't guarantee what. I asked her how dangerous it would be. She said I'll be fine if I'm not caught. If I am, my will better be up to date. I pointed out that wasn't much help. She told me to have dinner there like a regular customer, and no one would be the wiser.

Now I know where I'm having dinner tonight. The only hiccup is my security detail. If I try to shake them, Gabriele will flip out. If the guy tells Gabriele where I'm going before I can explain, he won't trust me. If I tell him, he won't let me go. I thought about how reserved he's been most of the time, and it's enough to make me think he's just being polite to me. But he's been really insistent about my safety. Is it because he wants his lawyer to live long enough to represent him? I want to believe it's something more. I want to believe it's about me personally. But he's been strictly professional.

I know where the Nowakowskis' favorite restaurant is. There's one two doors down that I've been to several times. It has a back terrace that has an exit onto the side street. The Nowakowskis favorite restaurant has a side door I can go through. I'll tell Afonso I'm meeting friends for dinner. I'll slip into the other restaurant but still be close enough to get to him if anything goes wrong. I'll just be a regular woman coming out of the ladies' room. If anyone notices I've been in there a long time, I'll claim I went to wash my hands and got in an argument with my boyfriend on the phone before I could get a table. He's refusing to come to dinner, but I refuse to let him ruin my night, so I'm dining alone.

I gather my stuff, text Afonso that I'm ready to leave, and head down to the lobby. I see him already there. He walks me around the side of the building to the part of the parking garage I used today.

"I'm headed to La Belle Maison to meet friends for dinner. Last-minute invite."

"I'll follow you, Ms. O'Malley."

"Thank you."

It takes thirty minutes to get there, but I have great parking karma and find a spot almost immediately. There's one right behind me, so Afonso pulls in. I hesitate because I'm not sure if I should get out. He answers that by walking straight to my door and opening it.

"I'll go inside and do a sweep of the place."

"Oh, all right. I think I'm the first one here. I'm a little early. I'll wait at the bar."

Shit. I hope he doesn't plan to stay in there all night. I walk to the door, and he opens it for me. But he immediately steps past me and looks around, taking in practically every person. He nods, and I head to the bar, where I order a drink. He heads back out to the car. I sip my drink before paying the bartender. I make my way toward the back door and out to the terrace. I look back over my shoulder, something telling me to. Just as I step outside, I spot Gabriele.

What the fuck? I dart outside, hoping he doesn't see me. What's he doing here? Is it a coincidence, or did Afonso tell him I was coming here? Where was he that he managed to get here so soon after I did?

I hurry across the terrace to the little gate. I push it open and look back again. I'm certain I see Gabriele approaching the door to the terrace. I can't see his face, but I can't think of any guy who'd be as tall, broad shouldered, and muscular as him unless they play for the NFL. I'm tempted to run down the street, but that'll attract attention and leave me winded. When I get onto the street, I blend into a clump of people probably headed to the subway. I look over my shoulder before I dart inside the Polish Mob's hangout, and I can still see Gabriele since he's so tall.

Him following me and the ridiculous danger I'm putting myself in stirs something within. The risk permeates the fog of determination I felt earlier. I should wait for him, explain what I'm doing, face his anger, then try to convince him to help me. I should abandon this altogether, knowing what I'm doing is beyond stupid. I can't believe my friend actually suggested this. I'm having major second thoughts. This is drunk girl in college walking home alone at three a.m. level belief in my immortality.

If I were in a movie, I'd deserve to get caught and lord only knows what else. But there's a thrill in Gabriele following me that is so utterly inappropriate for right now. I can't help it. I caught his expression when I glanced back. It's exciting.

It's quiet in here. Like makes me nervous quiet. Is this place a front for the Nowakowskis? The one time I've been here was for a friend's going away party, and someone recommended it to him. I spot the hallway to the bathroom and make a beeline for it. I just get into the shadows when an arm wraps around my waist and yanks me back. I know that scent.

Chapter Seven

Gabriele

I follow her down the hallway, certain she knows I'm there. Does she realize how soon she'll come to a dead end? That this hallway doesn't go anywhere? I watch her freeze as she discovers what I already know. She continues to stare at the wall as I walk up behind her. The door she must be looking for is hidden.

"I could have told you there is no way out, but you ran from me. You knew I followed you. I think you wanted me to chase you."

She says nothing, but I sense her anxiety. I reach past her and push the women's restroom door open. She steps in, and I'm on her heels. I sweep my gaze under the stalls, satisfied we're alone.

"Look at me."

It's not a request. She hesitates for only a second before she spins around. I encroach, backing her against the wall without touching her. All the possessiveness I felt when I saw Tyler floods back exponentially stronger. Every ounce of need to protect her thrums through my blood. She doesn't know what she's started.

"Is that what you're into?"

She stares up at me, unable or unwilling to say anything. That's fine. I'll keep doing the talking.

"That's a dangerous game you play, letting a man follow you down some dark and deserted hallway."

"You."

It's more like a puff of air than a word.

"Me what?"

"Not a man. You. I let you follow me."

"Why? You don't know me well enough to trust me following you like this."

"About this, I do. Gabriele, you are many things that terrify me. But I have never been scared that you'll hurt me."

"I won't. But can I say the same for you? Are you going to knife me? Lead me to men who'll try to kill me?"

Hurt fills her expression before she shakes her head. But why else would she come to a place known for the Polish Mob? If she's here, she must know that.

"It bothers you that I think you could do that."

It's a statement, not a question. Her coming here changes everything between us, everything I thought about her. Her voice is barely more than a whisper when she speaks. Is she breathless from me being so close, or does she still have an awareness of how precarious our situation is? Both?

"I'm many things you probably don't like right now, but I will never hurt you or make someone else do it."

I lean forward, my hands bracketing her.

"More fool am I that I believe you."

"Am I a fool to think you won't hurt me?"

"No. I will never hurt you, *piccolina*."

Her brow furrows. I let my right hand drop before I cup her jaw. Her eyes droop shut for a second, and I know she relishes me touching her as much I do touching her. This has been building since we met. Even right now when I no longer trust her like I did only hours ago. Her eyes pop open, and I see her chest rise with a deep breath. My hand slides down her throat until it rests at the base. I know it's heavy there, but I don't apply any pressure.

"You like me calling you that as much as you like your little game of cat and mouse."

"Gabriele, that's not why I like it."

Her voice grows softer with each word.

"Tell me why."

My voice is just as low, but the command is clear.

"That."

My eyebrows shoot up, but I say nothing more.

"The way it sounds when you say it. I like that."

I bring my lips only millimeters from hers, but I don't kiss her. Everything about this is heated in a way our attraction hasn't been since we met. Maybe it's the darkness of this hallway and dim lighting in the restroom. Maybe it's the fucking danger she put herself in. Put me in because there was no way I wouldn't follow her, and I think she fucking knows it deep down.

"Tell me why, *piccolina*."

She shudders as she opens her mouth, but whatever she was about to say, she refuses to let me hear. Does she have a name for me? Does she not want me to know that?

"It sounds— protective —possessive. You sound so certain."

"Because I am. You are mine."

I don't wait another second for what I've craved since the moment I first saw her. My lips press to hers, and she opens to me at the same instant. I drive my tongue into her mouth, and she sucks. Holy fuck. My hand leaves her throat to fist her hair. She knows I want her. She wants me to know she wants this, too.

I press my body against hers, trapping her between me and the wall. I grind my dick against her pussy. She fists my shirt for a moment then releases it. Her hands go to my waist, her fingers dipping beneath my belt and pants, tugging me closer. Her hips rock against me, and I nudge her legs open with mine. I slide my thigh between hers, giving her the friction I know she needs.

Her moan.

Fucking hell. That sound. I might come instead of making her come. I want to make her keep doing that. I want to hear it in the car on the way to my place. I want to hear it in the elevator up to my penthouse. I want to hear it as we walk through my door. And I sure as fuck want to hear it as I pound my cock into her as we lie in my bed. I might never let her leave it.

She pulls away, panting. I'm breathing just as hard, but I know how to be silent. I don't think she wants to be. I think she wants me to know what I'm doing to her. That or she has no idea and can't control it.

"More."

It's a plea that I want to satisfy, but I haven't completely forgotten where we are. Anyone could walk in and see us, and that is one thing I won't allow. No one will watch me pleasure my woman.

"Do want to fuck?"

"I want you to fuck me."

"You believe there's a difference."

"You know there is."

"I won't be gentle."

"Good. That's the last thing I want right now."

"And if I want to spank you while I fuck you?"

"Please."

"And if I want to bite your nipples until you fear you can't take anymore?"

She lets go of me and pushes her tits together as an offering.

"Birth control or condoms? Both? Because I am coming inside you, *piccolina*. And when I do, I won't let go of you. You are mine."

"Fuck. It's so hot when you talk like that. It's even hotter knowing you mean it."

"Is that what you want? To be mine?"

"We both know I have been since the moment we met. The moment we saw each other."

She's right. I just didn't think she realized it. I liked chasing her as much as she liked being chased. I'll make her admit it. This isn't the time or place, but I'm making it so. I'm staking my claim, and I want her to do the same thing.

"Why pretend otherwise? Was it so you could control me? Make me chase you like I did today?"

"I don't want control. Just the opposite. I can't go anywhere. You can do anything you want to me right now, and I knew that coming down here. I admit, having you follow me is empowering in a way. It feels good to be that desired. To know you pursued me and didn't stop until you had me."

"Did you want me to take without asking? Is that your real fantasy with a man?"

"You. These things I want— I only want them with you. Of course, I've wanted to be desired before. I'm not a virgin. But this— game or whatever it is —I've never played it before. I don't know all the rules, but I want it. I only want it with you."

She repeats herself. She wants me to understand that. She feels like she must prove herself to me. That's *not* what I want. I want her to admit it not feel insecure.

"I believe you, little one. Arrogant as this will sound, I don't chase women. No, it's not because they chase me, or they just give themselves to me. I've never wanted anyone the way I want you. I followed you because I wanted what we're doing now. To feel you against me. To clear the air. And to punish you for being so reckless. What if there was already someone down here? What if something or someone got in the way of me following you, and you came down here alone? Was this one time enough? Or do you want us to roleplay this fantasy again?"

"Again. And you're right about everything. It was short-sighted and reckless, but that's how much I trust you. I thought about the risk, but I was so confident you'd protect me I took it. I just knew, Gabriele. I know I'm safer with you than I will ever be with anyone else."

"You know who I am. You're my fucking attorney, which makes this utterly unethical. You know what I'm accused of, and the claims being made about my past to prove I did something I didn't."

"I'd very much like to be your fucking attorney."

She grins and waggles her eyebrows, but she grows serious. She cups my cheek with her left hand as her right rests on my chest.

"I know you're *Cosa Nostra* and what that means. I can guess at your past, but I won't ask. I will listen to anything you tell me, and I'll take it to the grave. But I won't put you in a position to divulge anything. Maybe it's having a clue what you can do that makes me know I'm safest with you. But I don't get the same feeling with any of the other men in your family. It really is you."

I lean forward and kiss her again. The first was hot, passionate, savage. This one is gentle and sensual. She slides her arms around my neck as I press against her again. My arm wraps around her waist as the other guides her hips to move on my leg.

"I'm going to make you come right now. Then we are going somewhere, so I can taste every inch of you. Then I'm going to slide my cock into your cunt and fuck you hard. I asked you before, birth control, condom, or both because I am coming inside you, *piccolina*. When I do, I'm making you—"

"I'm already yours— Gabe. I have an IUD. I've never had sex without a condom before. I want to with you. I don't want anything between us. I test regularly."

"I've never done it without a condom either, but I want to know my cum is inside you. That every step you take, you'll feel it in your pussy and on your leg. You are mine beyond fucking, Sinead. I am not your fuck buddy."

"We haven't even gone on a date, but you're so certain."

"We've spent hours together already. We're roleplaying a fantasy, so I think we're miles past a first date. Do you not want what I do?"

"I'm scared I want it too much."

I reach for the buttons of her pants and unfasten them before pulling down the zipper. I pull her blouse out and am about to slip my fingers down her panties when we hear voices. I yank her into a stall and lift her until she's standing on the toilet seat. I press down on her shoulder with one hand while reaching back to lock the door with the other. I'm crouching on the toilet seat with her a moment later. When we hear the door open, I pray whoever the woman is doesn't try our stall. It's the disabled one, so maybe she'll choose the other from habit, assuming her habit isn't to use the wider stall.

We squat together, my legs bracketing hers until the woman flushes then washes her hands. Sinead looks down at the floor and lifts her foot to get down when we hear the door close. I shake my head and press her thigh with my knee. I'm ready to reach to my lower back any second. My gun is holstered there. The door opens again.

"I thought I smelled men's cologne. It was faint, but I thought I did."

We hear a woman's voice followed by a deeper one.

"I don't smell it. Maybe some guy didn't read the bathroom sign. We've got that guy at the bar who's hammered. He broke the seal and has been going to the restroom between rounds."

I spotted him on my way in. I know who the man is talking about. I don't wear a heavy cologne, so the scent should be faint. This woman must have a nose like a bloodhound. We listen to the door close, but I still make us wait at least two minutes before I step down. Sinead cups my ear as she leans forward.

"How'd you know to wait?"

"Because we heard two voices. There was the chance that person might come in, too. The only other reason for a woman to be in this hallway— if she isn't spying —is to deliver food to the brothers."

I help her down from the toilet seat. That clearly killed the mood from earlier, which is just as well. I was seconds away from fucking her in the last place either of us should be. But we're here now. I take her hand and guide her to the wall I know separates this restroom from the secret meeting spot. I know about it because I've been in there. I forced my way in about a year ago and beat the shit out of a couple guys who were late paying us. The Nowakowski brothers didn't do shit to stop me. It pissed them off, but they knew I'd show up somewhere. I'm certain they preferred I kept the beating private.

I pull out my phone and turn it so Sinead can see the screen, too. I pull up a translation app that runs in real time, giving me subtitles to whatever it hears. I turn the mic all the way up. I'm just in time to hear the start of a conversation. I recognize the first voice is Jacek's.

"This Cohenour fucker is threatening to tell some bullshit story about overhearing two of our guys talking about that shit bag."

I've been called way worse. I don't know who the second person is.

"What do you want me to do about it?"

"Visit him. I called in a favor from Sergei Andreyev that's cost me at least seven favors in return. He scanned the video footage since it's one of their casinos. No one in the garage or the casino was one of us. He's lying. Make sure he understands honesty is the best policy."

I glance over at Sinead who also has her phone out and is furiously typing in a notes app.

Are they going to kill him?

I shrug. At some point, they will.

The next voice I hear is Jacek's uncle. The man is practically prehistoric. He's been shot at least eight times, knifed on the street, and shanked in jail. The man is immortal.

"Don't kill him until you find out who put him up to pulling us in. He isn't smart enough to come up with this on his own. He owes us for paying for that lawyer he hired. The only reason that's still a sound investment is because he'll be our bitch on the inside. The man can't shut up to save his life."

My gaze keeps jumping between my phone and Sinead. She points to her screen.

Do they mean he's going to be a mole or something in prison?

I nod. That's exactly what they want. They'll pay for his protection in prison, but they'll tell him nothing he can repeat. They'll expect him to tell them everything. I need to find out if Sinead knows Cohenour is a lackey for the Valentzas— Greek organized crime. We purposely keep them at arm's length, even though back in the day they were connected to the Lucchese family. That fell apart when someone in that old *Cosa Nostra* family turned on them and narced.

They have problems with the Albanians that go back generations. While the Greeks sided with the Lucchese, the Albanians sided with the Gambinos. Clearly, the good relations between their mother countries don't extend across the Atlantic. We've squashed our inner squabbling and don't need them reignited, especially after the recent issues we had with Carmine's dad's side of the family. Distantly related, the only partly Ciccones tried to resurrect their family's influence.

And being attached to the Greeks would have been one more reason for the FBI to look at us. Agents busted them right around the time Uncle Salvatore became our don. There was too much backstabbing between the Greeks and Albanians because of the *Costa Nostra's* tangled alliances in the past. He demands we stay away now and not instigate trouble. He's right since taking sides only invites people to think they can divide us again. It's none of our business. Those without sin can cast the first stone. We can't even pick up a pebble.

Cohenour's connection to what some call the Greek Crew is what makes me question what the fuck he's doing.

There's a lull in the conversation, or the voices are too low for us to hear. I take Sinead's phone and type in a message.

Do you know Cohenour is linked to the Greek Crew?

She shakes her head. I share a few things I learned from the guy who ratted out Cohenour.

He was an errand boy when he was a teenager. His family is still connected. He never officially left. Money he extorted went back to them.

She takes her phone back.

How do you know this?

I look at her, but I keep my expression blank. She scowls, but I can't and won't tell her that was a piece of information that came out of the guy I basically pulverized. Just as she's about to type something else, we hear voices again. I recognize Bartlomiej's now.

"Turns out Cohenour's attorney is dumping him to represent Scotto."

Sinead's hand grips my sleeve. Her expression tells me she's wondering how they know that. I'd like to know that too. It's the unknown man who speaks next.

"Nah. I heard she's still taking him to trial this week. But she's handing him over if he does anything to force her off the Scotto case."

I think it's Jacek who laughs. There's never any humor in it. It's more maniacal.

"Is Scotto fucking her yet?"

"I don't think so. Though I'd tap that ass in a heartbeat. Besides, he's got his thing. He won't fuck her."

It's my turn to fist Sinead's sleeve. I shake my head vehemently. I don't need her thinking I intend to make her a side piece. I don't need her to know about what I get up to at Cries and Whispers. At least, not yet.

I wish these fuckers would say something that's actually useful. The longer we're here the greater the chance we'll get caught. I'll end up killing someone right in front of Sinead. It'll fucking traumatize her and force her to turn me in.

It's Bartlomiej who gets them back on track.

"So what's Cohenour's deal? As far as we know, he's saying he heard two guys in the garage at the casino. But he also told someone else that one of the guys was his source and flat out told him. He needs to decide what lie he's going with."

"He needs to shut his fucking face for good."

Jacek again. The way he sounds, Cohenour won't even make it to trial in two days. I wait to see if he orders a hit, but hear nothing except chairs scraping on the floor. We wait, then we hear a door open and muffled voices in the hallway. That got us nowhere.

I put my phone away, and Sinead does the same. We look at each other, things still unresolved between us. But we can't do anything now. I take her hand and lead her to the restroom door. I ease it open and wait. When I hear and see nothing, I draw her out. When we get to the end of the hallway, she turns to the left when I turn right. I tug her hand. We can't walk out across the main dining room. I lead her to a back fire door, knowing that it won't sound an alarm. It's the door people go through to meet with Bartlomiej. It's not the one they use. They're arrogant and use the main door to come and go.

Once we get onto the street, I half steer, half drag Sinead to her car. I look at Afonso, who's standing between her car and the town car. He nods and gets into the town car's driver's seat.

"You're fucking lucky, *piccolina*. Did you see them in the dining room?"

"What? No. They were there when we left?"

"Yes. If you'd walked out the way you came in, they would have seen you. They intentionally made it difficult to see the back door from the dining room."

I cock an eyebrow to make sure she gets my drift.

"What the fuck were you thinking? I warned you away

from them. I knew you'd do this, but I want to know why. That's why I was in the car with Afonso."

"How'd you know?"

"Because you don't understand the game you're trying to enter. What were you thinking? Don't make me ask a third time."

"You seem to already know what I was thinking. That's why you hid, then followed me."

"Little girl, now is not the time to be stubborn."

I see her swallow. I relax my expression. I don't want her scared of me. I want her to have a healthy fear of what she did.

"I wanted to hear what's really going on. I wanted to know what they wouldn't tell me in a recorded interview."

"Sinead, you are not a stupid woman. Far from it."

"I know. This is probably the stupidest thing I've ever done. This isn't some book or movie, and if it were, I'd be dead and deserved it."

I see the self-loathing in her eyes, and I've pushed hard enough. I don't want her to feel worse.

"Don't risk your safety like that again, *piccolina*. You won't like the consequences."

I reach around her since her car blocks anyone's view from that side. I grab her ass and squeeze hard. She doesn't struggle against me, whimper, or push me away. She nods. I let go immediately. The way she looks at me says way more than she realizes. I lean into her and whisper, even though I know no one else can hear us.

"You want that, don't you? You want my hand on your bare ass."

She nods.

"Give me your keys. Luigi is going to drive it back to your place. You're coming with me."

"Where are we going?"

"My place."

This wasn't my plan. At least, not originally for tonight. But she will learn that her actions have consequences in my world. I lead her to the town car and hand the keys to Afonso.

"Call Luigi. Have him meet us and take her keys. Then take us to my place."

I help her into the car and slide in after her. Afonso closes the door, and the privacy glass is already up. It's how she didn't know I was in the car, too. She reaches for her seat belt, but I pull her toward me. Her shirt is still untucked, but she zipped and buttoned her pants at some point.

"Undo them and push them down. Your panties too."

"What?"

"Sinead, do it. You risked your life today, and I told you there would be consequences. Your expression told me you consent as loudly as if you screamed it, then you got in this car. Do you disagree?"

"No."

It's a soft murmur as she does as she's told. It's awkward, but she gets them down her hips. I tug her over my lap.

"I am going to spank you, and I am not talking about some little taps on your ass. This isn't anywhere near for pleasure. This is a punishment because you endangered your life. You knew I would follow you, so you endangered mine, too. Someone must have told you about this place, and my guess is a cop or a fed. They had to know you'd use that information and go. By telling you, they encouraged you. I don't want to know who because if it's a man, I'll just be adding to my sins. I can't punish them for something so stupid, but I will take out your recklessness on your very fine ass."

I run my hand over, squeezing and stroking and patting. She's unprepared for it to crack down across both cheeks. I'm not gentle, but I am restrained. I would never use more than a fifth of my strength on her. It wouldn't just hurt. It would harm her, and the thought of that happening is why I'm punishing her in the first place. I have a large hand that easily covers most of her ass. But she's not a small woman, even if she's much smaller than me. Her ass is perfection. Plenty for me to enjoy. And I will enjoy it soon. I don't see abstinence on tonight's plans anymore.

I rain down spank after spank. One to the left, one to the right, one under both cheeks at her horizontal crack. I keep this pattern up, each set of three serving as one in my mind. We get through twenty, and she's sobbing. She's kicked her legs several times, but she hasn't tried to pull away. It's obvious this isn't her first spanking. I don't know if her others have only been for pleasure or not, but she clung to my ankle to keep her hands from covering her ass.

"You're dripping wet for me, *piccolina*."

I reach across her and slide my finger through her pussy lips. I put my finger beneath her face so she can see and smell her arousal. That hand kneads and massages her sore ass while my spanking hand cups her pussy. Her pants make it challenging to pull her legs wide, but I get my fingers into her slick, tight cunt.

"I'm going to edge you until you think you're going to explode. Then I'm going to stop because orgasms aren't part of punishments."

But I will make her come once we get to my place. Many, many times.

"Gabriele, I'm sorry. Please. I already can't take it. My ass burns from the spanking, but my pussy burns from wanting you. Please."

"You sound so sweet when you beg. I won't relent, but I like listening to you."

I do, but it's a fucked-up thing for me to say, and I know it.

Then again, it's only fucked-up to a woman who isn't like Sinead. I feel her relax. I've told her what to expect, so she can now prepare herself for it. She won't exactly enjoy this, but I've given her enough control back not to panic.

I keep working her pussy, pulling my hand away when I think she's getting too close. I noticed we're headed toward my place, but I don't think she's realized we're moving. She's moaning and trying not to tremble, trying not to let me know when she's close. When we're a few blocks from my place, I stop. I sit her up and lick my fingers in front of her. Then I coil her hair around my hand before kissing her.

"Sinead."

I groan her name as her hips presses against my cock. I open my thighs enough for her sore ass to rest between them, not wanting my pants to irritate it further. I tuck her against me and kiss her forehead. Her tears subside as I hold her.

"You truly frightened me more than I have been in years. Please, never do something like that again. You know you're representing someone in the Mafia, but you don't know this world. I do. I'm not trying to control you when I tell you not to speak to someone. I'm doing it to protect you. I told you about those men, and you did it anyway. I was angry earlier, but I wasn't just now. I would never spank you out of anger. But I wasn't pleased with you."

"I could tell."

"If I spank you, I want it to be so I make you come."

"And edging? Is that always a punishment?"

"Not always."

She nods and curls up against me. It's been a long day for both of us. When we arrive at my place, Afonso pulls into the subterranean garage. I put her back on her seat as gently as I can and make sure she's presentable. I can't help the fucking tent pole I have in my pants right now. When I step out, I button my suit coat right away to hide it at least a little. I lead her to the private elevator to my penthouse unit. It's the only one that goes to that part of the top floor. I prefer having a way to keep the world out.

No one's getting up here without my security knowing it, since they can watch the fire exit through cameras placed in the stairwell. The people who live in the other penthouse units have their own shared way up. In the elevator, I keep her head tucked against my chest, shielding her from the cameras I know are installed in it. I had them placed there as part of my personal defenses.

Once we step directly into my home, I sweep her into my arms and carry her into my bedroom. We're already kissing, and once I set her on her feet, we're tearing off each other's clothes. Then I'm pressing her back onto the bed. She scoots back, and I prowl after her. But I stop when her head hits the pillows, and my head is at her pussy. I press her legs open and lick.

"Gabriele."

"Hmm?"

"Please, don't. I need you."

I hear the waver in her voice, and it's not like in the car. This one is sad, and I don't like it. That's not how I want her to feel. I shift to hover over her. I press my cock into her, easing in inch by inch until the last couple. I thrust hard, and her back arches off the bed.

"Yes!"

She screams, and I only want to make her do it louder and louder. I pound into her, over and over.

"Come."

It's a command as much as it is permission. She grabs my ass, her nails digging in as her pussy clamps around me. I pull out at the last minute, remembering that we didn't decide earlier. I look down at her, panting. My cum is all over her belly and just beneath her tits. She looks down too. I've branded her, and we both know it. She slides her right index finger through it, then licks it. Fuck. I'm ready to go again.

I roll onto my back and bring her with me. I feel my cum, now sticky on my stomach. She's stretched across me as I run my fingers along her back.

"That spanking hurt like a motherfucker, but you're so gentle with me now."

"It was supposed to hurt. I wasn't gentle just now, but it was vanilla."

"I know. I liked it."

That makes me wonder if she'd ever want kink with me. She doesn't know I know about her BDSM membership. Maybe she doesn't think— hasn't guessed —what I'm into.

"Gabriele, I don't want to fuck and run. But I need to go home."

"You can stay."

"I want to, but I can't. I'm not ready for that."

That breaks my heart. I want her to move in, and she doesn't want to spend the night. She bites her bottom lip before she speaks. It's not what I expect.

"I have that postponed date tomorrow night. I can't get out of it."

I don't know what to say to that. I just look down at her as she pushes herself up to rest on her forearm on my chest. I barely feel it.

"I don't regret this at all. But you and I both know we shouldn't have done this. Not yet, at least. And I didn't want to spend the night with you and then you find out I have a date with someone else. It already feels wrong that I'm going out tomorrow night with someone else after this."

"It's fine."

She can tell it's not, but she doesn't argue with me.

"Can I stay a few more minutes, then I'll go?"

She's backtracking, and I'm not stopping her. But it only lasts another fifteen minutes before she drags herself off me. I sit up and swing my legs over the side of the bed. She cups my jaw in her left hand as her other hand brushes back hair from my temple. She offers me such a tender kiss before she steps back and gets dressed.

All I can do is sigh. If this was a one-night stand, it was the best I've ever had and the best I ever will.

Chapter Eight

Sinead

JOSH

> You're famous. I saw you on the news a few
> days ago while watching the market.
> Numbers are looking good and so are you.
> Can't wait to show you off tonight. Pick you
> up at 7.

Fuck my life.

"This night's going to blow."

"Why's it going to blow?"

I look up to find Gabriele watching me in the mirror again. He arranged for Giuseppe to take me home last night after a guy around Gabriele's age picked him up from wherever the driver was. Gabriele said the man's name was Carmine. I was too dazed by what happened— all of what happened —last night for the name to register. When Gabriele picked me up this morning, he acted like nothing happened between us yesterday. It hurt. It still does.

So, why's it going to blow? Besides the fact the hottest guy alive is my babysitter on a date I don't even want to go on? It's the actual fucking date. Show me off? Dance, monkey, dance. Thank you, no thank you. That's a level of clingy I don't like after two dates, especially from a guy I'm not into.

"Josh saw us on the news the other day while he was watching the stock market. He's looking forward to tonight."

"He wants to show you off, right?"

"How'd you know?"

"Your expression and what you just said. Cancel."

"I wish. It's not for his sake, that's for sure. I told Andrea I would give it three dates before I decide anything. She wanted me to give him a fair chance. I was willing to before I met him. Now I just want to get to tomorrow morning and end it."

"You're going to a club tonight. You won't be stuck talking much."

"True. I just need to get through dinner. You said someone in your family owns Constantine's. Can you ask them to serve us really fast?"

I'm only half kidding.

"Yes."

He's not kidding.

"Thanks."

"Sinead, I'll be there. If you want to leave, just signal me. I'll get you out."

I nod.

"He said he'd pick me up at seven. When I rescheduled, I said I'd meet him at the restaurant. He conveniently forgot."

I'm watching Gabriele in the mirror, and I see the muscle in his jaw tick. Other than that heartbeat-long reaction, he appears unfazed by what I said.

"If you don't feel comfortable getting in a car with him,

then don't. Text him back and say you aren't coming from your place and will meet him at the restaurant. I'll take you."

I'll take you out for dinner.

That's what I wish he said. I'm infatuated. Last night has thrown me off. I thought my lust was one-sided. Now I know it isn't, but he's acting as though we didn't have sex, let alone amazing sex. I've never been so attracted to a man in my life. I've hooked up with some women at the BDSM club I belong to, but it was never anything romantic. I just wanted to know if it was something I was into. Not really. They weren't horrible experiences, but I don't feel like I need more. I'd still call Gabriele "sir."

"I'd prefer you take me, please."

I just want more time with him. I want to figure out if he's pissed about this date, and that's why he's blowing cold or if it's because of what I did yesterday. Did the punishment not resolve things? I hoped it might mean that we were past it. At least, sorta past it.

It's not even twenty miles from the courthouse to my apartment on Staten Island, but it's going to take close to an hour since it's the beginning of rush hour. Gabriele's taking the Hugh L. Carey Tunnel instead of the Brooklyn Bridge. I almost wish he were taking the slower route, but I don't want to sit here in silence and treat him like he's a hired chauffeur. That feels incredibly rude since he's giving up his evening to babysit me. It makes the chasm between us feel even wider.

I look down at my phone and inhale, bracing myself.

ME

I'm not coming from my place. I'll meet you at Constantine's. Besides it wouldn't have made sense to drive to Staten Island just to come back into Manhattan.

. . .

The response is immediate.

> **JOSH**
> No problem. It'll give us time to chat.

> **ME**
> I'll

Where the fuck am I supposed to be coming from?

> **ME**
> I'll be coming from Rikers.

He definitely won't meet me at Rikers Island. It's the biggest jail in New York City. Considering they're closing it, and I currently have a case against a prison guard there for unlawful use of force, it isn't somewhere Josh wants to go. He might get his loafers dirty.

> **JOSH**
> We can bump it back a little so you can get ready.

Asshole. He doesn't think I'll be presentable. I ought to wear some *Little House on the Prairie* style dress. Cover up from head to toe and see how he feels about taking me to such a chic restaurant and hot nightclub. Maybe he'd break it off, so I don't have to.

> **ME**
> It's fine. I'll be at Constantine's at 7. See you then.

If he texts again, I'm ignoring it. I just hope he doesn't show up at my door. That won't go over well with Gabriele.

"He knows I'll meet him at the restaurant."

"He didn't like that idea."

It's a statement, not a question.

"Not so much. He hinted I should go home and dress for the date."

"You should dress like an Amish woman."

I laugh, and his brow furrows.

"I told myself I should dress like Laura Ingalls."

"Same difference. Anywhere sell those?"

"Not that I know of. They were sorta back in style a couple years ago, but not so much now."

I was going to change, but now I can't unless it's putting on a pantsuit. I also didn't think this through. Where would I shove my work bag? There's privileged information in there. I couldn't just toss it in his car and leave it for the evening. And if I did that, I'd have to go back to his car. Then he'd want to drive me home.

I know what I'll do.

"I think I have a solution to not having any of my work stuff with me and being dressed for a date rather than work. If I'm stuck going out, I may as well be comfortable."

ME

Hey. I told Josh I'm not coming from my place. Can I say I stopped at yours to drop off my stuff and change? Maybe say I borrowed something of yours to wear? Pretty please with cottage cheese and a cherry on top.

ANDREA

You're lucky I saw this. I'm about to start a yoga class. Sure. Why don't you want him to pick you up?

ME

I told you I'm breaking it off with him in the morning. I just don't want him getting the wrong idea if he drives me home. He's tried to kiss me twice.

ANDREA

Is he really that awful? He's fine at work.

ME

He's not a pompous ass at work at a hedge fund management company? Shocking.

ANDREA

I'm a hedge fund manager too. Am I pompous?

ME

No. You actually work.

She sends me a smiley emoji with the hearts for eyes.

ANDREA

Say whatever you need to. I'll be a corroborating witness counselor.

ME

Thank you.

I put my phone back in my bag and look out the window as we cross the Verrazzano-Narrows Bridge onto Staten Island. We're making way better time than I expected. I might have a moment to catch my breath after all. It's all relative in New York, but traffic should have died down a bit by the time we need to leave a little after six. I should have an hour.

"My friend Andrea is going to cover for me. I'm going to say I got ready there since she lives in Manhattan."

"That's good. Then he won't ask where your work stuff is."

"You read my mind as well as I do you."

Our eyes meet in the mirror. I don't know what to make of the look in his. We've sat in silence most of the time, which is exactly what I didn't want. I've treated him like a chauffeur, being on my phone almost the entire way. But last night makes things awkward today.

"Other than the gym, what do you like to do?"

I can be conversational. Maybe he wants to forget last night ever happened. It feels off to ask something so mundane, but I suppose I should actually get to know him if I want to believe I'm truly into him. I want it to be deeper than lust.

"At least you assume I do things other than go to the gym. I like to read."

I try not to show my surprise. It'll seem like I'm shocked someone who looks like him can read. I don't respond fast enough.

"Shocking, right?"

"I don't know too many people in their early thirties who would name that as their first-choice pastime. I would. But I know most people wouldn't. What do you like to watch on TV?"

"I don't have one."

Wait. What?

"You don't have a TV?"

"I'm not interested in local stuff. If there's something I really want to see, I can stream it on my computer. But, like I said, I like to read. I didn't go to law school right out of college, so I've been studying and prepping for the bar most recently. That took up a hefty chunk of time for three-and-a-half years. When I wasn't at class, I was at work."

Dare I ask?

"Work?"

"Yes, Sinead. I worked before becoming a lawyer. I didn't spend all day whacking people."

"That's not— well, that's not entirely what I meant."

Fuck me.

"I own a few businesses like the two hardware stores, plus a moving company, some real estate, and I also guard the women in my family."

"Why didn't you go straight to law school? We're the same age. We'd have been in the same class."

He doesn't answer, pretending like he suddenly needs to concentrate more on the road. What did I say? Was it about being in the same class? Does that idea appall him so much that he has nothing to say? Did I just set back any progress we just made?

"I had some family commitments, so I took time off."

Not totally forthcoming, but better than nothing. If I really wanted to dig, I'm certain I could find out. But I'd rather he share it than be violating his privacy.

"Part of me wishes I'd taken time off. I was so driven to prove myself by graduating high school early and getting into a Seven Sisters. Then I felt like I had to go to an Ivy after that or it would be a big step down. Of course, that only meant I felt like I had to do all the things like moot court, the law review, intern. By the time I graduated, studying for the bar was relaxing."

"I can appreciate that. I would have gone straight into law school if things hadn't come up. Even with the break, I still felt I had to go to another Ivy."

"Where'd you do undergrad?"

"Brown."

Shit. He is smart. Brown and Yale. Brown may be D1 for athletics, but you still have to be smart to get in and stay there. I doubt he's a legacy at Yale, so it had to be grades and LSAT scores.

"You have a bit of an accent. Is it just because you grew up speaking Italian?"

I can't believe I'm asking questions most people use to get to know someone the first time they meet. I know he has a huge dick, but I don't know why he has an accent.

"I grew up speaking Sicilian until I was ten. I spoke Italian too, but I'm from Palermo. I barely knew any English at all when I moved here. I caught on quickly, though. I read everything I could get my hands on. I watched a lot of movies too."

"So, you speak three languages?"

"Six."

"*Six?*"

"Sicilian, Italian, Latin, Greek, Spanish, and Chinese."

"Mandarin or Cantonese?"

"Mandarin."

"*Xiǎo shìjiè. Wǒ zài dàxué xuéguò. Wǒ zài táiwān dùguòle yīgè xuéqí. Nǐ dú fántǐ háishì jiǎntǐ?*" Small world. I studied it in college. I did my semester aboard in Taiwan. Do you read traditional or simplified?

"*Yī kāishǐ hěn jiǎndān, yīnwèi wǒ de liǎng wèi jiàoshòu dōu láizì zhōngguó dàlù. Dàn wǒ zài táiwān zuòle hěnduō shēngyì. Wǒ xuéhuìle chuántǒng de yuèdú hétóng.*" Simplified at first because both of my professors were from mainland China. But I've done a lot of business in Taiwan. I learned traditional to read the contracts.

I realize I'm leaning forward when my seatbelt tugs across my chest. I don't get to use my Chinese like I would have if I'd gone into corporate law. But it comes in handy sometimes, and not just in Chinatown. Besides, I don't speak Cantonese, anyway.

"Is that your place?"

Gabriele's switch back to English and the harshness of his tone is jarring. We're outside my building. He sounds like he did last night when he found me in the hallway.

"Yeah."

"You have a basement apartment."

"I know."

His mouth sets in a thin line, and he looks pissed. Like super pissed. Like even worse than last night, if that's possible. He gets out and opens my door. He looks both ways several times before we cross. He puts his hand out and stops me, going down the steps first.

"What the hell, Gabriele?"

I see him reach behind him to his lower back as though he's going to take something from his belt. Like a cop on TV does with a gun.

"The door's not on its hinges properly."

"I know. It's been like that since before I moved in."

The look he shoots me could make me go up in flames. And it's not the sexy kind of heat. It's the even more royally pissed than he was ten seconds ago.

"Give me your keys."

It's a command. One I don't dare disobey. I hand them to him, holding up the key to my place. He gets out his phone and turns on the flashlight before he unlocks it. He eases it open as though he expects someone to be there. From the door, you can see my entire living room and kitchen and all the way down the short hallway to my bedroom.

"Stand by the sofa. Don't move."

More commands. Another time, another place they would be sexy as hell. If I hadn't been so stupid yesterday, they would be sexy as hell. Right now, he's freaking me out. He walks around the living room, his flashlight shining along the baseboards. He squats and picks something out of the carpet. He closes his fist around it. He works his way through the kitchen, running his hand along the underside of every shelf and every drawer. Whatever he found in the living room, he found two more of in the kitchen. Did someone bug my place?

He goes to my bathroom next, and that really freaks me out. Has someone been watching me, too? He comes out pretty fast, so maybe there was nothing there.

"Sinead, come here, please."

His manners are back, and I think he knows it's because I'm silently freaking out. He drops whatever he found into his pocket and reaches out his hand. He leans over to whisper in my ear.

"You're safe. Do you have any weapons in your place?"

I shake my head. I didn't feel safe a moment ago, but I do now that he's holding my hand.

"I'm going to search all your drawers and beneath your bed. I'm sorry if it embarrasses you."

For fuck's sake. He knows he's going to find my vibrators. If only that were all he was going to find. He starts with my closet. He must be searching every inch three times before he finally steps back as he drops stuff in his pockets. He moves to my dresser, where he finds something else. Knowing what he'll discover in a moment makes him going through my bras and panties seem like no big deal. Did he just run his thumb over the teddy I've never worn? It still has the tags on it. It was for an ex-boyfriend, but we broke up before I wore it.

I watch him get down on the floor and flip the bed skirt back. Not only does he have broad shoulders, but his chest is thick. Like he has big pecs kind of thick. It's obvious he won't slide very far under the bed. He looks around and pulls back. He rolls onto his back and inches under the bed again. When he's satisfied there's nothing there, he runs his hands over the bedframe, the footboard, and the headboard. I know when he finds the small groove. His thumb runs over that too. He checks all the walls, saving my bedside table for last. I try not to cringe.

He pulls open the top drawer and feels around among the condoms I have there. It's not like there's a mountain or anything, but there is a variety. Fuck me. He pulls open the bottom drawer, and I want to cover my face. Double fuck me. I hear him moving things around before he shuts it.

"Stay here, please."

I nod as he walks back to the kitchen. I lean to try to see, but I don't know what he's doing until I see him with a hammer. He goes to the front door and opens it. He squats after grabbing whatever was in his pockets. He smashes all of it into smithereens. There can't be much more than dust by the time he stands. I keep watching as he returns the hammer to the kitchen. Then he's in front of me and pulling me into his arms.

"I know you're scared, *piccolina*. But I'm certain I found all of them. You're safe now."

What does *piccolina* mean? It sounds so— so —gentle the way he says it. He's being gentle while he hugs me. I feel completely protected from anything and everything. I feel tiny against him, and I want to burrow closer. Knowing someone's been in my home terrifies me way more than entering the Polish lions' den. I would have had no one to blame but myself for that. This is different. This is my home where I live alone.

"How'd you know my place was bugged? How long could they have been there?"

"They're brand new. There wasn't any dust on any of them. The door being off alignment made it easy for them to jimmy the lock and get in. Whoever it was knows you're my lawyer. Either they found out before the reporters ambushed us, and it became public knowledge. Or they did it while you were at work."

"Who?"

I lean back to look up at him. There's genuine sadness in his eyes, and it makes me want to comfort him.

"Who isn't it? The obvious answer would be the Polish Mob. But they're not the only ones. It could be the Colombians, the Russians, the Irish, the Mexicans, the Albanians, other *Cosa Nostra*. I can't be sure yet."

"I didn't realize there were that many people who might want me dead."

"They don't want you dead, *piccolina*. They want to know what you know. This is why I wanted a detail assigned to you. This is why I was so pissed that you tried to ditch Afonso and me. From today on, you go nowhere without one."

"Today on? That sounds indefinite."

"It is. At the very least, until the case is over. Then I think you should have protection for several months after."

"I don't know how to pick a private security company. Do you know any?"

Did his arm just flex? It felt tighter for a moment.

"This changes things. You will trust *no one* outside my family, Sinead. No one. If the man or woman isn't related to me but says they're with my family, don't believe them. Don't go anywhere with them. Call me or text me immediately. I will answer. If you're alone somewhere, keep your phone unlocked and in your hand. Pull up my contact and have it ready to call if you feel threatened at all."

"Gabriele, you're scaring me."

Last night was a fucked-up kind of exhilarating when he found me. It triggered some kind of roleplaying fantasy, even though I knew it was not the right time or place. It was because I was certain he was there. He won't be here every night.

"I know, and I'm sorry. But someone broke into your house and put nearly a dozen devices in here. They wanted to make sure they missed nothing. I don't want you to stay here right now, but I won't force you."

"Where would I go? A hotel? I don't want to bring this anywhere near my friends, and I have no family around here. I grew up in Rhode Island."

"I understand. I want you to stay with a woman I've known since before I moved to America. She's like my second mom. She's my best friend's mom, and I've stayed at her house so many times I have a room of my own there. Her name's Paola Mancinelli."

"Like as in the political strategist and campaign manager? Like the woman who picks mayors?"

"To me, she's just Auntie Paola, but yes. She's influential. She also lives on her own, but has tons of security on her property. Her son, Carmine, goes there all the time. He and his wife have dinner there once a week."

"Like a big Italian family dinner?"

"That's Sundays at Uncle Salvatore and Aunt Sylvia's."

"You guys get together every Sunday?"

"Just about. We have a midweek snack at another family home on Wednesdays."

"Snack?"

"Yes. Three courses instead of five."

"The other Mr. Mancinelli?"

"Yes, but not the one you met. They have an adopted second cousin. We grew up with his sons."

"Just how many of you are there?"

"Salvatore, Sylvia, Pia, Natalia, Massimo, Nicoletta, Luca, Olivia, Marco, Lorenzo, Maria, Matteo, Domenico, Carlotta, Paola, Cesare, Carmine, Serafina, and me."

"That's nineteen!"

"Olivia is pregnant."

"Is she married?"

"Yes, to Luca. Luca, Marco, Lorenzo, and Maria are Uncle Massimo and Auntie Nicoletta's children. Luca is married to Olivia, and Maria is married to Matteo, who's Uncle Domenico and Auntie Carlotta's son."

"And they're all Mancinellis?"

"Sort of. Carmine is a Ciccone since that's his father's last name. He goes by Mancinelli because that was his legal last name for more than half his life. His parents are married, but that's super complicated. Uncle Domenico is the adopted second cousin."

"So, wait. Maria and Matteo got married, but they were already related?"

"Not by blood. Uncle Domenico's birth parents had nothing to do with the *Cosa Nostra*. A priest arranged his adoption."

"You said Domenico has sons. You didn't name anyone other than Matteo."

"Another complicated branch. His older son lives in Jersey."

Why do I feel it's more like they banished him to Jersey? I won't push. It's too confusing to add any more names to the list. I need to know all of this, but it's a lot for me to take in without having it written down in front of me.

"Wait. Who are Pia and Natalia?"

"They're Uncle Salvatore and Aunt Sylvia's daughters. They're little kids. Uncle Salvatore married in his forties."

"Why do you call her aunt when you called the other women auntie?"

So much for not adding to this confusing litany of names.

"Aunt Sylvia joined the family when everyone my age was already an adult. All the other women have been around since I moved to America and since everyone else's birth. Matteo's two hours younger than Marco. Their mothers are best friends from

113

childhood. Uncle Domenico and Uncle Massimo are best friends, too."

"You might need to draw me a family tree."

"In all seriousness, I will. You're going to need to know all of this because my family members will come up."

"And all of them are *Cosa Nostra?*"

"There's no way not to be in a family like ours."

"But you're not related to them."

"My father worked for Uncle Salvatore when we moved here. Before that and now, he works for Aunt Sylvia's father in Palermo. He's a Made Man. Have you heard of that before?"

My cheeks suddenly feel scorching.

"Yeah. I've seen *Goodfellas* a few times."

He laughs. Thank God. The tension's eased since we were in the car and while he was searching my place. Is he trying to distract me, so I don't freak out? Whatever the reason we're having such a casual conversation, it's soothing me.

"Mostly right, and maybe completely right back in those days. One thing I can promise you, Fridays aren't for girl-friends, while Saturdays are for wives. There is absolutely no infidelity in the family."

He hesitates and seems to hold his breath before continuing.

"There's no secret infidelity. Carmine's parents' marriage is—"

"Complicated."

I interrupt him since that seems to be the word of the day when we're talking about anything to do with him.

"Yes. They didn't have a good marriage when they lived together. After Carmine left for college, they separated. They won't divorce, but they live separate lives. They're close friends now. No one discusses it, but we all know they have other rela-tionships."

"Are they men within your organization? I'm not asking to pry, but you said you spent a lot of time with her growing up. I need to know about anyone who's closely connected to your family. Are the women with Carmine's father also *Cosa Nostra?*"

It may seem like we're chatting, but this is partly work for me. It's useful information while letting me get to know him more personally.

"Some. You're going to be late a second time today."

He lets go of me, and instantly, I feel cold. I miss having his arms around me. We could have stepped apart ages ago, but neither of us did. But this is my hint to stop asking for anything he doesn't volunteer. My head's spinning with all of it. I'll have to sort it out later. But I can almost guarantee everything he told me will come up in discovery then the trial.

"I can be ready in five minutes."

"I'll wait for you in the living room."

Chapter Nine

Gabriele

I pull out my phone and open the group text to all the men.

ME

Someone bugged S's place. I found them and took care of it. I don't want her staying here. The door's shit and too easy to get past. I'm pissed neither Giuseppe nor Afonso told me since they've both driven her home and should have walked her to her door.

I hear Sinead moving around in her bedroom. She has a one bedroom, but the bathroom has jack-and-jill doors. She can go into it without stepping into the hallway, or someone else could enter it without going into her bedroom.

CARMINE

I'm sure she can stay with my mom if you want.

I mentioned it but our family tree distracted us before she answered.

SALVATORE

She can stay here for now. She goes to a hotel tomorrow. We can't have any suggestion of impropriety.

That's a silent warning. I'm not to touch her. Way too late for that. I won't suggest she come to my place. How the fuck I kept her from feeling my dick while I hugged her is beyond me. She looked so shaken that hugging her was all I could think of doing. Then I realized she'd feel how hard I am for her. I'm glad last night happened, but it can't happen again.

The day we met, my cock calmed down while she was in court, but the moment I saw her, it came right back. The same thing happens whenever I'm around her. She did nothing to make me think she noticed while we were in her bedroom, but maybe she's good at pretending. We've both avoided talking about last night.

It didn't fucking help seeing what I did in her bedside table, either. It took everything not to command her to strip, then get on the bed while I cuffed her to it. I want to watch her squirm and tremble as I use her vibrator on her. I want to stick the plug I spotted in her ass while I fuck her pussy. I felt the chip in the headboard and suspected what I would find. She not only had the handcuffs, but she had a set of padded neck, wrist, and ankle cuffs too. The neck cuff has a ring for a leash. Goddamn. I'm going to be jerking off all night at this rate.

Shit. The text thread.

ME

I'll suggest you or Auntie P. If she won't agree, then I'll take her to a hotel. She already said she doesn't want to go to her friends and she has no family around here.

CARMINE

Let me know so I can let my mom know.

ME

Or I could text her like I have for years.

Carmine sends me the eye roll emoji.

LORENZO

C said she has that postponed date tonight at my places. Is that still on?

ME

Yeah. She's getting ready right now.

MARCO

I'll be at Spotlight.

ME

She asked me to see if they could serve her and her db date fast at dinner. She wants out of it all. I don't think she wants to have to talk any longer than absolutely necessary.

LORENZO

I'll make sure of it. I'm at the club tonight. But I'll text Manny to let him know.

MATTEO

Do you want me to come too?

ME

No. Go on your double date. I don't need your wife pissed at me.

MATTEO

She wouldn't get pissed knowing I'm guarding someone.

ME

She'd be pissed that she couldn't go dancing because you'd be watching S which means she can't go since you don't have two sets of eyes.

Matteo sends me the emoji with the raised eyebrow, then the guy shrugging.

LORENZO

How late do you think you'll stay?

ME

I have no idea but probably not late. I told her to give me a signal if she wants out. But I'm sure she'll come up with an excuse to leave before ten or eleven.

SALVATORE

Let us know what she decides. You know you can get into either place. She'll find whatever she needs wherever she picks.

ME

Will do. She's coming out.

I put my phone in my back pocket. Or at least I try to. I almost drop it because all I can focus on is how damn fine she looks. Her hair's down and it's way longer than I expected. Though I see a scrunchie thing on her wrist. She's wearing a mid-thigh length black skirt, only a little shorter than the ones she's worn for work. Not what most women would wear to a club. She has a silver and gray halter top on, but it comes high up her back and covers her entire chest. She looks hot, but she's not trying to get anyone's attention. Which is cool with me.

"Ready?"

"Yes. Thanks for waiting."

"Of course. We never settled where you're going to stay tonight. Auntie Paola's or Uncle Salvatore's offered."

"I don't want to be an imposition."

"We'll make a more long-term plan tomorrow. For now, we just get you through the night and off to work in the morning."

"Staying at Salvatore's, when he's the man who hired me, doesn't look good. Your aunt's house works. Should we skip Spotlight? I don't want to come in too late and disturb her."

"Her room is on the first floor, but at the opposite end from the stairs. I know the code, and her guards know me. We can slip in without a problem. She'll have anything you need already waiting on the bed."

"I should grab some stuff before we go. Give me a minute."

She hurries back to her room, and she's back out in what had to be barely three minutes. She has a backpack and a garment bag. She reaches for her work bag, which she put on the sofa when we came in. I take all three from her. When she opens her mouth to protest, she knows she won't win. She offers me a smile that makes my heart stutter. What the fuck was that? Lust I can handle. This? I'm not so sure about. I felt it last night when I held her in the car and after we finished having sex.

"Is that your driver?"

She nudges her chin toward the street while I lock the door behind us.

"Yeah. I asked him to meet us here while you were in court. You never told me what the fine was that day we met."

"It doesn't matter."

"Sinead, don't lie."

"I'm not lying. It doesn't matter."

"It matters to me then. How much of a fine did I cause?"

"Considering you waited out in the car for a couple hours, protected me from myself and the Polish Mob, and swept my place for bugs, which you found, the fine isn't a big deal."

"Was it more than five-hundred?"

She has no desire to answer.

"A little."

"How much is a little?"

We get into the car, and I help her with her seatbelt since she struggles to find the buckle in the dark. We get it, but I don't take my hands off hers.

"Sinead?"

"Fine. Twenty-five-hundred."

"That's outrageous."

"It is. But with the attention and retainer people guess I must be getting, they'll assume that isn't a big deal."

"It's the principle. Levying a fine just because they can isn't how the system is supposed to work."

"I know that. You know that. The judge even knows that. But he makes anyone held in contempt pay fifty percent to a charity. Since he doubles the fines, the city and state get their portions. Then what's left over goes to the charity."

"That's extortion wrapped up in a pretty bow."

She shrugs. I wait for her to say something, but she doesn't.

"What charity did you pick?"

"Alzheimer's Association."

She's quiet as she answers.

"I know about your dad, *piccolina*."

"What?"

She twists in her seat.

"There was no way my family would hire you without

vetting you. You've been through the FBI and DOJ background checks before. This was the same."

"Somehow, I doubt it was. I bet it was far more thorough. What did you learn besides my father has dementia?"

She doesn't enjoy having the tables turned where her history is the focus instead of mine.

"I know you have him in Manhattan, but you want to transfer him to New Jersey."

"How far back did your investigator go?"

"A year for that sort of stuff."

"He or she hacked my phone and email, didn't they?"

I won't incriminate anyone any further. She's getting testy, and I don't want this to devolve. She looks out the window while she speaks again.

"Could you change the subject or something rather than leaving these gaping holes in the conversation when we get to something you don't want to discuss?"

"It would be a ping-pong game. There's a lot I can't tell you, Sinead. We'd be jumping all over the place. It's not that I enjoy keeping secrets, but some of them aren't mine to tell. Some of them are dangerous for you. I'll tell you what I can."

"As long as it pertains to the case."

I want to scream *no*. But we're supposed to have professional distance from each other. So far, we're shitty at keeping physical distance. I have to regain some mental distance. I can't keep that if I share everything with her. Anything that involves me pretty much involved Carmine until he got married last year. Everything else I can think of off the top of my head involves at least one other person in my family.

"It's safest that way."

And that bothers me more than I care to examine right now. I've already shared more about myself than I do with anyone outside the family. I don't date, so it's not like I have girlfriends scattered all over who know my past or what matters to me.

"I don't want to be evasive, but I'm going to have to be. I'll tell you as much as I can for the case, but if there's something I won't say, it's because it endangers you or my family or people who rely on my family. I can never make decisions without considering who might suffer from it. I don't have that luxury."

As I gaze into her eyes, I'm drowning. Drowning in my desire for her. Drowning in all the lies I must keep. Drowning in the exhaustion that yet another fucking disaster adds to my life. None of it has ever been fair, but such is life. I remember as a child learning about the American Revolution. Life, liberty, and the *pursuit* of happiness. No one promises you actually get it. I prefer the original version, John Locke's life, liberty, and property. Sums up reality much better.

"I'm sorry I pushed. I don't know much about the inner workings of the *Cosa Nostra*, and I get I'm never supposed to. But common sense told me I shouldn't ask things I know you can't answer."

"I wish it weren't like that."

We ride in silence, both looking out our own windows until we're back in Manhattan and pulling up outside Lorenzo's restaurant in Chelsea.

"Pauly will walk you inside. I'll be right behind you. There's a nook near the restrooms where I can see everything. I'll stand there. Signal me or walk over if you need anything, including wanting to leave. Pauly will be just inside the kitchen."

We've done this so many times we all know our preferred stake out spots in an establishment we frequent. Lorenzo worked with Matteo— who's an architect —to design the entire restaurant that way. Same with the club. He made sure it all worked out with Carmine, who's a structural engineer and construction manager.

I tap on the window, and Pauly opens the door. I watch as Sinead swings her legs out before standing, careful not to flash anyone. I wait until she's on the sidewalk and away from the car before I get out. I shut the door, and she glances back. A moment of panic registers on her face when she realizes I'm not as close as she expected. My long stride allows me to catch up to them as I button my suit coat.

"It's all right, *piccolina*. I don't want people to assume we're arriving together. It's not good for your date, and it's not good for anyone watching either of us. Go ahead. I'm close."

I fall back and watch as Pauly opens the restaurant door for her. He enters and surveys our surroundings. He whispers something to Sinead before he moves toward the kitchen. I wait for her to look around until she spots her date. I watch her move across the restaurant toward a man I vaguely recognize from my building. I'm excellent with faces and names and voices and smells and all the shit. He's not memorable, but I know I've seen him before. I wander over to the hallway with the restrooms. I step into the shadowy nook and lean against the wall. It would be easy to get bored and think about wasting the time on my phone. But I'm working. The only reason I'm even standing here is because I'm protecting someone who matters to my family. Someone who matters to me.

In the time I've spent with her, she obviously matters more than some attorney working for a fat check. Putting aside our physical attraction and what happened last night, I could see us being friends if I had any of the female persuasion. The only women I'm friends with all have the same last name—Mancinelli. I watch as Josh smiles and waves, but the dipshit doesn't stand up when she arrives at the table. It's a fucking date, douche.

I watch the host hand Sinead a menu before he walks away. Only a moment later, a server arrives. Josh raises his glass, showing he'd like a second of whatever wine he's drinking. I bet it's the cheap house wine Lorenzo won't even let his chefs cook with. I notice she glances toward the kitchen. Josh catches her attention and makes her smile. Why? I want to know what the fuck he said that made her smile. Possessive much? What the fuck is the matter with me? We screw one time. I'm not kidding myself that's all it was. I want to roll my eyes and shake my head at myself.

I grew up with basically seven brothers— until Matteo's older brother fucked up and got banished to Jersey —and one little sister. I've shared everything with everyone and been happy to do it. It wasn't easy being a new kid who didn't speak the language and didn't have any siblings to rely on. Maria and Carmine are my age, and we used to sit together at lunch, trading our sardine sandwiches and salami sandwiches among us. We were the only ones who had fresh cheese our mothers made. I don't know any other ten-year-old who took bruschetta to school unless you count the other members of the Mancinelli family when they were our age. We're the babies of the family. With that many kids always around me, I didn't grow up possessive of anything. Now I look at Sinead sitting across a table from some guy I don't even know, and I want to go apeshit. I've known the woman a week, half of which she was in a courtroom nowhere near me. I'm totally fucked up.

"Do you want anything to eat, Mr. Scotto?"

Fucking Lolita. Like really, that's her name. She's way too close. We hooked up once like a year ago, and she still thinks I'm interested. It was not that great. It wasn't even good. She may look sexy as sin, but she sucks at sex. Most boring lay I've ever had. But now she's pressing her tits to my arm as though she's whispering sweet nothings to me. I shake my head and step away, but it's too late. Sinead's staring straight at me as someone opens the men's room door right behind me, shining light on Lolita and me. I cross my arms and raise my chin.

"No, thank you."

"Let me know when you change your mind."

"I won't."

She shifts her gaze to see who I'm looking at, but I'm looking in the far-left corner when Sinead is off to the right. Lolita saunters away, and I want to barf. Her nasty-ass cloying perfume is hanging in the air. I remember getting home after being with her and taking a shower because all I could smell was roses and cherries. You live, you learn.

I settle my attention back on Sinead, and she's smiling again. She looks like she's having a good time. It doesn't match the dread she had earlier. Did Josh turn out to not be such an a-hole after all? She looks amazing. Her hair looks black when it's up, but under the light, I can see hints of gold and copper. I watch as she leans forward, the muscles in her back shifting. I know the front of her halter top covers her up to her throat, but I hate the idea that he might look at her breasts.

Once again, the possessiveness is foreign to me and wholly disconcerting. It keeps coming back to me. I even declared she was mine while we were in the restroom, eavesdropping on men who would have killed us without a second thought.

I make sure I'm back in the shadow for the rest of their meal. I would have accepted something to eat if anyone but Lolita offered. I'm starving.

"Hey."

Manny, the manager— not like no one's teased him about that a thousand times —walks over and jerks his chin in a what's up.

"Hey."

"I saw Lolita come over here. Ruin your appetite?"

"Something like that."

"Figured you were hungry."

I look at the oddly concocted cheeseburger and fries. This is not a restaurant where you can get either of those. It's more like sliders, I suppose, made on pumpernickel bread. The fries are fresh because they were regular potatoes twenty minutes ago. But it's delicious and easy to eat. Though it always grosses me out having to eat near restrooms. Such is life when you're on the clock.

"I don't see your family, but Enzo said to make sure the woman who walked in with Pauly gets her food fast."

"Yeah. Special job for a family connection. I guess she wasn't looking forward to her date. I don't know her very well. Just met her the other day."

I'm reminding myself of that more than I'm letting Manny know. He probably doesn't care, and I better shut the fuck up before I say too much.

"You might want to let her know he was here last night with some other woman and a different one the night before. He comes here pretty often, and he's got Lolita as a side piece."

Motherfucking douchey asshole.

"I'll mention it. Thanks for the heads up."

"You're welcome."

I eat as I watch Sinead and Josh finish their food. I hurry to scarf mine down when I realize Josh just got the check. She gets up and turns toward me. I step back farther until I'm beside the ladies' room.

"We're walking over to Spotlight."

She doesn't stop to tell me, instead talking as she walks past and into the restroom. I wait for her to come out, and I've just finished my dinner. She's about to go by without saying anything. I grab her arm, and she whirls around on me. She tugs it loose and glares as me.

"What's the matter?"

"I'm scared as shit after what you found in my place. You said you were going to watch out for me. The first time I look to make sure you're there, so I feel safe, you're chatting with your girlfriend."

"Girlfriend? That woman is not my girlfriend. I've known her since she started working here because I'm here often. We hooked up once a year ago. You've had my attention the entire night. If I was with someone, last night never would have happened."

Why am I admitting all of this? Why do I feel defensive? She looks like she's questioning why she got upset.

"I'm sorry. I'm on edge. I'm trying to have a good time, but I'm freaked out about my apartment and staying in someone's house who I've never met. Josh is still boring as all get out, but I'm trying not to be rude."

"You don't look freaked out. You were laughing earlier."

"Because he was telling stupid jokes, and I knew I'd look like a bitch if I didn't."

"Do you want to leave?"

"I can't. I already told him I'm ready to go to Spotlight. Even though the service was great, we've already been here almost two hours. Let's see how long I last there."

"Okay. I'll let Pauly know to go out ahead of you. I'll follow again."

She hesitates before she nods.

"*Piccolina*, what's wrong?"

I keep calling her that, but I'm definitely not ready to examine why I call her little girl or translate it for her. She hasn't asked what it means. Does she know and is fine with it? Does she not care?

"Will you really be right behind us?"

"Did Josh do something?"

"No, not really. But I think he thinks he's getting laid tonight."

My gaze darts to him, and I know he's getting impatient. She has to go back there.

"If he does anything you don't want..."

She nods, and I don't have to finish that thought. She hurries back to the table. She only grabbed her cell phone, ID, and a credit card from her purse as we pulled up. She left everything else in the town car. I didn't realize her skirt had pockets. I'll never understand why most women's skirts and dresses don't have them. I get the whole it'll mess up the lines and how the clothes hang. But pockets matter more. At least they would to me if I were a woman.

I'm talking to myself to distract from how he wraps his arm around her waist, and she doesn't pull away. I leave my hide-away and hand my plate to Lolita without looking at her. It makes me the asshole; I know. But I'm not falling behind when Sinead told me she was scared and asked me to be where she can see me.

It's barely a five-minute walk to get to the club, and I spot Lorenzo immediately since I texted him we were on our way. It's hot as balls, and the place isn't even packed yet.

"She's cute."

Lorenzo waggles his eyebrows. I shrug.

"Can you keep an eye on her? I need to ditch my jacket and gun in your office. I'm way overdressed, anyway."

"Yeah. Marco's over by the DJ already."

I saw him there as I came in. There's a fire exit he's guarding. No one is coming in or out of that door without him saying yes. I hurry down the hall and punch in the code to open Lorenzo's office. I slip my suit coat off and toss it over the back of the desk chair before I punch in the code to open the left-side desk drawer. I put my gun in there with Lorenzo's second weapon. The man never sweats. He's wearing a suit out there, but he also won't be in the crush of people. He has his gun in the holster at his lower back. But if he feels like he needs to, he'll come and get his shoulder holster and put both guns under his arms.

I'm rolling up my sleeves as I reach the dance floor. I spot her easily. There are more people here than there were when I went in the office, but it's like she has a homing device on. I can find her without having to try. She has a bottle in her hand. I strain and look over at Lorenzo, who's still by the bar. He nods. None of his bartenders would ever roofie a drink, and they're excellent at watching out for anyone who is. But they can't see everything all the time. Lorenzo's letting me know he watched the bartender open the drink in front of Sinead, and she never let it out of her sight.

She's swaying to the music while sipping her beer. She doesn't like it. I wonder if he ordered it for her or she just doesn't like beer, and it's the least offensive. I notice he's drinking the same thing, so it was probably the former. He tries to draw her closer, but she dances away as though she doesn't notice. But she turns her back to him, and he wraps his arm around her waist, pulling her back.

I clench my fists. I have to let her deal with it unless she looks for me. He's grinding his junk against her ass. She pretends to misstep and puts her foot down on his. She spins and looks apologetic, but that gives him the chance to pull her closer. The motherfucker is trying to put his leg between hers. She stops and shakes her head before leaning in to tell him something. Now he's shaking his head and trying to wrap his arm around her again.

I inch closer until I'm behind Josh, and she can see me. She relaxes. A couple women dance around me, and I can't stand here like a statue without people wondering why I'm there. I might sway next to them, but I don't touch them, and I don't look at them. They lose interest and move on.

It's the same thing for four songs. Josh is keeping some space between them, but he still has his arm around her waist, and now she has an arm around his neck. When the song ends, they head back to the bar. I find a spot not far away, and I can hear them talking.

"I can drive you home if you want to go now."

"No thanks. I'm actually headed to Andrea's. She's only a couple blocks away."

"I'll walk you."

"Really, Josh. It's fine. The streets are well lit, and the fresh air will feel good. You don't have to worry."

"Of course, I'll worry."

He inches closer and tries to cup her cheek with his left hand. She pushes his hand away and backs into me. I got closer when the space opened up. She twists to see over her shoulder. I act like I don't notice. She turns back to Josh.

"You don't need to. Thank you for a nice dinner, but I don't think we're a good match. It's just not working for me."

"What?"

"I don't want to see you again."

He stands there with his mouth open, blinking like a beached fish. Someone needs to toss him back in.

"You just wanted the free dinners."

"Goodnight, Josh."

"Cocktease."

I straighten and turn toward him.

"What did you call the lady?"

"None of your fucking business."

"Yes, it is. Apologize and leave, or I'll have your ass dumped on the sidewalk."

"Make me."

"Are you five?"

I gesture to two bouncers who hurry over.

"Mark, Tony, can you see this guy out? Let Lorenzo know he should ban him from the club and Constantine's." I look at Josh. "That'll suck since you're fucking Lolli and taking every date there."

"Who the hell are you?"

I sense more than see Lorenzo walk over.

"He's my cousin, and I own the club and Constantine's. I also own several other bars and restaurants. You're now banned from all of them."

"You don't even know what happened. He should mind his own fucking business."

I turn to look at Lorenzo and the bouncers. I keep my voice low, so only they hear me, along with Josh and Sinead.

"She ended things, and he called her a cocktease."

The mood shifts on a dime. Lorenzo leans in until he's forcing Josh to lean back against the bar.

"Get out before I break you in half. Then I'll let my guys do whatever the fuck they want with what's left of you."

Lorenzo isn't as big as I am when it comes to muscle mass, but we're the same height. He goes to the gym twice a day most days, just like me. We're just built differently, but he can carry my ass up a couple flights of stairs and not get winded. My money's on him.

"I should call the police and have them arrest you for threatening me."

Sinead cringes. It's basically the same thing she said to the reporters when they cornered us. The rest of us laugh. It's my turn to talk again. Mark and Tony are just the muscle.

"Call the cops. See how that goes for you. See what happens when they arrive, and we offer them drinks on the house."

"Fucking mobsters."

"We're not Irish, dumb fuck."

Four voices respond at the same time. We've said the same thing so many times we ought to get it tatted across our foreheads. I glance down at Sinead, but she's glaring at Josh. I make sure he truly understands how fucked he is.

"By the way, you live in a building I own. Move. Tomorrow."

Mark and Tony handle getting him to leave. From the way he stumbles, the alcohol at dinner and here just caught up with him. I'll make sure some of my guys visit him tomorrow morning to remind him of what I said. I won't give it a second thought after that. Lorenzo signals the bartender over.

"You good?"

"Yeah, I'm fine. Sinead, do you want another drink?"

"No. I—" She looks toward the door. "I hope he won't make a big deal about this. You don't think he'll really call the police, do you?"

I lean over to whisper in her ear and inhale lavender.

"He can go ahead, but it won't do him any good. We pay a lot to keep the police away from here. If they have to come, they'll look around without getting out of their cruiser. Then they'll drive away like they never stopped."

"Don't tell me anything else."

"Why do you think I'm whispering? That's all you need to know, counselor."

Lorenzo's already walked away, and I'm not drinking. Sinead's empty bottle is on the bar, and she didn't say she wanted anything else. I take her hand and lead her out onto the dance floor. I have to lean in to whisper again.

"I don't want your night to be ruined. Have some fun for a bit, then I'll take you to Auntie Paola's."

She nods, and we start dancing together. My mother

thought I would be a child ballroom dancing star. She forced me into those stupid spandex fake tuxes and pushed me out on the dance floor from being five until I turned ten, and we moved to America. I still dance from time to time with Maria and my aunts because they all know how. So, I don't have two left feet as I move to the music with Sinead. She looks so much more at ease than she did with Josh. She's dancing for real instead of just swaying.

One song turns into two, turns into five. We've been getting closer with each one until we're now touching. I wrap my arm around her waist, and she leans into me. I have a fucking tent pole in my pants right now, and I know she can feel it because she just rubbed her pussy against me. We keep moving together, and all I want is to drag her into one of the storerooms, wrap her legs around my waist, and pound into her. I want more of what we started last night.

I look down to find her staring up at me. When I cup her cheek, she doesn't push me away. How has this woman I wasn't sure I could trust entranced me? I want to taste her like I want my next breath. I've had one-night stands before. Fucking Lolita for example. I've hooked up with women I met the same night, though I haven't done that in close to a decade. I get lust. I'm feeling it right now. But I don't recognize the feelings going along with it. It's a lot of what I felt last night, but it's even more. Last night was driven by fear, anger, lust, protectiveness, and possessiveness. Tonight doesn't have the fear. It has something I can't name.

I lean down as she lifts her chin, and our lips brush, then fuse. We can't get enough the moment the kiss starts. She fists my shirt as I slide my leg between hers. We move together with the music, and all I can think about is if this is dancing, then how the fuck will I survive kinkier sex with her? This is a gentler, more sensual version of last night, and I'm close to coming already. We're equal partners in this, but she's letting me control it. She's not pushing for more, but she's taking everything I'm offering. She's deciding as much as I am. My hand slides down to her ass, and she moans into my mouth.

"Tell me to stop, *piccolina*."

"I don't want to."

"You know we shouldn't."

"And I don't care right now."

"You will in the morning."

"Good thing it's still tonight."

I look around as I take her hand. I spot Lorenzo, and he grins. He nods, and I roll my eyes. He's going to give me shit tomorrow about how he knew from the moment he saw her I wanted her. He juts his chin toward the office. He knows I can't leave without my jacket or my weapon. I lead us to his office and enter the code. The moment she follows me inside, I slam the door shut and pin her against the wall.

"What do you want, Sinead?"

"You."

"To do what?"

"Everything."

I kiss up her throat until I get to the spot just behind her ear.

"Do you want me to taste more than your mouth?"

"Yes."

She pants the answer.

"Do you want me to slide my hand up your skirt until I feel how wet you are?"

"Yes."

She moans as my fingers glide up the inside of her left thigh. When I get near her hip, I pull her leg wider and step between them. I slip my fingers under her panties as I grind my cock against her.

"What else do you want?"

"Anything. Just please keep touching me like last night."

"Do you have any idea that you keep me hard all fucking day, every day? Do you know that I've wanted to be inside you since I laid eyes on you?"

"I thought you were more interested in the court documents."

"I can do more than one thing at a time."

"You sounded pissed when you heard my name. Bet that helped calm you down."

"Just the opposite. I wanted you even though I knew I shouldn't. I'd already guessed you were my lawyer. I knew I shouldn't want to do this. I shouldn't have wanted to keep going after we left the restaurant last night. We shouldn't have done any of that."

"You were angry with me last night."

"And scared for you. I meant everything I said."

I drop to my knees and lift her right leg over my shoulder. I push her skirt all the way up until I can see her pussy. I love that it's bare and smooth. Like she must have waxed within the last few days. I pull her panties out of the way again and breathe cool air onto her pussy as my index and middle fingers slip inside her. I lick her clit, and she presses her back against the wall. I lick her over and over as I work her cunt.

"Do you want to come?"

"Yes."

"Then ask me."

Chapter Ten

Sinead

Then ask me. I'll fucking beg you.

"Please, sir."

"Please, sir, what? Tell me what you want, Sinead."

Did his voice just get huskier? It's like the commands he gave at my place, but fucking sexier than anything I've ever heard.

"Please, sir, will you make me come?"

He doesn't answer with words. Instead, he works my fucking clit like he was born to do this. He slides a third finger into me, and my knees shake. He's rubbing the spot just south of my clit while he sucks on it. I press my hand against the back of his head. He pulls his fingers out and snags my wrist as he raises his head. *Everything* is changing between us yet again.

"No."

Oh, fuck. He's a Dom. This isn't just a little kink by calling him sir. This isn't getting over being angry at me sex. I lick my lips before I slide my free hand behind my back and tilt my head down to look at the floor. He lets go of the one he captured before diving back in. I put that one behind my back, too. I raise my head until it's pressing against the door just like my shoulders and upper back.

"Sir, I need to come. I can't stop."

"Come for *me*."

As though his wish is my command, I feel the tightening in my belly and the feeling I don't quite know how to explain in my pussy. Then I'm fisting my hands as I moan.

"Fuck... I'm coming... Gabriele, fuck. That's feels so good."

He doesn't relent as I suck in a lungful of air. His fingers keep working me, even more urgently. Thank God it's so noisy outside the office, or the whole club would hear me getting off. My second orgasms— if I get them —usually aren't as strong as the first. This one makes me fist Gabriele's shirt over his shoulders. He pulls back and pulls me down onto his lap, his legs wide enough to stroke and soothe the outside of my pussy. The heel of his hand presses lightly against my clit as I come down from my high.

He's kissing me again, and I don't enjoy tasting myself. But I do like how gentle he's being as he takes care of me. He's definitely a Dom. He grips my hair with his free hand as he kisses along my neck then back up the other side until he reaches just behind my ear.

"My sweet *piccolina*."

"What does that mean, sir?"

"Gabe. And it means little girl."

My head's resting on his shoulder, and I sigh. I like it. He's been calling me that for hours. I remember he called me that last night. I've lost count of how many times he's said it. I didn't ask before in case I didn't like it in English. But I do. A lot. That's something I'm not ready to analyze.

"I'm going to take you to my aunt's, and you're going to

sleep in the room next to mine. If you need me for anything, I'll be right next door."

"And if I wanted to slip into your room and slip your cock into me?"

"Then I'll fuck you until you can't see straight. But not tonight. I'm serious about if you need anything, Sinead. But we aren't doing more than this."

That's a reality check I don't love. His voice a moment ago made me think he was offering something more. Now, it's back to business. I cling to him when he stands, and I have no idea how he does it from kneeling while I'm on his lap. He wraps an arm underneath my ass as he moves to a couch in the corner. He tucks my head against his shoulder.

"Once we leave this office, we have to go back to attorney-client. But for right now, I'm going to hold my *piccolina*. If you get scared or need something and don't know where to find it, then come to my room."

"Are you a Dom?"

"I have been in the past. I don't have an arrangement right now. I know about Cries and Whispers, Sinead. I knew before I found that stuff in your drawer. I'm a member, too."

"You are?" I think for a moment. "Oh, shit. You wear the long sleeve black shirt with the jeans and the gladiator mask."

It's a leather mask that covers the front of his face with cutouts for his eyes. It has metal studs that run down the center from mid-forehead to his chin.

"You don't kiss."

He couldn't since it completely covers his mouth with no opening.

"No, I do not. You recognize me?"

"If you hadn't told me you were a member, I never would have made the connection."

Oh, shit. Oh, fucking shit. Oh, holy fucking shit.

"You just tensed, *piccolina*. You've watched me, haven't you?"

"Yes."

It's barely more than a whisper. Now that I know who he is, I want him even more. He's never naked, and that's part of the appeal. He's always with the same woman, or at least he has been for a long time. She's naked, but he's clothed, and it's fucking hot to watch.

"Do you mask?"

"Absolutely. I wear a lace Venetian cat mask. It covers my entire face too."

"Does it have rhinestones around the eyes and lace over the mouth?"

"Yes. You've seen me. We've never..."

"No, *piccolina*. I wouldn't have stopped with only once. But I remember you now."

I want to curl into a ball and roll into a hole. I don't know why I'm ashamed when he's a member too. But it's intensely personal for someone to know I've seen them have sex, and they know I have kinky sex with other people. It feels even more personal than having his face in my cunt.

"Sinead?"

"Yeah."

"You are so stiff you could snap in half. You were completely relaxed a moment ago. Will you let me kiss you again?"

He's asking permission. Was earlier some halfway scene, and now this is something different?

"I can practically hear the gears grinding in your head. This is all real. I'm not your Dom. What just happened was not a Dom with his sub, even if I had the advantage of knowing you're into that. Are you a Dom?"

"Sometimes."

"Power exchange?"

"Yes. But that is *not* something I think you'd ever be into."

Why the fuck did I just say that? That assumes there would ever be a time where we truly roleplay. Yesterday tapped into a fantasy, but it wasn't roleplaying in the least.

"No, that isn't something I'd be into. Is it a must for you?"

"I— I—"

I can't say it. He presses me away enough that he can turn my head toward him. His lips brush mine, and it's such a soft kiss that I melt. What the hell is happening here? This is, hands down, the absolutely most bizarre twenty-four hours of my life. I return his kiss because I never want to let him go. I don't want to step back into reality. His hands slide up the outside of my thighs until they grip my ass. God, all I want is to take him out of his pants and sit on his dick. Yes, I desperately want to fuck. But I also just want to feel him inside me.

"Do you wish to submit to me? Is that what you were going to say?"

"Yes."

"Have you had a Dom in the past?"

"Yes."

"Do you have one now?"

He doesn't sound like he likes the idea that I might. His question is demanding, and I don't answer right away. His hand cracks down on my ass, and I clench.

"Answer me, Sinead."

I still refuse, praying he spanks me again. He doesn't disappoint. He lays two more across my ass. This is definitely different from last night in the car.

"I'm going to spank you because you want it, but you are also going to answer me. Are you with someone?"

"No. There are two guys, but I'm not in a D/s arrangement with anyone. You said you don't have an arrangement" with anyone right now, but is there someone you meet or go with?"

"Yes. There is a woman who's a swinger. We have no relationship outside the club. We meet every other Thursday. If I don't show, I don't show. She and her husband do something else."

"Are you..."

"If he's fucking her, she's sucking me off. Is that what you want to know?"

"Yes."

"We aren't saying it, but we're both establishing what we want together. I will not share you, Sinead. Not at a club, and not outside of it. If we have sex again, I'm the only man— only person —you're with. Whatever we have going on with other people ends. It's all or nothing for both of us."

"You want to be my Dom?"

"No."

"I'm confused."

"Do you want me to be your Dom? I'll always need to dominate. I need the control, Sinead. There's a lot of my life that I can't control, so what I can, I cling to. I also want to be the one who takes care of you. We can't date right now, but that's what I want. We can meet at the club and use the anonymity to our advantage if you want to pursue a physical relationship. After the trial, if we win, and you want more, then we'll have more."

"How can you be sure you'll want more by then?"

"Because I want more now. I don't date. Like ever. I might hook up with someone every once in a while, and I have someone I see at Cries. But I haven't met anyone until you who I'd be willing to let into my life. Did it start because you're my attorney in this fucked-up situation? Yes. But I've told you things I didn't have to. Things I wanted you to know."

"Like that you read and don't have a TV."

"Yes. I've explained why I call some women in my family auntie and not aunt. I've told you who my father works for now. These are not things I tell just anyone."

"I want more too. I couldn't stop thinking how much I wished you were my date. How much I wanted to be dancing with you. Then getting to dance with you was so fucking hot. I couldn't stop thinking what it would be like to have another night like last night."

"Same. I do not want a D/s relationship with you with a contract and no emotional attachment beyond aftercare. I want a real relationship with you that involves kinky sex. Like I said, when the trial is over, if that's what you want, then we try it."

"But for now, it's just sex."

"You know it isn't just sex, but that's all we can do that won't get us in trouble, and it has to be at the club under the guise of not knowing who each other is."

"Can I think about it?"

"Of course."

"What if I decide to say no?"

I won't. There's not a fucking chance in hell that I'd say no. But I want to understand where this is going.

"Then I respect that, and we continue on the way we're supposed to."

"And it won't be awkward?"

"We don't let it be. Today was because we didn't talk about this last night or this morning. I want to date you because you intrigue me. I want to get to know you better because you're intelligent and assertive. I want to fuck you because you're hot. I'm old enough to separate the two."

I consider everything he's saying. It truly has been the most bizarre day and a half. But we're in a bizarre situation. If I weren't his attorney, he could ask me out, and I would say yes.

If we met each other at our club, then we could scene together without either of us being the wiser. That's sort of what we're going for. We can have the physical and emotional but in a limited setting. I think.

"Can we talk and get to know each other better while we're at Cries since we can't go out together?"

"Yes. I don't know who might join us for our pretrial meetings, but that is also a time for us to spend together. And that's about the most fucked-up way to say we can have a date."

He grimaces, and I giggle. I sit up and kiss his cheek. He turns his head and captures my lips again. Once more, it's such a soft kiss that you would never expect from a man like Gabriele. He strokes my hair, and I want to fall asleep against him.

"This is why I don't want to be your Dom, Sinead. I want this unconditional affection. I want it even when we're not having sex. I want you to give me affection too. The longer I hold you, the stronger my craving for it is."

I cup his cheek but wait for him to turn toward me. I start the kiss, and he lets me lead. I can feel he's still hard, but he hasn't tried to get me to do anything to him. He seems content the way we are.

"*Piccolina*, we need to get going. We can't stay in here for forever. I'm certain Lorenzo has needed to come in here, but he won't."

"He knows we're back here? He assumes we're having sex, doesn't he?"

"Probably. But if I tell him we didn't, and that we talked, he'll know I'm telling the truth. I've told a lot of half-truths, even to people in my family, but they know I don't lie to them. Will I tell him what we did against that door? No fucking way. That's between us."

"You know I've seen you. Do you want people to watch us?"

"Maybe sometimes. But you will see I have very distinct tats."

He unbuttons the top of his shirt and shows me a map of Italy over his left pec.

"Sinead, it's been more than a decade since anyone's arrested me, but I've had this tat since I was sixteen. My mother nearly killed me. I have feared for my life many times, but never have I been so close to death as my mother finding out I got my first tattoo. The police have photographed some of them, so you would know about these, anyway. But I can't let people see them. I don't want to always be fully clothed with you."

"So, no voyeurs when you want to be naked."

"When either of us wants to be watched, we can, but not if you want me naked. You said it was hot to see me fucking clothed. If you want that, and you want people to watch, then they can. But I have two conditions to that."

"Okay?"

I have no idea what's coming next.

"We never have sex in the main room. I can handle knowing someone might watch us through the two-way glass, but if we're having sex in the main room, then I will know there are people watching you. I will know seeing you is getting them off. No one ever joins us, Sinead. Don't ask because I will not even consider it. I told you, once we're together, there's no one else. I am not a possessive man in general. I come from way too large a family to be. But the idea of watching someone else arouse you or get you off, someone touching you, makes my head want to explode."

"Good. Because I will fucking tear a bitch apart if she comes near you. I feel the same about the voyeurs and the main room. It's too personal seeing who's watching, to know men and women are getting off from watching you. I want that to be mine alone. I won't share either, Gabriele. I've been in non-monogamous nonromantic relationships before. And because I always use condoms with guys, and we have to test regularly, I don't care if those two men are with other people. We fuck and say goodnight. I have no contact with them outside of the club."

"Do they know about each other?"

That makes me hesitate.

"Sinead?"

"Yes, they know about each other. They're bi."

"Are they a couple?"

"Yes."

"Is that something important to you? Do you want to be shared?"

"With them, I don't care. With you, no. I don't want anyone else with us, male or female. But I do want certain things a dildo or vibrator can do instead."

"That's fair."

I nestle back against him, emotionally and physically drained. My body still feels rung dry by those two orgasms. They were, like, cataclysmic. But I'm emotionally worn out from this conversation. It's been so fucking much to take in. I have *never* had a conversation like it. Not even remotely close. I feel better about the two of us being on the same page and knowing we want the same thing, but I'm suddenly exhausted. I can't help but yawn as my eyes drift shut.

"It's time to take you home."

Home.

It's not really home. At least, not his, mine, or ours. But I wish it were ours. Somehow, I think that would be the happiest place I've ever been. I'm fucking certifiable.

He helps me onto my feet, and I push down my skirt and

run my hand through my hair. I hear buttons being pushed, but he's squatting in front of a desk drawer. At least I assume it's a drawer. Maybe it's a safe. I can see him reach in and take something out, but I don't know what. Then he's standing and putting his suit coat back on. He reached for something at his lower back when we got to my apartment. He doesn't want me to see what he has, and he put his coat back on.

"Gabriele, are you carrying a gun?"

"Yes."

"You can't! They will throw you in jail with no possibility of bail. They've released you on a ridiculously high bail. You'll lose your freedom if the cops find out."

"Sinead, I will always take that risk because it's way less than being without one. There's no fucking chance I won't have one when I'm with you. I carry a knife too. I will protect you any way I have to, and you already know being my attorney, let alone anything else, comes with risks. This isn't negotiable. If you can't live with it, then you can't be my attorney or anything else."

I can only stand there and blink. My mind is scrambled eggs. He steps around the desk, but he doesn't get any closer to me. He waits to see what I do. I nod, but I don't have words right now. The gun isn't what freaks me out. It's knowing he might have to use it to protect me.

What the ever-loving fuck have I gotten myself into?

Chapter Eleven

Gabriele

I'm freaking her all the fucking way out. We managed to have an intensely personal conversation about our sex lives after only knowing each other a week. A conversation that detailed how our sex lives are joining. That was fine. This? This is not fine.

"Sinead, I'm not trying to give you an ultimatum. I'm telling you facts about the reality you've stepped into. All our bodyguards carry weapons. They're there to protect the people in my family from a lot more than someone looking in their direction. If I felt the need for you to have a detail from the very start, it's because I believe there's a real danger to you. I don't live in a world where calling the cops is the solution. Quite honestly, if I didn't know my life depended on it, I wouldn't carry a gun. I wouldn't even own one. If I didn't live in this world, I wouldn't feel like I need one. Not to protect myself. Not to protect my home. But I was born into this, just like the last six generations of my family. I'm surprised they didn't give me my first knife at my baptism, and my first gun at my confir-

151

mation. I will not risk your safety, nor will I apologize for protecting you. It's non-negotiable for me. If this gun is a deal breaker for you, then we go our separate ways."

"This is a fuck ton to take in right now, Gabriele. My head is fucking spinning. Part of me is surprised you have one somewhere like this, and part of me thinks I'm fucking stupid for being one bit surprised. Part of me is glad that you can protect yourself, and I appreciate you can protect me. But it's also terrifying to know you might need to protect me. I didn't consider whether your men would carry them. I guess I thought their presence would make people know I'm off limits. Now I feel supremely naïve and even stupider for it. The scared part of me says run. The ambitious part of me says pull your big girl panties up and get over it. The attracted to you part of me doesn't want to think anything could happen to you and wants you too much to have much common sense. I don't know what to do."

"I take you to Auntie Paola's. You sleep and think about it with a clear head in the morning. If you can't sleep, then you at least rest. When I was really little and hated taking naps, my mom would tell me to have a body rest. I still wanted to be up doing stuff, playing, but it did me some good. And if you get scared in the middle of the night, you come and get me. I'll stay with you until you aren't scared."

I hope she can hear the sincerity in my voice and see it in my eyes. I hope she knows I regret all of this shit coming even remotely close to her. I'm seriously fucking questioning why I'm doing any of this. I should stay away from her. I should insist Uncle Massimo and Uncle Salvatore find someone else to represent me. Someone with experience with syndicates; someone I couldn't give two shits about. I don't want this undertow to suck her down and drown her.

That's what it does to anyone else who gets too close to

syndicate life. Maria was born into this. She didn't have any choice. Serafina was born into two different Italian syndicates: Venice and Sicily. She's like Maria and has known nothing else. But Olivia met Luca because a cartel tried to suck her in, and now that she's married into the Cosa Nostra, she'll never be free of it. Not now that it's touched her life. Is that what I want to have happen to Sinead?

"All right. I have to be in court at eight tomorrow. It's getting late, and I'm exhausted. Let's go."

"Are you all right with this?"

"I have no choice, really. So, I'll get all right with it."

She turns toward the door, and I walk with her. I lean past to open it, and we come face-to-face with Lorenzo. He sweeps his eyes over us, but his expression shows nothing Sinead could interpret. I can tell he's certain we didn't go all the way to sex, and he's glad. He didn't stop me, but now that I'm not in a lust haze, I know he wouldn't have approved. It wouldn't have been a moral judgement. It would be him worried I wouldn't get the best possible defense because I compromised Sinead's ability to detach reason from emotion. He doesn't need to know about last night.

"We're headed to Auntie Paola's."

"Did you text her?"

Fuck.

"I will now."

Sinead looks up at me, her eyes wide.

"It's after midnight, Gabriele. You can't text her now. I'll check myself into a hotel."

I stare down at her, and I see the mutinous glare enter her eyes. I can wait her out.

"Oh, for fuck's sake." Apparently, Lorenzo can't. "Sinead, go to our aunt's house. She won't care at all. Hell, she's probably awake working on a campaign speech or something. If you go to a hotel, Gabriele will spend the entire night standing outside your door. Do us all a favor and let him sleep. He's fucking Grumpy from the Seven Dwarfs if you don't. You think he's stubborn now? Wait till he doesn't get his four hours of beauty sleep. He's fucking Shrek. Auntie Paola has the best beds in her guest bedrooms. She also loves soft towels and always has practically a buffet in her kitchen around the clock. You won't want to leave."

Sinead's listening to him but watching me. I'm not trying to push my will onto her anymore. I'll let Lorenzo's reasoning do it for me. She nods, but she still hasn't taken her eyes off me. Lorenzo steps aside to let us pass, and we walk through the club with Sinead a step behind me. I nod to Marco as we approach the door. He smiles at Sinead, and he knows how women react to it. But it falters before he looks at me. When he gets nothing from me, he goes back to Sinead. I feel her shift and step closer to my back.

"Sinead, this is Marco. He's Lorenzo's older brother. He's one of Uncle Massimo's sons."

She steps around me and extends her hand, which Marco takes. I'm surprised he doesn't do the whole air kiss over her hand and say "enchanté." He's goading me while trying to see if he's allowed on the field.

"Hello, Sinead."

"Hi."

I turn, so I can see both of them. She's watching me, not Marco. Her expression is expectant. Does she want more of an introduction? Or is she trying to get me out the door?

"We're headed to Auntie Paola's."

"Will I see you at the gym in the morning?"

I gaze down at Sinead.

"I usually go at four and will be back about six-thirty. Which court do you need to be at?"

"Queens Criminal Court."

"That's not too bad. Auntie Paola lives in Queens."

"She does?"

"Did you expect her to be a Manhattanite?"

"I suppose."

"Only the unmarried people seem to still be in Manhattan. Everyone else already lives in Queens or moved back there when they got married."

"So, you two and Lorenzo?"

"Yes."

"How long do you think it'll take to get to the courthouse?"

"About forty-five minutes. She lives in Malba."

She doesn't know what to say to that. Maybe she doesn't realize just how wealthy our family is. Malba is the most expensive neighborhood in Queens. Auntie Paola used to entertain a lot earlier in her career. She hosted tons of fundraiser dinners for various candidates. Now that Uncle Cesare and Carmine don't live there anymore, it's a big house for her to be rattling around in. But she enjoys being out on the coast. It's quieter.

"Could we leave at six-forty-five? I would feel better if we left an hour to get there."

"Absolutely."

"Thanks. Goodnight, Marco."

There's the not-so-subtle hint. I clap him on the shoulder.

"Night."

He does the same. It's the closest we get to a public embrace, and it's more than what we exchanged for like eighteen years.

"Night."

I walk out with Sinead, and Pauly's right by the curb, waiting for us. He gets out and opens the door for Sinead. She slides over, and I follow her in. Once we have our seatbelts on, she wilts. It's going to be an hour drive from Chelsea to Malba, so I wrap my arm around her shoulders and nudge her head onto mine. The strain of the day is too much, plus it's already close to midnight. She's asleep before we make it past the Flat Iron Building and onto Lexington Avenue, so not even four city blocks. I close my eyes and rest, too. I've fallen asleep in our town cars plenty of times. Sometimes, it's the only place I get enough time to sleep. But I can't with Sinead with me. My eyes snap open, and I'm looking out both windows, watching everything. I can't relax knowing someone bugged her place. It's been on my mind all night, but I'm finally letting myself really consider it.

I don't know what to make of this. The most obvious explanation is usually the right explanation, so that means the Polish. But I'm not convinced. The bratva categorically do not involve women in syndicate business. *Ever.* Luca and Carmine— which invariably means me —made some shit choices with a bratva then-girlfriend, now-wife. Things went way left, and shit happened that none of us intended. We've been on the top of their shitlist for two years. We finally seemed to have fallen down to maybe number four or five.

The Colombian Cartel could most definitely be behind this, but we've been getting along well lately. *Tres J's*— Javier, Jorge, and Joaquin— the *jefe's* nephews —did us a solid when traffickers kidnapped Maria in Miami. Enrique, their jefe, has been trying to get back on good terms with the bratva leader's wife. She grew up near Enrique's family in Jersey. Shit went down between the woman and another one of Enrique's nephews. He's in one of the circles of hell right now because of it. So maybe they aren't the ones. A strike against any woman, bratva or otherwise, is a battle call to that woman.

The Irish are a constant love-hate relationship for us. We've been rivals and allies for decades. Generally, we don't like them. But we do sometimes need them, especially when it comes to the docks. But we've had the upper hand there for a while, and they're paying us a tax to keep the customs inspectors away. They were willing to help us protect Maria too, so I can't see them suddenly flipping and going after a woman again. Not after what they've already lost from targeting bratva and *Cosa Nostra* women.

That leaves some smaller syndicates who might make a play to seize some of our business or territories. Only Uncle Salvatore, Uncle Massimo, and Auntie Paola's great-grandfather did it. It was when he took control of our branch from Carmine's father's family. We came out the winners in that. Very few have even plotted something so foolish, let alone tried it. Nothing good will come of this except destroying whoever it is.

That means it could be Italians from Chicago or LA. It's just as possible it's Greek-Americans, Jewish-Americans, Assyrians and Chaldeans, or Albanians. There's a good chance Mexicans in NYC or closer to the border like Texas or California are trying to gain power. For a while, smaller Colombian Cartels tried to oust Enrique by bringing us down. We've had a few target us directly, but it's never gotten past their planning stage before Enrique sweeps in and takes out the trash. The list for other Latin American cartels is pretty long, though. Mexicans, Brazilians, Nicaraguans, Bolivians, Peruvians, Dominicans, Guatemalans, Hondurans, Venezuelans. Take your pick. They all have active cartels, too.

It could be Triad, but as long as the Chinese syndicates get their drugs run through us, they stay out of the way. Same thing with the *yakuza*. The Japanese aren't that interested in us. There was a little ripple with an investment that didn't go through properly for one of our casinos Luca handles. You also have the Golden Triangle and the Golden Crescent in Asia. But I don't think they're looking in our direction.

Even Canada has a string of syndicates that wouldn't mind getting more territory across the border, eh. They are not the polite, "no, you go first; no, you" types either. You have the Italian-Canadian Mafias, like the *Cosa Nostra* and *'Ndrangheta*. There are a few syndicates in Quebec and British Columbia, but we're on good terms with them since our relationships are mutually lucrative. I can't see them trying to frame me for anything.

So that takes us right back around to I don't know who the fuck to blame for framing me and targeting Sinead. But when I find out...

I look down at Sinead, who's still sleeping against my shoulder. The bubble I put myself in when I met her is shrinking. It may have even popped since getting in the car and having time to think clearly for the first time in a week.

She's a fucking lawyer. What am I thinking that I can be with her and fulfill my commitments to my family? How do I keep any kind of a connection with her without getting her disbarred? She's not my wife, so they could compel her to testify. I can't let this slight go. I have no choice but to retaliate, or at least my family must. I'd let it go and move on with my life if I could, but that's not even remotely an option.

Maksim Kutsenko's wife, Laura— the one pissed at Enrique —balances being their corporate attorney and being married to the bratva leader. But she doesn't touch their criminal matters. Sinead only handles criminal cases. At least she's a defense attorney and not working for the District Attorney.

And once again, this is why I don't date. Because it's complicated.

But I've never wanted a woman like I do Sinead. I need to slow this the fuck down. What the hell is she going to think when she wakes up? She didn't drink at dinner, and she barely finished the drink she had at the club. She can't blame being drunk for a second hook up. I don't want to give her the cold shoulder in the morning like I sort of did today, but things need to slow the fuck down.

She isn't used to making decisions as fast as I am. She's incredibly intelligent, and I don't doubt her ability to observe, assess, and decide quickly. But I make life altering, life or death decisions that can't be mistakes all the time. I've had days to consider Sinead, and that's why I know what I want. A week is a luxury. I've gotten good at this, and that's why I'm still alive when guys I grew up with aren't. I can't expect that from her. Weeks, months, years are more reasonable.

"Gabriele?"

"Yes, *piccolina*?"

"Are we there yet?"

She sits up and pushes her hair back.

"We're three blocks away."

"I fell asleep fast."

"Pretty much as soon as the car pulled out."

"I'm sorry. I didn't mean—"

"I didn't mind, *piccolina*."

Well, that's not putting any distance between us. That's not slowing things down for her to catch up. She nods as she shifts to look out the window as we pull up to a gated property within a gated community. I feel her stiffen as she sees the man in the little guard hut. He's in all black with night-vision goggles on. He's got his rifle slung across his front, hand near the trigger. She sweeps her eyes over to my window and sees a couple men on patrol.

"This is like an embassy or a Miami cocaine dealer's house in an 8os movie."

I'm not sure she realizes she said that out loud. It was more of a mutter, but I heard her. She isn't wrong. Auntie Paola's security is top-notch, especially since she lives the farthest out.

Everyone else lives in Forest Hills. Long story short, Auntie Paola's and Uncle Cesare's fathers forced them to get married when Auntie Paola got pregnant at nineteen.

Our last don was Salvatore, Massimo, and Paola's father. He was a dick. He bought the house for them. Not as a wedding or baby shower gift. It was his way of keeping Uncle Cesare out of family business. Carmine's parents never intended to get serious, and were like oil and water living together. Uncle Cesare's family was the one the Mancinellis dethroned. Bad blood. Lots and lots of bad blood spilled back in the day. Even though Cesare doesn't live there anymore, she's kept the house out of nostalgia after raising Carmine there.

Right now, it's a blessing and a curse. It's far away from Sinead's place and tucked away where most people wouldn't think to look. But that also means we're isolated, our guard limited to just the men on duty right now. It takes a weight off my shoulders and settles it right in my gut. I don't want my second mom or Sinead to come to harm. I call her auntie because so does everyone but Carmine. But I've called her mom plenty of times, and she loves it. I do too. I may be thirty-one, but I miss my parents. It's nice having her around.

We pull into a garage, and I put my hand on Sinead's, stopping her as she reaches for the door handle.

"Wait until the garage door closes, and the engine is off. The driver will turn it off the moment the door hits the ground, but you never get out until he does."

"In case he needs to back out."

"Yes. Once you're inside one of our garages, you can get out on your own. Or the driver can come around if you'd feel better having him there."

"I can do it. It seems pretentious to have someone open my car door inside a house garage."

"I don't care how it looks to anyone. What I care about is you feeling safe and being safe."

Her shoulders relax for the first time since we arrived. My hand still covers hers. She turns hers over and squeezes it before letting go. She unbuckles her belt and reaches for the door again. I walk around to her side of the car and lead her to the door into the house. It pings softly, letting me know Paola set the alarm and is in bed. I turn it off and point to the stairs. When we get to the second-floor landing, I stop us.

"If you need anything, like a snack, wake me. The alarm has motion detectors inside the house and outside and on all the doors and windows. You'll set it off if you walk past here."

I point to a little object sticking out of the wall. Then I point to a matching one at the bottom of the steps.

"Will I set them off coming out of the bedroom? What if I need to go to the bathroom?"

"All the guestrooms have en suites. The first two rooms are mine on the right and Carmine's on the left. Then there's a laundry dumbwaiter on my side and a linen closet on Carmine's. The next three rooms are guest bedrooms. The one at the very end on the left is Cesare's if he crashes here."

She just nods. She knows: it's complicated. I should have that shit tattooed across my face. She whirls around when she hears someone open the garage door into the house. It's only Pauly bringing in her stuff. I didn't even think about her bags.

"I'll get those. Go check out your room and see if there's anything you need."

I head back downstairs as she moves down the hallway. Just as I get back up to the landing, my phone pings in my pocket.

CARMINE

We've got a problem. A big one.

161

Chapter Twelve

Sinead

I'm wiped. I enter the bedroom, and it's beautiful. The bed is more inviting than any I've seen in a posh hotel. I kick off my shoes before sitting on the end. My eyes are closed as I wait for Gabriele. If I lie down, I'll be asleep before he comes in. I actually really want to take a shower, even though I'm so tired. I don't know why, but I feel like I shouldn't get between the sheets unless I'm clean. Even with pajamas, I feel like I'd enjoy it way more if I didn't have any sweat or anything on me.

"Sinead."

I open my eyes to see Gabriele standing in the doorway. My brow furrows. This isn't the sweet man in the club office after he got me off or the one who let me sleep against him in the car.

"What's wrong?"

"Why don't you tell me?"

I shake my head slightly as it falls forward. He's holding out his phone, so I stand up. He won't come in the room. I take it from him, and it's like the entire world crashes down around me.

Mafia Attorney Snorting Her Retainer

There's a photo on a news website with a photo of a woman who looks just like me, leaning over and doing a line of coke. It's a profile shot. I know exactly where it came from, too. I shift my focus to Gabriele, but he's blurry as tears fill my eyes. All I can do is shake my head since I can't dislodge the lump in my throat.

"Sinead, what the fuck?"

I swallow and swallow, but I still can't speak.

"Answer me. This is not one of those times where you're going to enjoy the outcome."

I keep looking at his phone as I skim the article below it.

The Mancinelli crime family hired defense attorney, Sinead O'Malley, to represent the latest felon on trial. Gabriele Scotto stands accused of detonating explosives and extorting local gangs. Ms. O'Malley graduated from Yale Law school six years ago. Rather than pay her student loans, she's seen here inhaling at least one gram of what the drug community calls an eight-ball worth at least two thousand dollars, which Mr. Scotto provided his lawyer. Ms. O'Malley has a history of drunken and disorderly conduct from her youth in Rhode Island. Her drug use and memberships to a well-known BDSM club in Manhattan are going before an ethics review board in the morning. She is facing disbarment. The Mancinellis will be searching for a new defense attorney. Perhaps the person they find can represent Ms. O'Malley as well.

Tears stream down my face. I fumble for my phone and go into my cloud to a photo folder I have but prayed never to look at again. I can't hold back my sob as I tap on one of the files.

"Sinead, answer my fucking questions."

I don't even know what he's saying. I didn't hear any questions. My ears are ringing as I step back and forget I'm not as close to the bed as I thought I was. I lurch backwards and would have fallen hard if Gabriele's reactions weren't so fast. It's like slow motion as he drops my work bag, overnight bag, and garment bag. He catches my arms, but I sag. I can't anymore. I go limp, and he lowers me to the ground. My nose is running, and I can't catch my breath as I sob. All I can do is hand Gabriele my phone.

"What is this, Sinead?"

I stare blankly ahead of me. I know what he's looking at as though someone painted it inside my eyeballs. I let myself fall sideways and curl into a ball.

"I'm the one who's supposed to be dead."

I don't know if he hears me. I don't even know if I say it out loud. I close my eyes and try to breathe. It's so fucking hard, and I feel lightheaded. I'm right back there again. It's all happening in my mind as though I'm in that car.

"*Piccolina?*"

"Hmmm."

Did I just hum? I'm certain that's Gabriele's voice and his hands now picking me up. I'm floating, or at least it feels that way. He must be carrying me. This really is the softest bed I've ever felt. The mattress dips as he climbs onto it. He must be even heavier than he looks. He pulls me against him and strokes my hair.

"*Piccolina*, breathe. I don't understand what you showed me, but you're freaking me out. If you don't say something, I'm calling a doctor. We have two in the family."

I wish I could. But I can't. I know I'm breathing because I'm alive enough to hear Gabriele. But this blindsided me, and none of the things I've learned to handle this trauma response are going to work. I'm too far gone already.

I hear Gabriele speaking again, but it's not to me. I don't know who it is. I catch snippet.

"Maria...Auntie Paola's... Need you now... If you don't... ambulance... Shaking... pale... pulse..."

I'm only catching every few words. He moves, and I want to reach out to him. Beg him not to go. I hear him running then yelling.

"Auntie Paola! Auntie Paola! Hurry!"

I don't feel right. Like really don't feel right. Like worse than I ever have. I hear more feet running, but I don't know what's going on. My chest hurts so fucking much. I know Gabriele would never sit on me, but it feels like it. I try to move my hand to rub my chest, but my arms aren't obeying.

"Hello. I think my girlfriend is having a heart attack. She's thirty-years old, shallow breathing, pale and clammy skin, pulse is racing, and she isn't responding to anything I say. It's been like this for at least three minutes."

A heart attack? I'm way too young for that, aren't I? Maybe not. It would explain how I feel. Wait. Girlfriend? I— I—

"Sinead, can you hear me?"

Someone's shaking me. Not hard, but it feels like I'm rattling around in a can.

"Sinead, I'm Maria. I'm a doctor. Can you hear me?"

I try to make a sound, but nothing is happening. I feel someone wrapping my fingers around someone else's finger.

"Sinead, I need you to listen to me. Are you allergic to aspirin? Squeeze my finger if you are *not* allergic."

"Not allergic?"

Who is that? It's a man.

"Because I don't want to misunderstand if she is. I'd rather not give it to her than risk her having an allergic reaction on top of a heart attack."

I'm squeezing as hard as I can. Can she feel it?

"She's not allergic. Matteo, get my purse. There's aspirin in the first aid kit. Sinead, I'm going to give you a chewable tablet. I need you to try, okay? Gabe, help me sit her up. It'll take some of the strain off her heart."

This woman is gentle, even if she's authoritative. She's shoving pillows behind me as someone pulls me forward. I look up and see Gabriele. Once I'm positioned the way she wants, she helps open my mouth and slides in a pill that's already broken into smaller pieces. I let it sit on my tongue because I can't do anything else. I try swallowing, and it's not bad. I think I get the whole thing down.

"Matteo, there's the ambulance. Can you let them in?"

I don't know the woman's voice. Is that Paola?

"I'm Dr. Mancinelli. This is Sinead O'Malley. She's thirty years old and presenting with sudden stress induced cardiac arrythmia. She's got tachycardia with a pulse at one-twenty now. But it's dropped back to eight-six and eighty-two in the ten minutes I've been here. She's been minimally conscious and verbally unresponsive for twenty minutes and didn't rouse when I took her blood pressure, which was eight-five over fifty-five. She squeezed my finger earlier to show she is not allergic to aspirin. She took three-hundred milligrams about four minutes ago in case this is a heart attack."

While Maria's talking, someone's put an oxygen mask over my face. Finally. And twenty minutes? That's not possible. I would have remembered this lasting twenty minutes. What's minimally conscious? Did I faint? Is that what she means? I must have because I don't remember her arriving. But I didn't know fainting could last this long.

"Dr. Mancinelli, we'll take her now."

Before I know what's happening, I'm being lifted onto a stretcher. I have control of my arms again, and I fling my right one out toward Gabriele. I catch his sleeve and cling to it.

"Sinead, I'm going to follow you to hospital. I'll be there when you get there."

I tighten my fist as Gabriele tries to pry my fingers off. Where the hell did this strength come from?

"Can I ride with my girlfriend?"

"Yeah. We need to go."

"We'll follow, Gabe."

I shift my gaze to Maria's. I can see clearly now. I see a man standing behind her, his arms around her middle. Then there's a gorgeous middle-aged woman by the bedroom door.

"Auntie Paola, will you let the others know?"

"Of course. Keep us posted."

"I will. Thank you. Maria, tell Carmine to find her emergency contact. I need to know who's going to make decisions."

I tug hard on his sleeve and look up at him.

"You."

I don't know if he understood me. I think he did because he nods. I love Andrea dearly, but I trust Gabriele to make medical decisions. Somehow, I think he has way more experience with this than Andrea does. She's my emergency contact, but I want Gabriele.

It's so much easier to breathe now. The paramedics are doing things as they load me into the ambulance, and Gabriele's trying to stay out of the way. He's a giant, and the space is cramped. But he's with me. I'm not panicking anymore. Maybe that's all it was. A panic attack. I've had those before. Just not anything like this one.

"Who're you?"

I look over at Gabriele as he jogs alongside the stretcher into the emergency room.

"I'm her boyfriend."

"You're going to need to wait out here if you're not family or her proxy."

"All right."

"No!"

I try to scream, and I won't let go as Gabriele tries to pry my fingers from his shirt, which I'm clutching even hard then before. Apparently, the oxygen has revived me enough to find more strength than I expected.

"I'm staying with her."

I watch as someone in scrubs tries to disagree. Gabriele takes my hand as he straightens from leaning over me, pushing his shoulders back. I dart my gaze to the other guy, who nods.

"Shhh, *piccolina*. I'm staying."

The next hour is almost as much of a blur as what happened at Paola's house. They're admitting me for observations overnight, and Gabriele's staying out of the way as they get me settled into my room. He promised not to leave. Once it's blessedly quiet again, he pulls a chair closer to the bed.

"That's the worst panic attack I've had over that."

"I don't understand what 'that' is. I didn't have time to see what you were handing me. I have your phone, but I'm not showing you whatever you pulled up."

"You can look at it."

I hold my finger out to unlock it. Once I have, he sits down again. I watch as he reads the newspaper article. He scrolls back up and reads it a second time.

"Was this why you became an attorney?"

"Yes. I haven't talked about this in years. I haven't seen that photo in years. That isn't me. That was my sister, Delaney, when she was nineteen, and I was fifteen. She died the night whoever it was took that photo. She died, and I lived."

Gabriele remains quiet, holding my hand in his while his other strokes the inside of my forearm. It's so incredibly soothing.

"She started doing drugs when she was thirteen. It started

with pot and moved on from there. It was recreational. She never did it at home. She didn't need them to make it to the next day. But she partied a lot more than my parents realized. It started when our mom got sick. That's how she coped. I spent a lot of time with air fresheners and doing laundry to cover for her. When our mom died, she went completely out of control. She would go out and not tell my dad or me where she was going. Sometimes, she'd be gone for thirty hours. Just short of a missing person's report. She got arrested for possession, but she got off both times because our attorney found technicalities. She was guilty as sin, though."

I close my eyes and focus on my breathing. I'm choosing to talk about this, so I have control. I use the techniques I drilled into myself during years of therapy.

"She was a minor, so most of her legal issues were sealed. My dad didn't know what to do. He was trying to muddle through his own grief, raise me, and tame my sister. Delaney made it through high school and even got into a good college. She got great test scores and kept her grades up. She partied hard on Friday nights and all-day Saturdays, usually until the middle of the afternoon Sunday. She'd come home, shower, and do as much of her homework for the week as she could. That way she could get high during the week on pot. She saved the coke for weekends."

I point to my phone, which Gabriele's still holding.

"I was so angry at her that day. So beyond pissed. I absolutely hated her. It was my birthday, and she stole money our grandparents sent us. It was supposed to go into my college fund. Instead, it went up her nose. It wasn't just that year's birthday money. When I checked my savings account, she'd cleared it out. There was fifty thousand dollars in it that our parents and both sets of grandparents had been paying into since I was born. They'd done the same for her. She was using hers for her freshman year. She was stealing from me to pay for her drugs and for shit she thought made her fit in with the Hamptons-Martha's Vineyard crowd. Purses. Clothes. Shoes. Sunglasses. All of it. I told her what I thought of her, what she'd done, and what I wished would happen to her. I told her she'd either cave her nose in or die. I hoped it was the latter."

I close my eyes as the tears burn again, but this time I'm prepared. I can work through it. I just need a moment. Gabriele's not pushing me. He's still holding my hand and stroking my arm.

"It was one a.m. when she called. We didn't know some things we saw were signs of what was to come for our dad's early onset dementia. We thought it was stuff from being in combat. Some of it probably was. I didn't have a party that year because my dad wasn't well enough to organize it. So, I was home on my birthday while she was out wasting my money. When the phone rang, I ignored it. I knew it was her. When it rang a third time, I answered only long enough to hang up. Then a call from another number came in. Something told me I needed to answer it. It was one of her friends calling to tell me she'd OD'd. They wanted me to come pick her up. I couldn't drive. At least not legally. I'd been riding four wheelers and dirt bikes for years. I'd driven my grandpa's old truck on their farm plenty of times. Ever since I could reach the pedals."

I rake my teeth over my bottom lip. I can hear my breathing, but it's reassuring. Gabriele shifts how he's holding my hand, so ours are facing opposite directions. He curls his fingers around my hand and brings the back of it to his lips then his cheek. I close my eyes and find strength in him just being there. I know he's listening, but he's not asking anything of me.

"I found out they were at a farm about thirty minutes outside of Providence. We lived in the suburbs, but on the other side. I tried to wake my dad up, but he took prescription sleeping tablets. He never, ever abused them. But they worked well. I could have woken him up if I really tried, but trying to make my day special after learning what Delaney did exhausted him. He also spent the day getting ready for Christmas. My birthday is the twenty-third. By now, it was Christmas Eve. I was fifteen. I knew what I was doing was so totally illegal, but I figured it would be fine as long as I was careful. I grabbed my dad's keys and went to get her."

I close my eyes and curl into a ball on my side. I just have electrodes and a pulsometer clipped to my finger. No IVs or anything, so I can do that. My eyes spring open when Gabriele lets go of my hand.

"I'm not going anywhere, little one."

He walks around the side of the bed and drops the rail. He climbs on and spoons me. It's like having the most enormous teddy bear curled around me, but there's nothing soft about him. I want this story over with, so maybe I can fall asleep with him holding me.

"I made it across the city, avoiding all the highways. It took me forever. By the time I got to the farm, everyone was gone. But I spotted Delaney. As dark as my hair is, hers was that light. Like almost white-blonde. It was her natural color, and pretty much the only thing about herself that she didn't want to change. She was completely passed out. It took me forty-five minutes to get her to wake up enough to get her in the passenger seat. She was breathing, so I didn't call an ambulance. I didn't want the cops to come."

I pause because the hard part is coming. I take Gabriele's hand that rests near my belly and draw it up to my chest. He kisses my shoulder.

"Because I'd never taken Driver's Ed or driven on anything but fields, I didn't know bridges ice over faster than surface roads. That applied to the causeway, too. The roads were fine on the way there, but it was even colder by the time we headed back. We were halfway across the Scituate Reservoir Causeway when she woke up. Seeing me pissed her off, and it didn't thrill me to see her either. But I focused on the road. Nothing prepared me for her to lash out at me. She slammed my head against the part of the door just in front of the window when she punched me. It was just as we went over a patch of ice. I jerked the steering wheel as my head hit the door. We spun out. I was trying to push her away while getting control of the car again. She kept hitting me and swearing at me. She didn't know who I was. She thought I was some junkie who stole her stash. She didn't know where she was or anything. Even stoned, she was stronger than me. She used both hands and slammed my face into the steering wheel. She broke my nose."

I run my finger of the slight ridge that I have as one of several keepsakes from that night. But I never look at my other scars. Ever. They're way more than skin deep.

"I couldn't see straight when she finally let go of my head. She did that because we plowed into the guardrail, crumpling her door enough that she wouldn't be able to open it. I tried to correct the spinout and point us back in the right direction. I just wanted off the causeway. We were halfway across at this point. Thank God there was no oncoming traffic. I thought she'd stopped when we started moving again. She'd blacked out for a moment. We hit another patch of ice. I tried slamming on the brakes, but that only made it worse. She woke up and started flailing around, saying I should be the one who died. She even unfastened my seatbelt. It was freezing out, but I had my window open, hoping the cold air would sober her up. It saved my life. We hit the guardrail again, except this time, we went through it. I hadn't gotten my belt refastened."

Gabriele's cologne is spicy and masculine without being gross. I don't know what it is, but I like it. He draws me tighter against his body, and I haven't felt this safe since before my mom got sick.

"We went in the water, and I was completely disoriented at first. I somehow held my breath just as we plunged in. I tried to get to Delaney, but she was fighting me as I reached across to unfasten her belt. She grabbed my hair and tried to hold my head down. She didn't seem to realize what was happening. She wasn't doing anything to save herself. She wasn't trying to undo her belt. I raked my fingers across her face as I fought to get loose. I pulled away and got the belt off my arm. The car was full of water, and it was pushing me into the car when I was trying to get out. I reached out the window, and one hand grabbed the top of the outside of the door. She grabbed my legs and tugged. I kicked as hard as I could. I didn't want to die. I got my second hand out and pulled as hard as I could while I kept kicking. I got free of her, then I kicked and pushed off of anything my feet landed on. I got to the surface because the car wasn't sinking as fast as it felt when we went in. But we were over a deep part. I grabbed onto the broken part of the rail that had bent all the way into the water."

I need a breather. As though this part wasn't bad enough. The part that Gabriele read about is coming up.

"I pulled myself out, but I didn't know up from down once I rolled onto the road. I just laid there. It was a State Trooper who happened to find me. I almost died from hypothermia. I'd gotten too hot trying to drag her into the car. I took off my coat, then just sucked it up with the window open while I drove. If he'd been another few minutes, I would have. I told him my sister was in the car and that he had to get her. He wrapped me up and put me in the back of his cruiser. There are a lot of gaps after that. I remember my dad getting there. I remember him screaming when they told him Delaney was dead. There was no way she wasn't. I remember him holding me as I sobbed,

174

telling him everything that happened. They took me to the hospital for my nose and the other cuts I had from fighting with Delaney and the actual accident. While I was there, they scraped under my fingernails. I didn't understand why at the time. I do now. The next week was horrific. They dredged the lake and did an autopsy on Delaney. They knew she was stoned and drunk. I didn't know she'd been drinking, too. But I was fifteen and a day when it happened. People knew we'd fought and what I'd said on my birthday because she told them."

This is the part that takes me from despondent with sadness to stark raving mad with rage.

"They indicted me on voluntary manslaughter in the first to be tried as an adult. We both know that's still considered murder in the third degree. I knew the dangers of driving underage, but I did it. They claimed that was a blatant disregard for human life. They used the skin they collected from under my nails to claim I attacked her and lost control while it happened. They claimed I broke my nose during the crash. They claimed I ran us into the guardrail on purpose and hitting her side of the car was my first attempt to kill her. They knew about the stolen money and said that was my motive. My father stood by me. He testified to everything Delaney had put us through. The psychiatrist who saw us after mom died testified on my behalf too. The court psychiatrist stated I exhibited borderline personality disorder and sociopathic tendencies. She claimed my stoicism in court was proof of it. I was too terrified to do a single thing but barely breathe."

I roll over to face Gabriele, and he kisses my forehead, my nose, and my lips as he wraps his heavy arm over my waist.

"Because they were trying me as an adult, and they set bail at an amount no bondsman would pay. They detained me with real adults. I learned a lot really fast during those two months the trial dragged on. Part of the reason I'm good at what I do is because they incarcerated me in gen pop. I know first-hand how things work. I figured out how to stay under the radar after I got jumped my second day there. It released every bit of suppressed grief, which included rage. I beat the shit out of the woman. I'm lucky they didn't add aggravated assault. But they caught everything on camera. It was clearly self-defense, but I was probably four punches away from killing her. I would have too. I still don't regret it at all. It wasn't my only fight during those two months, but it was the longest. I learned to carry a shiv. It's not like I was in some super max prison. I was in the county jail, but it didn't matter to those women. Plenty of them had been to prison. Recidivism. But I was lucky my attorney was as good as she was. She got the acquittal. The state apologized for questioning me without a parent, poor evidence collection, and detaining me as a minor. I was exonerated, and all of it went away. But not before the news covered the trial every day we were in court. We moved that summer, and I went to a different school. It helped, but people still knew. It was a lonely two years before I graduated and escaped to Mount Holyoke. What you saw was a photo taken at the party Delaney was at. It got printed in a New England newspaper. You read only one of the articles. After that, I decided I would not only become an attorney, but I would be the best because I'd had the best. My lawyer is a senior partner at the firm I'm at now. She happens to be from Rhode Island, too."

I sigh, the weight of the world lifting from me. At least for now. I watch Gabriele, but he says nothing. I get nervous until he tucks me against his chest.

"Whoever did this will never do anything like it again. Don't ask me any questions, *piccolina*. This time, I really will blow someone's world up."

Chapter Thirteen

Gabriele

Sinead's asleep, and I don't know what to make of half the story she told me. I remember what I was doing at fifteen, and I lived with the guilt of killing people. But it was nowhere near the same thing as Sinead. What I did was premeditated. What I did was to save my family and our interests. It didn't take one of my loved one's life. I escaped being caught and tried as an adult. Though I should have been. I should be serving multiple life sentences with no possibility of parole. She did nothing and lost so much. She was a naïve fifteen-year-old trying to do the right thing. My naivety disintegrated when I was twelve and started carrying a knife because our rivals carried them too. I was the same age as her when I was involved in an enormous melee among the syndicate members in high school.

It's utterly fucked-up, but we went to school together. Members of the bratva, mob, Cartel, and *Cosa Nostra* wound up at the same party one night. Maria stood up for her friend who liked one of the *Tres J's*, but he was being a douche. He called Maria a flat-chested bitch. One of the Kutsenkos heard and got in the brothers' face. Maria came and told Carmine and me. Next thing I know, guns and knives were out. Anyone not associated with a syndicate got the fuck out of there. No one died. Somehow. I truly don't know how. But none of us came away without injury. I have a bullet scar in my left arm from Misha Kutsenko shooting me. It stopped being about Maria and became a turf war.

To this day, I have never seen Uncle Salvatore so angry. He couldn't decide what language to yell in. It switched between English, Italian, and Itanglese— a combo of Italian and English —by the word. Even after the shit with Luca, Carmine, and me and the bratva woman who wound up injured, then kidnapped because of us. After that shit show with Anastasia Kutsenko, he took a turn with us and broke Luca's arm before he exiled us to Sicily for several months. The vineyard owner resented Uncle Salvatore sending us because the man owned him a favor. The guy beat us daily. We could do nothing. But I digress.

My mind's wandering because part of it doesn't want to process everything Sinead told me. Because they tried her as an adult, they wouldn't have sealed her record. Anyone who dug a little would have found it. The photo is super incriminating because the angle doesn't show the girl's hair color. I didn't know it wasn't Sinead, and I've been looking at her for days.

Shit happened between a soccer coach and me when I was fourteen. I swore I would never be that vulnerable again. It was also when I knew I would be loyal to Carmine for the rest of time. He came into that locker room just in time to stop the guy from forcing himself on me. After that day, I started working out twice a day. I was the same height I am now, but I was half my weight. By the time I turned fifteen, so Sinead's age when this shit with Delaney happened, I was three quarters of my current weight, so one-hundred-and-eighty pounds. If they'd sent me to jail, I would have been bigger than most guys in county. It would have been a different story in federal prison, but I already knew how to protect myself. Sinead had to learn among women who'd already committed plenty of crimes. She didn't have anyone to teach her. She carried a fucking shank and used it.

As I watch her sleep in my arms, I could get used to this. I want to protect her and ruin whoever did this to her. I want to know who the fuck dug around, who the fuck sold the story, and who the fuck the reporter and editor are. Journalistic integrity my fucking ass. If they got the photo, then they got the rest of the story, too. They purposely did this to be prejudicial to any jury. As it said, there's going to be an ethics review.

And that's fucking stupid in and of itself. When they admitted her to the New York State Bar, they did a full background check. If I fucking got admitted, with my obvious family ties, then there shouldn't have been a problem for her with an exoneration. Belonging to a sex club isn't against any rules for attorneys. They tossed that in for the sake of sensationalism.

Being with Sinead right now, knowing I shouldn't leave her and don't want to, is the only thing keeping me from tearing the city apart to find out who did this. She didn't deserve this just because she signed on to be my attorney. This is more extreme than I expected, especially this early in the case. To have some asshole bugging her place and a story like this planted, someone is working overtime to fuck with us.

A soft knock pulls me out of my thoughts. I twist to see Maria and Auntie Carlotta coming in. Auntie Carlotta's a general surgeon at this hospital. Maria did her radiology residency here. Auntie Carlotta walks over and rests her hand on my shoulder as she leans down to kiss my cheek. Maria stands at the foot of the bed. Our fucking family tree.

I'm distantly related however many generations back, but the Mancinellis have pretty much adopted me. The Mancinelli family legally adopted Auntie Carlotta's husband, Domenico, as an infant sixty years ago. He's Uncle Salvatore, Uncle Massimo, and Auntie Paola's second cousin with no actual blood relation. Uncle Domenico and Auntie Carlotta have two sons: the exiled Emilio and Maria's husband, Matteo. She's Maria's mother-in-law and something like her second cousin once removed-in-law.

Auntie Carlotta keeps her voice low as she watches the monitor then Sinead.

"How's she doing?"

"Better now. They ruled out a heart attack and believe it was an extreme panic attack brought on by exposure to a childhood trauma. They said it was rare that the response should be so severe but not impossible. Maria, did you speak to Carmine?"

"Yeah. He's in the hallway. He didn't want to come in if it wasn't appropriate."

"Can you stay with her while I talk to him, please?"

"Of course."

I do what I can to ease my arm away from her waist, but her eyes flash open. She grips my hand as tightly as she did my shirt earlier.

"Shhh, *piccolina*. I'm not going far. I need to talk to Carmine in the hallway. Auntie Carlotta and Maria are here. You probably don't remember, but there was a man who came with Maria. This is his mom. She's a doctor too."

"Don't go. Please, Gabe."

"Shhh. Maria, can you push back the curtain?"

She hurries to do what I ask, and I point toward the door. I can see Carmine through the little window. I noticed it when we came up to her room, and I hate it. Glass can be broken, and guns pointed through the opening. Most hospital doors these days don't have the window. Why the fuck does this one?

"That's Carmine. He's my best friend and Maria's cousin. I'm just stepping outside to talk to him. You'll be able to see me the entire time."

"Can't he come in here?"

"You can't listen to what I have to say. Neither can Maria nor Auntie Carlotta."

I give her a meaningful look. She nods as she looks at the two women, who both stand at the foot of the bed. I roll off and resist the urge to kiss any part of her. I walk out as I hear Maria greeting her. Carmine pushes off the wall he's leaning on across from the door.

"I had no idea that wasn't her. I checked shit before I sent it to you. But it all came back as her."

"Hold on." I hurry back into the room. "Sinead, can you unlock your phone and let me show Carmine the article I read?"

"Does he really have to? I don't like people—"

I see her getting upset. I lean over, my hand taking hers as I whisper to her.

"My family will find about all of this. I'm sorry that it can't stay between us, but it's as much about protecting you as it is my case. Carmine is an expert at gathering intelligence. Lorenzo is an expert hacker. He has a degree in Computer Science. Between the two of them, they will figure this out, but they have to know that evidence exists to disprove the article that just came out."

She looks at me for a long time before she nods. She unlocks the phone when I give it back to her. She taps the screen a couple times.

"This is the folder with everything. All the articles from the trial, all the evidence that's been digitized, the case findings and rulings, and the exoneration letter."

"Thank you, *piccolina*."

I kiss her temple as I head back into the hallway. I scroll until I find the article she showed me. It detailed everything that went wrong from start to finish without going into the details she told me about that night. I hand it over to Carmine. He does the same thing I did: read it twice.

"Holy fuck."

He whispers as he looks up at me and gives me the phone back as he looks past me and into the room. But I pulled the curtain behind me the second time I walked out, so he can't see much.

"Right?"

"From the way Lorenzo and Marco described her, they never would have guessed she'd survived gen pop jail as a teenager. She seems so well-adjusted."

"So do we."

"True, and that's not saying much."

"Carmine, I need you to find out who the fuck is doing this. I'm assuming it's all the same people. I want to know how they're getting shit done so fast. And I definitely want to know the journalist and editor who ran this. If they got this photo out of public records, then they saw the rest of what happened, too."

"I'm working on it. You saw it doesn't have a byline, but I'll know within a few hours. It's almost four, so I can start making some calls soon."

"Do you have any guesses?"

"None that aren't complete speculation. I should have asked right off. How's she doing?"

"Exhausted and badly shaken. I had no idea seeing a photo could trigger such a reaction from anyone. I've feared dying too many times to count. I've almost died plenty of times. I've seen you and the others near death, too. But this was the scariest shit I have ever experienced. When it started, her eyes were open but completely unseeing. It was like she was catatonic. She didn't move when I put her on the bed. Not at all. The only movement was her chest while she breathed. Her heart was racing, and I've never seen anyone so pale without blood loss."

"You're lucky Fina and I had just finished the movie with Maria and Matteo, and we were still near the College Point theaters. Otherwise, it would have doubled the time it took for them to get to Mama's."

"I know. Why were you at such a late movie?"

"Maria got delayed with an MVA that came in and needed imaging. We waited and didn't have dinner until almost nine. How're you doing?"

"Fucking shaken like a shitty martini."

"Glad to see you still have your sense of humor."

I scowl. I wasn't trying to be funny. I've been calm for Sinead's sake, but I haven't wanted to cry this hard in years. I am not a crier, but I don't know what to do with all these feelings. It scared me shitless, then it broke my heart when she told me what happened. There is so much I know she didn't tell me.

"I want to get back in there. Let me know as soon as you find anything."

"I will. Is she getting discharged today?"

"Yeah. As long as nothing else happens, they said they'd release her midmorning."

"Are you taking her back to Mama's?"

"I don't know. I don't want to take her anywhere that'll upset her again. But I definitely don't want her at a hotel. We can't control that like we can one of our places."

"Papa's the most removed, so it would be great if she could stay with him. But that'll looked fucked up if anyone finds out.

Luca's our underboss, and people know that, so he and Olivia are out."

"Plus, Olivia's pregnant. I doubt she wants a houseguest she doesn't know."

"True. She can stay with Fina and me."

"You're my best friend, and that's not a secret from fucking all the stupid blogs and newspaper social pages we've been on. Maria and Matteo or Uncle Dom and Auntie Lotta are the best choices. Both women are doctors, and Uncle Dom and Matteo are high level but way lower profile."

"True. Are you going to ask Auntie Lotta or Maria now?"

"No. I'm going to talk to Sinead first. If she refuses and gets upset, I won't push. We'll work something out with a hotel or her place."

"You really like her, don't you?"

"Yeah. You and Sera knew each other as kids, but you weren't around each other at all except for once in nearly twenty-years. You didn't get along when you were around each other back then, but somehow you knew it was different when we went into her bakery with Maria."

Only Carmine calls his wife Fina. The rest of us call her Serafina or Sera.

"True. I'd say it's a lot more like Luca and Olivia."

"Yeah, but I can't move her in with me to protect her. That's the last thing I can do."

"I know. But Luca said he just knew. He said from the get-go, he knew there was nothing he wouldn't do to protect Olivia. And he couldn't get enough of the time they spent together. He just really enjoyed being around her."

"It's the same, but it's only been a week. Don't go getting me married off with a picket fence quite yet."

"Fina's turning me into a hopeless romantic."

"Ha. Only for her."

Carmine waggles his eyebrows before growing serious.

"Go back in there and talk to her. Decide what happens next, and I'll keep you posted when I find anything."

"Thanks."

We embrace, and I turn back to the door. He'll wait out here until Maria and Auntie Carlotta join him. When I step inside, I hear three voices laughing, and I feel way more at ease.

"You should have seen him. There he was on Carmine's shoulders while I was on Matteo's. He's like eight inches taller than me and like twenty times stronger than me when we were eleven. I knocked him off Carmine's shoulders. He came up looking like a drowned rat. I kept my undefeated title as the Chicken Queen."

I hear them laugh again. Maria is shockingly good at playing chicken in the water. It doesn't matter how much bigger or stronger her opponent, she always manages to knock them off their partner's shoulders. She's wily and strategic.

"I seem to remember tossing you a good four feet across the pool after that."

I step around the curtain, and Maria giggles.

"And I loved that way more than you did having me beat you. *Again.*"

"Rematch. Any time, any place."

"Care to put your money where your mouth is? In the water or on dry land."

She thrusts her hand out while winking at Sinead. All the guys can carry me if they have to. But a fireman carry over their shoulder is way different from me sitting on their shoulders and shifting around. She knows that. But I shake anyway.

"I'm starting rounds in half an hour, but I'll try to swing back before they discharge you."

Auntie Carlotta pats Sinead's legs before she and Maria say their goodbyes and head out.

"They're super sweet. Maria's hilarious, and Carlotta reminds me a lot of my mom."

"They are. Though be forewarned, Maria will get you in trouble. You'll have a blast doing it, but you will regret it."

"She doesn't seem to regret a thing."

"Because she has all of us guys wrapped around her little finger. Her mom and our aunts, not at all. The rest of us, completely."

"I don't think any of you mind."

"We don't. She's kind, funny, wickedly smart, and has managed to live her entire life as *Cosa Nostra* and not come out jaded. She was one of my first friends when I moved here. She helped me meet other kids and stood up for me when they made fun of me for not speaking English or for being so tall for our age. She did the same thing for three guys in the Cartel when they moved here from Colombia as teenagers."

And that's why the melee happened. The Kutsenkos stuck up for her as a girl. They have no tolerance for any threats or insults to women. My family was pissed because of that, but also because of how ungrateful it was of the Cartel guys to disrespect her after she'd been nothing but nice to the *Tres J's*. It was Javier who started it, but Jorge and Joaquin made it worse.

"I could see that."

"She also covered for Finn O'Rourke when they were at a party a few years ago. His date OD'd on some fentanyl his cousins supplied the party hosts. He'd gone to get her another drink, and she took some pills. Maria was in med school and tried to resuscitate her, but it was too late. She sent Finn away and covered for him with the cops. After that, she doesn't leave the house without Narcan with her."

"Wow. And she helped me. She said she didn't think it was a heart attack, but since she couldn't be certain without any tests, she erred on the side of caution and gave me the aspirin. She said she carries it just in case of situations like mine."

"Yeah. That time in med school really shook her. She carries a pretty well stocked first aid kit in her purses most of the time."

"Well, I appreciate it."

"You still look tired, *piccolina*. Why don't you try to sleep?"

"I am, and I will. Was your conversation with Carmine helpful? I get I can't ask what you guys talked about, but was it at least useful?"

"Sort of. He's still doing some digging."

She nods and sighs.

"You're supposed to be on your way to the gym right now."

"I think I can miss a day."

"You haven't slept. I forced you to come here. And now you're missing part of your routine with your family. You should go."

"Sinead, no. Even if I wanted to— which I definitely don't —I wouldn't. Maria and Auntie Carlotta have their guards, and I know someone in my family must have arranged for some here. But you don't have nearly enough protection for me to leave. If they decide to keep you past midmorning, then I'll arrange for more men. Until then, I'm staying as your guard."

"You don't have to babysit me."

"No one is babysitting you, Sinead. Babysitting implies you can't be trusted to be alone or can't do shit for yourself. Nothing about tonight made me think you're a little. Even if you were, you would have bodyguards, not babysitters. The men assigned are there to protect you from outside threats, not to make sure you don't drink bleach from under the kitchen sink or choke on a hot dog."

She just stares at me for a moment before nodding. I didn't mean to get heated, but the way she said it made me think she doesn't believe she's worth the effort for anyone to watch out for her. It wasn't that she thought I was making a mountain out of a molehill. It was more about her self-worth in this situation, and I don't like it. It's all too new to her, and I don't want to explain it. I sure as shit hope nothing proves she needs protecting.

"I'm definitely not a little, Gabriele."

"Gabe. I don't think you remember me telling you that in the office."

"I thought that was just for after..."

"Whenever you want."

I walk around to the chair that I sat in earlier, but she reaches out her hand.

"Please?"

I climb back onto the bed and wrap myself around her. She's asleep within minutes. I feel her relax. I tell myself to do the same, but it takes at least half an hour before I can. Then I only get forty minutes before a nurse comes in to check her vitals. I'm off the bed and in the chair the moment I hear someone touch the door handle. I am not a deep sleeper. I stay in the chair after that and doze.

"Gabe?"

"Good morning, *piccolina*."

"What time is it?"

"Seven-o-five."

"Shit. Can I have my phone? I need to call my boss and the court clerk. I'm supposed to meet my client there before it opens at nine. We're first on the judge's docket for today. Shit, shit, shit, shit."

She scrambles to sit up as I hand her the phone. She's

looking at the wall clock now, and I can tell she's getting anxious. She's waiting while the phone rings.

"Marta, it's Sinead. I know it's early, but I can't make it in today... Delaney's— she —it came up. I had one of my panic attacks...Yeah, way worse, though... Remember when they first brought me into the courtroom in cuffs?... That times about twenty. I'm in the hospital."

There are pauses when she listens to Marta. Her boss sounds like she was the lawyer who represented Sinead all those years ago. At least, she has someone who understands that she's not playing sick.

"They're supposed to release me midmorning... Tomorrow off too would be great. I need a continuation since the Cohenour case was supposed to start." She glances at me. "I still feel like shit, Marta. I should be good in two days, but you need to know something was printed about me. They used that photo that looks like me to claim I'm a drug addict and that Mr. Scotto is my dealer... It also mentions something about my sex life and says I'm going before an ethics review."

She listens again, and she's looking at me every few minutes.

"I don't know that we have any choice but to resign from Mr. Scotto's case. Between this press and filing a defamation or libel complaint, it's going to compromise Mr. Scotto's defense. A retraction won't be enough to prove to some people I'm innocent. What if one of those people winds up on the jury?"

She goes quiet again as she watches me. I understand her reasoning, but I am not pleased. Despite my attraction to her, I believe she would be my best defense. I point to her, then hold up two fingers, then point to the chair.

"I'll speak to Mr. Scotto about that. Perhaps I could sit second chair to someone else... All right... I will... Thanks, Marta."

She hangs up and looks at me.

"Gabe, I will not risk this influencing anyone on the jury. Whether or not the newspaper prints a full apology and admits to gross negligence and a violation of journalistic ethics, this article could sway people. You know how jury selection goes. Even if we specifically ask if they would be prejudicial to you based on the claims, we can't be sure someone isn't lying. I won't risk your life for this."

"We're still a long way from jury selection. We'll cross that bridge when we come to it. Until then, please don't resign. I trust you, Sinead. I don't say that to many people outside my family. Not even everyone in our branch has my trust. But I won't risk your career for this."

We stare at each other caught at an impasse. We nod at the same time, and we put the subject to rest for now. We still have other things to discuss.

"Where do you want to go after they discharge you? Your place?"

"Fuck no. I want to break my lease and never go back."

"Do you want to go to a hotel?"

"I thought that wasn't the safest choice."

"I don't want to take you somewhere that will re-traumatize you."

"Do you mean Paola's? I felt safe there. What happened wasn't because of where I was."

"If that's where you want to go, then I'll take you there."

"Would she let me come back? I caused a huge disturbance for her."

"*Piccolina,* I know Auntie Paola as well as I know my own mom. She'll feel better knowing you're with her. She'll worry otherwise. She's a kind woman, and the worst thing that'll happen to you there is you'll eat more in one day than you have in your entire life."

"Thank you. I know you're busy and lost a day's work yesterday— guarding me. I'll be fine there since I'll probably sleep most of the day."

"I'm glad you didn't say babysitting."

"I already have one spanking waiting for me. Maybe I shouldn't add a second one. Yet."

She grins at me with the last word, and I could maul her and fuck her into next week. My palm itches to land across her ass. I want to see it ripple and jiggle as I do it right before I spread her ass cheeks and thrust my dick in her pussy.

"Gabe?"

"Hmm?"

"What're you thinking about?"

How do I answer that when she's lying in a hospital bed after I put her here because I caused her massive panic attack?

Chapter Fourteen

Sinead

Is Gabriele blushing? I think he is. Holy shit. Is he thinking about sex? I grin even wider and shoot him a knowing look. Now he's definitely blushing.

"Gabe, are you picturing spanking me?"

"Among other things, *piccolina*. Many other things."

"You know, if I withdraw from representing you, then there wouldn't be a conflict of interest."

"Sinead, you know I want to agree to that. But I also want to stay out of prison. Carmine told me your track record for wins and acquittals. You held your own against me without batting an eyelash. I told you. I trust you. I need your legal mind more than my body needs to sleep with you. Not by much, but I do."

He sighs, and it's the most beleaguered sound I've ever heard. It matches his expression. I know he's right. Even if I wasn't representing him, we should slow down. We've gone from zero to two hundred miles an hour way too fast. But even if we don't have sex again for a long time—which might be what truly pushes me around the bend— I don't want to give up the way it feels when he holds me.

Something from when I was studying for the bar pops into my head as clearly it would if I were reading it out of a book. The American Bar Association rule one-point-seven on conflict of interest with a current client. Lawyers can't have sex with their clients unless they were already in a relationship before becoming their attorney. Since I only know Gabriele because of this case, that rules out— literally —the possibility for us. Unless...

"Do you remember what the ABA states for conflict of interest with a client?"

"There are several points, but I assume you mean the part about having sex with a client."

"Yes."

"Vaguely. I assume it states only if the relationship predates the attorney-client relationship. I never imagined I'd need an attorney who wasn't Uncle Massimo, and I doubt any client I might have had would be a concern."

"Might have had? You make it sound like you'll never practice."

That derails where I wanted the conversation to go.

"While I know who might hire me, I also know no judge or jury is going to take me seriously."

"You don't know that. I sense you can be very persuasive."

I smile, hoping that lightens his mood. He just nods. I persist.

"Are you sure we never had sex before going to your place?"

I cock an eyebrow, but this time he shakes his head.

"I've touched you. Tasted you. Regrettably, I know we didn't at the club."

"But we could have since we're members of the same club."

"Sinead, if anyone were to ask, they could easily say they've only seen me with one woman in the last year or so. She doesn't fit your description. And even though I wear a mask and never undress, I don't blend in. One look at you and me together, and people would know I haven't been seeing you there."

I sigh. I know he's right. But I feel like the sex would be about more than just getting off. Even if it was rough and kinky fucking, I still feel like it would be more. It was the other night. I want it to be more, which is completely stupid and pointless right now.

"Sinead, if I thought there was any way around this, I would seize it. I already thought about using our mutual club membership while I waited for you in court yesterday and while you slept. It's not worth the risk, considering what's going on right now."

"I know. I can't believe I even considered it. That's utterly out of character for me to dream of doing anything that could endanger an acquittal for a client."

"I want you that much, too."

I didn't realize my shoulders were almost up to my ears. They droop as I concede. I'm not thinking clearly, anyway. They gave me a sedative last night just before they settled me into the room. I suspect there are some lingering effects since I feel a bit sluggish, too.

"Try to sleep some more."

I curl up, and Gabriele adjusts the sheet and blanket over me. I feel like an idiot now, but when he kisses my temple, everything gets a bit better.

"If I come up with a way around it, *piccolina*, you'll be the first to know."

"Thanks."

I barely get the word out around a yawn. I feel like a Mack truck ran over me again. I'm out within a minute or two.

As I come back to the land of the living, I feel something vibrating under my hand. I curl my fingers around the object and realize it's my phone. My eyes snap open as I look down. I turn it over and see my boss's number on the screen. I also notice it's the middle of the afternoon. I've been asleep for another eight hours. Was it a sedative or a tranquilizer they gave me last night?

"Hi, Marta."

"Hello. How're you feeling?"

"Much better."

"You sound groggy. Did I just wake you?"

"Yes, but that's okay. I've been asleep since the last time we spoke."

"I thought they might have discharged you."

I look around and find Gabriele watching me. He offers me a sweet smile before looking down at his phone.

"I thought so too. Maybe they've just been letting me sleep, and I'll leave soon."

Gabriele looks up again and nods. He probably told them to let me sleep on pain of death.

"Are you going to your place? Would you like me to swing by? Do you need anything?"

Well, fuck.

"No, I don't need anything, but thanks."

That sorta answers all of her questions.

"Do you think you should be alone right now? Do you have a friend who can come over?"

I keep watching Gabriele, even though he appears to scroll

something on his phone. I know he's keenly aware of everything in this room. He could probably tell you exactly how many strands of hair I have on my head.

"The Mancinellis have offered me a security detail."

"Sinead—"

I hear the censure and wince.

"—That is not a good idea. They are your clients. Our clients. The firm will handle that."

"Marta, you know who they are. You can't not, and the firm agreed to take them on knowing full well what they charged Mr. Scotto with and who he's connected to. I'm entering their world, not the other way around. I think any protection they offer me is protection I should take. A regular bodyguard wouldn't know who to look for. Even if you pulled me from this case, it would be the same for anyone else."

"Your place isn't the safest in the world."

"I know. I'm going to stay somewhere else. I'd rather not say where."

"Don't you trust me?"

I hear hurt in her voice, and it's a stake to the heart. Marta has been like a second mother to me since the day I met her. Our relationship shifted when she became my boss, but there's still a maternal feeling to it.

"I trust you more than anyone else."

As I continue to stare at Gabriele, and he pretends not to notice, I realize that statement is no longer true. It has been for years, but in the space of a week, Gabriele ranks right up there, making it a tie between Marta and him for who I trust most.

"Where are you going, then?"

"The Mancinellis have somewhere safe I can stay while still going about my day-to-day."

"No."

"Marta—"

"Sinead, that is not how it works. Legal firms may put their clients in safe houses, but clients do not put their attorneys in safe houses. We will pay for a hotel and for your security. You will not rely on the Mancinellis for either."

I know that tone. It would not be wise for me to argue.

"All right. Thank you."

"I spoke to the editor-in-chief, and the paper already posted a retraction. Unfortunately, they went into some detail explaining the confusion between your sister and you in the image and the date."

"Some detail?"

"A very abridged version of your sister's death and your trial. They used it as a weak excuse for why they believed the allegations brought to them. I've already filed a defamation injunction to keep them from pushing this further. But you know libel isn't easy to prove despite this meeting the three conditions. And you know injunctions for defamation are hit or miss. But my hope is it will slow things down. Since we acted swiftly, and I know the editor-in-chief, they'll see this will cost them far more than they will gain. And I mean truly cost them money."

"Thank you."

"You're welcome, but this is why you must remain squeaky clean, Sinead. There can't be even a hint of impropriety. The firm won't tolerate it, and your career won't survive it."

"I know, Marta."

"I'll have Ashley make the arrangements and text you the hotel confirmation. I'll send a driver once you let Ashley know you're being discharged."

"I appreciate it."

There's not much more I can say, so we end the call. I haven't taken my eyes off Gabriele, and now he's openly watching me too. I don't know if he could hear any of what

Marta said, but I think he's already guessed what's coming. He appears casual in his seat, but he's anything but. He's more like a lion surveying the surrounding savannah, poised to strike when he needs to, while completely in control of everything.

"What did your boss have to say?"

"She doesn't want me staying in a safe house your family provides. The firm will get me a hotel room and a bodyguard."

I tense.

"Good."

Is that all? He was resistant to that idea only hours ago. Now he's fine with it? What the hell changed while I was sleeping? Hurt and disappointment make tears burn the back of my eyelids.

"Sinead, we will get the rooms beside and across from you. Men will be in the lobby and stationed outside any back or side doors. They can hire whoever they want to stand outside your room. Let them think they're handling it. It'll smooth things over and make your boss worry less. But you are not protected to my standards unless it's my men. They will be discreet."

He says it so nonchalantly that it almost feels flippant. At least until that end bit. *Protected to my standards.* It sends a shiver along my spine, and I hear not only the promise in his voice but a warning manifested into the universe to anyone who might come near me. He stands and shoves his phone into his pocket before two wide steps bring him to my bedside. He tunnels his hand into my hair and holds my head in place as he leans forward.

"We might be on pause, but you are still mine, Sinead. No one touches what's mine and lives to tell the tale. If you want to walk away, all you have to say is you want out. But as long as you agree, I will take care of you."

"Thank you."

I stop myself there. I want to say more, but I would regret it if

I did. We're on a pause, but I'm still his. It sounds contradictory, but I get it. We can't date, and we can't fuck. But I don't want anyone else. I don't want to sleep with anyone else, and I don't want anyone else emotionally close to me either. When I repeat the words to myself, they sound possessive and controlling to an extreme. But when Gabriele says them, I feel safe. Not for a moment do I think he'd keep me from friends or family, imprison me in some metaphorical or real prison, abuse me for disobeying him. Just the opposite. I think he would give me all the freedom I could ask for and make sure I'm happy and safe with it.

"You're mine, too."

"I have been since the moment I saw you, *piccolina*."

Goddamn, that voice. It's like Charlton Heston and Jensen Ackles had a voice baby, and it makes my pussy ache. It's the perfect blend of gravelly one moment and smooth the next. Even though we're alone, he leans forward to whisper in my ear, and it makes my tits silently beg for him to suck them.

"The next time we have sex, you can fuck me however you want because I'm yours. After that, I decide."

"Yes— sir."

Once more, I catch myself. I hope I sound breathless with desire and not like I'm trying to hide something. When he leans back, I know I failed, but he doesn't press me. He drops a soft kiss to my lips and lets me go. I want to grab his arm and hang on as he backs away, but then I hear someone opening the door. Did he hear them before me and know they were there?

He nods, and I realize he knows what I'm thinking. It's disconcerting.

"Ms. O'Malley, I'm Dr. Halgren. I'm glad to see you awake this time. How're you feeling?"

"Much better. More rested than I have in ages."

He looks at my monitors and reads the printout that's practically floor length at this point. He seems satisfied with the peaks and troughs that represent my heart rate and I'm guessing my oxygen levels or something like that.

"You're ready to be discharged. I'll have a nurse come by with your paperwork. I'm prescribing you three one-milligram tablets of lorazepam to have on hand in case another panic attack begins. This is meant to abate the symptoms long enough for you to reach your mental health provider not to treat an anxiety disorder."

"I understand, Doctor. I'm not currently under the care of a psychiatrist, but I have one I can begin seeing again. A psychologist, too."

I don't think I need to go back on medication or have more talk therapy at the moment, but I'm calling both to make sure I'm right. I never want to experience something this severe ever again. If either of them says I need help, I'm taking the first available appointment.

"Good. I wish you well, Ms. O'Malley."

"Thank you."

Once he's gone, Gabriele reaches for a clear hospital bag I hadn't noticed. He lays out all my clothes at the foot of the bed, my shoes right below. The kind of quiet he is now— I'm not sure if he's retreated and withdrawn or just giving me time to breathe.

"Gabe?"

He looks up at me and waits.

"Did something just change between us?"

His brow furrows.

"No."

"Then why do I get the feeling you're being distant?"

"Because the doctor didn't ask you if I should step out before discussing your care. If you'd wanted to tell me what he said, you would have. He didn't give you the chance to have a private conversation. I feel bad."

"But that wasn't anything secret."

He shrugs.

"Maybe not, but you are well enough to decide things on your own. It was presumptuous on his part and mine to stay. I still feel bad."

I can only sit and stare. Last night, he had his tongue up my hoo-ha, and now, he's embarrassed that the doctor said I should talk to another doctor. I laugh. I can't help it.

"Gabe, you didn't invade my privacy. But I appreciate that you care enough for it to bother you. If I hadn't wanted you to hear any of it, I would have asked you to leave. Even if it had been something more private, I'm glad you were there. If it had been something scary, I would have appreciated your support."

We don't get to say anything else since the nurse arrives. She goes over my discharge orders after I tell Gabe to stay. I have no choice but to put the clothes I was wearing last night back on, and we stop by the hospital pharmacy on the way out. I checked my phone and saw Ashley's text with hotel and car service information. I don't want to wait around for a car to get me, but I show Gabriele the hotel confirmation. He tells his driver where to take us. On our way to the hotel, I text Marta the truth, and she responds that someone is already there. I don't see him, but Gabriele does.

"The one in the khakis and red polo shirt. He's your bodyguard."

Gabriele nudges his chin toward a man sitting on a sofa in the lobby, angled to see the doors and the elevator. He's in shape, but he's nowhere near Gabriele's size. He looks like a scrawny tween in comparison. When he stands, he's close to Gabriele's height, which puts him at least six inches taller than me. He spots us. His gaze takes me in, but he's fixing his attention on Gabriele. Something's off.

"Do you know him?"

"Yes."

I wait for more.

"And?"

"He'll do for appearance's sake."

"Should it scare me to only have him protecting me?"

"You'll never have only him. I already texted Carmine in the car while you were looking out the window. The hotel's arranging for us to have the rooms beside and across from you."

"How can you do that? There are probably people already staying in them."

"Hotel maintenance issue."

They have the influence to make people switch hotel rooms. I watch the man with a deep suntan and dark hair approach. Gabriele's standing close to me, but not enough to touch. I wish he was since I'm filled with trepidation. I watch Gabriele extend his arm to this man.

"Armando, this is Ms. O'Malley."

"Hello, Ms. O'Malley. Gabriele."

No pleasantries from either side. They shake, then Armando offers his hand to me. I see his gaze sweep over me, and it's appreciative. But I almost get the sense that he's doing it to goad Gabriele more than to make me think he likes what he sees. When he gets no reaction from Gabriele, his attention immediately wanes, and he becomes more professional.

"Ms. O'Malley, your firm hired the company I work for to provide you with twenty-four-hour protection. My associates and I will rotate eight-hour shifts. I will be outside your door while Hunter will be down here in the lobby."

He points to a man near the door, sitting on a sofa similar to the one Armando sat on when we arrived. Gabriele doesn't turn to look when I do. I realize he already noticed him, but somehow knew Armando was the one who'd approach us.

"Once you're checked in, I'll take you up to your room. We can exchange numbers, and you can either text or call me, but don't open your door once inside. I'll take the spare key to pass along to my replacement. If you order room service or food delivery, let me know."

He opens his arm toward registration as though he's ushering me forward. When I take the first step, he tries to fall in behind me, but Gabriele is too close. It forces Armando to walk beside me rather than protecting my back. He steps away when it's my turn to check in. Gabriele hangs back too, but I look over my shoulder at him and raise my eyebrows. He moves to where he's standing mostly beside me, but if he shifted even a little, he would once more protect my entire back.

"Welcome, Ms. O'Malley. We have you in a deluxe king suite. It comes with a kitchenette, but we have a full-service restaurant that offers around-the-clock room service. Our guests park free, so I can validate your ticket if you're parked below."

"Thank you. I didn't drive."

"Very good. We already have your company card on file, so I just need to see a valid driver's license."

I pull mine out, grateful Gabriele thought to grab my purse. At least, I assume it was him. I don't remember anymore. Once I've signed a few things, the man behind the counter offers to send a bellman to gather my luggage, but frowns when I say I don't have any. I assure him it's arriving later. The few things I have are still at Paola's.

"Oh, may I have a third key, please?"

I think I'm covert when I hand one to Gabriele. At least, I hope I am. I believe he's blocking Armando's view, but I don't know where Hunter is. I don't dare turn around to look. I wonder if he'll introduce himself today. Once I have the third key, Gabriele and I join Armando before walking to the elevator. When it dings and the doors open, Armando once more holds out his arm, ushering me forward. This time he tries to step in front of me to hide me from the doors, but Gabriele is too close.

"Scotto, I hear you've been busy these days. I figured you'd spend any spare time at one of your clubs."

I tense. Does he mean a BDSM club? Wait, clubs?

"You know Carmine handed those to Matteo when he got married. Matteo turned them over to Marco when he got married. I bounce at them and nothing more. I don't spend my leisure time there like you do."

Gabriele sounds like he doesn't enjoy these places, and I don't get the feeling they're nightclubs like Lorenzo owns. Strip clubs?

"I figured you'd soak it up while you can."

"Armando, you have the subtlety of a hog in slop. I do not frequent strip clubs for fun. I have all the time in the world since you can clearly see I'm not in jail. And I'm here to meet with Ms. O'Malley, my attorney, to ensure I continue to enjoy all that free time. Feel free to text Enrique or Pablo now and let them know. Or better yet—" Gabriele pulls out his phone. "—I'll call them."

"Don't be petty, Gabe."

There's so much more going on here than I understand. I almost feel like I'm intruding, but I have nowhere I can go, stuck in an elevator with them both.

"I haven't chatted with either of them recently. It might be nice to catch up. I'm certain they want to know how I am. After all, you're here."

"It's a coincidence that Ms. O'Malley's employers hired my company."

Gabriele snorts. I tilt my head as I look up at him. He looks over his shoulder and grins down at me as though he's going to let me in on the joke.

"Armando works for a top security company run by *the* Diazes. It didn't surprise me at all to discover the *jefe*, Enrique Diaz, assigned one of his senior men to protect a client who happens to be my attorney. How many cousins removed are you from Enrique anyway, Armando?" Gabe looks at me and shrugs. "Nepotism runs in all our families."

Now I just stare. Diazes, as in Colombian Cartel Diazes. Oh, shit. Gabriele must be pissed, but he's not showing it. Which must mean Armando knows how angry Gabriele is. They're baiting each other. That much is obvious. Armando has to know Gabriele isn't happy another syndicate is guarding his attorney— guarding me —when they could be the very ones who set him up.

The elevator pings, and I look at the sign on the wall. I say nothing as I hurry down the hall, Armando rushing to get in front of me since he already knows any attempt to walk behind me is futile. When we reach my room, he uses the key I handed him.

"Behind me, Sinead."

I look up at Gabriele as he steps around me and reaches to his lower back. I watch him pull a gun from beneath his suit coat as he steps across the threshold. Someone brought him fresh clothes while I slept. He reaches back to me, and I lift my hand. He takes it and tucks it onto his belt as he inches forward, sweeping the room. He doesn't trust me to stay behind with Armando, but he definitely doesn't want me walking carelessly into the room. We move throughout the suite so that I have a wall to my back the entire time. Armando is sweeping the room too from the opposite direction until they cross over. When Gabriele's satisfied no one is here, he holsters his gun. I let go, and he turns to me before leaning forward to whisper.

"If we have the power to make people move rooms, other people have the power to make this room yours. Do not say a word until I sweep it for bugs."

I nod before he leads me to an armchair. He pulls up the cushion and sweeps his hand over the chair before unzipping the cushion and sticking his hand in. He pulls out something and shows me. It's like what he found at my place. My eyes hurt they're so wide. He puts the cushion back on the chair and points to it. I shake my head, but he eases me onto it. I glance at Armando, and he appears shocked. I don't know if he's shocked that there's a bug, or that Gabriele found it already.

Gabriele uses his phone flashlight to look everywhere. Baseboards, drawers, cabinets, doors, window frames. Everything gets examined. He finds four others before he flushes them. When he returns to squat in front of me, Armando speaks up.

"She can't stay here."

"I know. She's coming with me."

Chapter Fifteen

Gabriele

It didn't surprise me to see Armando Jimenez in the lobby, but that doesn't mean it thrilled me either. Enrique's security company is legitimately one of the best in the city. So it's reasonable that a top law firm like Sinead's would already have them on speed dial. Even if it hadn't been Armando and Hunter, I would have spotted anyone who was a bodyguard within five seconds of walking in. If you know what to look for, we stand out.

It didn't surprise me to find the bugs in the room, either. The only surprise there was that I only found five. But they were high end, so super sensitive with almost perfect sound quality. It pleases me that Armando immediately suggests Sinead needs to leave. At least, that tells me he isn't in on this, even if it turns out to be Enrique. It means I don't have to kill him. It doesn't mean I trust him.

"Sinead, we're going to stick to the original plan."

She nods, but remains quiet. I'm certain she fears I missed a device, so she wants to say nothing. It's why I'm not giving any more details. I reach out my hand, and she takes it without hesitation as she stands. I slide my arm around her waist and draw my gun again. I let it rest against my thigh as we head to the door.

"I'll call Enrique in the car, Mondo. Stay here and make it look like Sinead's still inside. Order room service for her in an hour and insist upon taking it inside yourself. Do you know who's relieving you?"

"Yeah, Manny."

"Your brother?"

"No, Manny Vasquez."

"That fucknut? Fuck no. Sinead would leave regardless of this shit. Now I'm really going to speak to Enrique. The fuck Manny's ever going near Sinead."

I feel Sinead stiffen next to me, and I don't mean to scare her. But making Armando understand I'm not playing is more important.

"I was going to call Enrique to tell him to switch Vasquez for someone else. We all know how you feel about him."

"Good."

Sinead's still staring up at me, but I shake my head. I'm not getting into how Emmanuel Vasquez shot me. The shitbag was fucking around, thinking he was Wild Bill Hickok doing some Wild West show, twirling his weapon while we were both at a shipyard guarding goods bound for the same ship to Amsterdam. Motherfucker got me in the thigh. This was two years ago. So not like we were teenagers or some shit. Stupid sack of fucking ass.

Just as we get to the door, my phone vibrates in my pocket. While I checked for bugs, I texted Carmine, and now he's calling me.

"*Ciao.*"

"*Ciao. Siamo qui accanto.*" We're next door.

"*Stiamo uscendo ora.*" We're walking out now.

I end the call as I gesture Armando to go ahead of us. I hear another door open and watch Armando nod. I know Carmine is out there, so I guide Sinead into the hallway. Across from us, the door opens, and Marco and Lorenzo step out. I look over my shoulder and see Matteo and Luca come out of the room on the other side. Armando's shut out of the circle we make around Sinead, but that's fine. He knows I expect him to stand outside her door and not fuck up.

I glance down at Sinead, and I follow her gaze. She's looking at the gun in Carmine's hand as he walks in front of us, then her gaze darts to Lorenzo, who's walking beside Carmine. He has his gun resting against his right thigh, just like Carmine and I do. Anyone approaching wouldn't easily see them, and when we get on the service elevator, no one watching the camera will be able to tell. But we can't wait around. We shouldn't be on the freight elevator, and that'll raise the alarm. As soon as we step off, we're near the loading dock. Lorenzo pushes open the door, and an SUV is parked out front. One of our most trusted Made Men, Luigi, is in the front seat.

Luca, Lorenzo, and Matteo clamber into the third-row. It's an insanely tight fit since it's a seat made for two. I hear Luca grumble and roll over the seatback into the trunk. Carmine and I sandwich Sinead between us. Marco gets in beside Luigi. When we pull onto the street, I watch a black sedan pull into traffic after us. I know it's Damian, another one of our Made Men, and he'll trail us until we get to Auntie Paola's.

I help Sinead with her seat belt, then wrap an arm around her shoulders. I glare over my shoulder at the smirks I'm already sure are on Luca, Lorenzo, and Matteo's faces.

"*Fanculo.*" Fuck off.

I see Marco's expression in the mirror as he rolls his eyes.

He's intentionally leaning on the center console to make sure I see him. Sinead lifts her head from where she'd just rested it against my chest.

"Don't worry, *piccolina*. It's all right."

The air shifts in the car, and Sinead feels it. She continues to watch me, but I give her arm a squeeze before I stroke it. Luca, Carmine, and Matteo are all married, and all call their wives *piccolina*. It's not something any of them said before they were with the women they fell in love with, and I sure as shit have called no one that. They get I'm not just looking for a good fuck.

"I need to call Marta again."

"Not yet. When we get to Auntie Paola's, Carmine's going to go through the hotel security footage. We need to know who did this. Then we can plan better. She means well and cares about you, but Marta's suggestions won't keep you safe. We need to decide what happens next so you can convince her to go along with it."

Sinead sighs with acceptance, and I'm glad I don't have to convince her as well as Marta. It shows me how deeply she trusts me already, and I want to do nothing that might ruin it. Protecting her is the most important responsibility I've ever had. It rests on me like I'm Atlas, bearing the weight of the heavens on my shoulder because I hate knowing I'm the reason she needs the protection. Someone else is doing this, but she wouldn't be in the situation at all if she weren't representing me. But I like knowing I'm the one safeguarding her. I like knowing I have the final say. It calms me.

When we arrive at Auntie Paola's, Carmine's mom is at work. He goes into her study and sets up his laptop. The other guys raid the kitchen. I take Sinead into the living room where I'm ready to sit beside her, but at the last minute, pull her onto my lap. She curls into me, and I stroke her hair.

"Who could have gotten in there so fast, Gabe? I was just assigned the room."

"When the woman from your office made the reservation, someone was ready. Or they found out right afterward. Either way, they hacked the system to assign you that room just like we got the surrounding rooms. Carmine texted me just before they arrived. All three were actually vacant, so no one had to move."

"So they had at least an hour or two head start to get in there and bug it."

"Yes."

"Do you sweep every hotel room where you stay?"

"If someone makes a reservation ahead of time, yes. If we walk in and request a room, then we just sweep it for anyone who might be lurking."

"Isn't it exhausting to be anxious all the time?"

"It's just the opposite. At least for me, anyway. I don't let myself worry until there is a reason to, but checking everything out calms me. It's reassuring that I was right not to worry."

"But you live in a constant heightened sense of alert."

"I suppose. I only remember being a kid and not knowing these things then, at some point, just knowing to be vigilant. I remember learning how to be, but I don't remember when it just became a part of me."

"Are all—"

I can practically hear the gears grinding in her mind as she tries to figure out how to word whatever she's about to say.

"—men like you like this?"

"Men like me? As in criminals or Mafiosos specifically?"

She freezes. She didn't want to come out and say it outright, and she doesn't like that I did.

"No, little one, they are not. That's why they're in prison or dead."

I feel her hand clench my shirt, and I'm uncertain she realizes she did that again.

"Then I'm glad you are exactly who you are, Gabe."

"Thank you."

I try to lighten things by grinning when her gaze meets
mine, but she doesn't see any levity in this, and I can't blame
her. If I weren't trying to make her feel better, I wouldn't either.
This isn't the time to swap childhood stories or chat about fun
times in college. So we remain quiet, both lost in our thoughts
until Carmine comes in with his laptop. He sits on the edge of
the coffee table— only because his mom isn't home to yell at
him —and turns his computer toward us.

"They turned off the feed on the floor. The best we can see
are two people getting off the elevator in what looks like cover-
alls. Then it goes dead."

He plays the video, and it's what he said. Two figures step
off the elevator, and before they turn toward Sinead's room, the
screen goes black. Carmine advances it until the feed goes live
again, and it's the back of them getting into the elevator. He
toggles to something else, and it's the inside of the elevator.
They have hats on, heads down, gloves on, and no way for the
cameras to capture anything identifying. They're pros. They're
doing just what we would.

He toggles again, and we see the lobby. It's a time lap video,
showing these two approaching the elevator with hats pulled
low and chins tucked. We watch people moving around the
lobby and getting on and off the elevator. Then we see the pair
exiting the elevators. The video shifts to another camera angle,
and we can see a partial profile as one looks up to open the
hotel's main door. Then it jumps to another feed and them
getting into a van that's parked right out front.

"I'm running the tags right now, but you know it's going to
come up legit now and stolen within the hour or fakes already."

Carmine's grim expression shifts to Sinead and eases. He doesn't want to scare her any more than she is by what we've already seen. She sits up and moves to a spot beside me.

"May I?"

She gestures to the laptop, and Carmine nods. She picks it up and rests it in her lap. She replays everything, pausing here and there, zooming in a few times. She points to the screen, paused on the culprits' return to the lobby.

"There. Look."

Her fingernail is almost touching the screen. There's the slightest reflection of a face in the gold plating around the buttons. I lean forward and peer at it before shifting my gaze to Carmine.

"Can you zoom in more and clean it up?"

"I don't think so, but Lorenzo probably can."

Sinead looks at Carmine questioningly. He glances at me before answering.

"I'm good at gathering and analyzing intel, but Lorenzo has a degree in computer science. He can handle these things better than I can."

He takes care of everything to do with any software or programs we use, both legally and illegally, and he's been our computer forensic analyst more than once. Carmine's old defense mechanism used to be knowing everyone's business right up to the result of their last colonoscopy. Information was the only power he felt he had for a long time, and I can't blame him. But it also meant he became our best intelligence gatherer since he could use his genius for good rather than evil. For all his faults, of which there were plenty, he has always put our family first, for better or for worse. Now that his secrets aren't only his and mine to keep, people understand and appreciate him as much as I always have.

"Eagle eyes, *piccolina*."

"I was an open water lifeguard during my summers in high school and college. I got to spend my days at the beach, and I paid for a chunk of undergrad that way. I've also been to enough crime scenes to know to look for anything shiny that reflects."

"I'll get Lorenzo to work on this now."

Carmine excuses himself, and Sinead turns to me.

"We know nothing more, but I'm going to have to call Marta again, and soon. If she finds out I'm here some other way, she's going to be pissed."

"I know. Call her, but put her on speaker, letting her know I'm with you."

"Are you sure?"

"Yes."

She sighs and pulls out her phone and does what I ask.

"Marta, it's me again. Something's come up."

"Are you all right? You're wearing years off my life."

"I'm sorry. I'm here with Mr. Scotto."

I speak up.

"Hello."

"Hello, Mr. Scotto."

"Marta, Mr. Scotto found listening devices in my hotel room. We left and are now at Paola Mancinelli's home."

"What? Why was Mr. Scotto with you at your hotel? Did you have a client meeting?"

"No. I—"

"I escorted Ms. O'Malley to her home yesterday after she left court and found several listening devices in her apartment. I insisted she have a security detail last night when she went out. I also insisted she not return to her apartment because someone we haven't identified easily opened her front door. We were together last night when I received a text with the image of her sister. I showed it to her and intended to question her. It was my fault. I triggered the panic attack. I called the ambulance and took her to the hospital, where I stayed all night. Upon her discharge, I escorted her to her hotel and insisted upon inspecting it. Fortunately for all of us, I did. I found four bugs, which I disposed of. It clearly was not safe for her there, and the security detail you hired is not up to the task. I will speak to Enrique about that personally. She is now with my family and me at Paola's home. She can stay here until we secure a safer location."

"Mr. Scotto, you don't need to sound like an expert witness. You are not on the stand. Yet. Sinead, this is not a good idea. But frankly, I don't think there are any good ideas left. My guess is the Mancinellis don't know who bugged your home or your hotel suite."

"Not yet, but they are actively working on it."

"Don't tell me anything more, and Sinead, don't ask them anything else. We hired Mr. Diaz's firm years ago to protect high profile clients because it's a legitimate business. We know his ties and know that is why his team is so well-trained. However, it's clear we cannot trust anyone affiliated with other — groups. Mr. Scotto?"

"Yes?"

"Can Ms. O'Malley remain at Ms. Mancinelli's home tomorrow and rest?"

"Of course. Paola is happy to have her for as long as Ms. O'Malley needs somewhere safe."

I watch Sinead, who nods. I'm not sure what she's thinking.

"Mr. Scotto, I will speak to Mr. Diaz."

"So will I. As his client, you can express whatever you feel is appropriate. Whichever way this goes, it's personal between my family and his."

There's a pause before Marta responds.

"Fine."

Sinead cuts in as things get terse.

"Marta, I have my computer and can work from here. I'll try to stay on top of everything."

I can think of something she can stay on top of, but this is so totally not the time to imagine her riding my cock. Though now that thought is in my head, and my dick's ready to oblige. Fuck me. Like, seriously. Please fuck me, Sinead. Fucking hell. Fucking pay attention.

I push my thoughts away from that momentary distraction and listen to Sinead and Marta finish the call. When she hangs up, Sinead leans back against the sofa.

"She's pissed."

"I figured as much. Would she have said more if she didn't know I was here?"

"Maybe. I don't know. Are you going to call Enrique?"

"I will, but I have to do that alone. I don't know what else might come up."

"I understand."

She rests her head on the couch and closes her eyes.

"Are you hungry? You've eaten nothing all day."

"Starving now that I think about it."

"Come."

I stand and stick out my hand, which she grasps. I help her to her feet, and we walk to the kitchen. It looks like a high school football team tore through it. Carmine's sitting at the table with his laptop between Lorenzo and him. The guys covered the counters in open containers of pasta, chicken parm, meatballs, antipasti, salad, cold cuts, bread. They barely look up as they continue to scarf down any and everything in sight. You'd think they'd just escaped prison or were gearing up to hibernate for the winter.

"Anything left that you haven't all slobbered on?"

Marco grins.

"I think we left some celery for you, Gabe. Ms. O'Malley, we made you a plate. We didn't know what you might like, so we put a little of everything on there."

He offers her a plate heaped with food that's practically spilling off the sides. It's more than any of us could eat, but she's sure to find something she likes.

"I'll zap it for you, *piccolina*."

"I can't eat all that."

She laughs as she hands it to me.

"I'll take your leftovers."

"Eat with me."

She picks up two forks as I move to the microwave. While we wait, I pour two glasses of lemonade and take them over to her. The guys chat amongst themselves, but I can tell she's not sure if she's allowed to join in. When the timer goes off, I take the food to her and pull out a barstool. She climbs on while I stand beside her.

I know the guys don't want to bombard her. They don't want it to sound like they're interrogating her if they ask questions to get the conversation going. I twist to look at Carmine.

"Car, where are the pastries you promised us?"

"I ate them. Fina knew they were my favorite red velvet cupcakes and the strawberry tarts. It's her fault for trusting me to bring them over. She knows better."

He shrugs unrepentantly. It's a good thing he works out as much as he does. His wife is a gifted baker who owns two shops. I think I remember their vows included her bringing home any unsold pastries or bread.

Lorenzo nudges him none too gently.

"She was going to send over two dozen cupcakes, *stronzo*. You said she forgot." Asshole.

"She did forget. She forgot not to trust me. And it was one for each of you, not two dozen. And I didn't eat them all at once. I sneaked two at the bakery, then a few more on the way to and from the hospital. I ate the last two while I was in Mama's office."

Marco's pissed. He loves Serafina's baking as much as Carmine, but he gets it far less often.

"*Figlio di puttana*, you had them here in the house?" Motherfucker.

Carmine shrugs again.

"Find your own hot wife to bake for you."

Marco pulls out his phone.

"I'm telling on you."

"Go right ahead. I'm not worried. She can scold me all she wants. I'll just have to make it up to her."

He waggles his eyebrows.

"You're supposed to make it up to us."

Marco unlocks his phone.

"Rosella's single. That would solve your problems. I'll let her know you're looking for a woman who bakes almost as well as Fina."

"Don't you fucking dare."

"Tell her she only bakes almost as well as Fina or that you're looking for a woman?"

Carmine offers the innocent expression he perfected when we were kids. It was the surest sign he was guilty as sin. Marco puts his phone away, knowing Carmine doesn't issue empty threats. Rosella is nice and attractive, but she is not Marco's type at all. She's a put a ring on it kinda girl, and Marco is a running as far and fast from the altar as he can kinda guy. Carmine wouldn't lie to Rosella and say Marco was interested, but he might plant the seed that he likes women who bake.

Throughout this exchange, Matteo, Lorenzo, Luca, and I keep eating as though nothing's going on. Sinead's finding what she likes and eating silently, but she's listening to the cousins go back and forth.

"Cry to Auntie Carlotta and see if she'll make you those cookies you used to beg for whenever you got hurt trying to keep up with Luca and Emilio."

Auntie Carlotta is the next best baker in our family with sweets. All the mothers and wives— including Olivia now — can bake bread. But Auntie Carlotta— Matteo and Emilio's mother —finds it relaxing. She's a general surgeon and says she far prefers the smell of her kitchen with the oven full of dough and batter than an operating room. I watch Luca, then dart my gaze to Matteo.

Emilio is someone we almost never talk about. He gets mentioned in passing, but that's it. He fucked up even more than Carmine and now lives in Jersey. Matteo still sees him, and so do his parents. Which means Luca's sister, Maria— who's Matteo's wife —sees him too. But rarely. Emilio and Luca were best friends until Luca wound up with a scar from a knife blade. It runs along the side of his cheek to beneath his collar, and Auntie Carlotta was the one who stitched it. Maria's also Marco's sister, and Matteo is both Emilio's younger brother and Marco's best friend.

"Uh-uh. Mama promised Maria and me her next batch of anything."

Marco snorts as he glares at his best friend who's three hours younger than him.

"She promised Maria— not you —because you ate all the wedding cookies at Sunday dinner and tried to blame Pia and Natalia because you gave them each two."

Pia and Natalia are Luca, Marco, Lorenzo, and Maria's cousins through their dad and Carmine's cousins through his mom. The girls are still in elementary school. Uncle Salvatore didn't marry Aunt Sylvia until he was in his late forties. When older members of our branch pressured him to marry and have an heir, he would say God promised him good things come to those who wait. He accepted an arranged marriage because it was good for our branch to keep ties with Sicily. He and Aunt Sylvia hadn't known each other before she arrived in America for the wedding and fell in love almost immediately. He swears that was what God really meant.

I glance at Sinead as we continue to eat, and she can't help but smile at the guys' bickering. I'm only in my early thirties, but could God have made me the same promise, and I just didn't know it? If I wait, will Sinead be that good thing? I hope so. I know I'm in lust. There's no point in denying it or calling it anything more than it is. I still feel like there could be way more. It's a good thing that we can't sleep together again. I keep telling myself that.

It's true. And if I have any sense at all, then I'll appreciate the divine wisdom and use the time to get to know her non-biblically.

"Gabe?"

I'm so lost in thought that I don't hear Matteo at first.

"Huh?"

"Your phone is vibrating. We can hear it."

I pull it out and look at the screen. I hold it up for the guys to see.

Carechimba

They know that means Pablo Diaz, but it literally means face of a vagina in Colombian slang.

"Sinead, I need to take this. It's Enrique's nephew, his second-in-command."

I answer it as I step away from the breakfast bar and turn away from the group.

"You saved me the trouble of calling your uncle."

"Yeah, we already heard. Armando filled us in. He said the

attorney-client privilege you have has nothing to do with the charges pending."

"Fuck him. He might not know what the fuck's going on, but did you do this, Pablo? Did you bug the suite?"

"No."

His answer is quick and confident. He could be telling the truth, or more likely, he knew the question would be the next thing I said and was ready.

"Why should I believe you?"

"Because we don't give a shit what's going on with you right now. Mama's sick."

That stops me in my tracks. I'm halfway to the living room.

"Margherita's sick? As in really bad flu or looking at types of treatment sick?"

"The latter. We found out three days ago Mama has breast cancer. We have more important things going on in the family right now than listening to your lawyer making dinner or ordering take out. We know her reputation. She wouldn't be discussing a case over the phone in a hotel room after work hours. She might send some emails and shit. Read files. But she wouldn't meet you there, and she wouldn't be chatting with anyone about things she can't divulge. If she's seeing someone, we don't need to listen to them having sex."

"So, you might be off the hook for the bugs, but that doesn't make you off the hook for fucking me over and framing me."

There's no response to that since it isn't a question. Whether the Cartel is behind the trumped-up charges or not, I'm not wrong. Margherita being sick and the Cartel not being interested in my lawyer's personal life doesn't mean the Colombians couldn't be responsible.

"I just called to let you know we didn't bug her place, and I don't know who did. If you want Armando and Manny to look into it, I can tell them to. We'd do it as a gesture of good will since Ms. O'Malley is no longer one of our principals."

I'm certain Sinead's firm didn't fire Enrique's security team altogether. They just relieved them of guarding Sinead. That's fine with me. As for a gesture of good will, the Cartel's been showing us more of that lately than I'm comfortable with. They're not going soft. Just the opposite. I'm waiting for them to turn it on us and demand something in return.

"If your curiosity won't let it go, then by all means, go ahead. But I'm not accepting favors from you, Pablo."

"Consider it a favor to Ms. O'Malley."

"Nope. You wouldn't do her a favor unless you believed you'd get something in return from me. You don't know her. She was your company's principal for a hot second, so there's no loyalty or guilt to make you do it."

Principal. There was a term I had a hard time understanding when I heard it the first time in this line of work. I was eleven and had only been in the U.S. for about eighteen months. I knew principals ran schools. So, I didn't understand why Uncle Salvatore and my dad kept calling my mom a principal when they were assigning her a detail. I finally asked Papa one night, and he explained that's what bodyguards sometimes call the person they protect. It makes sense here since Sinead's firm is the client, not Sinead personally.

"Maybe we want to stay in her good graces in case we need to hire her one day."

He's goading me. Armando must have told him I'm into Sinead. Actually, there's no way he didn't. Pablo's fishing. Let him. He can dredge the bottom of this lake and still come up with nothing.

"My spaghetti is getting cold."

"Somehow, I don't think you're being facetious about that."

"You know I carbo load."

That earns me a snort.

"*Hasta luego*, Gabe." See you later.

"*Ciao.*"

If I believe him, then one crime family down. Two to go. Plus all the other little shits who want to sit at the grown-ups' table. No steps forward, two steps back. Who the fuck is doing this?

Chapter Sixteen

Gabriele

I head back into the kitchen. No one but Sinead looks up at me. I shoot her a smile I pray is reassuring. I move to stand beside her and rest my hand at the small of her back, but only for a moment. When I slide my phone back into my pocket, she looks up at me, questions clear in her eyes. I sweep my gaze over the guys.

"Margherita's sick. Pablo says it's cancer."

Lorenzo is standing across the breakfast bar from me. His eyes widen as he speaks.

"How bad is it?"

"I don't know. Pablo didn't say, and I didn't ask. But they only found out a few days ago. I shot Uncle Salvatore a message as I walked in here. He'll do what needs doing."

Usually, that means scooping someone up and sending them to the garage. In this case, it'll be call Margherita's husband, Luis. He's Enrique's younger brother. He'll offer any and all contacts he has to the best doctors in the world. He'll send flowers, and he'll make sure my aunts know, so they'll send food the family can freeze. Those four women alone will make sure that entire family's fed for a month with what they send.

Even though Carmine, Luca, and I seriously fucked up the women and children are untouchable rule, it still applies. We suspend all rivalries when it comes to the women. It's why the Irish and the Colombians helped us when Maria was kidnapped. It's why we and the Irish helped the bratva when one of their wives' sisters was in trouble. It's not like we used to carpool with Pablo and his younger brother, Juan. But she was a snack mom on our peewee sports teams. Yeah, not only did we go to high school together, but we played kids' sports together before each of us turned twelve. That's when we started carrying knives to protect ourselves from each other.

Fucking rites of passage. Our fucking families. It makes me watch Sinead as I consider whether I should truly bring her into this shit. I want to. I've tried pushing the thought from my head, but it's pointless. I wouldn't have touched her if I didn't want this to be permanent. I'd still care about her safety, but I wouldn't be driven to the point of tearing down and destroying whoever set me up and is fucking with her. I wouldn't have called her mine if this wasn't for keeps. I want us to be taking *our* kids to peewee and little league sports.

Carmine's voice breaks into my thoughts when he comes to stand next to me. He keeps his voice low enough for Sinead not to hear him on my other side.

"Gabe, I got the weather report."

It means he knows which way the wind's blowing. He found out either who bugged Sinead's apartment and hotel room, or the journalist and editor responsible for the article. All the men need to speak privately. I glance down at Sinead's plate, and I see she's eaten a healthy portion, but most of it's still on my side of the plate. I put my hand back on the small of her back and keep it there this time.

"Do you feel better now that you've eaten?"

"Yeah, but all these carbs are making me sleepy."

"Do you want to go up and rest? You can watch TV up there if you want. I need to talk to the guys."

"I need to get some work done."

I give her the Wi-Fi username and password, and she heads upstairs. I watch her until I can no longer see her on the second-floor landing. Once she's out of earshot, I turn to Carmine. He gives us the rundown.

"I found out who wrote the article. You won't believe it."

"Don't tell me an O'Rourke."

The bratva wouldn't target her, and the Cartel has a family crisis.

"Not exactly. Sinead's related to them through her mother, but both sets of grandparents had ties to the mob here and Sinn Féin."

"The IRA?"

"Yup. Sinead's family has only been here for three generations on her mom's side. Her paternal family's been here for four generations. They came over when the war ended."

Sinn Féin and the Irish Republican Army were Irish nationalists. Depending on whose side you were on, they were patriots or treasonists. Either way, people described Sinn Féin as the propaganda machine. The voice of the public and political movement, while the IRA was the—muscle. That's the best I can describe it since I don't know enough beyond that to take sides.

"How does this link to the O'Rourkes or matter to Sinead?"

"Remember Duffy O'Toole?"

"Sorta."

I look at Luca since the guy's the same age as him. Luca grimaces.

"I remember him. He ran the school newspaper from sophomore year until we graduated. He thought he'd walk into a position with CNN the moment he graduated college. He wound up working for some Westchester newspaper. Is he working for the newspaper in the city?"

Carmine nods.

"He stuck to print journalism. Remember how tongue tied he used to get? No one wants to listen to that. He's moved up from Westchester, but he's not a stand out at such a large international paper. Anyway, his grandfather was Liam O'Rourke's mentor or something."

Thanks to the bratva— actually thanks to the Irish fucking with the bratva —the Irish went through a high turnover in their leadership recently. Liam O'Rourke died when I was a senior in high school in an airplane crash. His son, Donovan, took over. He led the mob for nearly ten years. He fucked around with the Kutsenkos one too many times, and when he went after Maksim's wife, Laura, he went one step too far. Next came Declan, who was Donovan's cousin through their dads. He thought he'd avenge Donovan and went after the bratva. That was a shitshow for them, too. He didn't last a year. Their current leader, Dillan, was both men's cousin through another one of Liam's brothers. Liam came from a big, stereotypical Irish family. Yet another brother has Finn and twins Sean and Shane. Somehow the family tree wrapped its way back around to Cormac and Seamus being Dillan's cousins on their mother's side. Their father actually took their mother's last name, which makes them O'Rourkes, too.

Oh shit. Now it clicks. Luca must remember too because he explains what we both realized.

"His grandfather was Liam's mentor, but Duffy's dad is Cormac and Seamus's uncle. He's their father's brother."

Carmine's eyebrows rise while his mouth turns down. He shares more of what he learned.

"Duffy's grandfather was Liam's mentor or whatever, but he was also Sinead's paternal grandfather's best friend before he died in Vietnam. Their parents arrived in New York on the same ship. Sinead and Duffy used to play together as kids. Sinead has a flashback photo on one of her social media accounts with them making a sandcastle at a beach."

"But she grew up in Rhode Island."

"Her parents moved there when they got married to get away from the mob."

Luca interjects, but he says what I think all of us figured out.

"He's pissed Sinead's representing Gabe because he's *Cosa Nostra*. And he thinks his Sinn Féin roots mean publishing propaganda against you. He thinks he's going to win a Pulitzer from this shit."

Carmine agrees as he shrugs and shakes his head.

"Pretty much."

I clench my fist.

"I want him at the garage in an hour."

Matteo speaks up, shooting me a skeptical expression.

"This is worth killing him over?"

Mmm. That might be a little rash.

"Maybe not yet. Carmine, is there anything linking Duffy to the O'Rourkes and Sinead?"

"No. I don't think they have any clue."

"Is there anything that connects Duffy to whoever's spying on Sinead?"

"No. But it would be logical that it's him."

I drum my fingers on the counter as I think.

"Is he purely angry that Sinead is representing me, or did he also print the article to sandbag my case? Is he working with whoever set me up?"

Carmine shrugs.

"I don't know yet. Do you want me to find out if Dillan knows anything about Duffy's article?"

"Sure. I don't want Dillan knowing Sinead means something to me personally."

"All right. All of you stay quiet."

Carmine pulls out his phone and dial's Dillan's number on speakerphone. It rings four times, and it's probably going to voicemail.

"What do you want, Carmine?"

"Such a pleasant greeting. Sounds about right for the manners you have."

"I'm in the middle of something. What do you want?"

"Duffy O'Toole."

There's a prolonged silence that makes all of us look around.

"What about him?"

"He wrote that article that trashed Gabe's lawyer. Did you put him up to that?"

"No. I read it though."

"Have you talked to him about it?"

"We're having a chat right now, aren't we, Duff?"

There's a muffled sound in the background.

"Is he at the shop?"

Another silence. That's a yes. It means Dillan's working him over before he kills him.

"He pissed you off that much? I was calling to see if we needed to pick him up then blow some of your shit up."

"It didn't take you long to connect him to us. You won't be the only one. I didn't sanction this, and I don't need this falling back on us. I don't know Sinead well, but we'd play together when she came down from Rhode Island to see her grandparents. They'd come with us for Midnight Mass on Christmas Eve, and we went to her birthday parties a few times since it's on the twenty-third. Before Gabriele gets in a fucking huff since I know he can hear me, no, we are not friends now. Sinead has had nothing to do with our family since her mom died."

"So, Duffy took it upon himself?"

"Yeah. And now I'm pissed."

Well, Duffy definitely done fucked up. It also means I won't have a chance to question him. I speak up since he already knows I can hear the call.

"Are you pissed because you set me up, and he drew too much attention your way?"

"The only thing I care about is not having some shit newspaper article fuck me over because you assume we're to blame."

That doesn't answer my question. The evasion makes me think they are to blame.

"He's family. Are you going to deal with him? Or will I be cleaning up your mess?"

"Don't worry. He and his editor will get the message just fine. If they don't, then they're yours."

Ah, so they aren't at the shop. They have the same rules there as we do. Anyone who goes doesn't leave alive.

"You just smashing kneecaps?"

"Among other things. Let me get back to it."

He hangs up before anyone can say something. I grit my teeth as Luca says what I'm thinking.

"There's no way Dillan's going to share anything he learns. And you know Duffy's going to have a broken jaw and broken fingers. He won't be telling or typing anything any time soon."

"Fucking-a."

I pound my fist on the counter as I swear, just like I did during my first conference with Sinead. I'm just as pissed as I was then.

Lorenzo leans forward on his elbows as he looks at Carmine's phone, which is still on the counter.

"Did he only pick up Duffy, figuring the editor will learn his lesson from what happens to Duffy? Or did he pick up the editor too? Maybe he's the one we talk to."

Marco disagrees.

"It's fine that Dillan has Duffy. Fucking D names. Really? He can do whatever he wants to the shitbag, and Duffy is smart enough not to say a fucking word because they're family. Duffy grew up with the mob. He knows how much worse it could be. But the editor didn't. If he's left alive, then he might talk. If he dies, it's too close to the article's publication. No one will think it's a coincidence. They'll just try to add his death to your charges, Gabe. Duffy can claim he was in some car accident or something."

That's a fair point. If we go anywhere near the guy, he could fuck us over. If he lives while we bribe him or threaten him, he might not fear us enough. He could print another article or go to the cops. If we kill him, then it'll make us look suspicious.

"So, what now? We know Duffy can't hurt Sinead again. But we don't know about this other person. Carmine, who's the editor, anyway?"

He goes back to his computer and pulls something up before he answers.

"Ezekiel McSwain. Never heard of him before."

I look at the other guys, and they shrug. We all read plenty of news, but none of us pay much attention to the bylines or the publications' editors.

"Do you think he has an axe to grind too, or he just thought this would be good press?"

Carmine sighs before he answers.

"McSwain sounds Irish. I'll dig into this guy too and find out."

I consider our options before I say anything else. Luca's our underboss and second in command to Uncle Salvatore, but the rest of us are all equals as *capos*. This is about my case and more importantly, my woman. They'll let me lead as long as it isn't to our death.

"Let's see what you come up with. Regardless, his place needs some redecorating, and the tires on his car might need to be slashed."

Those are things we can send men to do for us. We don't have to do it personally, and it's better that way. Unless it's happening at the garage, the further removed we are from the small hands-on jobs, the better.

The afternoon shifts into evening, and everyone but Sinead and I go home. We have dinner together in Paola's kitchen because she's at some work event. We watch a movie, and it feels like domestic tranquility. I sit with my arm around her, but we do nothing more. We exchange a brief kiss goodnight, then we go to our separate rooms.

I'm barely asleep when my phone rings. Three rings, then it stops. Three rings, then it stops. It's work. I answer the next time, looking at the screen to see it's Luca.

"What's up?"

"Finn called. He said Duffy's ready for us to take our turn."

"Now? It's like two in the morning."

"Yeah. I know. He woke Livy up, and she already sleeps like shit because she can't get comfortable."

Olivia's due in the next few weeks. Luca was already

protective of her. He's like a bear with a thorn in his paw right now. I'm certain Finn knows it wasn't a good time to call.

"Where's he at?"

"They dumped him at a bodega in Harlem."

It's not near any of the Irish territories that matter. I can guess which one. Enrique won't be pleased.

"Is someone getting him?"

"Yeah. They'll take him to Palermo's. He can chill in the fridge if he gets too heated."

Palermo's in Queens is a restaurant we go for private conversations that don't need the garage. The walk-in fridge is a good place to mellow people out who might not be ready to talk.

"All right. I'm on my way."

I hurry to dress, then I slip into Sinead's room. I shake her shoulder until she rolls over and opens her eyes a crack.

"*Piccolina*, I need to go out for a while. I should be back by breakfast, but if you need anything, call me."

Unlike at the garage, I'll have my phone on.

"Okay."

She's so groggy I'm not sure she'll remember this when she wakes up. I press a soft kiss to her temple, then I'm gone. There's a town car waiting for me by the time I get downstairs. I don't need to tell Pauly where to take me. I slip into the restaurant through the back alley. Marco's already there with Duffy sagging against a wall. He's had the shit beaten out of him. He looks like he can barely stand up. That's why Marco isn't letting him sit. It's part of the punishment. Our guys stripped him for two reasons. One, to humiliate him. Two, to ensure he's not wearing a wire.

"Why'd you write the article?"

I ask without preamble. I want to get back to Auntie Paola's. I don't like leaving Sinead there alone. I know Auntie

Paola isn't there, but I don't ask questions about where she is. I also need sleep. Last night was horrible. The few minutes I caught here and there at the hospital hardly left me rested.

"What article?"

"Duffy, don't. You know what I mean. Clearly, Dillan knew about it too. That's why you look like shit warmed up. Why?"

"Because her family would never approve of her representing some Guido who should already be serving life."

"But she doesn't have family to tell her no. So, it's not your concern. Why'd you make it your business?"

"You should be locked up. She shouldn't be keeping you out of prison where you belong. She can represent anyone who isn't a rival."

"Even if Sinead were a close relative to someone in the mob, she would be untouchable because she's a woman."

He scoffs at me.

"Bah."

"Women aren't involved. Men don't pull them in. She's free to represent whoever her firm tells her to."

He's getting heated as he continues to speak. He sounds like he believes he's fulfilling a just cause.

"Bullshit. If women weren't involved, she wouldn't represent you. Your family specifically demanded she represent you. Your family sucked her in, and she agreed. She's a traitor."

"To what? She's never sworn loyalty to anyone. She's Irish-American, but she's not mob. Who are you to decide this shit, anyway? Dillan makes those calls. You took this upon yourself, and your face shows what a bad choice that was."

"I'm loyal to my family and the cause."

It's my turn to scoff now.

"The cause? What the fuck cause are you talking about? What propaganda are you peddling?"

"The Irish have run New York for generations. That's the way it's going to stay. You fuckers aren't shit."

Marco and I laugh. Hard.

"You are batshit bonkers. The Irish have *never* dominated New York City. The Italians have. The Irish have worked for us, not the other way around. You're fucking delusional."

He scowls at me and looks down his nose at me. It's hard to do, considering it's mangled. He flicks me off, and I just laugh again. My guess is Dillan left ten little piggies on his hands and his feet for me to break. I walk around a counter and pull open a drawer where I know they keep the meat mallets. I say nothing while I pull out dish towels and a couple gallon-size plastic storage bags.

I nod to Marco as I set up my workstation. He yanks Duffy away from the wall and shoves him toward me. He opens a drawer with a key. A key that even the restaurant owner doesn't have a copy of. He pulls out a pair of cuffs that he quickly shackles around Duffy's ankles. Now he can't kick or run. He grabs Duffy's left hand as I pull up his right. I slip a clear storage bag over it and place it on top of a dish towel.

"This hand is just punishment because you pissed me off trying to interfere with my case. The other hand will be simply because you're a douche. I will shatter every bone in both feet for going after Sinead. Scream as loud as you want. No one will hear you outside this building. And no one in this building could scrape two shits together to save their life."

I lift the mallet to shoulder height and slam it down on his thumb. He howls with pain. I don't wait. I drop the mallet onto each finger without pause. I'd cut off fingers, but that's too permanently obvious. These injuries will heal with no significant outward signs. My goal is to make sure he never types another word.

"You tried to derail my case by prejudicing any possible

jury member and judge. You assume your reach is much further than it is. There are millions of New Yorkers who haven't read the article. It was your intent that's gotten you here."

Marco releases his other hand as I trade places with him. He holds the other hand up for me as I slip on a bag. I want no fingerprints left, and if I break the skin, I don't want blood shooting all over the place. We'll have a team come in and clean, so there's no DNA evidence left behind. No point in making their job harder.

"You are some peon with delusions of grandeur that will never happen. You aren't good enough for CNN or any broadcast news. You're a dime a dozen reporter, even if it is for a big publication. You're a nothing in the mob. If you were, Dillan wouldn't have handed you over. You matter to no one of importance."

"I matter to you."

"For tonight. Believe me, I will sleep just fine and not think about you again. Unless you give me reason to. Do that, and I'll kill you. Then I definitely won't think of you again."

I strike each finger twice on this hand for good measure. When I'm done, Marco and I shuffle him into the cold storage where there are sides of beef hanging. Marco lowers a hook that he attaches to a link connecting the cuffs around his ankles. I push a button, and a pulley yanks him off his feet, lifts him into the air, and flips him upside down. He's shorter than Marco and me, so I don't have to raise him very high for his head to clear the floor. Marco gets a chopping board and holds it against the soles of Duffy's feet.

I step forward into position like when I played baseball. For good measure, I swing the mallet a few times like I'm warming up with a bat. Duffy watches me, pure terror in his eyes. I grin. I keep doing warm up swings until I know he thinks I'm just showing off. Uh-uh. It's keeping him unprepared. I strike his foot with no hint. His body convulses with pain, all the blood already draining to his head. I broke two toes on his right foot with that blow. I'm working from his pinkie toe inward. I take out the next two without a word. I single out his big toe and hit it harder than I have anything else.

He gags and pukes. He splatters it on himself. But Marco and I know where to stand, so we aren't in the spray zone. I slam the mallet across the bridge of his foot, and I have a flash of that scene with Kathy Bates taking a sledgehammer to James Caan's legs in the movie *Misery*. Inspirational body of work, that one. I move to the outside of his ankle and fracture that bone. Then I attack the inside of his ankle. He pisses himself. He douses his own face. Perfect. Exactly the reason we strung him up like this. I strike his heel in just the right place to break the bone and damage his Achille's tendon.

I repeat the entire process on his other foot. He's puked two more times and pissed himself again. I think he almost shat himself once. He's a sobbing and sniveling mess. He passed out halfway through the second foot. The mallet to his junk woke him fast. He may never have kids. That's fine. One less shitbag procreating in the world isn't a bad thing.

"Women and children are untouchable. You gonna remember that now?"

"Yes. Please, no more. I can't take it."

"Oh, you'll take whatever the fuck I give you. If I decide to shove this mallet up your ass, you'll take it and say thank you. I don't give a fuck what you want. You hurt Sinead, so you paid for it."

I grab a butcher's knife and put it against his balls.

"If you want to remain a bull and not be a steer, then answer this question. Did you bug her place?"

"No. That wasn't me. I don't know who did that."

"Your editor?"

"No. Ezekiel approved my article, but he had nothing to do with writing it or how I got any of the information. I knew what happened to Sinead from back in the day. It wasn't hard to find the photo. When that bitch from Sinead's firm forced a retraction, all the details I included came from memory. I didn't need to look anything up."

"You did it purely to torture her. You abused your connection to her family and exploited her. If you knew what happened to her, then you knew the toll that took on her. This wasn't about sending a message or even making her regret accepting my case. You mind-fucked her."

I walk to a bag at the far end of the counter. Whoever brought him over pulled it out of the trunk of the town car they used. It has very specific items in it. It's a tool bag, if you will. I push some stuff aside and pull out what I want. I prowl back to Duffy, making him watch my slow return. His brow furrows when he sees what I have. Marco knows what to do. He already put the chopping board down. With the hook through the link that connects both sides of the cuffs, Duffy remains in position when Marco unfastens the right one. I slip the first leg into the adult diaper. I do the same for the left. I pull it all the way up, then pull the right leg hole wide, exposing his dick and balls.

"And Jacek?

"Who?

The confusion is legit. I've been an enforcer long enough to read expressions, body language, and tone to detect innocence and guilt, lies and truth, real confusion and feigned misunderstanding.

"Polish Mob."

We've heard murmurs they're involved somehow, but I don't know if they are, how, or to what extent.

"What about them? I don't know who that is. I didn't know

there was a Polish Mob. Don't they all just work for the bratva?"

"Uh, no. Learn your Eastern European politics."

I don't need to say anything beyond that. Russian relations with the rest of Eastern Europe, especially the former Soviet Bloc are— complicated. That may be my least favorite most frequently used word these days. The same is true for Eastern Europeans here. Though the New York bratva does a shit ton better working with their motherland neighbors than anyone would expect. The Kutsenkos rule with an iron fist, but they offer positive and negative incentives. It keeps would-be enemies under their control and on good terms.

Since there's nothing left to learn, it's time to finish.

"You've received your punishment. Now you're going to get a reminder to stay the fuck away from Sinead, me, my family, our business. Anything to do with us."

I take the butcher knife and slice a diagonal line across the bottom of his nut sack. Then I carve a semicircle around the base of his dick. I'm quick to do it, so I can put the diaper back in place. With so many veins down there, these will bleed fast. The diaper keeps my workstation clean. I ball my fist and drive it into his junk. He wails like a little bitch, then passes out. It's Marco's and my turn to strip. We take everything off by the deep sink. We have soap and hand towels in that toolkit. We wash every inch of ourselves before putting on fresh clothes. We've already put our old clothes in a bag to be destroyed. Once we're dressed again, we turn back to where three of our guys are redressing him.

"Drop him in Camden."

It's the most dangerous city in New Jersey. Whatever happens, happens there. They'll make it look like he got carjacked. They'll steal the stereo, his laptop if he has it in there, and they'll strip the hubcaps. He'll be out for a while, so they'll dump his body next to his car. It'll look like he either tried to fight back or the carjackers roughed him up for the hell of it. He's an investigative reporter. He could have been there for a story for all anyone knows.

Marco and I get into the car Pauly's driving and head back to Auntie Paola's first. Pauly'll drop Marco off in Manhattan afterwards. The privacy glass is up as we talk.

"You did that purely out of spite."

"Yup. And it felt vindicating."

"But you learned nothing new."

"True. We still have no idea who bugged Sinead's place or hotel room. It could be Bartlomiej or Jacek. We need to know more about them."

"There's a guy who likes Paradise. He's there more nights than not. He works for Bartlomiej on the side. He might know something. He's a sloppy drunk. If something happened to him, it would surprise no one."

"Pick him up and take him to the garage. He can be a guest for the weekend."

Chapter Seventeen

Sinead

I spent the rest of the week and weekend recuperating at Paola's, and I feel world's better than I did. Gabriele and I came close to a stand-off last night over me continuing to stay at Paola's instead of going home. Not once did Paola make me feel like I wore out my welcome. But I wanted privacy. I wanted my things in my place. Turns out, not only is Gabriele an attorney, he owns several hardware stores. I never guessed. He'd already sent men over to repair my door, but he also had one of those camera doorbells installed. I think he would have gutted the place and started over from the studs if I let him. I think it had nothing to do with my place so much as loathing the idea of me returning to an apartment where an unknown intruder violated my space.

It angered him when I dug my heels in, but I know he understood. We compromised when he offered, and I agreed to a car parked outside my place with two guys in it. He also insisted on an additional guy in a car at each end of my block and one on the street behind my place. I think it's excessive, but if it lets him feel in control of an uncertain situation, then I can accept it. I'll admit I feel better for it.

Control. That's something I've already realized Gabriele craves. I think a shit ton is beyond his control within his world, so the little he can have, he clings to. He has such an air of command no one could ever imagine him not being fully in control. I see glimpses of him through what must be at least partially a facade. But I'm positive that's only because he lets me see it. If he wanted to shut me out entirely, he would. I wouldn't have a clue what he's thinking or feeling. That'll be good in court, but I don't know that it bodes well for a romantic relationship.

A romantic relationship is practically all I could think about over the weekend. I had the time to let my mind wander while I watched TV in my room. When I wasn't dozing, I was bingeing my shows. I have a secret addiction to the reality TV shows about the crews sailing around the world and the wealthy women who drink too much and fight all the time. Sometimes, I just need to not have to think very hard. It's why I don't get people who listen to public radio in the car. I don't need to be bombarded by the news everywhere I go. I want to just chill out and listen to music when I'm driving. Gabriele admitted he feels the same way. At least about the music. I still can't get over the fact he doesn't have a TV. Not needing a boob-tube either makes him the most cultured person I know, or the biggest heathen in custom-tailored suits. I'm undecided.

He came back to Paola's during the week. He went to work while I telecommuted. I figured he was at the businesses he owns. I had the time to think about us over the weekend because I didn't see him at all until Sunday night when we had our showdown. He said it was his turn on a rotation that I assumed meant guarding a family member. He said he wouldn't be available to talk since Salvatore expects him not to be distracted. I wonder if he was guarding Salvatore's daughters. I sent him a text late Saturday night, thinking he'd respond since he was probably at his place by eleven. But I got no answer. I didn't push it.

The more time I spend with him, the more time I crave. Paola invited Carmine and his wife, Serafina, over for dinner on Sunday. Apparently, the entire family usually gets together for Sunday dinner. There's like twenty-something of them who go to Salvatore's. But Gabriele wasn't the only one working, so Paola had her son and daughter-in-law over. I helped Paola cook, and Serafina brought the most delicious cinnamon and rhubarb pie with a flaky crust I've ever tasted. Paola teases Carmine mercilessly, and it's one of the sweetest things I've ever seen. The guy is huge. Not quite as big as Gabriele, but I wouldn't want to find him at the end of a dark alley. The man is terrified of his mother. She's lovely and kind, but she looks in her son's direction, and he's asking how high he should jump.

They also told me about some things Gabriele and Carmine got up to when they were kids. Most of the stories also involved the other cousins, but Carmine and Gabriele were the focus. It seems like Carmine was the instigator, and Gabriele kept him from being throttled by all the adults in their family. I deduced he was a gentle giant as a kid, head and shoulders taller than his classmates until high school. I still see that in him. The way he touches me speaks of tenderness that I doubt has much of an outlet these days. Even when he's insistent about something, he doesn't intimidate me or come across as forcing his will upon me. It's always reasoned out and with my best interests at heart. When I think about it, it makes me all gooey inside.

What doesn't make me gooey is walking into court this

morning. The Cohenour trial begins today. I spot my client and walk over to him.

"Good morning."

He barely glances at me when he returns the greeting.

"Hi."

He's antsy as fuck.

"What's wrong?"

Here's one of those blunt moments Jason mentioned the other day.

"Huh? Nothing. Just regular nerves I suppose."

He's jumpier than a frog on a frying pan. This is making me anxious.

"Has something come up, Mr. Cohenour?"

"No. No. It's all fine."

"Today we may only have time for you to formally enter your plea and the prosecution to give its opening statement depending on how long it is."

"Yeah, you already told me that."

Rude much. He completely snapped at me. Given how many times I've had to repeat other things, I figured he might need the reminder. Fine. I have nothing else to say to him, so we can wait in silence. It's not long before the courtroom opens, and we make our way to our table. I gesture toward it, and he's ready to take the first chair.

"That has to be mine."

I whisper it twice since he doesn't seem to hear me the first time. That or he just doesn't want to get up. He glances over his shoulder three times. The third time, I look too. There are two men in the middle that he's looking at. I get a sinking feeling about them. I pull out my phone and rest it in my lap. I pull up a browser and type in two names.

Jacek and Bartlomiej Nowakowski

Sure as shit. The men in the courtroom are the brothers I

eavesdropped on. Fuck. I pull up my text messages and scroll down.

> **ME**
> The brothers are here watching us

It takes a moment, but then there's a response.

> **Gabriele**
> How close to you are they

> **ME**
> About four rows back and across.

> **GABRIELE**
> Look around. Do you see Carmine

I try to look inconspicuous as I sweep my gaze over everyone gathered in the courtroom. Just as I'm about to turn back, Carmine walks in with a guy who has a scar on his cheek.

> **ME**
> He just got here with Luca. They just spotted the brothers.

> **GABRIELE**
> That's fine. Carmine will sit right behind you. Luca will sit behind them.

> **ME**
> Yeah Luca just sat down and Carmine's about to.

> **GABRIELE**
> Don't acknowledge them

I guessed as much. I'm certain the Nowakowskis had to

recognize Carmine when he walked past. They have to be wondering what he's doing here.

ME

Won't it seem suspicious to them that Carmine and Luca are here

GABRIELE

No. I'm certain they know we know one of their men supposedly knows shit about me. They can't be surprised that C and L came to listen to the man in the middle of all this.

"All rise. The New York City Criminal Court is now in session. The Honorable Judge Simmons presiding."

ME

I gotta go. Starting.

I shove my phone in my pocket as I stand.

"Everyone but the jury may be seated. Ms. Homestead, please swear in the jury."

I zone out for a moment while the jury recites their pledge. Something is going on. How'd Carmine and Luca know to be here? Are they just my regular guards assigned to me during this case? Will Mancinelli men be inside the courtroom every day? I didn't get a chance to ask Gabriele that.

I tune back in when the judge addresses Diane.

"Is the prosecution ready?"

"Yes, Your Honor."

I can practically hear her smirking. Cunt. I got a particularly snarky email from her saying that they intend to throw the book at Cohenour. They had no intention of considering a plea agreement or reducing the charges.

"Is the defense ready?"

I stand.

"Yes, Your Honor."

I sit. I sense Cohenour is about to do something as the judge speaks again.

"Prosecution, you may make you Opening Statement."

Cohenour shoots out of his chair. I try grabbing his arm to pull him back down, but he yanks it away. Oh, fuck. I know what's coming. *No.*

"Your Honor, I plead guilty."

Fucking hell. I spring out of my chair like a fucking jack-in-the-box.

"Your Honor, a moment to confer with my client."

The murmurs running through the courtroom will hopefully drown out my voice.

"What are you doing? You already entered your plea at the arraignment."

"I changed my mind."

"Did the Nowakowskis change it for you?"

He remains silent.

"Now you decide to plead the fifth? You can't do this."

"They'll kill me if I don't."

He's likely right.

"Counselor?"

I look at the judge.

"Does your client wish to officially change his plea?"

"Your Honor, may we approach?"

I glance at Diane who looks like she's ready to dance a fucking jig on my grave. The judge waves us forward and pushes aside her mic.

"Ms. O'Malley, what is going on?"

"I believe my client is under extreme duress to change his plea. Known leaders of the Polish Mob are in the gallery. I believe they're coercing him to plead guilty."

"Why do you think that?"

I can't exactly share what and how I heard my info.

"Mr. Cohenour may be a witness for the state in another case where he is naming a member of the Polish Mob as a witness to a crime. I think the Nowakowskis don't want him to involve their people in the trial and want him to be their informant on the inside."

"Do you have any proof of this?"

"They're sitting here."

That's not even close to evidence, but it tumbles out of my mouth. I scramble.

"My client heard the Polish Mob talking about another crime and called Detective Morris. He will testify for the state in that trial."

"Which he cannot easily do while a guest at one of our fine correctional facilities."

The judge surmises the situation with the sarcasm of a woman who's sat on the bench for nearly thirty years. Diane tries to sound like she's not gloating when she speaks up, but she fails miserably.

"Your Honor, the defendant wished for immunity in exchange for testifying in the Gabriele Scotto trial. We refuse to allow a man guilty of embezzling millions from senior citizens to walk free. We intend to request maximum sentencing, but we can still compel him to testify even if he goes upstate."

"I know, Ms. Stanton. That does not negate the fact that the defendant might be changing his plea under duress."

"Your Honor."

All three of us turn to look at Cohenour who takes a step around the table. The bailiff immediately rushes forward. Cohenour raises his hands.

"Your Honor, I'm sticking with the guilty plea no matter what Ms. O'Malley recommends."

I glower at my client. Even if we lose the case, at least he wouldn't be admitting fault. Now there's no chance Diane won't request maximum sentencing. I'm still facing Cohenour, but I shift my gaze toward the Nowakowskis. They're watching me like hawks. I quickly shift my focus elsewhere, pause, then shift again and pause. I don't want them thinking I was staring at them specifically.

"Mr. Cohenour, I will give you only this chance to change your mind and rescind your guilty plea."

"No, Your Honor. I'm guilty."

Fuck me. Fuck me. Fuck me up the ass with a pogo stick. Fuck me. I maintain my bearing when all I want to do is rub my eyes and let my shoulders droop.

"Your Honor, I request a recess to further discuss this with my client since I clearly did not know he would take this course. I believe an inquiry into him changing his plea would be appropriate."

"This court is in recess for fifteen minutes."

The gavel taps the sound block, and I suck in a breath that I hold as I approach my client, slowly exhaling as I sit. I turn to him and want to choke him.

"Art, what are you doing?"

I'm never this informal, but maybe it'll sink in if I'm kinder.

"I changed my mind. You're right. The preponderance of evidence says I'm guilty. Why drag this out? I have a family. I need to think about them."

"And getting shanked in prison is going to help them?"

"I— I —That won't happen."

"Because the Nowakowskis are going to pay protection money for you? Is that what you think is going to happen? You'll be their mole, and they'll keep you safe. But what happens when you run out of usefulness? What happens if they don't like what you have to say?"

"I'm not going to be a—"

"Don't lie to me. Why else are they here but to be sure you send yourself to prison? Cohenour may not sound Greek, but I know your connection. Why aren't they representing you? Why aren't they here to protect you from the Polish?"

"Because they washed their hands of me. Some of my victims were members of our community. They're more likely to have someone go after me than the Polish are. I trust their protection way more. There are former Soviets locked up with Polish Mob ties. Bartlomiej promised they'd help out. They're ruthless."

"And when they turn on you? Because they will, Art. What happens when you have no one, and you're in there for years?"

"I might die in there, but I will definitely die out here if I don't go."

"Then you admit you made your plea under duress."

"That I won't admit to. Ms. O'Malley, this is my choice."

"And as your lawyer, I must advise you against this."

We're going to go around and around, but I keep trying until the bailiff calls the court back into order. I stand to address the judge, but Cohenour stands again.

"Your Honor, I confer—"

"Ms. O'Malley, you're fired."

I blink twice before I turn toward my client who has clearly gone around the bend.

"What?"

I hiss at him.

"You're going to keep trying to defend me."

No shit.

The judge is not impressed with this spectacle. Neither am I.

"Your Honor—"

"No, Ms. O'Malley. Your client has made his view clear. Bailiff, escort the defendant out where he will be remanded into the custody of the New York City Police to await further inquiry."

At least, the judge is going to examine into his plea, even if I no longer represent him. I watch the bailiff leads Cohenour away, now in handcuffs. I look over at Diane, and for once, she's stunned silent. I gather my belongings after I nod to her. I focus on the judge as I slide my laptop into my bag. She looks annoyed and bewildered at the same time. She looks the way I feel. Once I have my stuff together, I turn toward Carmine. I notice most of the gallery has cleared out, but the Nowakowskis remain, Luca still sitting behind them.

"Are you ready?"

Carmine's voice permeates my clouded thoughts.

"Yeah. I don't even know what the fuck just happened, but I suspect they happened."

"They did. We'll discuss this in the car. Gabriele's outside."

"He is?"

"Yeah, the moment Cohenour stood, Luca and I both knew shit was going down. We both texted him."

Everything has just happened way too fast for me to understand. Or rather, I understand perfectly. It all happened way too fast for me to control. I don't know if I should ignore the brothers or stare them down. The latter would be as fucking arrogant as slipping into the restaurant and listening to them. That arrogance is likely to get me killed. I keep my eyes locked on the door, but as I'm about to walk past, the one I assume is Bartlomiej stands. Luca does too and steps into the aisle, blocking the man from reaching me. Carmine shifts so Jacek can't get to me either. Bartlomiej and Jacek glare at Luca and Carmine, the latter clearly giving no fucks.

Bartlomiej opens his mouth, and Carmine's hand is already pressing against my lower back.

"Ms. O'Malley—"

Luca interrupts and hisses at him.

"Shut the fuck up."

"We only wish to talk."

Luca and Carmine ignore him, now sandwiching me between them as we file out of the courtroom. I don't sense the Nowakowskis following us. I'm glad, but I'm also curious.

"Gabriele will decide whether they speak to you and where."

Carmine whispers it from behind me. Part of me wants to rebel at the idea that he'll decide who I can and can't talk to, especially about work. The other part of me is completely content with that. I let them steer me toward the elevator, then out through the lobby. Gabriele is there, and I want to run into his arms and hide from what's been a shitty morning. But we're in public. He guides me to an SUV, and I want to groan. It means no privacy glass. It makes me want to doubly groan when Carmine and Luca climb in. Luca goes in the front seat, and Carmine is on my left while Gabriele is on my right. His thigh presses against me while Carmine tries to keep his leg a respectful distance from mine.

Chapter Eighteen

Gabriele

It's a tense ride from the courthouse, so I try to lighten the mood. We had little time to talk yesterday, and it was more of an argument than talking. I still hate that she's back to staying at her place, but I respect her choice.

"How was your weekend?"

I already know the answer to my question. But I'm trying to be polite. Carmine already filled me in.

"It was surprisingly nice, considering the circumstances."

She'd worked a lot last week, even if it was telecommuting. Paola wasn't home much either since an election is coming up.

"Paola is such a sweetheart, and I really enjoyed hanging out with Serafina during dinner. I never would have guessed all the guys in your family took ballroom dancing classes. I definitely wouldn't have guessed you were a star pupil and won a bunch of contests, but Carmine told me all about it. You'll have to show me your ribbons and medals one day."

Of course, he would tell her that. I glare at him over

Sinead's head, but he pretends not to notice.

"He looked better in spandex than I did, but I had a gift, according to our instructor. I hate to disappoint, but Mama took all my trophies back to Palermo when they moved. She said having them around was like having a little of me, so she wouldn't miss me so much."

"That's so sweet."

I can tell she's still frazzled, but talking is helping. We keep chatting about the stories Carmine and Auntie Paola told. I keep a tally of how many punches I need to get in at the gym the next time he and I spar. Our conversation remains light-hearted until we get to her office and close ourselves into the conference room.

After learning the Nowakowskis showed up, I need to discuss something vital with her. I've hinted at what I need to say a couple times, but now it has to all come out. If she wants to jump into a lifeboat and row away to safety, then it has to be now. She needs to know enough to make an educated decision.

"Sinead, we have to talk about something that concerns my case, but also if there's an 'us' in the future."

"Okay."

She eases into her chair beside mine. I sit and swivel toward her.

"If you were a typical woman I met somewhere and was into, I wouldn't tell you who I really am. I wouldn't say anything about the Mafia. I wouldn't give any hints about my previous arrests. At least, I wouldn't tell you until I was sure there was a real future for us. I wouldn't bring you anywhere near this world if I could help it. But you know who I am. You must have looked up my record before we even met. You may not know the intricacies of the Mafia, but you're intelligent enough to sort out fact from fiction. For this case and in the future, there are things I cannot tell you. I will *never* tell you."

I pause to see how she reacts. Her expression is neutral, but I can see it in her eyes. She's dreading what might come next. She's preparing herself for something bad. She won't be wrong.

"There are so many secrets I could fill the ocean with them. I will keep all of them from you. I will lie by omission, and sometimes, I might have to lie to you for real. But if I can help it, I won't. If I can tell you even a little of what's going on, I will. That's likely to be rare. The one thing I can promise is I won't lie to you about us. I won't lie about how I feel or what I want. I won't lie about why I'm hiding things. That's the easiest thing to explain. When I don't tell you the truth, it's not because I enjoy being deceptive. It's because I'm protecting you, my family, and the people who depend upon us. What I can give you, I will give you completely. But you'll never have all of me."

She sits there, digesting what I've just vomited at her. It's a lot to unpack, so I won't rush her. She's staring at the table while I watch her. It has to be at least five minutes before she turns and faces me.

"You weren't guarding someone this weekend, were you?"

"No."

"But you let me think you were."

"A lie of omission."

"And there will be a lot of those."

"Those are the ones you'll probably figure out. I hope you know that when I speak them, it's because I'm protecting you."

"It'll be when you're committing a crime."

I say nothing to that. She observes me for a moment before she nods.

"There will be times when I'm away and won't know how long I'll be gone. I didn't get your text until Sunday night just before I went to Auntie Paola's to see you. There's a reason for that. I need a promise from you."

"All right. Normally, I wouldn't promise something without

knowing what it is. But I trust you, Gabe."

"There's somewhere we go to take care of things. Somewhere completely under our control. When I'm there, I never have my phone on. If it's a true emergency, you contact someone in my family, and they contact me. I need you to promise you will never look for this place. You won't find it in the city records, but I know you're resourceful. Don't do it. I can't say what the outcome would be because I don't know. But it wouldn't be good. Don't think torture or death. I don't mean that. But it just wouldn't be good."

I hope she gets the gravity of this. That's why I repeated myself.

She scrubs her hands over her face.

"I already know all this, Gabe."

Her voice is little more than a whisper. I don't get the feeling it's because she saw it in some movie. She runs her hand through her hair before our gazes meet. She inhales so deeply I can hear it.

"I don't consider myself an O'Rourke, but I am distantly related. Dillan O'Rourke's great-grandfather was a distant cousin of my great-grandfather on my mother's side. Second cousins a couple times removed, I think. Before our family even moved to America, my great-grandfather was an enforcer. My maternal grandfather got away from all that when he left to fight in Vietnam. He came home injured. He had a TBI. The O'Rourkes let him off the hook, and he no longer had to work for them. But he told me stories. I didn't know until I was a teenager that he shouldn't have. I think some of it was the brain injury, but I think some of it was a warning to stay far, far away from them. I asked my dad about it, and he told me to never repeat a thing I heard. My parents met because both of my grandfathers were being trained to be mobsters before they left for the Vietnam War. My dad's dad didn't come home."

She bites her top lip before continuing.

"I also spent time with the O'Rourkes and another family, the O'Tooles, when I was really young, and we'd come down for Christmas and over the summer. I know they have a fake storefront somewhere in Brooklyn or Queens. I don't remember. I know they do shit there, and it sounds like you're describing the same thing. What you told me is hard to hear. The part about the lies is the worst. I know it shouldn't be. But it is. I get it, though. I knew this when I accepted the case. Marta knows my family history. It's why they assigned me to you. She figured I'd know which questions not to ask. At least, that's what I figured until another managing partner told me Salvatore and Massimo insisted they hire me."

"Can you accept lies between us in our private life?"

My chest aches. Depending on her answer, there may be no going forward once the case is over.

"Yes. I know it's not the same by any stretch, but I won't be able to tell you things about the cases I represent. It hurts to know that I can give you all of me, but I'll— at best —get half of you. I don't know that I'll get even that much."

"I'll give you as much as I can. If I ever tell you to stay away, that I can't see you, it's not because I don't want to. It'll be because something happened. Something went wrong. I may need to calm down or get cleaned up. Please don't offer to help because I won't accept. I don't want to reject you that way, but you can't get involved. Whether or not you were a lawyer, I would shelter you from that."

Maybe one day it'll get to where we're living together. That would make it harder, but I believe she'll understand this part and respect it.

"I can do that, Gabe."

"Good. Does that mean you can still see a future for us?"

"Yes."

I glance out the conference room windows and see no one paying attention to us. I take her hands in mine and give them a squeeze. There's nothing left to say about this, so we turn our attention to the evidence we now have more time to review since the Cohenour case fell apart.

We're sitting close enough for our legs to press against each other. Knowing she's willing to give us a try got me hard in an instant. I test the waters and place my hand on her thigh. She does nothing, so I start to pull away. Her legs snap shut, capturing my hand. We continue to talk as though nothing is going on beneath the table. I pull just enough for her to know I want to slide my hand up her legs. She wheels the chair closer, and I angle my body to appear like I'm intently reading something. I can feel the heat coming from her pussy. When I slip a finger into her panties, I feel how wet she is for me.

"Naughty, *piccolina*."

She glances down at my crotch and cocks an eyebrow.

"Exactly. Naughty for being so wet and for getting me so hard. Should I reward you or punish you?"

"Reward."

It's a breathy whisper that makes me twitch. I shouldn't be doing this. We agreed. But who am I kidding? The only thing that's kept me from fucking her again is the threat the ABA could discipline or disbar her. I could be disciplined too, but I worry more about her.

My hands are large enough to cup her pussy, and I use the heel of my hand to rub her clit. I don't press inside her. Not yet. I run my fingers on each side of her pussy lips, and she fights not to wriggle.

"Tell me what you want, little girl."

"For you to put your fingers in me."

"Like this?"

I dip two into her cunt. She moans. I caress the inside of

her, and it's smoother than any satin. I keep using the heel of my hand since it's too awkward to twist and use my thumb.

"Yes. Daddy..."

I don't drop a beat, even though I feel her tense.

"Tell me what else you want."

"Your cock. You know that."

"And if I want you to suck me off instead of putting it in your hot, little cunt?"

"If we wouldn't get caught, I'd slide under this table and suck you off until you came down my throat."

"And if I want to come on your face and tits?"

"Then you'd brand me as yours, Daddy. Is that what you want?"

"Yes."

It's my turn to sound breathy. Hopefully, it's more husky to her ears than it is mine. Since I didn't object the first time she called me Daddy, she tries it again. She's told me more than once that she isn't a little, and I don't believe for a moment that's changed. But I also guessed she wanted to call me that before.

"Do you know where else Daddy would like to come, *piccolina*?"

Her eyes widen for a moment, pleased that I'm playing along. We'll dissect it later. For right now, it's making us both hornier.

"I don't think you mean only my pussy."

"I don't. Say it. Where do I want to come, Sinead?"

"In my ass."

"Why?"

"Because then I really am yours."

"True. But do I really need to come inside you at all for you to know that?"

"No. But I don't need to make you come to know you're

263

mine."

"That's right, *piccolina*. But fucking would be so much fun."

"Oh, God. Gabe. I'm close. You're going to make me come."

The moment she admits that I pull my fingers out and stop rubbing her clit. Her hand flies to my thigh and fists my trouser leg. I feel her legs trembling against the back of my hand and my wrist.

"Please."

She's begging, and I love it. The risk is too great that we'll get caught to really indulge in orgasm denial. I thrust my fingers back into her and work her until she begs again.

"Please, may I come?"

"Yes."

She shifts her hips a few times, then goes stiff. Her hand clenches and unclenches my pants. I pry her fingers loose before they leave wrinkles. She squeezes my hand instead. When I pull them out, I spin the chair toward the windows overlooking a park. I lick each one, and I know she's watching me.

"Tastes like *mine*."

She releases a ragged sigh.

"Thank you."

Watching and listening to her tempts me to adjust myself, but I can't stand seeing men do that in public. I refuse to do it.

"Come with me, *piccolina*. I'm treating you for lunch."

"For lunch? Not to lunch?"

"I didn't drive today, and the town car has privacy glass."

I infuse my voice with the authority I use when I'm a dom. She knows what I mean. It's not a question of what we're going to do in the car. It's a question of what I'm going to do to her.

"Where are you taking me?"

"Wherever you want, as long as it takes an hour to get there

264

and an hour back."

She gathers the papers we've been examining and shoves them into folders. When she stands, she appears a little unsteady on her feet. She rests her hand on the table for a moment and composes herself before brushing down her skirt. She heads to the door, and I follow her.

"I'll wait by the door. Gather your things, *piccolina*. Tell whoever you have to that you're going to a meeting at Mancinelli Developers. You're not coming back until tomorrow."

She looks up at me, then nods. I watch her walk to her office, and no ass has ever looked finer. The things I want to do to it. I want to fuck her from behind, and I want to fuck her ass. I want to fuck our way through the Kama Sutra. She glances at me as she walks out, but turns away from me. I watch her knock on someone's door and stick her head in. I don't know who she's talking to, but she better tell them she's not coming back this afternoon.

"I think Marta knows."

She whispers to me as we walk out to the elevator.

"I'm certain she does. That's why she was adamant about you going to a hotel and having your own security detail. It wasn't about propriety and appearances. She didn't want us to be an 'us.' But I also think she's accepted it. I hope she knows I have your best interests at heart."

"She does. She said so. She just told me I should listen to whatever you tell me because she can tell my safety is your highest priority. She believes it means more to you than your freedom."

"It does."

She watches me for a moment, then the elevator pings, and the doors open. We face each other as we go down. Her smile dazzles me.

"It's been a long time since I've felt like someone would do anything to protect me. It's been a long time since I've felt like someone's top priority. Not since before my dad started forgetting who I am."

"I know, little one. I know you haven't had that, but you deserve it. Your safety and happiness will always be a priority. I think you understand now why your happiness can't always be my top priority, even when I want it to be. But nothing will ever be more important than your health and wellbeing. I won't budge on that."

"You make me feel safe."

I offer her a half smile.

"You wouldn't need to think about that if you weren't in danger because of me."

"No. I wasn't even thinking about that stuff. I mean, I feel safe from life in general. I feel like I can talk to you about anything. I feel like I can trust you. I feel like I can relax with you. I don't have to be some hotshot lawyer. I don't have to be someone's overwhelmed and frightened daughter. You're you, and it always feels like you're in control. Like even if something bad happens, you'll still make everything okay."

"I want you to always feel that way with me. I want to give you all of that and more, Sinead. I want to take care of you. Not smother you or treat you like you can't take care of yourself. Not like some sugar daddy who gives you an allowance and pays all your bills. I want to take care of your emotional needs as much as anything else."

"That. All of that is why I called you..."

She trails off, and her cheeks turn pink. She was so confident a moment ago. Now she's nervous. I hit the stop button and slide my arm around her waist, pulling her against me. My free hand cups her face. I press a tender kiss to her lips as my thumb brushes over her cheekbone.

"*Piccolina,* I understood as soon as you said it. I think you wanted to say it before, but caught yourself."

"I did. It shocked me each time. I thought it would freak you out. I decided to see if it did. I needed to know because I didn't want to blurt it out one day."

"How do you feel now that you've said it?"

"Relieved. Happy."

She shrugs.

"You know I've called you little girl in English and in Italian since nearly the beginning. It's not a coincidence. Maybe that's what made you think of it. Or maybe we've been thinking along the same lines all along. I don't know. But I think it works for us."

"The other people in your family all speak Italian. What if they overhear you call me *piccolina?*"

I push the stop button again, and the elevator continues its descent.

"I know we're not the only couple that comes to this point in their relationship. Luca, Matteo, and Carmine call their wives that. And I know their wives call them Daddy too. None of them are into Daddy Dom/Little Girl. Not the husbands nor the wives. It's the same situation we're in. We don't discuss it because it's private between husband and wife, but no one in our family is blind to it. It wouldn't surprise me in the least if all our parents are into similar stuff. They just never, ever let any of us hear it. Thank God."

I grin. One time, Carmine and I walked in on my parents. Not into their bedroom or anything. We didn't see them just heard them. We were in like eighth grade. He and I have never moved as fast as we did running out of that house. I know I heard my dad call my mom *bambina,* or baby girl. I'm absolutely certain my mom isn't a little. I've belonged to a BDSM club long enough to recognize tells from couples who are in

DDLG relationships but aren't open about it. Fuck. It creeps me out thinking about my parents like that. Fuck. Sinead. Fucking her. Sucking her tits. Coming in her mouth. Anything to not think about them.

"My mom and dad — they — uh — they were into that."

Her face flames red. I don't know what to say.

"I was getting a sweater from my mom's dresser one day and opened the wrong drawer. Everything in it was like what a doll would wear, except they were all my mom's size. I was twelve and nosey. Once I saw one thing, I couldn't not look for other stuff. I found toys— sex ones and little girl ones. I didn't understand it until I was much older because I could never ask. I wasn't supposed to be in that drawer, and I definitely couldn't admit poking around. Once I learned about DDLG, I realized what I'd found years earlier. I also knew that wasn't what I was into. I've never called another man Daddy since I was probably five. That's when my father became Dad. And I definitely don't feel the same about you and him."

"You might feel taken care of again like you once did. But I know your other feelings are decidedly very adult."

We step off the elevator and make our way across the lobby. My eyes sweep our surroundings. Something feels off, but I can't tell what. I glance over my shoulder, but I see nothing suspicious.

"Gabe?"

"Keep walking. Look straight ahead like you normally would."

I slip her hand into mine, trapping them between us. She holds on for dear life, like she fears someone will snatch her from me if she doesn't keep a tight grip. I can't wait to feel it wrapped around my cock like that. I steer us toward the far-left set of glass doors.

"Stand next to the wall, your back to it."

She follows my instructions as I look outside. I don't see any of our cars. Luca and Carmine took off once Sinead and I came inside. Luigi should be waiting for us, but I don't see him. I pull out my phone and tap an app. All our vehicles have trackers, but the car Luigi drives isn't appearing anywhere. Not even at the garage where we keep the fleet.

"Car, where's Luigi?"

I don't bother with a greeting.

"He isn't waiting for you?"

"No. Neither his tracker nor the car's is pinging."

"Are you still at Sinead's office?"

"We're in the lobby."

"She's with you?"

"Yeah."

"Hang on."

I hear him tapping his phone, then it goes silent. A moment later, I hear Luca join the call.

"Gabe says Luigi isn't there, and he's not on the tracking app. Does he know he's on duty with Gabe?"

"I'm sure he does. I sent out the schedule on Thursday and got the confirmation from him. I know Pauly and Giuseppe were talking to him earlier. Beppe took Livy to see her mom, and Pauly was with you and me when we went to the courthouse."

Carmine cuts in, and I could hear him tapping his phone while Luca spoke.

"Pauly just answered my text. He said Luigi was on his way to you before we even dropped you guys off."

I glance down at Sinead, whose face is pale after blushing so beautifully in the elevator.

"*Mi sembra che qualcuno ci stia osservando. Luigi non c'è e mi si rizzano i peli sulla nuca. C'è qualcosa che non va. Non voglio che stiamo insieme nell'atrio, ma non mi va bene portarla*

269

fuori." I feel like someone is watching us. Luigi's not here, and the hair on the back of my neck is standing up. Something's not right. I don't want us hanging out in the lobby, but I'm not all right with taking her outside.

I switch to Italian because I don't want what I say to freak her out, even though I can tell switching languages makes her realize something's not right.

Luca speaks as my gaze shifts back out the glass doors.

"Pauly isn't that far away, so he'll be there in five minutes or less. He was having lunch with his sister and brother-in-law."

"*Bene. Ma ho ancora la sensazione che qualcuno ci stia osservando. Non riesco a capire chi. Non vedo nulla qui dentro che confermi i miei sospetti, ma lo so e basta.*" Good. But I still feel like someone is watching us. I can't tell who. I don't see anything in here that confirms my suspicions, but I just know it.

Sinead gives my hand a little tug. I offer her what I hope is a reassuring smile, but it does nothing to soothe her. Her brow's still furrowed, and her eyes are darting around.

"*Piccolina*, I see Pauly. He just pulled up. Let's go."

I say it as much for her as I do Carmine and Luca. I get off the phone with them as Pauly hurries toward the building. Neither he nor I say anything but position Sinead between us, so Pauly leads, and I follow. My shoulders are broad enough that I can walk slightly to her right side and still shield her entire back.

"It's all right. We're going to my place."

Pauly opens the door for us, but the dome light doesn't turn on. I yank Sinead back and spin us around. Pauly and I wrap our arms around her back, our shoulders bumping as we push her forward into a run. The explosion propels us off our feet. I twist, so I land beneath Sinead, and Pauly lands on top of her. I pull her head onto my chest, and Pauly's is practically on my shoulder.

People scream, and I can hear feet running. Most sound like they're moving away from us, but a few people rush to help us. Pauly scrambles to his feet and helps Sinead up. I'm fighting to catch my breath after having both of them land on me. Pauly's not a slim guy. A few too many chicken parm sandwiches. I'm just relieved he didn't crush Sinead. His size surely protected her.

"Pauly, you hurt?"

"Nah, boss. Suit's a bit singed, but I covered my head. I'll have some bruises from shit— sorry, stuff —hitting me. But I don't feel any cuts or burns. You?"

"Fine. Sinead?"

"I'm all right. Just— uh —dazed. What happened? How'd you know?"

"I'll explain everything, but we need to go. NYPD will be here any minute. We don't want to answer questions. This is an uncontrolled place and clearly not safe. I want you away from here now."

Pauly and I sweep up the bags Sinead dropped, then Pauly's hailing a cab. He gets in the front passenger seat, while Sinead and I climb in the back. He gives the driver the address to the Mancinelli Developers' building. It's the closest safe place for us right now. Ironic that I told Sinead to tell her boss she was going there.

"Lean against me, *cuore*."

"What does that mean?"

We're both whispering as though Pauly and the driver can't hear us.

"Sweetheart."

I won't call her *piccolina* in front of Pauly. At least not in a car like this where it feels crowded compared to our town cars and SUVs.

She rests her head on my shoulder, and I wrap both arms

around her. I stroke her back, and it calms me as much as it does her. I drop kisses on the top of her head and forehead, and she wraps one arm around my waist.

I'm watching her as she rests with her eyes closed. But five minutes later, she sits up and puts her lips to my ear.

"You are so rigid, you might snap if I move your arms. I know whatever is going on isn't over. But can you breathe for now?"

I press her head back to my shoulder and inhale. I hold it for a moment, then slowly exhale. I do it over and over until I relax. Or at least until my body does. My mind is still going a mile a minute.

Who did this? How long ago did they plan it? Was it intended for me, Sinead, or both of us? Who's watching us? Who's following us because someone definitely wants to know if they killed us? How am I going to get Sinead inside? How do I explain this?

My brain quiets momentarily when I see our men pouring out of the office building. We have security there around the clock, even though we don't use the building often. Other companies do, and it's no secret our family owns the property. They surround the cab as I shove cash at the driver. He's looking around, trying to figure out what the fuck is going on. Six men my size in black suits are facing away from the vehicle as Pauly opens the door for me. I slide out and reach in to help Sinead. The moment the door closes, the men form a tight circle around her. People might see her bare legs among the trouser legs, but other than that, she's invisible.

"Mr. Scotto, Don Salvatore called me. Tony's in the garage waiting for you."

"Thanks, Mario."

Pauly, the six guys, and I crowd into the elevator with Sinead still in the middle. Word travelled fast if Uncle Salvatore's already involved. Luca and Carmine didn't wait around. Mario was the driver who met my parents and me at Laguardia when we arrived in America. He was the first Cosa Nostra man I met in America. Now I can relax. I trust Mario implicitly.

Sinead doesn't. She freezes when the circle opens for her to step into the car. She looks up at me, and I recognize the blank stare from when her panic attack started. I push her into the car a little rougher than I liked, but I follow her in. I yank the door shut myself and pick her up, placing her on my lap. I press the button to drop the glass an inch.

"*Il mio posto.*" My place.

I raise the glass and wrap my arms around Sinead, pulling her against my chest.

"*Piccolina*, you're safe with me now. I'm holding you, and I won't let go until you tell me to. I've known Mario since the day I moved to New York. He was my mama's bodyguard the entire time my parents lived here. He's driven all my aunts and Maria around for years. He won't let anything happen to us, and neither will I."

"Daddy?"

Her voice sounds so tiny and hollow, but at least she's speaking.

"Yes, little one."

"How'd you know?"

"The dome light didn't turn on. It's a feature our vehicles have to detect explosives."

"But Pauly had already driven the car, and we saw no one go near it. I don't understand."

"Someone activated it while we walked to the building. It was set to detonate when the door opened."

"Do you think having your car explode will prove you're not the one blowing things up?"

Chapter Nineteen

Sinead

Gabriele's fingers. *Holeee fuck.* The moment he put his hand on my thigh, I hoped he'd finger me. It didn't prepare me for how good it would feel. The angle was awkward, but he still made me come hard. I kept thinking back to how he ate me out in Lorenzo's office and the sex we had the night before that. When he wouldn't let me come, I thought I would combust. I almost burst into tears. But it wasn't my first-time experiencing orgasm denial. I pulled myself together and enjoyed it. The way we talked during it. Fuck, that was hot. I want more of it.

As we left my office after I gathered my bags, I couldn't help but wonder what was next. An hour car ride each way? There was a lot that could have happened during that time, and I think none of it would have been about trial prep. We got on the elevator, and it was practically perfect when he stopped it and held me close. Then it all went to shit.

I felt the change in him like a wave crashing over me. He's

always vigilant, but he practically pulsed with I don't even know how to explain what. Determination? Confidence? Authority? It made me nervous and calm at the same time. Totally disconcerting. I was nervous because I knew something was up, but I was calm because he was with me. It didn't feel rude when he switched to Italian, but I didn't like not knowing what was happening. But it was the first test as to whether I could handle the secrets he would keep from me. Frustrating as it might have been, I accepted it easily enough.

It was like that wave crashed over me and spun me around like I was in a washing machine when he and Pauly dragged me back from the car then herded me forward. I thought I was flying for a moment, then I landed hard on top of Gabriele. His arms came around me the moment we touched. He tucked my head against him as I felt Pauly land on my back. They both protected me, risking their own lives to do it. There had to be almost four hundred pounds pressing down on him between my weight and Pauly's, but he rose to his feet with ease. To say it blew me away seems grossly inappropriate right now. But it did.

"*Piccolina?*"

"It's all right. I was just thinking."

"Do you want to talk about it?"

I shake my head.

"Later."

As we reach the elevator in the basement garage of his building, he's holding the door open for me. His hand's resting in the air just inches from the small of my back, and it feels so protective. I love it.

"There are cameras in here, *piccolina*. If there weren't, I'd have you against the wall."

"I want that."

We're riding up alone in an elevator that only has a

biometric panel. There's only one destination, his penthouse. Thinking about fucking right now is exactly the distraction I need. Some people might think that's crazy after nearly dying, but it's a relief. Like it confirms we're still alive.

"Elevator sex?"

He cocks an eyebrow as he asks.

"Yes. I've never had it, but I want it. I want it with you."

I clarify that. I've thought it was hot in movies. I've even thought that I'd like to try it. But I've never thought about it with a specific guy. Now it's all I can think about. When we step out of the elevator, his hand returns to my lower back, but now he's adding some pressure to it. It feels possessive and protective. I love that even more.

When we walk into Gabriele's place, I take time to look around. I didn't do that the last time. We were too focused on something else for me to notice anything about it. When I left, it was dark in most of the place. Now I sweep my gaze around the living room. It's the comfiest looking place I've ever seen. Every overstuff armchair and the sofas scream "take a nap on me." The sunshine pours in through pristine windows. There are floor to ceiling bookshelves brimming with books. There's not even enough space for all of them to stand with their spines out. There are some stacked on top of each other or standing in front of the others.

He leads me into the kitchen and opens the fridge, which I can see is overflowing with fruits, vegetables, and freshly sliced deli meat. I don't think there's a single thing in there with a preservative.

He laughs when he sees my face.

"I can cook, Sinead. I don't order out that often. My mom made sure I wouldn't starve when I moved out and went to college."

"But your kitchen is huge for one person."

That thought— or rather one that goes along with it — makes my smile drop.

He pulls me close and kisses me so hard and passionately that my toes curl in my shoes.

"You are the only woman I've ever brought here. I've lived here five years. I haven't been a monk, but no one's been here other than family. I like my sanctuary. I've never lived with a woman other than my mother."

He has a look on his face I can't read. But it's gone a moment later when he lets go of me and grabs a glass from the cabinet. He pulls a carafe of freshly squeezed juice from the fridge and hands me a glass of it.

"I was scared you were about to have another panic attack. You're still really pale. You need some sugar."

I sip, then practically inhale it. It's a blend of orange, pineapple, mango, with a hint of carrots and something else. It's delicious. He pours me another glass, which I down just as fast. When he reaches to pour me a third, I shake my head. While he pours himself one, I rinse my glass, then get ice and water from his fridge door. I sip that at a more graceful rate.

He takes my hand and leads me back into the living room. I take a seat on a sofa as I watch him take off his suit coat. I try not to flinch when he takes off his gun holster. He takes the weapon out, checks it, puts it back in the holster, before setting it on the coffee table. He kicks off his loafers as he rolls up his sleeves. I squeak when he picks me up and takes my place on the sofa. He swings his legs up and arranges me, so I'm draped over him. I kick off my shoes and rest my head on his chest. I don't know how long we stay like that, but we both appreciate the silence.

I can feel he's hard, and I know I'm wet. But neither of us makes a move until we both seem to need something more at the same moment. Before I know it, we're kissing, and he's rolling us, so that I'm lying on the sofa. My hands roam all over him as his hand squeezes my breast. His other hand slides up my thigh and under my skirt. He yanks down my thong. He pulls back and kneels while tugging it off my legs. He flings it behind me, making it land in the fireplace.

"Wear panties again, *piccolina*, and I will light that fireplace and burn them all."

Burn them all? That sounds as though I'd be keeping them here. Maybe it's a figure of speech. He moves to settle his shoulders between my legs, but I put a hand on his shoulder and push.

"You told me the next time we were together, I would decide. After that, you'd be in control. You also said that I had a spanking coming for not answering you when you asked me a question. Is all of that still true? Can they happen today?"

"If that's what you want."

"Daddy, I want to taste you. I want to make you come that way. Then I want you to take over. If that means spanking me, then whatever else you want, fine. If it's the other way around, fine. I don't want to decide right now. I feel too scattered to do more than know I want to give you a blow job and have more incredible sex. I need..."

I'm not exactly sure what I need to be honest.

"You need me to take care of you. You need me to have control because you feel you don't have any. You need one of us to have it, and you know I need it after what happened. You know I feel just as out of control as you do, but we need opposite things right now. We need what the other can give."

"Yes. All of that. Exactly that."

We shift positions, and I get off the couch to let him lie down. Except that isn't what I want. I kneel on the floor.

"Sinead, are you kneeling because you expect me to be a dom while you— you —service me? I can't think of a better term right now. That isn't the right one, but I have some brain fog. Or are you kneeling because you're offering your submission?"

"Yes. I guess it's both. You've gotten me off so many times and not asked for anything in return. You haven't made me feel like you expect anything in return. I want to offer this to you. I want to do this for you."

"Do you want this as a one-off? Or do you want me to be your dom?"

"Once or twice-off. I guess time to time. But I don't want you to be my dom. And I don't want to be your sub. I want more."

I wait to see what he thinks of that.

"Sinead, I'd be your dom if that's what you wanted. But it's not what I want. All I've wanted since the beginning is more."

"Me too."

I whisper as I reach to unfasten his pants. He stands, so I can pull down his pants and boxer briefs. He whips off his socks, then unbuttons his shirt and peels it off as he steps out of his pants and underwear. He sits, and I'm ready to start.

"Uh-uh. Strip. I want to see your tits, play with them while you suck me off. I want to see you play with your pussy."

I grin at him.

"I thought this was supposed to be the way I want it. You can't help but take control."

He looks guilty, and I wish I hadn't said anything. I stand and straddle his legs.

"Daddy, I was joking. I like the idea of you being naked and me being clothed. Somehow, it fits with this moment of submissiveness. And you're so fucking hot. I want to stare at all of you.

Normally, I want anything that allows you to touch me. That's why I'm not saying no."

I drop a quick kiss on his lips before I stand and drop my clothes on the floor, adding to his pile. I kneel again and wrap my hand around his cock. Fuck. Everything about him really is proportionate. I glide my hand up and down three times before I feather my thumb over the tip. I graze my fingertips along his length before I lick the side closest to his belly. I swirl my tongue over the bulbous head before curling my tongue around him as I lick the rest of his cock.

I shift and rise higher on my knees as my mouth sinks down onto him. I put my hands behind my back, crossing my wrists. My head bobs as he brushes his thumb over my cheek and along my jaw. He inches forward to the edge of the sofa, making it easier for me to angle my head and take him deeper. His hands caress my shoulders, neck, and upper chest before he massages my tits. He tweaks the nipples until I moan.

"Play with yourself."

His voice is soft, but it's a command, not a suggestion. My left hand runs along the smooth skin before my middle finger slides along my clit. I'm dripping. I do as he says, and press my fingers into me, coating them before I work my clit in earnest. But I can't concentrate on two things at the same time. I go through the motions and play with myself like he said, but I only want to focus on him.

He's gentle when he pulls my other arm from my back. He brings my hand to cup his balls. When I do, he rests his head back against the couch and closes his eyes. But it's only for a moment. Then he's watching me again. I take him as deep as I can; the tip brushing the back of my throat. I relax, remembering to measure my breathing through my nose, so I don't gag when I take him farther past my uvula and down my throat. I'm not super skilled at this since I haven't been with anyone as long *and* thick as Gabe. I've fucked other guys with his length, but none with his girth. I'm swallowing a fucking Coke bottle. From his groans and the way his dick keeps twitching, I'm doing something right. My fingers find his taint, and I rub it. The moment I do, he pulls free from my mouth.

"Stroke me."

I follow that command too. It takes nothing to have him spray his cum across my lips. He covers my hand with his, directing the rest of it onto my tits. I swallow, then lick my lips. I don't love swallowing in general, but I do with Gabriele.

"Daddy, I'm yours."

I lean forward, pressing my tits around his cock to titty fuck him. He scoops me up, and I wrap my legs around his waist. I marvel at his strength. I'm not light, but I know he can carry the other guys. I don't weigh as much as any of them, so it shouldn't surprise me that he can. It still makes me feel petite. At five-nine, that's not easily done.

He carries me into the bedroom and places me on the bed. When he reaches toward his bedside table, it makes me think of what I keep in mine and how he found it. He reads my mind.

"I remember what you had. I want you to remember that I've never had a woman here. I know I got ahead of myself, but after having you in my bed once, I knew it wouldn't be the last time. I did a little shopping."

I peer into the drawer he opens. Holy fucking shit. It's like a sex shop crammed into a box. I stand up and step beside him. I lean forward, my hands between my thighs to keep from pulling things out.

"You decide this time, *cuore*. Flogger, paddle, or crop?"

"Crop. That one."

I point to the one with the wider leather slapper. I think I heard that end called a popper once. Either way, it's the part that lands on me. He takes it out of the packaging, which he puts on the bedside tabletop. After seeing his place and being in his bedroom, I realize dropping his clothes on the living room floor was out of character for him. Everything looks precisely positioned. It's not for appearances. I think it's for practicality. A place for everything, and everything in its place. It makes the penthouse inviting.

"Nipple clamps?"

"Yes, please."

I point to a metal set that has rubber between the prongs. It's been a while since I've worn a set, so I think I need a little padding.

"What size plug can you take comfortably? I want you to feel full, but not stretched."

I glance up at him. I don't know that anyone has asked that before. It's either been one small enough to not do much for me, or big enough to stretch me for a cock. He's asking me because he wants to get it right and to ensure I enjoy whatever we're about to do. It's not about prepping me to get him off. He is the definition of a generous lover.

I watch him pull out a set of soft cuffs like I have. He also has a collar with a ring like mine. I stick out my left arm, and he wraps a cuff around it, buckling it tight but with enough room for him to stick a finger down it. He repeats the same steps for my other wrist and both ankles. When he stands and grabs the collar, he pauses.

"I will never ask you to crawl. I will never ask you for pet play. I won't yank or drag the leash. If I fasten it, it's to demonstrate control. It's not a leash to me, Sinead. It's more like a handle. If you want those things, tell me. I'll oblige if that's what you want, but I won't initiate it. You aren't my sub or my slave. We're always equals even when it seems like I'm in control."

A lump rises in my throat. That's exactly how I've wanted BDSM, but it's never quite been like that. Even when I've been the dominate one during fluid power exchange, I couldn't get my partners to accept that. I had to be the one to accept that it was always truly about domination and submission. It was fine, and I liked it, but it always left something missing.

I'm not falling for Gabe. I've already fallen. I place my hands on his chest before sliding them around his neck. I stretch to kiss him, and he lowers his head to make it easier. The kiss seems to last forever before we both need to breathe.

"Little one, do you need vanilla first?"

"I do."

I think he does too. He puts the collar aside, and I ease back onto the bed, lying parallel to the pillows. He climbs on and hovers over me. He looks at me before he shifts as though he's going to lie beside me.

"Wait."

He freezes as he watches me.

"I want missionary, Daddy. I know that's boring, but I want to see you on top. I want to see the muscles in your shoulders and your abs. They're a major turn on."

"There's nothing boring about you, about sex with you, or how I feel about you. If missionary is what you want— if it's all you ever want —I will love every moment."

"I definitely don't want only missionary. But I want that for right now."

He positions himself between my thighs and eases into me. He presses in, then pulls back, coating his cock. When he can glide smoothly into me, he thrusts hard. Driving every inch into me as I lift my hips to take him. Fuck. This is amazing.

"Just entering you is enough to make me want to come, *piccolina*. Goddamn, that feels amazing."

"I know."

I'm panting already. My hands roam over his chest and abs as I watch his muscles flex. I've always been drawn to the more muscular types, but not necessarily as cut as Gabriele. His body is a work of art. He's what the Italian Renaissance artists carved out of marble. Fitting.

"Tell me how you want it. Harder? Slower?"

"Both. Thrust hard into me like— like —"

"Like I can't get enough of you and want every bit of you. Like I crave you and want to possess you."

"Yes!"

I scream my answer. He'd punctuated every couple words with a thrust hard enough to push me up the bed. But he was agonizingly slow withdrawing. He's driving me crazy. My fingers are digging into his ass. He's giving me exactly what I want, and all I want is more. I need him to move faster, but I love how he torments me. I don't know what to ask for, so I let him decide. When my eyes drift shut, he alternates his pace. I truly don't know what will happen next, and I love it. I love the surprises.

"Daddy, I'm close. May I come?"

"This is vanilla, *cuore*. Don't ask. Take."

"Ohhh...Yes...God, yes. Gabe!"

My orgasm grips me as it makes my pussy practically vibrate. I Kegel and clench around him, but he keeps thrusting over and over. I relax as the orgasm subsides, but it's only a few heartbeats before I'm rocking my hips again. I keep expecting my second orgasms to be milder than the first, since that's how they've always been in the past. But I should have known. With Gabe, each one gets better. I come again as I moan.

"Louder."

He demands it, and I'm happy not to hold back. I know he has neighbors, but I don't give a shit. Besides, it's the middle of the day. They're probably not home. He'd been leaning forward, resting his weight on his left hand and right forearm. He uses his left hand to draw my leg over his hip. He changes angles, and I cry out again. How's he still going when I've already come three times?

"I need to come, *piccolina*. I can't wait much longer. I'm trying, but my cock's got a mind of its own."

He rears back, grabbing both hips and slams into me. His fingers will leave marks on my ass, and I love knowing that. It heightens my arousal. I can't move on my own anymore. I don't know how his hips flex as fast and hard as they do, but this is still what I consider vanilla but rough. His right hand reaches forward and cups my breast, squeezing. He leans forward again, his right elbow near my head. As he thrusts while he comes, he speaks close to my ear. He doesn't whisper. There's no chance I can miss anything he says.

"You are mine. I want all of you. I have your body. I will get your heart and soul."

I watch him as he speaks, his eyes boring into mine now that he's no longer leaning toward my ear. I fist his hair and push him toward me.

"I will settle for nothing less from you. Leave me before you ever stray, Gabriele. I know I can't have all of you, but I won't accept anything less than all of what you can give me."

He rolls us then sits up, so that I'm straddling him on his lap. His left arm pins me in place around my waist. His left hand squeezes my breast as his thumb brushes my nipple.

"I will never be unfaithful to you, Sinead. Never. It's dishonorable and cruel. If we're not working out, then we end it."

"Same."

Our kiss starts fiercely, but it mellows into something tender. It finishes with little pecks, then we rest our foreheads together.

"Gabe, you're on your way to having all of me. My heart and my soul. It scares me that I'm going to give you all of it, but you'll always hold something back from me."

He kisses my nose before he lifts his head.

"I didn't explain it well because I wasn't sure how. You won't always be my top priority, and I hate knowing that. There are things I do I will never tell you about, but that's the part of me I never want you to see or hear about. It's the part that makes me fear you'll reject me. It's the part of me I loathe exists. But it does because I can never walk away. I can't walk away from my family because I love them, and I'm loyal to them. But I also can't walk away because it would put a target on me that would never go away until I'm in my grave. My family is everything to me. I— I— hope maybe one day..."

I think I know what he means. I hope so, too.

Gabriele's body no longer cooperates with staying inside me, and neither of us likes it. He pulls back the covers, and we slide into bed. But he draws me back onto his lap to straddle him.

"We have some intense conversations. There's a lot we need to talk about after what happened today. Some of it will sound repetitive, but I won't feel at ease if I don't say it again. I need to know I told you everything, and I need to know you heard it."

"I get that. There's stuff I may have forgotten. A lot's happened between my panic attack and a car exploding with us nearly in it."

"Never get into a car without the driver opening the door. Never open your own door unless you are at a house, and the garage door hits the floor. If the dome light doesn't come on or the car doesn't start immediately— like it splutters —get out and run. Don't wait for your driver or guard to open the door. You do what we did today. Get away as far and as fast as you can."

"Is this because I need guarding during the case? Or is that a rule that will always apply?"

"Always. If we're a couple, you'll have a guard at all times. Never do what you did when you went to spy on the Nowakowskis. You won't sit for a week if you do that again. Unless it's to and from work on a regular schedule, you will have someone from my family with you."

"Your family?"

"Yes."

I wait for him to say more, but he doesn't, so I do.

"I can't picture Don Salvatore Mancinelli being my bodyguard."

That gets a chuckle from him.

"No, not Uncle Sal, Uncle Massi, or Uncle Dom. None of them will guard you. I mean Carmine and his cousins."

"Aren't half of them married?"

"Yes. Carmine, Luca, and Matteo are. But Marco and Lorenzo are still single. That doesn't matter. We take turns guarding the women in our family."

"But I'm not family."

He tucks hair behind my ears and shifts me to draw me closer.

"Sinead, the way people in this world decide things differs from the rest of the world. A lot of it is instinct. But a lot of it is taking in a shit ton of information, analyzing and processing it immediately, and deciding, knowing we can't take it back. We've known each other less than a month, but I know what I want. I've thought about it nonstop. I've considered the good, the bad, and the ugly about us being in a relationship. I'm thirty-one-years-old and haven't had a serious girlfriend since high school. I dated a little in college and after, but I always knew it was for their short-term company. It was never going to be serious. You are a different story. I will never force you to stay. The 'if you leave, I'll have to kill you' bullshit is for the movies. You aren't trapped with me. I want you to want to be with me as much as I want to be with you. If that changes, then you walk away whenever you want. But I pray you won't."

"You told me the other night at the club that we'd be monogamous from the start. You didn't just mean sex, did you?"

"No, I did not."

"You really do want me heart, mind, soul, and body."

"I won't share you, Sinead. Ever. If you want someone else, then we end it. You will never share me."

"And if you want someone else?"

He kisses my neck as his hands grip my hips.

"There won't be anyone else. If I haven't found a single woman in thirty-one years that I would let into my life like I have you, I won't find another. I won't look for another."

"You sound as though this is all an absolute."

"It is on my part. I get you aren't there yet."

"How do you know that? I haven't said I'm not."

"You haven't said you are."

"Gabe, you make it sound like you want something beyond just long-term."

"I do."

"Something permanent?"

"Not right this very moment. But that's the direction I want us to go."

I stare at him, then I lean forward and kiss his cheek just in front of his ear before I whisper.

"If that's the case, I'll take my chances with the Bar. I don't want to wait to be in a real relationship with you."

"*Piccolina*, nothing will keep you from me. Not the fucking Bar Association. Not this case. Not whoever is trying to ruin me. Let them try."

His hands grips my bare ass and squeeze.

"No one is taking me from you, Daddy. We belong together."

As I lean back, he grasps my chin and turns my head. His kiss consumes me. He doesn't let go of me, and I don't want him to. It goes on and on, and I can't breathe. But neither do I want to end it. When he releases my chin, I let him know I don't like it. But he flips me around until I'm on my back again. His hand caresses my hip down to the back of my thigh, over to the front and up to my pussy.

"I wasn't joking earlier. Do not wear panties again, Sinead. I will rip them off you and spank you if you do."

My nipples tingle from that command.

"Yes, Daddy."

I believe him too.

"Do you have other rules, Daddy?"

He growls as he scoots down the bed, lying on his belly and drawing my left leg over his shoulder.

"Yes. One. If you put yourself in danger again, Sinead, I will spank you far harder than the last time. I know you're into kink like me, and trust me, we will explore that. But if you risk your safety, I will punish you each and every time. You will not find any pleasure in it."

"But you would."

That makes him pause. He lowers my leg and shifts forward to cup my face with both hands. His thumb sweeps over my cheekbone as he drops the softest kiss to my lips.

"Would it make me hard? Probably. It did last time. Any chance to touch you makes me hard. But will I enjoy punishing you? No. I definitely didn't enjoy it last time. It made me miserable. I don't want to be scared that something's going to happen to you. I don't want to be angry that you let something happen to you. There's nothing pleasurable about fearing I'll lose you."

He's gentler when he moves back down the bed and lifts my leg over his shoulder. He unfastens the cuff on that ankle, then does the same on the other. When he brings his mouth to my pussy, he licks the crease where my leg meets my hip with tantalizing flicks of his tongue. He slides it over my clit, in no hurry, as he twists and turns it. But he keeps it away from his cum, which still fills me. Then he clamps onto it and sucks hard. My hips buck as he worships it. He wants me to know I'm precious to him. I run my fingers through his hair, but I don't press him closer. I know he won't let me, and I don't want him to stop. I want to show him affection, even in my reignited haze of lust. This time when I come, my body feels replete. I could roll over and fall asleep peacefully.

"Gabe, I don't know if it's your skills or something about us, but you get me off like only a vibrator can. I've never been with a man or a woman who can make me come as many times as you do."

"You've been with women? Is that something—"

I cut him off.

"No. I've tried it out to see if I'd be into it. It's okay, but not what I want. I don't regret it, but I don't need or want it again."

I grin and puff out a chuckle.

"That wasn't the part of what I said that you were supposed to focus on."

"That I'm your human vibrator? That part?"

"Yes."

He tickles me, and I squeak my response. He rolls me over so easily, but I never feel manhandled or fear that he'll squish me. He's always so careful, aware of how much bigger he is than me. Never mind that he weighs more than me. He's six inches taller than me, too. I reach down and try to tickle him, but he snags my wrists and pins them over my head before he licks my nipple and sucks. He fiddles around but gets the wrist cuffs off. As I watch him, he seems to relax as he suckles. He must be a tits man more than ass. Then again, he has said he wants to fuck me there. I'll take either or both as long as he keeps taking me.

Chapter Twenty

Gabriele

We've spent all afternoon in bed, and it's been glorious. We both fell asleep, and we both agreed it's the best sleep we've gotten in ages. Better than even before all of this started. We know it's because we were together. When we woke up, we had another round of incredible sex. We made dinner together, and now we're both reading. She loved looking at my library and picking something out. She said we have similar tastes for some genres, and she has read many of them. But she admitted my choices are far more eclectic than hers, pointing to several books she'd never heard of. There are some collector's items and some I'm yet to read. However, I've read most of them. You have plenty of time to read when you don't have a TV and haven't since college.

We're on the sofa together. I have a pair of basketball shorts on, and she has on one of my button downs. I love the look of women in men's shirts when you know they have nothing on underneath.

"Should one of us text Paola to say we're not going over there tonight?"

"Yeah. That's a good idea."

I grab my phone off the coffee table and notice a text I missed.

UNCLE MASSIMO
Call me.

Shit.

UNCLE SALVATORE
Turn your ringer on and answer it.

They're on a thread together, and I wince as I read them.

"Something wrong?"

I have my arm around her shoulders as she leans her head against my chest. I keep stroking her glossy raven's wing hair.

"I missed a couple texts. Could you let Auntie Paola know? I need to speak to my uncles."

She sits up and moves away from me. She figures I need to make this call alone, and I do. I head to my office and shut the door. I dial a three way call and wait for them to answer. When Uncle Massimo answers, I hear Uncle Salvatore in the background. He never answers his phone, but Uncle Massi puts them on speakerphone before he talks.

"What the hell, Gabriele? You nearly get blown up, and you can't bother to call me or Salvatore."

"I'm sorry. My priority was getting Sinead away from there."

Uncle Salvatore's voice gets louder with each word as he snaps at me.

"And in the hours since then?"

He must have stepped closer to the phone. I know his

different tones. This is his scared equals angry tone. It's different from the truly angry one. I feel guilty now.

"I'm sorry. You're right. It was rude not to let you know we're okay. Sinead and I have been talking."

Which isn't untrue. We just haven't talked the entire time. Uncle Massimo harrumphs.

"Talking, huh?"

I don't answer.

"Gabriele."

My dad may live in Sicily now, but Uncle Massimo sounds like him. There's warning in that one word.

"Uncle Massi, we're together."

I sigh.

"Shocker."

I don't really need his sarcasm right now, but I know he feels the same as Uncle Salvatore. His fear for me has settled into anger.

"I know this is shit timing, and there's a lot to lose if we're discovered and she has to step down from representing me. But time won't change how we feel. You can order me to stop seeing her, but that may be the one order I can't obey."

Uncle Salvatore's voice is unbending steel when he speaks up.

"Can't or won't?"

"Both, Uncle Sal."

"What? Two weeks, and you're in love?"

"Don't you always say it took you two minutes to fall in love with Aunt Sylvia? I'd say I'm working at a snail's pace by our family's standards."

"This isn't the time for your sarcasm, Gabriele. We've talked to Pauly. We want to hear what happened from you."

"Sinead and I met in her office conference room. When we

went down to the lobby to head out for lunch, I felt like someone was watching us. I couldn't spot anyone, but I couldn't get rid of the feeling. I looked outside for Luigi, but I didn't see him."

Just before we got dinner, I got a text from Carmine saying Luigi had broken down in Queens. The electrical system malfunctioned, so the tracker wasn't working. It made me wonder if someone tampered with it just like the car bomb.

"I called Carmine to see if he knew what happened. He sent Pauly over. Everything looked fine when he pulled up and met us at the door. We walked to the curb, and I still felt watched, but I still saw nothing. Pauly opened the door, and immediately, we both noticed the light wasn't on. We spun around, both of us protecting Sinead's back. We ran, but the blast knocked us over. I landed on my back to catch Sinead. Pauly landed on top of her. She's unharmed. Physically, at least. She's handling it well today, but it may hit her tomorrow. So, Luigi's really okay?"

It relieved me to get Carmine's text, but I felt guilty for not asking about our man. Salvatore's answer is only partly reassuring.

"Yeah. We don't know why his personal tracker wasn't pinging."

"Do you think he does, but isn't telling?"

"No. it completely surprised him when Afonso showed up. He was underneath the car."

I trust Luigi, but I'm realizing with Sinead's life, I'm far faster to stop trusting someone than I am to start trusting them.

"And I assume no one is claiming this? No chatter at all?"

"None that Carmine or Lorenzo have found. They would have called you by now if they had."

"The Polish have been on our radar. Would they do this because they're feeling a squeeze?"

Uncle Massimo jumps in to answer that question.

"I doubt it. They don't have the means to fight us if we find out they're responsible."

"Does someone else think we're getting too close to discovering them or me getting off?"

"Mmm. I don't think so."

"Is someone pitting two of us against each other?"

"Possibly. Probably. But we still don't know why that lumberyard and construction site were the target. The company that owns it does business with us, but they're not affiliated with any syndicate. Who gained from that? No one. But that wasn't personal. A car bomb is about as personal as it gets."

"Gabe!"

I spin toward the door.

"Gabe!"

I hear Sinead running toward my office. I yank open the door and step into the hallway.

"What's wrong?"

"It's Cohenour. He's dead."

I put the phone back to my ear.

"Did you hear?"

"Yeah."

Uncle Massimo and Uncle Salvatore answer together.

"I gotta go. I'll give you an update if I get one."

Uncle Salvatore ends the call with one word.

"Same."

The line goes dead. I look at Sinead.

"How?"

"Marta called me. His ex-wife found him. Supposedly natural causes, but no one will know until the autopsy."

"Are you sure they're doing one?"

"Yeah. There's no reason to think he'd die. No health concerns or anything."

"Fucking around with the Polish is bad for the health."

Her eyes dart from me to the floor to the wall back to me. Her brow's furrowed as she thinks.

"He dies today despite pleading guilty, and we're nearly blown up not that long after. Was I the target, and you would have been collateral damage? Was this about his case? Or was this about you, and I was collateral damage because of your case? Or was it about both of us and Cohenour?"

"I have no idea."

She looks down at her phone, then up at me.

"One reason NYPD and the feds have nothing on the syndicates is because they can't get any wire taps or pick up anything via cellular. Do you have frequency jammers or something? I don't know what they're called."

"Yes. All our homes do, and we have features added to the cars we share."

"So, if I make some calls, would the NYPD be able to trace it to here? If I turn my location services off, could they still find me here?"

"No."

"I have some calls I want to make. I have questions, but are there any you'd want me to ask? I know people on pretty much every team that could be even remotely connected to you or Cohenour."

"Let's think about it and write them down."

I grab a notepad and a pen before we head back to the living room. We spend the next ten minutes coming up with general questions and ones specific to each cop's assignment. I listen as she makes one call after another, shocked at some cops she knows. Most are clean, but some are on our payroll or another syndicate's. A few are probably working for more than one of us. She knows which are dirty, and she uses that to her advantage. She plants little seeds we hope will grow when they run to tell their bosses or other syndicate heads. Then we'll know who they are.

While she talks, I replay in my mind what we know about the night the site exploded. I think about the men who died who'd worked for me in one of my hardware stores. Who could have gotten to them and convinced them to set the explosives? Did they make those guys think they were doing it on my behalf?

I have more questions than I have answers. I picture the men, how they dressed, any jewelry they wore, the cars they drove. Had anything changed recently? Did they start wearing stuff they hadn't before? Did their stuff get better?

After Sinead makes her last call, I have a question for her.

"Were any cell phones entered into evidence? I don't remember seeing any on the list."

"Not that I know of. I guess the fire incinerated any the men had."

"One guy drove for a rideshare company. I don't know if he worked that night, but I think some record their different customers. I think some have dashcams that look out."

"The police impounded one car, but the other was too close to the explosion and caught fire."

"Was the one that survived a small Honda coupe?"

"Yes. A red two-door."

"That's the one Marcus owned and used for his rideshare. We need to know if there was a dashcam. It might have recorded what happened."

"If anything existed, the prosecution had to hand it over."

"I know. But this is a case about a Cosa Nostra member. I have little faith the NYPD handed over any evidence that might exonerate me. If the camera exists, it must have something on there that clears me."

"But the crime scene investigators would have logged

everything. Even if they didn't want to share it, it would have been in the report. I've read it four times, Gabe. I haven't seen anything out of the ordinary, nothing redacted."

"Call your friend from forensics back. Ask where the two mounts were."

"Okay."

Her brow furrows, but she does what I ask. Well, not ask. Told. But she does it and puts the call on speaker again.

"Hey, Ryan. It's me again. I forgot to ask you something. Where were the two mounts?"

"What mounts?"

"The ones on the dashboard or display?"

We don't know if there's even one. But I figure if she acts like she already knows something, he'll go along.

"One was on the dashboard just above the center of the display. The other was attached next to the steering wheel. Why?"

"You know how anal I get."

She's watching me as she speaks. She smirks at her last comment. I lift my left palm and scratch it with my right. She knows what an itchy palm means. She grins.

"I wonder what kind of camera was on the dashboard."

"From the brand on the holder, it was a higher end one. For some kid who worked in a hardware store, his whip was tricked out. There's no way he wasn't still dealing. You don't get something that nice from working minimum wage at a hardware store. I hate to say it, Sinead, but your client had him doing a lot more than stocking paint."

I take the notepad and scribble a message before pushing it back to her.

"Was all the nice stuff aftermarket?"

There's a pause, then the guy hedges his bets.

"Well, yeah. But that stuff couldn't be cheap."

I scribble another note.

"But the car was a late model, right?"

Another pause.

"No. The car was ten years old."

"Even for an older car, it sounds like the guy took good care of it. Aftermarket parts, good quality dashcam and phone holders, high end camera, and I bet a good stereo system."

"Yeah. Nicer than what I drive."

She shoots me a look. The guy didn't say there was no camera.

"Was it damaged at all?"

"No. Everything in it was fine. The car probably shook from the blast, but it was far enough away that the debris only dented it in a couple places and scratched the paint in several."

"How far was it? I don't remember what the report said off the top of my head."

"About eight meters."

"So that's what, about twenty-six feet?"

"Yeah. Twenty-six and some change."

"And it was undamaged? I thought blast perimeters were like four hundred feet?"

"Not everything within a perimeter gets damaged. That's a safety specification for a particular blast. The perimeters vary. This wasn't a large explosion. It was the resulting fire that did most of the damage. The car got lucky, I guess."

Once again, I jot a note. She needs to press for the camera fast before he gets suspicious.

"I wish I could have seen it."

"You haven't?"

"Not yet. I need to get it from evidence."

Sinead stares at me and shrugs.

"Yeah. I tagged the camera myself. It should have been part of discovery."

"Do you remember what the tag was? It'll make it faster for them to look up."

"No. I've been to too many scenes since then. I can't remember all that."

"Okay. Well, I'll just set aside some time to check for it."

"Good luck."

"Thanks, Ryan. Have a good night."

They hang up, and we both stare at her phone for a minute. She sits back on the couch and wiggles her mouth from side to side, something I've seen her do when she's at ease and thinking. She'd never do it in a professional setting. I think it's sweet that I get to see it. She twists to look at me as she speaks.

"The blast wasn't as big as the prosecution said. The fire chief's report made it sound like it was. There's a camera that's been withheld. I need access to the evidence locker because I have some serious concerns."

Serious concerns is putting it mildly.

"We can't do anything tonight, but you can go tomorrow."

I wish I could go too, but that's out of the question. I'll have to wait for her to tell me.

"I know, but I'm pissed now. I'm pissed on your behalf that you're being sandbagged, and I'm pissed that Tyler has something to do with this. I don't expect him to care enough about me to personally take an interest in being ethical. I'm pissed that he's being a little bitch to whoever is railroading him."

"Slow down. Tyler might be totally innocent. He may have no idea evidence exists that he hasn't seen. Depending on the evidence's chain of custody, it may have disappeared well before they even assigned Tyler to the case."

"True."

"Let's go to bed, *piccolina*. There's nothing more to do tonight."

She gazes up at me when I stand. I offer her my hand, and

she doesn't hesitate. When she's on her feet, I tug her against me. My right hand snakes around her waist and grasps her ass. I squeeze as hard as I dare until I know her limits.

"That crop needs breaking in."

"Yes, Daddy, it does. So do those cuffs."

I wrap her ponytail around my left hand and pull until she's looking at the ceiling.

"What's your safe word, Sinead?"

"Mmm."

I like that she has to think about it.

"How about cabbage? I think it smells revolting while it's cooking."

I grin.

"So, you won't be making it on St. Patrick's Day?"

"Who says I'll be making anything? You're the one with the gourmet kitchen."

We both pause, realizing the implications that we'll still be together next spring. I pull her tighter against me until there is no space.

"My kitchen is your kitchen."

Does she understand what I'm suggesting?

"Daddy, I'm not a very good cook, but I think I could learn anything in— our?"

She tests it, and she almost flinches once she says it.

"Yes, our."

I lower my head, and she presses harder against me. We can't get any closer, but she can let me know she wants what's happening. When our lips meet, I slide my tongue into her mouth. She sucks lightly. I back her against the nearest wall, taking her hands and pinning them over her head with my left one.

"That's right, *piccolina*. Our. We can deny this as long as we want. We can pretend to fool others. But you know, just like

I do, that there's a shit ton more going on between us than amazing fucking."

"There is. Gabe, you've made your confessions to me. Now I'm making mine. Ever since the accident and the shit-storm that blew in from it, I've been very selective about who I let into my life. I haven't had a boyfriend in years because I don't trust easily. I also don't want to lose another person I love. In spite of all Delaney's issues and the way things went down that night, I loved my sister. My dad doesn't know who I am. My mom and sister are dead. Everyone I've loved is gone. But I trusted you as soon as I met you. Maybe not always as much as I should have, but even when my trust wavered in one direction, it remained strong in others. I wasn't working the entire time I was at Paola's. There was a lot of time to think. I know how fast a situation can change and how close to death you can come. I know what it feels like to truly believe you're going to die. To fear it. To accept it. To fight it. You told me if you hadn't found any other woman you wanted to let into your life in thirty-one years, then you prob-ably won't find another. It's the same for me. I've gone on dates, and I've fucked. But this— you and me —this isn't anything like my past. I refuse to think about a future that isn't you."

"I made love to you earlier, Sinead. I'm going to fuck you now. For appearances' sake, we won't let the world know yet. But that is your bed now. Once this case is over, I expect you in it every night. Can you live with that?"

"I can move in tomorrow. Can we fuck now?"

I think I growl. I definitely pounce. I pin her against the wall, my body pressing hers. I'm careful not to take it too far, but she would have to push me or safe word to get free. Her kiss is frantic as she spreads her feet enough for me to slide my leg between hers. She rocks against it, grinding her pussy, needing to get off. When we break our kiss to breathe, I ease some of the pressure I'm putting on her.

"No."

She snaps the one word. I raise an eyebrow, unsure what she means. I lean back more, worried I'm hurting her.

"No. Don't move away. Keep me here."

"You like being pinned to the wall? No way to escape whatever I want to do to you?"

"Only because it's you, but yes. It's— it's something I didn't know I wanted. Some fantasy I didn't know I have."

I spin her around, pressing her wrists together against her lower back. She turns her head, so her right cheek rests against the wall. Her eyes are closed, and she looks relaxed. I use my free hand to push down, then kick off my basketball shorts before lifting my shirt she's wearing. I pull her hips back enough to impale her. Then I trap her against the wall once again.

"Is this what you want, *piccolina*? You want me to take?"

"Yes."

"What's your safe word?"

"Cabbage, Daddy."

I sense she not only wants it rough, but she wants me demanding. She just told me everyone she loves is gone. They've left her in one way or another. Her fantasy is about someone wanting her enough to not let go. To refuse to be apart from her. To insist they be together. My sweet *piccolina* has been on her own a long time. I've always had my family to keep me company and to protect me. She hasn't had that in at least ten years.

I thrust into her over and over. I watch to make sure this doesn't go from erotic to harmful. That I can't stomach. I release her wrists and move them to beside her head, my hands covering hers.

"You are mine, Sinead. I might have control of your body right now, but you also know I'm shielding you from anything or anyone who could come near us. You know you're safe with me."

"I know. That's the only reason I can do this. It feels so good to have your cock in me, fucking me. But it feels good to let you have control. And I do feel protected by you being behind me. I feel small, and you feel big enough to shield me from all the shit in my life."

I keep fucking her as I kiss her shoulder and along her neck. Her moans make my cock twitch, and I'm getting close to coming. I pull out, and she screams. I spin her around just as easily as I did before. I heft her over my shoulder and carry her into our bedroom.

Chapter Twenty-One

Sinead

I don't know what it is about Gabriele. What makes one person the perfect match for another? What I told him is the truth. I don't trust easily. I haven't wanted to let anyone into my life. I have a small group of friends, and I'm fine if I don't have any more. I can see how I could let Gabriele subsume me, but I don't think he wants that. I think he wants me to be separate and independent from him. I think he wants me to know I'm safe to do that. That he'll be here no matter what.

When he had me against the wall, it released something in me. It was the same as having him chase me. I knew that would make him angry, and a fucked-up part of me wanted that. I've had no one care enough about me to get angry about anything I do. Marta's probably the closest as far as someone older than me, and Andrea is my closest friend. But neither of them would demand I stay safe. Neither would make me relent and hand over control to them. I like it when I can do that with Gabriele.

Because as fierce as he is, as strong and imposing as he can be, I have never felt calmer than when I'm with him.

He does horrible things to horrible people. He's violent for a living, and his lifestyle only promotes it. His family business is to hurt people among other things. I can tell he's good at what he does. His command of every situation tells me that. When he was angry with me in that restroom, when he had me pinned against the wall a moment ago, as he carries me into what's now *our* bedroom, there's a gentle man beneath the surface.

The one who wants to be tender with me and take care of me. The one who wants to make me happy. No one would ever guess it— at least no one outside his family —but I think he's a gentle giant. He certainly proved he can be while I was in the hospital. But I think that's his true nature. He said if he didn't have to carry a gun, he wouldn't even own one. He's a man of many contradictions, but he's been unwavering in his feelings for me.

"*Piccolina*, lie on the bed and don't move. Face down."

He lowers me to my feet, pulls the shirt over my head, and I can't get on the bed fast enough. I rest my right cheek on the pillow, looking away from him. I don't want to know what's happening until it does. He's quick as he puts the cuffs back on me. He wraps his hands around my waist and lifts me straight up until he kneels on the edge and can put me in the center of the bed.

I hear a bar extending and know he must have a spreader. He connects it to my wrists before I hear a snap. He tugs on the bar, but my arms go nowhere. He's fastened it to the headboard. He moves around, and I hear another bar being pulled apart. My arms are at a comfortable resting width, but he spreads my legs as wide as the bar can go before he fastens it to the footboard.

"I know I told you I owed you a spanking for not answering

my question. I don't even remember what the question was. We wiped the slate clean. I want to be your boyfriend, Sinead. And I want to be more than that one day soon. Is that what you want?"

I turn my head to look at him.

"Yes. Were you serious about the kitchen being ours? That this bed is ours?"

"Yes. If you're not ready to move in after only a couple weeks, I get that. I won't pressure you. Most people would think I was insanely possessive to ask it. And I don't think I really did. I think I commanded it. But that's what I want."

"I wasn't exaggerating when I said I would move in tomorrow. I know I can't yet. But I'm even more determined than ever to get your case dismissed or to fucking ruin Tyler when I get you off."

I look at his cock and lick my lips.

"I'm going to get you off, Gabe."

He strokes himself and steps closer, his cock rubbing against my lips. I open to him as my eyes drift closed. I'm unprepared for the crop to land on my right ass cheek. I squeal. It's a good thing he wasn't in my mouth, or I might have Lorena Bobbitted him with my teeth. The crop lands again, and I want to kick my feet, but I can't move them at all.

"This is for pleasure, *piccolina*. Our pleasure. If it's too much or you don't like it, say your safe word."

"Yes, Daddy."

I won't though.

He grasps my hair and leans close to my face.

"You don't have to say what you're thinking for me to hear it. If you're in pain for real, if I harm you, and you don't tell me, we will only have a vanilla relationship. Do you understand, Sinead? If I hurt you, I won't trust either of us to be like this."

"Time out, Gabe."

He lets go of my hair and reaches to unfasten my wrist.

"No. Don't take those off. Just hear me out for a moment. Can you squat or lean forward, so I can see you?"

He squats, and I can't help my eyes going back to his cock. It's magnificent.

"Sinead."

His gravelly voice. The warning.

"I know I won't safe word because I know you'll never let it get to where I need to. I know you fear hurting me. I don't want that to diminish the pleasure you can get from being with me like this. But I know you'll be vigilant. You'll always be aware of your strength. You'll always read me and know what I can and can't take. If you realize you're pushing me too much, I know you'll adjust. I won't safe word because I'll never have to."

All of that is true. I've had to use safe words before because I've had partners who were experienced and good doms, but they just couldn't read me the way I know Gabriele can. I close my eyes and sigh. I'm ready for more. His massive hand grips my ass cheek and squeezes before feathering over the skin. He starts a pattern of right cheek, left cheek, double right, double left. My fingers and toes curl. It hurts like a motherfucker, but I love it.

"Fuck!"

He lands the crop against my pussy. It burns. He moves his pattern to the inside of my thighs, but between the double slaps, he nails my cunt. My instinct to get away rocks me forward, rubbing my clit into the mattress. I know he knows what he's doing to me. Sweat breaks out along my forehead, and I'm panting. I kick my legs when he leans down and bites my right ass cheek. It's not like a fucking vampire, but my skin is already tender. He nips at it, his tongue flicking the spot to soothe it.

I feel him pushing my legs together, shortening the spreader. Then he climbs onto the bed behind me. He pulls me up onto my knees. Just when I think we've moved onto something else, he brings the crop down on my left ass cheek. He wraps his right arm around my waist as he nuzzles my pussy. I'm focused on his tongue swiping my pussy, so I don't hear the crop whizz through the air. When I jerk forward, his arm pulls me back, pressing my cunt to his mouth. His tongue enters me, and I moan. He switches arms while his tongue continues to tantalize and torment me. He lands the crop again and again, but these swats are much lighter than before. They don't hurt at all.

Instead, he leaves me aching with need when he pulls back. He spreads my ass cheeks, but nothing more happens. I wait. And I wait some more. Just when I'm about to shift to try to look back at him, I realize he's doing this on purpose. I don't even know if he's looking at my asshole, but he's making me curious. And he's making me worry about what's coming next.

That's why I'm unprepared for him to thrust into my pussy. He's rougher than he was against the wall or earlier. He reaches around me, and I feel something clip onto my nipple. I hadn't realized he'd brought the clamps with him when he got on the bed. He fastens them to me, and I whimper. There are so many sensations whirling through me I don't know how to separate them.

"How are you doing, *piccolina?*"

He's breathless, so I know he's exerting himself. But his tone is different from anything I've heard before. This isn't just another fuck in a long line of fucking. When I don't answer right away, I hear him mumble.

"Shit."

He's reaching over me, but I shake my head.

"I had to catch my breath for a second. Don't release me

311

unless it's to do something more. I'm all right, Daddy. Keep going."

He still releases the cuffs, the bar staying attached to the headboard. If it weren't in the way of the pillows, I'd tell him to keep it there. He's quick to twist and release each foot. He's still buried inside of me. His body and arms are so long that he can do all of this without pulling out. He helps me to kneel before he pulls me back against his body. It's like reverse cowgirl, but we're both kneeling. I don't know what this one is called, but he urges me to ride him as he tugs on the chain between the clamps. He's kissing my shoulder and neck again, and it all feels so good. When he rubs my clit, it moves to divine.

"May I come, Daddy?"

"Yes, *piccolina*. I can't hold on much more. I'm going to fill you with my cum until it's dripping down your thighs. Every drop will remind you that you are mine, and that we are in our bedroom, on our bed, with me inside my girlfriend."

I move faster, more urgently while one hand rests on my belly, and the other rubs my clit until I can't take it anymore. My orgasm washes over me, and I moan.

"Fuck me harder, Gabe. Hard."

And he does. His hands grip my hips as he surges into me as I bounce on his cock. He clutches my hair and pulls my head back as he comes.

"One day, Sinead, when you decide the time is right, I'm going to fuck a baby into you."

Holy hell. If any other man ever said that to me, I'd be running for the hills. It's the most possessive and domineering thing I've ever had said to me. His tone is unwavering, but the moment the words come out of his mouth, his kisses along my neck and jaw are tender. He's easing the nipple clamps off, and his hold around my waist is loose. When he tosses them aside, I pull his arms around me, and I lean forward. He follows me, pressing me into the mattress. But he's more lying on his side than on me. He knows I'm tender, and he knows it's different having all his weight pressing my belly into the mattress than my back.

"*Piccolina?*"

I hear the uncertainty.

"You're perfect, Daddy."

I sigh with a bone deep contentment that I don't think I've ever felt.

"What I just said, I..."

I want for him to continue, but he doesn't. I look over my shoulder at him.

"I liked what you said. Whether you fuck me or it's something gentler, I've already thought about having a family with you. I want that to happen. And it'll be when *we* decide the time is right."

He remains quiet, but he doesn't loosen his hold on me. He keeps kissing the back of my shoulder as I stroke the arm he has wrapped around my belly.

"Gabe?"

"I'm moving things too fast. I meant what I said, and I'm glad you like it too, but I shouldn't have said it."

"What?"

I push his arms away and roll over. I want to see him.

"We haven't been together long enough to be talking about moving in and having children."

"Who says we haven't been? Where are the rules, Gabriele? Show them to me."

My voice is demanding, and it surprises me. It hits me like a train that I don't want him to retract anything. I try to take the edge out of it.

"We've explained to each other why we make decisions the way we do. We've talked about why we like things between us the way they are. We're both risking a shit ton. If we didn't both want this to move to something permanent, we wouldn't be together in *our* bed. This is mine now too, Gabe. Unless you want things to end altogether, we aren't moving backwards."

"But—"

"Gabe, do you want to slow down? Do you need more time?"

"No. But you—"

"Don't put words into my mouth or my mind."

I'm faster than he expects. I shove hard, pushing him onto his back. The moment he starts to roll, I grab his wrist with one hand and cuff him with the other. He stares up at me as I straddle him. I have not a moment's doubt that he could stop me in a second. Bat me away like an annoying fly. Pin me down like a pro wrestler. But he indulges me.

I get both wrists fastened, knowing that with his strength, he could rip the headboard apart if he tried. He's remaining where he is because he wants to. I think he's simply curious. I reach behind me and wrap my hand around his cock. I stroke him as he watches me. I slide him between my ass cheeks as my wet pussy glides over his pelvis. I lean forward, my right hand beside his head as my left hand continues to work him. Thank heavens for being tall.

"I'm done talking about whether we are or aren't. Let me make it clear to you, Gabriele. I understand your fears, and I've seen enough danger when I'm with you to believe every one of them. I understand your worries that we're moving faster than I can keep up. I think you also worry people won't approve of us, approve of you. I hope they approve of me. Unless you tell me we're done and you don't want me here, we're not going to keep going around in circles. Share with me how you feel about things. Don't hide what you don't have to. But I want us more than I've ever wanted anything."

I lift my hips and slide down onto him. He groans as his hips thrust up. I set the pace as I ride him, and I'm relentless just like he's been when he's in control.

"Fuck, Gabe. You're so deep."

I've been on top before, and I love it as much as I love missionary.

"Come soon, Sinead. I won't last."

"Then don't. I don't care if I don't come in time. I want you to."

I rock against him the way we both like it, no longer bouncing on him like a fucking pogo stick.

"Ah! Yes!"

My fingers dig into his chest as I come. He tugs against the restraints, but he can do nothing as I ride out the last of my orgasm. I don't think he came, so I keep moving. But he sighs, and his body goes lax. I wrap myself around him and curl tight over his chest, my head resting on his shoulder. I reach up, feeling around until I can release his left wrist, then his right. I've just pulled my arms down to curl up even more when he roars and flips us. His hand grabs my right leg and pulls it over his hip. He slams into me. I realize he lulled me into complacency, and now he's back to being in charge.

"Daddy, fuck me as hard as you can."

He happily obliges with a smile that's pure sin. I will be sore in the morning, and I want that so much. I want every step I take to remind me he's claiming me just like I claimed him. He leans forward, his breath warm against my ear.

"You made your point, *piccolina*. You had your fun being in control. You needed it just like I needed to listen to you. But do not doubt for a moment that when we fuck, I decide."

"Yes, Daddy. Holy hell, Gabe. You're so fucking hot when you say shit like that. I'll do anything."

And I would. I'd be Bonnie to his Clyde. I'd be Cleopatra

to his Mark Anthony or Caesar or both. Whoever the fuck he'd want. I'll be his to command during sex because I know he listens to me as an equal when we're not fucking. And even when he commands me, I still feel like we're sharing what we do in equal parts. He knows what I need, and he gives it to me. I'm doing my damnedest to do the same.

"Did you enjoy seeing me at your mercy?"

His grin is wolfish to the nth degree.

"Yes. But I knew the entire time that you could get loose if you wanted. You might have pulled the bed apart, but you could get free. You chose to submit, and I appreciate it. But that contained strength is super-hot to me, too."

We move together until I feel another orgasm building. He thrusts over and over until we cling to each other. Waves of emotion crash over me as big and as strong as the ones during Hawaiian surf competitions. I wrap my legs over his and my arms tighten their hold. I'm coming down hard from the endorphin rush, and it's leaving me depleted and raw. Gabriele reaches over to where he laid a moment ago and pulls the covers down. He rolls us again, and I'm back to clinging to him like a koala. He draws the covers over us, then he strokes my back.

"Sinead, I'm here, little one."

I nod. I release a shuddering sigh. I know why I feel like this. Because something I've never felt before envelops me. It's so intense that it could be scary if it didn't feel so right. I know I fell into lust at first sight with Gabriele. I know I've been infatuated with him since the very beginning. But what's happening today isn't false intimacy. I've never felt like anyone knows me as well as Gabriele does. He understands me like no other romantic partner has. For sure, no other sexual partner has. Not even my closest friends or my family when I still had them.

I've been in love twice before. Those emotions were similar

enough each time for me to recognize the second time was the same as the first, and it confirmed the first was love. But this is different. This is everything the first two times had, but so much more. Those relationships ended because love wasn't enough to overcome our differences. With Gabriele, I love him as much for our differences as I do how much alike we are.

"Sinead?"

"Yeah?"

"Don't leave like you did last time."

I lift my head. There's such vulnerability in his voice.

"I didn't want to go last time. I felt obligated. I have no reason to leave this time. I only have a cornucopia of reasons to stay."

I grin at him as I stretch to kiss him. I settle back against him and close my eyes.

"Cornucopia, huh? Are you giving thanks for having me?"

I giggle.

"I think we had each other."

"That we did, little one. Sleep in my arms. I'm not ready to let you go."

"The only place I'll go will be beside you."

When I lift my head again, we both know that was a metaphor. We're where we both belong. Heaven help the world if anyone disagrees. I'll burn it all down around them.

Chapter Twenty-Two

Gabriele

Sinead shocked the shit out of me when she rolled me over. The moment she did, I knew what she was going to do. I just didn't expect it. I let her restrain me because I was curious. She was right. I could have gotten free if I wanted. It would have involved me destroying the headboard, but it wouldn't have taken my full strength, even though the furniture is sturdy and solid wood.

I didn't mind being restrained as much as I thought I would. When someone's strung me up with my hands over my head in the past, it wasn't for such pleasurable pursuits as having sex with my girlfriend. It was so someone could torture me. It's happened more than once, and none of those times bring pleasant memories.

But Sinead. Having her cuff me and being at her mercy was hot. Watching her stroke me and rub her clit against me made me stiff as iron within seconds. I agree with everything she said, and she was right. Her tone was so emphatic while pragmatic.

Who knew that would be one of the greatest turn-ons I've ever experienced? I didn't feel weak or vulnerable. Just the opposite. The way she looked at me— like she wanted to devour me — fuck me into next week —keep me until her last breath. I couldn't get enough.

So, I was happy to stay right where I was. But I also laid in wait. The moment she released me, I seized control back. I knew she'd like that as much as we both enjoyed having her dominate me, albeit temporarily. It might happen again before I die, but it won't happen often. We indulged each other, and it gave us both what we needed.

I know I've been in lust with her since the beginning. I think falling in love with her was easy. We're past that now, though. I feel like she knows me better than anyone. Even better than Carmine. She gets me in a way he never could through no fault of his own. It's just different. I'm certain Carmine feels that way about Serafina. I didn't plan to tell her I want her to move in already.

I've thought about it, but it just sorta came out. I don't regret it at all. I'm glad I said it. I hate where she lives for one thing. But I hate the idea of either of us going home at night and not being together. When we go home, I want it to be to the same place. I'd even move into hers if it was really important to her.

I'd like to spend the morning daydreaming about this, but I can't. I'm at the garage again. We pulled in a low level Polish mobster because we caught him cheating at an underground card game last week. It was before Cohenour flipped out, changed his plea, then died the same day. We pushed the guy to get more information about how his bosses were involved with Cohenour. Now we're going to get that info and make sure no one knows he squealed. I pick up a set of pliers before approaching him.

"We didn't beat the shit out of you for cheating because you were going to spy for us. Now you're holding out. Maybe pulling out some teeth will give you more room to loosen your tongue. Speak."

I step in front of him and snap them open and closed four times. The last time, I jerk them forward, and he tries to get away. The problem is, he's strung up like a side of beef. We have hooks in the garage door chains that allow us to dangle people when the doors open and close. They must feel like their arms are about to be ripped off through their skin. No one can hear them scream over the sound of the metal doors. And even if someone could, the people in the neighborhood know which side their bread is buttered on. It's an old *Cosa Nostra* one. People stay quiet, and those same people stay alive.

"Jacek is pissed and won't leave Bartlomiej alone about that fucker Cohenour saying two of us were discussing the shit you did."

"Allegedly did."

I correct him because I'm pretty certain he knows who really did it.

"He wants Bartlomiej to get rid of anyone who could implicate them because Cohenour lied. The re—"

I raise the pliers to his face, knowing what he was about to say. I swear like a fucking sailor, but there are certain words I don't tolerate.

"The asshole was probably getting paid to say it was us, anyway."

Now there's two things to weed through.

"Get rid of anyone who could implicate them. Does that mean Ms. O'Malley?"

He won't look at me, so I answer for him.

"Your silence tells me that's a yes. Was the car bomb for both of us?"

I snap the pliers around his nipple and twist. I watch as the skin breaks, but I ignore his howls. I stop before I cause so much pain he can't concentrate on his story.

"Yes. They didn't want Ms. O'Malley to push for the police to investigate Cohenour's claims. That's why they showed up in court. Not only to intimidate Cohenour but to scare Ms. O'Malley, too. When she didn't flinch, they got pissed. They flat out don't like you. Since it was obvious you'd meet after court let out since Cohenour's plea affects your case, they figured they needed to move fast."

"Did they make one of our cars break down?"

"Yeah, but I don't know how. I know they set a bomb and watched you, but I don't know who actually did the leg work for that."

"Did they kill Cohenour?"

"Yes. They sent someone to give him a shot of adrenaline or something like that to give him a heart attack. To make it look like natural causes. They faked a break in to make it plausible. Like he died of fear or shock."

That seems weak, but it worked for them. Motherfuckers.

I frown as I consider what I'm learning. I need to make sure I'm on the right track, so I use my next opportunity to speak to check.

"Their only involvement is because Cohenour made up a story that involved them."

"Sorta."

"What the fuck does sorta mean?"

"It means that none of their men were involved until after the fact. None of us knew anything about what was going on until we saw it on the news. I was there when Bartlomiej and Jacek supposedly found out about what Cohenour was doing. They didn't seem shocked enough to me. You were already forcing me to spy. I didn't want to. I figured I'd get back at them by hiding in the ladies' room at their favorite restaurant and listening to them through the wall."

Not a well-kept secret from anyone but the brothers, apparently.

"What'd you hear?"

"They hired those two kids who worked for you."

"Hired?"

"Maybe not hired. Both guys had sisters. The Nowakowskis threatened to take the women and rape them."

I don't want to know whether they are capable of that, but I wouldn't put it past at least Jacek.

"They had photos of the women. Those guys were barely more than kids. I know they'd already done time, but they were like twenty or something. They didn't know shit. They obviously didn't know to go to you. They'd be alive if they had."

I've thought that dozens of times.

"Keep going. What else?"

"They don't like you, but it wasn't their idea to blow up the lumberyard and construction site. Someone else pressured them into it, but I don't know who. As far as I know, that place doesn't belong to anyone in our world."

"They don't. They belong to someone who buys lumber from for my stores. The buildings were full of wood. It's why the fires swept through so fast."

"Look, all I know is that they're involved. I don't know why, but I know they don't like you and want to see you go down. Whoever hates you more knew they could get the brothers to do their dirty work. When they didn't want to dirty their hands or risk one of us getting scooped up, they hired those two kids. I don't know who started this. I don't know why they did. And I don't know how it will end. It definitely didn't with Cohenour's death since they tried to blow you up an hour later."

I release the pliers from his nipple. I step back to think.

Someone hired Jacek and Bartlomiej to blow up a site I don't own but do business with the owner. They— or whoever hired them —set it up to look like I somehow did it or ordered it. Having Cohenour come up with a story that slipped a little too close to the truth meant he had to go. They don't want Sinead to disclose any information about her client. They resent me for obeying Uncle Salvatore's orders to maintain control over them.

What I need to discover is who hired the Nowakowskis. I also need to know who helped those young ex-cons get into the lumberyard. They went away for possession charges. Unless they learned it from video games, they wouldn't know how to set those explosives. In fact, they didn't. They triggered the alarm before they failed to set the bomb. Their failure got them trapped inside. But who wanted them in there? My guess is Jacek rigged the explosives to go off while the guys were in there, so there were no co-conspirators to testify against him. He's the one who probably did the car bomb that nearly killed Sinead, Pauly, and me. Jacek served in the U.S. military in Explosive Ordinance Disposal.

His parents came here from Poland before he was born. His uncle was their mob boss, and his cousin would have taken over. Both were killed in a skirmish with the Albanians. Bartlomiej was the next in line. He's been the most reasonable leader they've had in a few decades, but he can't control his brother. Apparently, Jacek came home a different man after too many war zone deployments. It would be sad if the fucker wasn't trying to kill Sinead and me.

We need the dashcam to see who was there that night. I have an alibi since I was guarding Serafina. But the DA claims I organized it. If there's anyone from another syndicate there, and the camera caught it, that'll be the first step in poking holes in the prosecution's arguments. We really need to discover who hired Jacek and Bartlomiej.

"Who's been threatening the Nowakowskis lately?"

"No one that I know of."

I believe him, which means he's outlived his usefulness. I pull a knife from my pocket and flick open the blade. I position myself out of the spray zone and slit his throat. Nothing fancy or drawn out. I need to get cleaned up and meet Sinead. She should be done with the police department soon.

I signal a couple guys to dispose of him while I go into our office and strip. I put all my clothes in a metal barrel. When I'm done cleaning up, I'll push it outside the back door. Luigi's here today. He'll burn the evidence I was here. I hop in one of three showers we installed. I lather up and scrub everything from head to toe. I'm quick, but I'm thorough. I've had plenty of practice.

It's not long before I'm dressed again. I purposely picked something to wear this morning that I knew I had a duplicate of here. It's a good thing we're rich because we go through custom-tailored suits at a ridiculous rate. Our tailor is Cosa Nostra, so he asks no questions. We bring him more business than he can handle, so he stays quiet. What we don't slip him under the table is laundered so many times you could eat dinner off the cash. It paid for his kids to go to college debt free without catching the IRS's attention.

I drove myself today, so I head out to where we park. It's tucked away in a separate, smaller garage. I like the SUV I drive. It's large, which suits me. I can't imagine trying to drive a Smart car. I'd look like a Great Dane that needs to stick its head out the window to fit. I pull out of the smaller garage and check everywhere.

We have security cameras in the main garage, so we'd know if anyone was within a mile of here. But it still pays to be cautious. I'm meeting Sinead in the Bronx. She lives— lived — on Staten Island. I live in Manhattan. My family is in Queens.

It's Brooklyn or the Bronx to avoid anywhere obvious. I don't think anyone would believe I'd arrange a meeting in the Bronx, so it's perfect. I make sure I'm early because I don't want Sinead waiting for me.

I took her by her place this morning, so she could get fresh clothes and her car. She's driving to meet me. I'm always worried someone might follow me and might photograph me. Unless they're using a drone, they won't be able to get close enough for clear photos where I'm meeting her. And it's cloudy today, so a drone would have to fly low enough for me to see it while it tried to see me. I wait in the car until I see her pull into the vacant parking lot. She pulls up next to me, our cars facing opposite directions.

"I think someone followed me, Gabe."

I'm not happy to hear that as her greeting.

"It wasn't Giuseppe?"

I look around and spot her guard. He's blocking one entrance, but the other is open. I watch a car pull in, and I recognize it immediately.

"What the fuck?"

"Gabe?"

"It's all right. Stay in the car."

"Ga—"

"Sinead, stay in the car."

My tone tells her not to argue as I get out. I draw my gun, not taking my eyes off the new arrival.

"Roll up your window. Do not get out no matter what. If anything happens, leave. Don't be a hero. Don't try to avenge me. Leave."

"Yes, Daddy."

I don't love hearing her voice so vulnerable, but she has to listen to me. I walk around my car until I stand where the other one is pulling up. It surprises me when the engine turns off. I definitely didn't turn off mine. Cormac O'Rourke climbs out.

"Put your gun away, Gabe. I come in peace."

"Why'd you follow Sinead?"

"Put your gun away, and I'll tell you."

"Fucking tell me, then I'll put it away, Cormac. Speak."

I raise the gun to point at him from beside my thigh.

"Calm the feck down. I came to talk to you about O'Toole."

I want to roll my eyes. They have no accent whatsoever except for the word fuck. So *fecking* stupid.

"Is he dead?"

"No, but we all wish he were."

"I'll make all our wishes come true if you can't do it."

"He works for a fucking newspaper, Gabe. He prints a shitty story about you and Sinead, then within days, he's gone? That's perfect for the headlines."

"He's your family. Deal with him."

"We are. But he's causing trouble."

"For who? Sinead?"

"Yeah. He's got an informant in the NYPD. He knows she went to see evidence from your case. He knows she was asking about a camera. He plans to leak details in upcoming articles."

"How do you know all this? Following him?"

"Actually, yeah. After what he did to Sinead, we decided he needs an extra shadow. We haven't had to do anything yet, but if he prints something else about her, we will."

"Why?"

"What do you mean why?"

"Why wait? Why get involved?"

"We're waiting so we don't draw unnecessary attention. Did you not get the part where I told you him going missing would be bad timing? As for getting involved, we all remember Sinead from when we were kids. She was my first crush to be honest. I think she was Sean's, too. She was sweet back then. But she's had a shit hand dealt to her. Her sister was a bitch even back then. But her parents were cool. She's kept her distance since we were teenagers, but Duffy's pissed she's representing you. Dillan's told him to lay off. If it doesn't bother him or the rest of us, then Duffy needs to back down. But he isn't. Dillan's ready to rip him a new one for some things he said."

"Did he threaten Sinead?"

"Yes."

I didn't expect him to be that blunt. It must be bad. He wants me to know he isn't exaggerating when he says Dillan's pissed. The man has patience a mile long, a mile wide, and a mile deep. He's a fucking strategist who could win world chess championships if he played. He's never rash. It's why he's survived as long as he has. He pulled Donovan's and Declan's strings for years. It was only when they each did what they wanted and didn't listen to him that everything went to shit, and they both wound up dead.

"What's Dillan doing about it?"

"That's private family business."

"Then why even come here?"

"To reassure you we know what he's up to. We're handling it. It doesn't thrill us that Sinead's with you. Oh, feck off, Gabe. Don't look at me like that. You think we haven't been paying attention? The moment we found out a childhood friend with strong family ties to ours was representing you, we got curious fast."

I step forward, raising my gun.

"Did you bug her place? Was it really you?"

"No. Put that fecking thing down. You can't kill me if for no other reason than you don't want your girlfriend to see you murder someone."

"Girlfriend?"

"For feck's sake. You're meeting her in the Bronx. You don't want anyone to know or guess you're here together. You would have met at her office or Mancinelli Developers if you only cared about her professionally. You'd have more control of the location. You want no one knowing you're meeting. You're protecting her. I only knew to follow her because Duffy was whining to Dillan about her going to the evidence department. I followed her from there."

I need to speak to Giuseppe about why Cormac made it all the way here. He should have noticed. He should have called me. He should have called Sinead and told her to go somewhere else.

"Chill out. Don't kill the guy. I arranged for a semi to be in the way, so he couldn't see me."

"You went to a lot of trouble to stalk her."

"It's not fecking stalking. Shut the feck up, you ass."

"Who's the informant?"

That's what I really need to know. I shouldn't have let us get distracted.

"We don't know. That's the problem, and why I came to see you. Sinead has to stay away from the police. She can't keep making calls to suss out shit. People are talking, and you know they're going to bleed blue before a single one of those motherfeckers is going to do shit to help you."

That's what I feared. Hopefully, Sinead found something, so she doesn't have to keep digging. I'm going to get Lorenzo to hack whatever the fuck needs hacking to keep her out of it.

"Thanks for the heads up."

I can try to be gracious.

"You love her already, don't you?"

I stare at him. I am not discussing my feelings about Sinead with Cormac O'Rourke.

"You don't scare me, Gabe. You haven't since the day I met you. You may be bigger than anyone but Sergei, but I remember before we all became what we are now. Back when we were just kids."

Sergei Andreyev is the bratva leader's cousin and head of their intelligence gathering. The Russians have an official position for that, whereas Carmine just wound up as ours. Sergei's what most people would consider a meathead. We have that in common. No one ever believes either of us have Ivy League educations.

"You were a nice guy for way longer than the rest of us. We all come from a fecked-up life and live in a fecked-up world. None of us like Sinead being involved in this, but she was long before she met you. She's kept her distance, but if it hadn't been your case, it could have been another. If it were anyone besides you— another Mancinelli, a Diaz, or anyone else —we'd step in. We'd keep her from the guy one way or another. But we trust you with our childhood friend. Disappoint us, and your little stay in Napoli really will look like a vacay under the Tuscan sun."

"You need to learn geography."

"Deflect all you want. Protect her and make her happy. Fail, and we will kill you."

"Do the same. Keep Duffy away from her and out of her life. Fail, and I will destroy everything, then I'll kill all of you. Slowly."

He has the audacity to grin.

"We know. That's why we trust you with her."

"Are you going to find out Duffy's informant? Watch out. Stand in Duffy's way, and he's likely to turn on you and use that informant against you."

"We know. We're working on it. If we find out, we'll let you know."

I stare at him again, and he grins even wider.

"Don't worry, Gabe. We don't expect you to reciprocate the favor. She still has a lot of housebreaking to do with you. You can barely do better than not pee on the rug."

Insulting my manners aside, this has actually been the most productive conversation I've had with Cormac since we were eleven. We stole Misha Andreyev's soccer cleats before a game against our team. That's when Cormac and I discovered Sergei's overprotective about his little brother. We had matching black eyes for two weeks.

"Keep me posted, Cormac. I'm serious. I don't give a shit whether you want me dead or alive. If you know something that endangers Sinead, and you don't tell me—"

"I know. I know. Destroying my world and torturing me. I get it. Fecking finish this shit, so you can take her out to a nice dinner."

I watch him get back into his car, and I wait until he leaves the parking lot before I walk back around to see Sinead sobbing in the car. I wrench the door open and lean in to unfasten her seatbelt. I pull her into my arms as I squat beside her.

"Oh, thank God. Gabe, that took forever, and I couldn't see you. I didn't hear any shooting, but I didn't know if I should check to make sure he wasn't killing you some other way. How am I going to do this? How am I going to survive when you have to go to that place where I can't call you? Worse. How am I going to survive when you can't go to that place?"

"Shh, *piccolina*. I'm fine. I'm going to call Mario. He lives near here. He's going to take your car back to your place. We're going to go home."

"Home? Your place?"

"Our place, Sinead. At least for now. If you want us to live in your place after this is over or you want somewhere that's new to both of us, then we can do that."

"I— Somewhere new? I can't— I have student loans."

"I know you're a successful lawyer. Your money will go a lot further when you don't have that noose. But even if you became a managing partner at your firm, you won't make as much as I do. Between the stores I own, my investments, my moving companies, and my legal practice, I'm very wealthy. Very, very wealthy."

"Your place speaks to that. But I don't want to have to—"

"If you say rely on me, I will spank you. We can sort out our finances when we need to. If you want us to share things, fine. If you want things to be separate, fine. If you want a prenup, fine. Whatever you want. But we rely on each other. Flat out. You can depend on me, Sinead. And I know I can depend on you."

"Prenup?"

Fuck me.

"That would be the one word you caught."

I run my hands through my hair.

"Oh, I caught all of it. That's the one I want to focus on."

"I'm not proposing to you in some parking lot in the Bronx. And I'm not proposing to you while I'm still on trial and may face life in prison with no possibility for parole. But that's what I want. I won't have a child out of wedlock, Sinead. I know how old-fashioned that sounds, but I won't do it. I saw what it did to Carmine to have his mom get pregnant before his parents got married. Most of the old members who sided with their fathers and forced them to get married are dead. But there are still enough people my parents' age, Uncle Salvatore's and Uncle Massimo's ages to make life even harder than it has to be. I want a future with you that includes a family. I won't do that without being married. I won't cause my children the hardships Carmine experienced. He and I kept a lot of shit secret because we were too young to know we could trust the other adults in our lives. The ones who would have protected us. There's nothing I won't do for you and our kids, and that includes creating a situation where people might mistreat you or them. You know I can't walk away, but I will do anything I have to, to protect you and our family."

I stop just short of admitting I'll kill for her. The way she cups my cheek and kisses the other, I know she knows what I mean.

"You want to marry me and have bambinos and bambinas?"

"*Si.*"

"Me, too."

"Let's go home and discuss what Cormac told me and what you found out. Anything that gets us closer to being done with this hell storm. That way we can start working on our future."

Chapter Twenty-Three

Sinead

I don't know why I started balling when I waited for Gabriele. Maybe it was because I recognized Cormac as he drove in. I haven't seen him in ages, but he still looks the same as he did when we were kids. He was the one who was always getting in fights. He was the one people said had a chip on his shoulders. I think it was because he was the opposite of Gabriele. He was short until he was thirteen. Then he grew like a foot in a year. But until then, kids used to give him a hard time. Even the ones in his own family. Now that I think about it, Duffy O'Toole was one of the worst. Such an asshole. It doesn't surprise me he was behind the article. Sounds about right for him.

Waiting for Gabriele to stop talking to Cormac was nerve-wracking, and wondering about it didn't help. I kept waiting to hear a gun or windows shattering. I debated with myself about whether I could leave like Gabriele told me to. I know I can't. I won't. Unless I'm pregnant or we already have kids, I won't leave. I'll take my chances and stay with him.

That was something that only made me cry harder. What if I'm left a widow? What if we have kids who grow up without a father? Salvatore and Massimo are in their fifties and have lived this long. I want to believe Gabriele will too. But I don't know their family history well enough to know when they stopped doing what Gabriele probably does. I don't know if they still do. I just don't know. And that freaked me out.

"Lean back, *piccolina*."

Gabriele opens his legs as wide as his soaking tub will allow, and I nestle between them, my heading resting back on his chest. He swirls bubbles around us as I wrap my hands around his thighs. When his arms encircle me, I sigh. Everything feels right again. Maybe the bubble bath helps, but I know it's being with Gabriele.

"Do you want me to wash behind your ears, Daddy?"

I infuse humor into my voice because I know my freak out freaked him out. He's been so gentle with me since I finally stopped crying on the way to the penthouse. I told him what scared me, but I didn't tell him about me deciding there wasn't a chance in hell I would leave him.

He tweaks my nipple, and it pulses straight down to my pussy. His hand drifts down between my thighs until he's cupping me.

"I know what I'm going to wash."

He eases two fingertips inside me, but that's as far as he goes. It's just enough to make me shift restlessly.

"Do you need something? Are you not comfortable?"

His tone taunts me, and his thumb and index finger playing with my nipple only intensify my need.

"You know I need more."

"Mhmm."

He hums beside my ear as he looks over my shoulder and down to where his hand hides beneath the suds. He pulls his fingers from me, spreading them to slide along the outside of my vag. He's tormenting me, and I love it and hate it in equal measure. I shift again so my ass rubs against his hard cock. Two can play this game.

"Stand."

"Yes, Daddy."

I happily oblige. He turns me toward him, wiping bubbles from my smooth skin above my pussy. He keeps me steady as he slides down enough for his head to rest on the edge of the tub, then moves my feet to be on either side of his waist. He peels me open and licks his lips. Then his mouth is on me. My hands fly out to brace myself against the wall. His hands wrap around my thighs until I'm sure I won't slip. Then one lands across my ass. I jerk, and immediately, both hands are back on my thighs to keep me from falling. I'm more prepared for the next spank. It stings, but this is all about pleasure. His tongue is doing things to me that make me dizzy. I have to close my eyes. I don't know how long it takes because time is relative whenever we're together, but I can feel my orgasm building.

"Daddy, may I come?"

"Yes."

It's a muffled response because he barely pulls back enough to form the word. He keeps sucking on my clit until my legs tremble. He's so strong that as I come, he's lifting me off my feet and bringing me back down into the water. His cock slides into me easily since I'm a sloppy mess, and he's so hard it's standing straight up. I fall forward, my arms wrapping around his neck. Neither of us moves, savoring the feel of our bodies being connected. As the moments turn into minutes, I expect him to move. But he stays still. He's still hard, but he's not trying to get either of us off. I relax against him, and his arms drape around my hips.

"I like this, Gabe."

"Me, too. I'd stay like this forever if we could."

That might be one of the most romantic things anyone has ever said to me. When he strokes my back, I fear I'll fall asleep. I play with the hair just above his nape, running my fingers through it despite it being short. He turns his head, and our kiss is languid and so incredibly tender. He tucks hair behind my ear as he holds me. We pull apart just enough to gaze into one another's eyes.

"You liked me following you. Is that a fantasy you want to explore?"

"Yes. With you, it excites me. It's one of those things where I've thought about it before but never been with anyone who tempts me to try it. It's one of those that I would never want to have happen in real life, but I like the idea sexually."

I pause for a moment, then pull back.

"Is that— is it — mmm —too close to what you really do?"

"Chase women down dark hallways to fuck them? No. I've never done that before."

He chuckles, and it takes away some of my fear that I put my foot in it.

"But you know what I mean."

"Nothing about that scenario reminds me of work."

"Is this one of those lies to protect me?"

His fingers curl under my chin as his thumb strokes my jaw.

"No, *piccolina*. I would never bring that part of my life into my intimacy with you. Have I been in fights in alleys? Yes. Have I pursued people? Yes. But I don't see those things as being remotely the same as roleplaying with you. Once I catch you, do you want me to pin you against the wall like earlier?"

"Yes."

Do I sound desperate with how breathy that word was?

He flexes his hips to push himself deeper into me. His arm tightens around me, pressing me down. He does nothing else to really turn this into sex. It's just melding us closer together. I love it.

"What you said about getting me pregnant?"

I wait to see how he reacts. He just nods.

"I'm not ready to take my IUD out and start talking about kids. I know you want to be married before having them, and so do I. But even then, I want to wait a couple more years. But what you said. I loved it. Would you— I want you to say stuff like that."

I find my courage to say what I want. We're partners. This isn't something I want to ask permission for. And I don't think he expects me to.

"I'd like to. I wasn't sure how you'd feel about it. It's the truth, but I don't mean right this second."

"For all the possessive things you say, never once have I felt — I don't know —threatened by it. I think you'll encourage me to spend time with my friends, to go see the little family I have left. I don't think you'll isolate me at all. I don't think you'll make me question myself or diminish me. Just the opposite. I think it would upset you if I did. I don't think your type of possessiveness would— could —ever be emotionally or mentally abusive. I think your protectiveness of me is so that I can be who I want to be."

"You continue to read my mind, little girl."

"I know."

"I like it."

"For now."

I grin.

"No, really, Sinead. I like it. I feel understood like I never have before. There's been no one else romantically or sexually that I've wanted to give the opportunity to learn about me. Carmine understands me in much the same way, but my friendship with him is nothing like how I feel about you. He's like a fraternal twin, I suppose."

"Hearing that makes me happy. I guess I'm possessive too. I like knowing you haven't shared this with anyone else before. I know I haven't."

"Hinting at marriage doesn't freak you out?"

"No."

"Hold on tight."

I'm confused for a moment, but cling to him as he stands. We're in the middle of a conversation, and we haven't even finished taking a bath. He pulls open the glass door that connects the tub to the shower. There's a door that opens to the regular floor, too. He steps in and turns on the water. I'm holding onto him, but he moves as though there's no extra weight tugging on him.

There are three shower heads with warm water pulsing down on us. He lowers me to my feet and pushes open the door we didn't use. He reaches to a drawer beside the sink. I see him pull something out that's still in its packaging. It only takes me a second to realize it's lube. He rips it open and tosses the wrapping into the trash. I've already realized that he won't leave something like that on the counter. He likes things tidy.

"Turn around, *piccolina*. Lean forward and pull your ass cheeks open for me. All of you is mine, and I will prove it."

I do as he says, looking back over my shoulder as he pours lube onto his fingers. He rubs it around my asshole before pressing a finger into me.

"Pull wider and flex it."

I do as he says, and I feel the lube drip into me. I can't see that far around, but I watch him pour lube on his dick until it's slippery and glistening.

"I didn't plan to do this. You haven't worn a plug, so if this goes from uncomfortable to painful as I enter you, we stop immediately. I want this, but not enough to hurt you. Do not grin and bear this. You don't need your safe word. Say stop, and it ends."

"Can I stand up for a moment?"

"Of course. This is intimacy as your boyfriend not roleplaying. I should have made that clear."

"You did. I understand, but I didn't want you to think I want us to stop. Just the opposite."

I stand and turn toward him.

"Gabe, I don't think you'd forgive yourself if you hurt me at all. Ever. You wouldn't trust me anymore if I let that happen. And that terrifies me and hurts. I don't want that. I thought I'd ruined your trust when you had to chase me into the restaurant. I regretted what I did because I thought I ruined us. I don't want to feel that kind of fear again. I don't want you to doubt yourself or not trust yourself. I can't reconcile that with how confident you seem. I trust you to always take care of me. That's why we roleplay the way we do. That's why I can call you Daddy and not think it's something different from what it is. It's affection that I feel because you care about me. I want this with you. All of it. The feelings and a good ass fucking."

I try to lighten how heavy I got. I turn around and bend forward again. He wraps his arm around me and lands a ringing slap across my ass. If he wasn't holding me, I would have gone headfirst into the wall.

"Cheeky. A good ass fucking is exactly what you're going to get."

And that's what he gives me. He's slow as he enters me. Ever so careful, giving me time to adjust. But once he's inside me, I can't get enough. I've had anal before, and I don't mind it. It's something different, but it's never gotten me off before. I heard the bottle of lube land on the tile right before he started thrusting. His hands are all over me. One's always holding me, so I don't lose my balance. But he alternates. One moment he's rubbing my clit, the next he's squeezing my tits, another he's spanking me. I pushing my hips back to meet each time he surges forward.

"Fuck, Sinead. I've wanted to fuck your ass since the first time you walked in front of me. This is even better than I imagined. You're so fucking tight. And now you're all mine. I've had your mouth, your hands, your pussy, and now your ass. There isn't a part of you I haven't claimed. I'm going to do it over and over."

He thrusts hard enough to push me onto my toes. I press my hips back to meet the next one.

"You're going to take my cum, and when I pull out, you're going to squeeze your ass and keep it there. Only when I tell you to, can you let it out. When it slides down to your pussy and along your thighs, you'll remember you're mine."

"When you fill me with your cum, you're going to remember I'm the only one who gets it. No one else ever again. Your cock is mine just like the rest of you, Gabe. All mine. Your cum only fills me."

He leans over me as he thrusts hard, pinning me against him.

"Is that so?"

"Yes."

I practically growl.

"Tell me again."

"Your cum and your cock are mine, Gabe. I'll never share. I know you won't cheat. But I will— I won't allow any woman near you."

What the fuck has come over me? I was ready to say I'd kill any woman who tried to take him from me. And I truly believe I would.

"Mmm. My lioness."

"You know I don't mean I'll freak if you talk to women, right?"

"*Piccolina*, I know exactly what you mean. I wouldn't stop you."

I glance over my shoulder.

"Are you gloating?"

He answers it by rubbing my clit until I'm moaning and begging.

"Please, let me come. I need to. I can't stop."

"Come while I fill your ass."

"Gabe!"

I claw at the wall before pressing my palms against it. It's so fucking intense, it almost makes me cry. I feel him pulsing inside me as he bites my shoulder. He eases out of me, and I clench my ass. He turns me and envelopes me in his arms.

"Shh. I know, *cuore*. I know."

His voice wavers, and it's thick with emotion. I love him. And I think he loves me.

"Relax for me. Let me finish taking care of you."

I sigh and let my entire body go. I feel his cum, but I'm distracted from the shower puff he's sliding over me. He uses his hands gently to clean my pussy and ass. Then he's down on one knee to wash my legs and feet. When he glances up at me, I know he hasn't missed the significance of his pose.

He washes my hair as I run the mesh poof over him. I kiss his chest over and over before I kneel to wash his cock and between his legs. I wrap my hands around it loosely, stroking it as I wash his legs. It twitches, and I know I could get him hard if I wanted. When I'm certain he's clean, I lick him before standing. I appreciate that I'm tall because I can wash his hair easily when I stand on my toes.

His towels are so fluffy they're like slipping on a robe. He rubs me dry before doing the same for himself. We walk back into the bedroom naked and crawl into bed. He sits, propped up by the headboard. I nestle against him, my head resting where his chest meets his shoulder, my arm across his abs. His hand holds my hip. I fight against a yawn as I speak.

"We still need to talk about today."

"I know. Did you find anything among the evidence?"

"I did. It took some digging after a call to a supervisor and a warning that I would get a warrant. And if I discovered anyone hid evidence from me or kept me from seeing all of it, I would have every single one of their badges and pensions. Apparently, I have just enough of a reputation for them to believe me. I was just pissed enough to mean it. Gabe, there was a camera. It was in another evidence box for an entirely different case that happened that same day. They still had it tagged for yours but accidentally put somewhere else."

I use air quotes with the hand on his abs.

"Have you watched it?"

"Not yet. I stood where cameras could see me opening boxes of evidence from your case. Then, I asked the officer to look into other boxes where I couldn't see the contents. I asked him to hold it up, so I could see it when it came out of the box. I asked him to read the tag. I never actually touched it. It'll be clear someone examined the label before I had access to it, and I never took it into my possession, so there's no chance anyone can claim I tampered with it. I asked for a printout of the chain of custody and of the bar scans when they entered the evidence. The chain of custody ended between the forensics officer I spoke to and the camera's storage. The record shows he entered it as an item gathered at the crime scene, but no one entered it into the records for the box. It just stops as though it never existed. I filed a motion for a subpoena to view the videos filmed in the evidence room on the day of and throughout the week after they brought the evidence in. At some point, someone moved it, and I want to know who."

"Go back further. Someone watched that video and decided it needed to disappear. If it proved my guilt, they would use it."

"There is one other possibility."

I hesitate, but he says what I'm thinking.

"If it disappeared to help me, I would know. I would distract you from it or flat out tell you not to pursue it. I want to know what's on that video."

I nod. How do you say there are dirty cops on your family's payroll without saying there're dirty cops on your family's payroll? You phrase it just like Gabriele did. I don't like the idea of him distracting me from it, but I think that would have happened before we grew— close. Telling me would definitely get me brought up before the ethics committee if anyone found out.

"Along with the subpoena, as soon as I got back to my office, I filed a demand that they turn over the evidence. We can work on the assumption that the reason it went missing was to keep it from proving your innocence. But if there is anything on there that could implicate you— if the prosecution could imply it connects you —they will see it before we do."

"The chain of custody's been broken. Even if the video somehow implicated me, there's more than enough to make it inadmissible."

"And that's why I wanted to be sure the evidence room cameras filmed everything closely. But the converse is true. The broken chain of custody makes it inadmissible for us, too."

"But it could be grounds for a dismissal."

"I'm certainly going to try. But even without the video, the court still believes there's enough evidence to convict you. That's why we're going to trial."

"But if the evidence they hid proves my innocence, then there's no basis for the charges."

"This video has to irrefutably prove your innocence."

I sigh. This is complicated, but not impossible. I just have to play our hand carefully. I need to gather all our evidence to present to Judge Hutchens at one time. I can't look like I'm grasping at straws.

"We can't do anything else tonight, *piccolina*. Let's get some sleep."

A good night's sleep is what I need before I go into battle.

Chapter Twenty-Four

Gabriele

It's been three days, and Sinead still hasn't gotten the videos from the evidence room. It took two days for the subpoenas to come in and the demand for evidence to get processed. Judge Hutchens had cataract surgery.

Thank God the woman is a workaholic. She's already back in the office. Sinead refused to let me come to the conference. I trust her to share everything with me, but I feel like a caged animal, prowling from one end of the room to another. I'm back at Mancinelli Developers, waiting for her to arrive. I've been to this building more times in the past three weeks than I have in the past three years. Well, maybe more than in the past year.

I hear the elevator ding, so I spin around from where I was staring out the window near the office suite's door. Sinead's grin is ear to ear, and I squeeze my eyes shut for a moment. I feel her take my hand and tug it. I open them and follow her to the conference room. I know Uncle Salvatore and Uncle Massimo are following us, but I don't care. She's excited and holding my hand. That's what I can handle thinking about right now. When we get inside the room, she pulls open her bag and starts spreading out papers.

"This documents the chain of custody. It shows they gathered the camera at the scene and logged it. It shows they brought it to the evidence room, but then there's nothing else."

She points, and I know what I'm seeing since it's a standard record.

"This is the evidence record for the box in which the officer found the camera. There's no record of a camera. However, the label clearly shows it was for your case. Whoever put it there was never on the chain of custody form for either case."

She points to a piece of paper she put beside the other one. She holds up a thumb drive and beams.

"All of this shocked Judge Hutchens, and she was not a happy camper seeing all these documents. But this was the silver bullet. I thought Tyler was going to piss himself. He sure as fuck won't have a job by the end of the day."

"What's on it?"

"He's seen talking to the forensics officer I know right after the guy stepped out of his lab. Based on Ryan's digital log, the conversation happened right after he finished tagging your evidence. It shows Ryan giving Tyler some papers. Ryan gave a sworn statement today that the papers were a full list of the evidence, including the camera. I don't have evidence to show who, quote-unquote, lost the camera, but it shows Tyler knew of its existence. When it didn't show up in discovery, he never mentioned it was missing."

Uncle Massimo shakes his head, but he's smiling.

"That's not enough to get him fired immediately, but it will put him up before the OIG and an ethics panel. It'll also get him withdrawn from the case."

We all know Sinead was exaggerating with her comment,

but Uncle Massimo is right. The NYPD Office of the Inspector General will be very interested to know how evidence went missing. The DA's Internal Affairs will be just as curious.

Uncle Salvatore jumps straight to the most important question.

"What has Judge Hutchens decided?"

"Right now, the evidence is inadmissible because of the failed chain of custody. She reserves the right to consider a motion to dismiss once we view the video. We'll have to wait for a new ADA to be assigned to the case. But given how close we are to trial, it won't take long. I expect to hear by the end of the day."

I listen to the conversation as it swirls around me. What I want to know is who the fuck, quote-unquote, lost it. And even more importantly, why? Who paid for it to go missing? Those are questions to ask my uncles without Sinead around to hear them. The outcome will be very different if I ask them in private.

When she looks at me, my eyes narrow for a heartbeat. She's waiting for me to ask those very things. They're the next logical step, but when I remain quiet, she says nothing. I shift my gaze to Uncle Massimo, then Uncle Salvatore. They know the same thing I do. They're waiting to see if Sinead presses, but she doesn't. Just the opposite.

"I have enough to deal with right now, trying to get the case dismissed."

She's watching me as she speaks, and my heart races. In the most fucked-up way, she's accepting not only my life but agreeing to entering this underworld. I want to hold her and kiss her senseless. That'll have to wait.

Uncle Massimo stands and buttons his suit coat.

"Let us know when you know who the new ADA is. I'm curious who Suarez will assign now."

There's as much humor as there is menace in his voice, and it makes Sinead freeze. She recovers, but she seems on edge now. I stand and step behind her chair. I lay my hand on her shoulder, and she looks up at me. She misses Uncle Salvatore standing too, so when he speaks, she jumps.

"Good day, Ms. O'Malley. Gabriele, stop by the house."

"Will do."

"Wait."

We all look at Sinead. Her brow's furrowed.

"Someone needs to look at Duffy O'Toole's emails or phone records. He knows enough to have printed that inflammatory article. He tried to influence this trial before it started, but making me look like a drug addict isn't enough. The only reason he believed it would have an impact is because he has something he wants to follow up with. He has to be getting the info from someone. Find out who that is, and I bet it'll lead to the cop who interfered."

"The most obvious person is Detective Morris since he was there."

"I know, and he was the lead detective on the Cohenour case, too. I really thought he was clean."

Uncle Massimo's jaw sets, and I know that look. Fuck whoever is about to be on the receiving end of what's coming.

"Detective Philip Morris? I knew he was involved with this case, but I didn't know he was on the Cohenour one, too."

Sinead glances at me before looking at Uncle Massimo.

"Is that a problem?"

"It won't be."

Sinead stops herself from asking more. I wonder what he knows and whether he'll tell me when I go to Uncle Salvatore's later. We watch as my uncles of sorts leave. I sit in the chair next to Sinead's and swivel it so I can see her. She does the same.

"Gabe, I won't ask what's going to happen. But will you be safe when it does? Will you be at that place?"

"Yes."

"There's a lot I want to know, but I won't ask. That weekend you were gone, and I thought you were guarding someone, I know that's where you were, but only because you let me know after the fact. You told me I couldn't communicate with you while you're there. I get why. You need to be untraceable. But could you saying something like— I don't know —like you're going to be working on the car? Something like that, so I know that you're somewhere safe while you're gone. I know your family won't tell me anything."

"They will. When this is over, and we don't have to hide anything, people will see us together. I won't lock you away in some gilded cage or refuse to do things with you in public. We aren't a dirty secret to keep. But even before that, if something happens unexpectedly, and I have to be gone, my family will get you. You'll go to one of my aunts. They won't leave you wondering what happened. I'll tell you when I can, but if I can't, you won't be alone. At least not yet. Not while it's so new."

"What do I do if we're out together and something happens? Like you get arrested or get hurt? I can be your attorney, but there must be some chain of command to let your family know. What about if you need to go to the hospital?"

I smile at her and feather my thumb over her forehead, smoothing the creases. I turn us farther, so my legs bracket hers, and I'm holding her hands in her lap.

"I'll put everyone's numbers in your phone. You can call any of the men or send a group text. Someone will get you, and someone will come to me. Under no circumstances are you to act as my attorney, Sinead. I'm serious. I don't want you there when they process my arrest. It will only draw you in. It's one thing for you to represent me after they've charged me. But I don't want you scooped up in their net. You get away from me as fast as you can. Go somewhere safe until my family can get you. Promise me."

I'm demanding, and it makes her flinch. I'm scaring her.

"I'm sorry. I don't mean to be so harsh. I know you'll want to protect me, and I— I appreciate it."

Fuck. I almost said I love you for it.

"But it'll also remove any question of impropriety, and you can't defend either of us well if you're locked up, too."

"Fine. I don't like it. I'll promise as long as I believe it's the right thing to do."

"Sinead."

"No, Gabriele. Protection goes both ways if we're really partners. You cannot convince me otherwise. If I believe the best way to protect you is to get away, then I will. But if I believe staying will keep you safer, then you will not get me to leave. You can try."

I see a tenacity in her that affirms she can take on the life I'm dragging her into. But it scares me she'll try to do more than she can handle or that she'll get herself entangled in something she doesn't understand.

"Please, at least promise you'll err on the side of caution. Me getting arrested will be because some other syndicate is involved. We make sure the police ignore us. When they don't, it's because someone else's money is speaking louder."

I've just confessed to a shit ton right there.

"I will not say more than that about this. It's not safe for you and for my family if I do. I've already told you more than I should, but it's important for you to understand."

Her lips flatten, but she nods.

"As for the hospital, if I'm shot or stabbed, you do not call an ambulance unless I will bleed to death. Not that you think I might. Not that you worry I might. I seriously have to be within an inch of my life ending before you get a hospital involved. Gunshots and knife wounds wind up with the police involved. Like I just said, we don't want that. Auntie Carlotta is a general surgeon. Luca trained as a paramedic in college and keeps his certifications current. Maria is a radiologist, but she's still completely capable of stitching me up. If you're in doubt, you call my family. If I wind up on the way to the hospital, you call them. Don't follow me there."

"No. Absolutely not. I will think twice about sticking around for the cops. But if you're going to the hospital, God help anyone who thinks they're keeping me from you. You just said you have to be nearly dead to go to the hospital. If that's true, then I will not leave you. Spank me. Edge me. Do whatever you want, but this I absolutely will not budge on. If you die, I will not spend the rest of my life wishing I'd said goodbye. That I trusted someone would heal you, and they didn't. No."

I believe her.

I reach across the table to a remote. I click a button and shades lower to block anyone from seeing into the conference room. I click another, and the blinds at the windows lower. I pull her onto my lap, and she curls up as though she's not wearing a suit. She tucks her arms in between us. I feel her shuddering sigh. She's my lioness again one moment, but she's my *piccolina* another. She will control any situation she has to, but this is one she doesn't want to.

"I'm scaring you, *cuore*, and I don't want to. But this is yet another thing we have to talk about. Knowing my favorite food or color can come later for us. I know we're dating completely out of order."

"Your favorite color is Kelly green."

"How do you know that?"

She's right.

"The throw blanket on your sofa is Kelly green. Your dish towels are that green and chocolate brown. Your bathroom rug is the same green with white. Your bath towels are closer to emerald and muted, but close enough. When you got dressed this morning, I saw three different ties with Kelly green in them."

I kiss her, and I hope she can tell just how I feel about her. If I asked anyone but Carmine, and maybe Maria, what my favorite color is, none would know. Not even my aunts.

"And I know your favorite color is lavender because it's your favorite scent."

"You do?"

"Yes. Your dish soap and hand soap are lavender. You have lavender scented dryer sheets you must use in your laundry but also keep in your drawers. You have two lavender dresses; one's long, and the other is short. You have a lavender winter scarf and hat set. And your bedding is closer to a royal purple, but close enough."

It's my turn to get a kiss that melts me. She cups my cheek, and her touch soothes the beast in me.

"Sinead."

I exhale the word as we pull apart. What has she done to me?

"When this is over, I'm taking you on a vacation, *piccolina*. Anywhere you want to go. Just the two of us." I frown. "For just the two of us, but I won't travel with you without guards."

She smiles and gives me a playful shake of her head.

"As long as they aren't in bed with us, I'll trust you to make whatever arrangements we need."

"They won't be in the bed, in the bath, in the shower, in the pool, in the ocean with us. No one is watching me make love to you."

She watches me for a moment, a speculative look on her face before she leans back against me.

"What is it?"

"Nothing, Daddy."

I won't press her. If she doesn't want to share her thoughts, then they're hers to keep. I'd rather hear her call me that again, anyway. She knows because she obliges.

"It's a good thing I think green and purple look good with each other, Daddy. If we're really thinking about living together, then you'll be seeing it in a few places."

"I'm not thinking about it. I've thought about it. That's what I want, but I'll wait until you're ready."

"After living with Delaney, I didn't look forward to having roommates in college. They weren't bad, and that's how I met Andrea. I want her to get to know you. But once I moved into a place on my own, I swore I wouldn't live with anyone else until I got married. I'm willing to ease off on that rule. But my point is, I enjoy living on my own. I've never lived with a man before. You're awfully special to get me to change that rule and to give up my solitude. I haven't done it for anyone else."

"You know it's the same for me."

"And that's why this feels extra right."

"Extra? Not a little. Not sorta. But extra?"

"Yes."

She gives me a smacking kiss on the cheek before she pulls away. I let her, but I miss the feel of her against me already.

"Don't look so sad, Daddy. I don't enjoy getting up either, but there's stuff we have to do. I'll be sleeping next to you in a few hours."

I stand too and grumble, but she knows I'm doing it playfully. I haven't been playful in years. Decades even. She brings this out in me, and it makes the world not so dark, not so heavy.

"By the way, my favorite food is steamed carrots with salt, pepper, and butter, *piccolina.*"

She stares at me, then laughs.

"Of course they are. Mine are tortilla chips with a hint of lime. Yours is a vegetable. That's why you look like you do, and I look like I do."

Her smile drops when she sees my left eye narrow.

"What's that supposed to mean? How do you look?"

"Not toned like you. Not like—"

I pull her against me, then back her against the closest wall. I rest my hand on her throat. It's just the weight of it that adds pressure. I'm not squeezing.

"I work out twice a day to stay alive and to protect the people I love. I like how you look just as much as you like how I look. I've seen it. If you don't know that by now, then I've done a shit job showing it. You are the most beautiful and enticing woman I've ever met. Your body is perfect for you and for me. I will not always look like this. I hope to watch your body change when we have kids. I will still desire you just as much, and I hope the same is true for you."

I lean forward to whisper in her ear.

"I love how you taste. The way you feel when I slip inside you. The way my palms itch to touch you, then how I hate to let you go. When you're dressed, I want to strip you naked. When you're naked, I want to devour you. So don't you ever doubt that I'm attracted to you just as you are. I can't decide for you how you feel about your body. But I won't listen to you suggest it's anything less than perfect to me. I know what I want. I'm not a little boy trying to pick out a toy I want to play with. I will fuck you right here, right now if you need me to show you how much I want you. You can feel I'm hard. I'll take you against this wall. On that table. Do you know why?"

"Because I'm yours."

"That's right, *piccolina*. Take me out."

I push her skirt up, knowing I won't find any panties. We stopped by her place the other day to pick up more clothes. She tried to pack some, and I tore them apart. I threatened to go through her entire drawer.

She unfastens my belt, then my pants before she unzips them. She demanded I not wear boxer briefs. I warned her everyone would know I have a constant hard on for her. I took them off at her place, and she told me I could put them back on by dinner. Her exact words were, "put those fucking things back on before I tear those women's eyes out for looking at how big you are." She pushes the underwear down and frees me. I lift her with ease, my hands gripping her ample ass.

"Oh, God."

I thrust into her, eliciting her moan. I keep her pinned against the wall as my hand goes back to her throat.

"Breath play, *piccolina*?"

"Yes."

I progressively tighten my hold, watching her every second for any sign that it's too much.

"Snap if you need me to stop."

She dips her chin. I continue to squeeze as I pound into her. Her eyelids are drooping but they don't shut. I work harder to make her come. When she grabs my shoulders, fisting my suit coat, I release her and replace my hand with my lips on her mouth. I swallow her scream as I demand she accept my kiss. She wraps her arms tightly around my neck as she returns my ardor. She rides me with an urgency I haven't felt from her before.

I feel like I'm exploding inside her. I keep coming as I pound into her. She fists my hair and bites my lower lips. Not hard, but it's possessive as fuck, and I love it. What is wrong with us? Nothing, I suppose. How we feel isn't detrimental to us. It's just how we are together.

I rest my forehead on her shoulder as she strokes my hair and back. My hands are once again gripping her ass while we both pant. I carry her to the table and sit down. The office chairs won't be comfortable for her legs if she straddles me. She cups my other cheek this time.

"Daddy, you make me feel perfect."

I want to tell her how I feel so badly that I'm practically biting my tongue for real.

"If there are things about your body you don't like, then I won't diminish your feelings by saying you're wrong. Whatever it is, is real to you. I won't suggest you change anything or tell you how to. I just want you to know I crave you now, and I always will. There will never be enough time or enough ways to get enough of you."

"You are the sweetest man ever. How'd I get so lucky?"

"You're amazing at what you do, so my uncles demanded you represent me. Then you were just you, and I fell head over heels."

Our foreheads rest together before we share several quick pecks. Then I put her down, and we straighten our clothes. We gather our things. I leave the shades down because raising them would scream what we've been doing. I know Lorenzo is meeting with some IT people for our legit businesses, but they're working in some cubicles with computers in front of them.

"I need to head back to my office and see if there's any news about Tyler. I have other cases to prep for, too."

"All right, I'm headed to Uncle Salvatore's now. Depending on how long this takes, would you like to have dinner with me there? It won't be anything formal. Matteo, Carmine, and Luca will go home to their wives if they're there. Uncle Massi will probably be, so maybe Auntie Nicoletta will come over. But chances are, he'll go home, too. Lorenzo and Marco will stay for the dinner they don't have to cook themselves. I can ask since he's over there."

I nudge my chin toward the voices.

"Do you think Salvatore will want me there? I'm still your attorney, and your family is still my client."

"He's not stupid or blind. He knows we're together. He saw us holding hands. Whether or not I tell him, he could know by checking with our bodyguards. He's said nothing, so he's okay with it."

"The other day when Luigi didn't show up. You said something about a tracker. Do you wear one?"

I look around when we get to the suite's door. I turn my belt buckle over and point to something that looks like it's just part of the backside of the prong. Then I point to the end of the buckle that looks like solid metal.

"Yes. The little gold piece on the prong is an activator, in case I need help. The tracker is covered up. All the men wear them in their belt buckles. The women either have a bracelet or a necklace that only a special key can unlatch."

I watch her as she digests that.

"It's not to keep tabs on us. No one's monitoring our every movement. We go where we want without having to ask permission or notify anyone. They're there in case of trouble. If we can't reasonably reach someone by pinging their phone or car, then we'll go to the belts or jewelry. I pinged the tracker on Luigi's phone and got no answer. He knew I expected him to pick us up. He's one of the most reliable guys we have. That's why I let him drive you. It was so unusual that I knew something was up right away. If it had been someone other than him, Giuseppe, Mario, Afonso, or Pauly, I would chalk it up to them not paying attention to time or some shit. Those five men have protected me and other people in my family for longer than I've been in America. They are the only ones outside my family I would trust with your safety. Until this is over, I only trust my family. That's not knocking the other guys. They're practically family, but the Mancinelli men are different. They know what you mean to me, Sinead. I don't have to tell them."

She watches me, and I wonder if she's going to ask me to elaborate. If she does, I will.

"Will I have to wear one?"

"I'd like you to."

"Would it be requirement?"

"No. Your body and what you wear are your own. But I would like you to. Once our relationship isn't a secret, I'll be anxious if you don't. I don't want to smother you, and I don't want you to feel like my family watches your every step. Wearing one means I won't do that. I'll know that if something happens, we can find you and get to you."

I won't say anything about how Maria's tracker didn't ping for hours when men kidnapped her in Miami.

"Are all the pieces of the jewelry the same?"

"No. Maria and Serafina have bracelets. Olivia has hers in a necklace. My mama's is in a watch my dad gave her for their wedding. The other women have a couple they choose from since they've been married so long."

"Can I choose?"

"Yes. There are some limitations, but you can choose what it is, and I can have it designed."

She glances back to where Lorenzo must be working.

"If you had to turn your alert on, would someone in your family tell me? Or is that something only family can know about?"

"My family will not only tell you, someone will come and get you. They'll either take you to one of their homes or take you to me. It depends on what's happening. I haven't told anyone about us, but I haven't had to. Like I said, they know what you mean to me."

I guess I'm hinting and wanting her to take it. I can admit I'm scared to confess how I feel in case she doesn't reciprocate. I'd rather her ask and me be honest than have to admit it on my own.

"Can we pick out something this weekend? I'd feel better in case we're together and something happens. If I can't get to your alert, I want to set mine."

I kiss her, and it's too short and too chaste. But it's all I can manage right now if we're ever going to get out of here.

"Will you come to Uncle Salvatore's, or would you rather go home?"

"I'd like to meet more of your family."

"All right. I'll ask Lorenzo to pick you up. I'll take you to your office, and Afonso will be your guard while you're there. When you're ready to go, text Lorenzo. Let me have your phone, please."

I enter his number and ask her to wait for me. I wind my way back to where I know people are working.

"Enzo, can I talk to you for a minute?"

He looks up and nods. We step away from everyone else.

"Uncle Sal wants me to come over. I'm going after I drop Sinead at her office. When you're done here, or if she texts, could you pick her up and bring her over?"

His brow furrows for a second as his gaze darts in her direction.

"You love her, don't you?"

"Can you let me sort out how I feel and tell her before I tell you or anyone else?"

I could knock his smug look off his face. I inhale, and it

makes me even bigger than him. He laughs and rolls his eyes. I don't intimidate him in the least.

"Yeah. I'll bring her over."

"Thank you."

I return to Sinead, and we head out. It takes an hour to drop her off and get to Uncle Salvatore's place in Queens. I don't need to knock to enter the house. I just enter the code, but I knock when I get to his office door. Pia and Natalia are still at school, and Aunt Sylvia is probably at her office in a meeting. She works from home most days since she can do plenty of tasks as corporate lawyer from here.

"*Entrare.*" Enter.

Fuck. Uncle Salvatore's not in the same mood as he was when he left our meeting. I step into the converted den and look around. The gang's all here except for Lorenzo and Carmine's dad, Cesare. He's in insurance and prefers not to get involved with the inner workings. He's saved us and made us millions. But he's been happy to stay at arm's length since he and Auntie Paola aren't together anymore. His father-in-law made it obvious he wasn't welcome when the older man was still don. Uncle Salvatore's told him he doesn't share the same belief as his dead father. Cesare politely declined.

So, I'm looking at Uncle Salvatore, Uncle Massimo, Uncle Domenico, Luca, Marco, Matteo, and Carmine. It's a good thing this office is a converted den, or we wouldn't all fit in here.

"What happened?"

Uncle Salvatore taps his fingers on his arm rest. It's an unusual pattern. He says it came from his mother making him play the piano for hours. It's more like an arpeggio than a scale.

"A little birdie with red hair and freckles called."

An O'Rourke.

"Oh?"

"Yes. Turns out O'Toole's been talking to a few cops, but Morris is the one feeding him the most shit. Finn did some looking at Duffy's files, and there're a series of exposés he plans to release when the case gets dismissed. He's going to allege we coerced the judge. Apparently, Hutchens drinks a little too much and got in an accident a year ago. Duffy's sources told him, but he's been holding onto that little nugget. He's going to blame Hutchens, and he'll blackmail the woman not to disagree. Either way, her career's over."

"What else?"

"He has photos of you with your gun out as you went in Sinead's apartment. She's not in the photo, so he's going to allege you threatened her. He also has a photo of you holding hands the other day as you got into your elevator. He's going to claim you're forcing her into a sexual relationship with you."

I listen, and I fight the urge to react. I need to hear everything with a clear head. I can't go apeshit yet.

"Has he sent those photos to anyone?"

"Finn doesn't think so. Apparently, Duffy has the O'Rourkes so pissed they can't agree how to kill him. It didn't thrill them to hear a woman with such close ties to their family was representing you. However, they know her grandparents and parents purposely kept her removed. A few summer and holiday visits don't count to them as her being a part of the mob. Just a family friend. They like her and respect her. They don't like or respect you, so they don't love the idea of you being with her. But they won't stop it as long as she's happy."

I nod. I wait for more, but everyone's looking at me.

"What made them investigate?"

Uncle Massimo answers instead of Uncle Salvatore. I shift my focus to him.

"Duffy came to them, claiming he could get an officer to tamper with evidence if they wanted. They trust him not at all. They want him nowhere near their operations since they're certain he'll flip on them just as fast."

This matches up with everything Cormac told me. Interesting how they felt it wasn't enough to just tell me. They decided Uncle Salvatore needs to know, too. I can guess who made the call.

"Why'd Finn tell you?"

"Dillan's asserting himself more and trying to crawl out of the cesspool Donovan and Declan left him. He followed through on what they started because he had to. They had too much wrapped up in what those two ass hats started. But he's proving he's his own man now. He's always been the brains of the operation, but he's been strategic in asserting himself. He doesn't agree with targeting women, and he doesn't agree with anyone going after Sinead."

"Is it personal to him?"

It sounds like it. What the fuck does Dillan want with her? Does he want to be with her?

Uncle Domenico speaks up. He's technically still a capo and will always be. But he handles a lot of our international business arrangements. It surprises me when he joins the conversation. How much did they discuss before I got here?

"Apparently, her dad had a really serious bout of pneumonia last winter. It's significantly weakened him. He knows her dad's dying. When the time comes, he wants her to be able to be with him. He wants you to be with her because she'll need you."

I feel like shit. I knew about her dad's health and that he's in memory care, but I never asked her how he was doing. I never asked if this was keeping her from visiting him. I never asked a lot of things I should have. Fucking selfish. It makes me wonder if she feels like she can't share this with me.

"Don't beat yourself up over it. Dillan only knows because his grandmother is in the same place. He saw Sinead there last winter when her dad was sick. I guess they talked a little. They're friendly, but they aren't friends. He's probably seen her dad or even asked about him when he visits his grandmother. He goes every Sunday instead of going to Mass with his mom."

That doesn't help at all. Have I kept her from visiting him? That's what keeps playing in my head. Have I been too busy fucking her to think about anything else? No. She'd tell me if she wanted or needed to see him. She wouldn't prioritize sex. As important as it is to us, she knows I'd never keep her from her dad. Doesn't she? I don't even know.

Luca's sitting next to me since I took a seat while Uncle Salvatore was talking. He nudges me with his knee.

"What do you want to do about Duffy? It's your call. Let the O'Rourkes deal with him or grab him before they do?"

"Grab him."

I don't have to think twice. The Irish might do Sinead a favor by getting Duffy out of the way, but I want to hear and see him when he lies, then when I drag a confession out of him.

Chapter Twenty-Five

Sinead

I wonder if and when Gabriele and I will ever have a mellow, uneventful day. We talk about such intense shit that it should be exhausting. But it isn't. At least, not always. Some of it actually invigorates me. Sorta. Understanding more keeps my mind from going into a tailspin. I feel confident about us and that I matter to him when he shares stuff. It gives me hope.

And it's fucking sexy as fuck. I've only done breath play a few times because it's scared me too much. When he asked me, I didn't hesitate. It intensified everything. Every move either of us made. It was like I was floating above us and watching while still feeling every bit of it. The way he said things wouldn't have been every woman's cup of tea. And that's fine. I'm the only one drinking it. It was perfect. I have imperfections I don't like about myself, but I'm okay with them. I have been for years, but I will admit that some insecurities flared the first couple times he saw me naked.

It startled me when he took what I said as belittling myself.

It really bothered him. It was like someone else had insulted me, and he wouldn't stand for it. He said I was perfect for him, and I appreciated that. If he'd tried to convince me I was perfect in general, I wouldn't have believed him. I would have taken the hyperbole and disagreed with all of it in my head. But he phrased it just right. He knew that, too. He knew what I needed.

Right now, however, what I need is to get this shit moving along. But I can't help myself as I search the web.

clinical psychology how long does it take to fall in love

I read the previews on several search results. I know there's no definitive answer, but I want to know if what I feel truly is love or just infatuation. The top result says it can take between two weeks and four months to fall in love. Clearly, I'm on the shorter end of the spectrum.

It fascinates me that these articles say men, on average, profess love sooner than women. The first article I open all the way notes men are ready to say it in eighty-eight days or about three months. But women take one-hundred-thirty-seven days or four and a half months. Apparently, I am not most women. Another says ninety-seven days for a man and one-hundred-forty-nine for women. Only the first preview I saw makes me feel better about this.

The rest makes me think I'm just infatuated. But I've been infatuated before. I've been in lust before. I started that way with Gabriele, but it feels so different now. It's where I'd expect to be after dating for several months, but we're here already. These articles may be based on scientific evidence, and I don't doubt the validity of at least some of it, but we don't fit. We're just outliers. I know what I feel.

Moving on, I'm checking my email, and there's nothing there that makes me think the judge has reviewed anything. I'm reading an email about another case when the notification of new mail pops up. I don't recognize the email address, so I ignore it. It's probably spam that slipped through. A moment later, my phone vibrates. I check and see there's a new text.

Read the email, Sinead. You're going down.

What the fuck? Who still talks like that? Reading it makes it sound juvenile, but I'll heed the warning. I open the email and check the sender address. I don't know the domain, and it's just a series of letters and numbers before the at symbol.

Keep digging and find out what happens. You should have quit when you discovered we bugged your place. You should have quit when we bugged your hotel room.

We? Who the fuck is we?

This is your last chance. Otherwise, everyone drowns. Tyler's already getting fired. Judge Hutchens isn't so squeaky clean. And you. There's more to you than killing your sister.

What the fuck does that mean? I've never gotten a speeding ticket after what happened the first time I drove. I've never been busted for drugs or underage drinking. The only thing I can think of is this fucker knows about Gabriele and me. If that's the case, I need to know who this is, and I need to get the judge to decide before this person leaks anything. I remember what Gabriele told me a couple nights ago. I dial my phone.

"Lorenzo? It's Sinead. I need you to come get me when you can. I need you to come up to my office and look at an email."

"Are you okay? Is it a threat?"

I hear urgency in his voice as he demands answers.

"I'm fine, but I'm concerned."

It sounds like he muffles the phone, then I hear the elevator ping.

"I'm on my way. Don't open anything else on your computer. Do you have an Apple or Android phone?"

"Apple."

"Don't call or text or do anything on it until I get there."

"Okay."

Now I'm getting freaked out. Now I want to talk to Gabriele.

"Sinead?"

"Yeah."

"Call Gabriele if it'll make you feel better. But touch nothing until I get there. Use your office phone."

"Thanks."

We hang up and immediately I'm looking up Gabriele's number. I don't have a choice. I need to memorize his number. It keeps ringing, but he doesn't answer. Oh, God. Is he at that place? I'm trying not to panic. I call again, and it rings and rings. For fuck's sake, Gabriele. Please. I try a third time.

"Who is this?"

"Gabe."

"Sinead, what's wrong? What happened?"

"I got a text and an email. Lorenzo's coming, but he told me not to touch anything. It sounded like he doesn't like that I have an Apple phone. I don't understand, and I'm scared."

"I'm coming. Do as Lorenzo says. He'll get to you faster than I can, but I'm on my way."

I hear him talking to someone, saying that I need him. I do, but what are they going to think about me? We were just together. What if this turns out to be nothing? I'm going to come across as so needy. I want their approval because Gabriele's entire world revolves around them. If they don't like me...

I sit, trying not to fidget for what seems like hours. I'm trying to think about other cases and other things I could be doing. But I haven't dusted off a law book in years. Everything is online. Any precedent I need, any law I need, I can find all of it online. But I can't use my fucking computer.

"Sinead?"

I jerk my head up when I hear Ashley's voice. I was lost deeper in thought than I realized.

"Mr. Lorenzo Mancinelli is here. He said you're expecting him."

"I am."

I stand and wait for Lorenzo to enter. Ashley definitely thinks he's hot, but he barely acknowledges her. He walks straight to my desk, but he waits until he hears the door close before he picks up my phone.

"Unlock it, please."

I press my finger to the screen, and he taps my screen. I try to see, but he's in parts of it I've never seen. It has something to do with the operating system and memory I think.

"Is Gabe coming?"

"Yes. He said he was on his way. It sounded like he was still meeting with your uncle."

"He was."

I wait to see if there's more, but he's not forthcoming. He has me unlock my computer, then he checks some shit that I don't understand either. He pulls a laptop out of the bag he was carrying and connects it to my work one. Then he's typing things into both of them. I see a blue bar on a small window on my screen while information's populating on his. I'm standing off to the side, looking over his shoulder while he sits at my desk chair.

"Ms. O'Malley, you can sit. This is going to take a little while."

He gestures toward a chair on the other side of my desk. I'd rather be in my chair and feel in control of what's happening, but I'm not. Not in my chair, and not in control. He's doing other stuff, but I can't see now. He's clicking and typing. What's happening?

My door opens, and Ashley steps halfway in.

"Sinead—"

"Thank you."

Gabriele steps around her as he speaks. He doesn't slam the door on her, but he makes it clear she needs to step back.

"It's all right, Ash."

I walk forward and smile at her.

"Something's come up with a family member, and they're helping me."

"Your dad?"

"No. Nothing like that."

I glance up at Gabriele as he grimaces. I realize that was a stupid lie. As my client, he shouldn't be helping me with anything personal. I don't know why that came to mind. But it gets Ashley to back away. Gabriele closes the door softly, then I'm in his arms.

"Shh, *piccolina*. I'm here. What happened?"

He's speaking softly, but Lorenzo answers before I can.

"She's got spyware on her phone. It's been hacked. They've gotten into everything that has a saved password. Fortunately, there's very little work-related stuff, and you've kept your texts discreet."

Fuck. He read those? Thank God we haven't had phone sex. I rub my right fingers over my eye as I lean against Gabriele. I'm so glad he's so tall. I can put my head on his chest and not have the top of it jamming his chin.

"Sinead said something about an email."

"Yeah. Come and look."

Gabriele keeps his arm wrapped around me as we approach the desk. Lorenzo turns the computers toward us. Gabriele

reads the email on my laptop, then reads something on Lorenzo's. He looks at me before meeting Lorenzo's gaze. Something
is going on that I don't understand. I want to, but I don't think I
should ask.

"Lorenzo is going to take you to his parents' house. His
brothers are going to come over too. Uncle Massi will join you
guys in a bit. Auntie Nicoletta will probably feed you until you
pop. If I don't get back until late, she'll make sure you have a
guest room you can go to when you get tired."

I glance at Lorenzo before I look up at Gabriele.

"Should I expect not to hear from you?"

"Yes."

"Could it be a few days?"

"Yes."

"Will your friends have to go too? Or will someone be able
to stay with me? Or do I stay with Massimo and Nicoletta?"

"Carmine and Matteo will be with me. Lorenzo, Luca, and
Marco will take shifts guarding you. I want you to go about
your day just like normal, even if I'm gone for a while. Just
don't go anywhere without one of them."

"How scared should I be, Gabe? Don't tell me not to be
because I'm with your family."

"I don't want you out of their sight, but you can still go to
the office, the courthouses, client meetings. Whatever. But I
don't want you going to the police, and I don't want you talking
to any of them."

"What if the judge calls me in?"

"Then you go, and one guy stands outside the door."

"This person said they bugged my place. Are they the ones
responsible for the car bombing?"

"No."

His answer is immediate, and that makes me blink away
tears. Who else is after me? He draws me away from the desk

and positions us, so he's shielding me from anything Lorenzo could see. But I'm certain his friend can tell he's kissing me. I melt into it, and for a moment I forget why I asked him to come.

"*Piccolina*, I'll be back as fast as I can. But this ends now. You'll be safe."

"Will you be safe, Daddy?"

I barely make enough sound to count as a whisper. I more mouth my question than say it.

"Yes. I'm going to take care of this. No one is going to threaten you again."

"You sound so sure."

"I am. I love you, Sinead. There's nothing I won't do to protect you."

"I love you, Gabe. I trust you completely."

And I do. Our kiss is way too short, but we hear Lorenzo moving around. We look toward him, and he's packing up both laptops. He drops my phone in the bag, too. When he looks at Gabriele, he grins.

"You know what Car's going to say about this."

"*Fanculo*."

"What does that mean?"

He keeps looking at Lorenzo when he speaks.

"Fuck off. Gloat all you want, but you've gotten the same lecture as I have more than once."

"Gabe?"

"Carmine insists we're all asking for trouble using Apple products instead of Android. He and Maria are the only ones who do. He insists ours are easier to hack, and this proves his point. But we also have other resources available at our homes and in our cars to make sure no one's hacking them or wiretapping them."

"I'm getting a new phone. I want Carmine to tell me what to get."

I'm dead serious.

"We can do that this weekend. In the meantime, go with Lorenzo. I'll go listen to Carmine's 'I told you so's.'"

If they're jesting, does it mean that it isn't such a big deal after all? Or are they distracting me from some catastrophe? I don't want to know. I gather the rest of my stuff, and we head out. I see Marta as we approach the office door.

"Sinead?"

There's censure in her voice, and for once, it grates on me. I usually appreciate any concern she expresses. But right now, not so much. She and the managing partners accepted Gabriele and his family as our clients. If they hadn't, I wouldn't need their protection. I also wouldn't have found the love of my life, but I can acknowledge that later.

"Someone hacked my phone and sent me a threatening email. The Mancinellis have the resources to deal with it."

She opens her mouth then decides better of it. She just nods and steps aside. I know that isn't the end, but she'll wait until I'm alone. That's fine. By then, I'll have thought up an excuse. I recognize Pauly and Afonso when we get to the lobby. The four men surround me as we go to the car. I can't keep up with who's on what rotation anymore. I'm just happy to see them and know that Gabriele trusts them. It surprises me when Lorenzo follows me into the backseat and Afonso gets into the front passenger. That means Pauly's driving. I lean across Lorenzo to see Gabriele.

"Who's your guard? Why are you alone?"

"I go places without one. You know that."

"But..."

"It's all right. It'll be over soon."

Chapter Twenty-Six

Gabriele

I didn't tell Sinead it would end now just to reassure her. I meant it. Carmine and Matteo brought Duffy to the garage, and he's strung up naked, waiting for me when I arrive. I sneer at him as I head into the office. I strip off my suit coat and change into a looser fitting shirt. I put the surgical booties over my shoes since those are one thing we don't want to constantly replace. Suits are fine. But a well-fitting pair of Italian leather shoes is a work of art. I remove my watch, and as I do, I look at my left hand. Specifically, my left ring finger. Carmine and Matteo are getting ready too, and I watch them both slip off their rings and put them in our safe. I want to be doing that too. I want to be taking off the ring Sinead slips on my finger.

But I pull myself out of my fantasy and head into the main area of the garage. I grab the baseball bat and stride over to Duffy. I crack it against his ribs with more force and speed than he could have anticipated. He howls as I pull back. I shift my hold on the bat and drive it into his junk like a battering ram. I

377

step back and wait. Anything more, and he'll pass out. Then we'll have to wait. I'm not feeling as patient as usual.

"You're pissing a lot of people off these days, Duff. Even more than usual."

"Fuck you, you worthless Guido."

"I'm worth to the tune of twenty-five million dollars. Call me whatever the fuck you want. Doesn't change the fact you're the one strung up, and I'm the one who's going to kill you. Since you're dead regardless, you can decide how you go."

I point toward an enormous vat. There's a set of steps with six on each side. That's the only way to get to the lid, which stands about fifteen feet from the floor. It gives off steam, and it's easy to see the temperature dial from where we are.

"You know what that is, don't you?"

"I can guess."

"You have to since you've never been to the store. The O'Rourkes have never considered you good enough to be part of their inner circle. They know they can't trust you. They know that you're worthless to them. But you pissed them off. They plan to kill you for causing trouble. I just wanted to have the joy of doing it myself."

I slam the bat into the other side of his ribs. I'm certain I've broken a couple on each side. The bruising is starting faster than I expected.

"You threatened my girlfriend."

"Girlfriend? She's just some cunt you're fucking to make sure she gets you off."

He laughs at his double entendre.

I grab a set of pliers and step in front of him. I open the pliers wide enough to wrap around his dick. Then I squeeze. His screams are blood curdling, but I've heard worse, so I barely notice. I'm in the zone if you will.

"I already know you sent the email and text, which means I

know you bugged her place. I already suspected that. But the listening devices weren't what you can usually buy. They're law enforcement grade."

I didn't mention that to Sinead because I didn't know enough to do anything with that information. But now that I'm positive someone's leaking info to Duffy, I can admit that I know. Whoever's been filling his ear is likely the one who stashed the camera in the wrong box. I think we can all agree it's Detective Morris.

I release the pliers, and he sighs. Dumb fuck. I gesture to Carmine to lower him. When he's on his feet, his arms are low enough for me to reach. I snap off his left pinky before he knows what's coming.

"Tell me what I want to know. Every time you make me wait, I snap off another finger. I'll go through all your toes if I have to."

I take off his ring finger to further my point.

"How'd you find out Sinead was representing me?"

"It's public record, but I have other ways of finding out."

"Evasiveness will not serve you well."

I jab my fist into his belly, making him double over, which only makes him scream because it feels like his arms are about to be ripped off.

"Who told you?"

"Someone who knew."

I snap off another finger. Blood gushes from his hand. Keeping it above his heart is on purpose. It'll slow the bleeding a little. Enough for me to keep questioning.

"Did they come to you?"

He's breathing harder. His head is lolling to the side. All the pain is catching up to him.

"Yes."

"Why?"

"They know I'm connected to the mob. They know I can't stand you or your family. This was perfect. I could fuck you over and punish the bitch for forgetting whose side she's on."

"Mine. That's the only side Sinead picked."

"Cunt."

My hand whips out as I backhand him across his cheek. It's enough to not only turn his head, but knock him away from me. He swings back, and my fist connects with his right eye.

"Who told you?"

I know he won't tell me yet. Which is fine. It's what I want. I take off another finger. I grab a nail from the table that had the pliers and start with the stump that's left of his little finger. I stick the nail into the open wound.

"This little piggy went to market."

I move to his ring finger.

"This little piggy stayed at home."

Now to his middle finger.

"This little piggy had roast beef."

His index finger.

"This little piggy had none."

I release his hand and grab his thumb as I yank his arm behind him. Matteo and Carmine step forward, each grabbing an ass cheek.

"And this little piggy cried all the way home."

I shove his thumb up his ass.

Then I take the pliers to it and cut it off, leaving the digit behind as I drop his hand. Carmine and Matteo let him go, laughing as he pisses himself. They grab metal pipes and circle him as I step back into his line of sight.

"Start speaking, and it'll only be me who beats you. Keep being awkward, and my friends will join me. How long do you think you'll last?"

"Long enough to die without telling you shit."

"What school does your daughter go to again?"

His eyes widen, and his nostrils flair.

"You wouldn't go after her."

I pretend to frown.

"You went after my girl. Why wouldn't I go after yours?"

"She's only a kid."

"Exactly. If you don't want anything to happen to your defenseless child, tell me what I want to know."

I step up so close that I have to make sure I don't step in his piss.

"You think you know so much. If you did, you'd know I'm my family's enforcer. I have no limits. I have no boundaries. You fucked up going after me. You guaranteed I'll wipe out your entire family by going after my woman. You have one last chance to save them. Who gave you the information?"

I step back. I adopt the most menacing stare I can, and he believes me. He pisses himself again. I wait, knowing what will come next. The anxiety he feels increases the serotonin in his belly. It'll cause his colon to spasm.

"Did you just shit your own thumb out of your ass?"

Uncontrollable bowel movements. This isn't the first time I've made someone shit themselves out of fear. I doubt it'll be the last. Carmine and Matteo laugh as they each take a swing with their pipes. With synchronicity that comes with practice, the pipes land across his kidneys. This time he shits and pisses himself. What the fuck does he have left in there?

"Philip Morris. He did it."

Confirmation.

"Who's he working for?"

"I don't know. Maybe no one. He hates your entire family. He's been passed over for promotion twice because of your uncle's ties to the police commissioner. He hates Sinead because she's humiliated him on the stand before. The chance to get back at both of you at the same time was too much for him to pass up."

Someone else knew that. Morris wouldn't do this without incentive and assurance that his ass is covered. Duffy couldn't offer either of those. Who? There are the obvious big players in this game, but we can't rule out the Polish Mob yet. We know they were involved in the car bomb and Cohenour's death. The only ones we can rule out are the Kutsenkos. They wouldn't target Sinead.

"You bugged her place, but whose idea was that?"

"Morris."

"Him or whoever's paying him."

"Definitely his. He threatened me if I told anyone. Whoever he's working for didn't tell him to do it. He wanted anything on Sinead that he could use to blackmail her."

"What did he want from her?"

When Duffy just looks at me, I know exactly what he means. Now I'm going to do even worse to Morris than I am Duffy. That fuck face was going to blackmail my *piccolina* into sleeping with him. I don't want to imagine what he'd do to her when she refused. Because she isn't someone who would ever succumb to that. He'd have to force her. And that idea only pisses me off even more.

I won't get anything else from Duffy, but that doesn't mean I'm going to kill him yet. Nah. He can suffer a few more days. I never liked him, and getting Sinead involved guaranteed I hate him.

It's getting late, and I know Carmine and Matteo want to go home to their wives. I tell them to take off. I'm going to crash here. I'll set my alarm clock to wake me a few times, so I can torment Duffy some more. Marco and Luca will bring Morris in tomorrow. I want Duffy as close to death without being dead as I can get, so Morris knows what's coming. Seeing a dead body won't do shit to him. He's seen plenty. I want him to see the agony.

"Gabe!"

I look out the office window as I scrub my hands and arms. Duffy's unconscious partly from the beating I just gave his abdomen and partly because I sent him twirling and spinning. He's on the chain connected to the hook on the garage door belt.

"In here!"

I call back to Luca. I watch him drag a bound man into the garage. He's got a hood on, but I know he's gagged because that's how we always do it. Lorenzo follows them and kicks the guy in the kneecap. I hear the muffled scream and watch as he tries to stand up. But Luca yanks on him, keeping him from getting his feet under him. Lorenzo kicks the opposite ankle, barking at him to stand up. They keeping doing their routine until he's sprawled on the floor beside Duffy. I step out as I finish drying my hands and drop the paper towels in the burn barrel.

"Morris."

His head turns in my direction, but he's not sure where I am. I take ten silent steps to the left.

"Morris."

He tries to tell where I am again as he lumbers to his feet. I move silently again until I'm behind him. I grab a pipe as I pass the table.

"Morris."

He spins around, right into the bat, as it lands across his ribs. I actually hear them crack. He retches. I nod to Luca, who yanks the hood off. Philip gasps and gags as he looks up at me from his bent over position. I see no surprise, so he knew he'd be seeing me. I walk over and grab a handful of hair, wrenching his head back, forcing him to stand as I also pull up. I shove him toward Duffy. His scream is garbled, but we all laugh.

"Now look what you did."

I point to Duffy with the pipe.

"You got him to bug my girlfriend's apartment and her hotel room. That means you hacked into more than one system to find out where and when she was going and to control which room she got. I think someone had to help you with that."

Neither Duffy nor Philip has those level hacking skills. It's what convinces me another syndicate was involved. It's like the puzzle Sinead told me she looks to put together as a criminal defense attorney. I've had the various pieces, and I've been turning them around for a while. I wasn't sure where they fit when I looked at each one alone. But now that I'm putting them together, they're finding their exact spot.

"You have a choice, Morris. Take his gag out, Enzo."

"What choice?"

He practically spits at me as he speaks. His voice is already hoarse, and it makes me wonder how much of a fight he put up if he's already been screaming in pain.

"Tell me who put you up to this, and it's a clean kill. Make me work for the answer, and you'll be worse off than O'Toole. Which is it?"

"I'm not telling you shit."

"Do they have your family?"

That's usually the one thing that people believe they can hold out for. They can't. If they know, they eventually break. If they don't know, I can tell. I don't bother with them. That's why I haven't tried to get anything else out of Duffy. He reached the end of his usefulness last night. I've kept him alive to punish him.

"Fuck you."

"No thanks. I know you wanted Sinead to fuck you. And you knew she'd never do it willingly, so you thought to blackmail her. But you had to know she still wouldn't have consented. That means you planned to force her."

Nothing about him makes me think he'll deny the allegation. He just looks straight at me. Motherfucking cock sucking piece of fucking shit. He wants a reaction out of me just as much as I want one from him. I won't give it to him. I'm in control, and I won't give that up to him. While Lorenzo and Luca strip him and string him up, I take a bucket of water and toss it at Duffy. It revives him enough for him to lift his head. His face is entirely unrecognizable.

I watch Philip as he sees what happened to his coconspirator. Nothing. No reaction. Either the man deserves an Oscar, or he's a sociopath. I doubt the academy trained him the way we've been taught to hide all our emotions. He's Kutsenko level good at hiding his thoughts. They are sociopaths. All fucking eight of them— well, six Kutsenkos and two Andreyevs —same difference.

"Anything you want to say to Morris before I kill you, O'Toole?"

He opens his mouth, and I finally see Philip react. I cut out Duffy's tongue, licked his asshole with it after he shat himself, then shoved it back in his mouth until he puked it out. Now Philip can see he doesn't have one. All Duffy can do is make unintelligible sounds.

"Missed your opportunity, I guess."

I gesture to Luigi and Afonso, who came in with Luca and Lorenzo. They walk over and take Duffy down.

"Hook him up."

They know what I mean. It's all perfectly choreographed. Lorenzo's yanking Philip's arms above his head, then he's lifted onto his toes by the garage door. Luigi hits the button, and the lid to the acid vat slides back while Afonso connects Duffy's wrist restraints to a new pulley system. It hoists Duffy over the vat.

While Luigi controls the lever that dips Duffy into the acid, then pulls him out, Luca's manning the garage door. He opens it the same time as Duffy's feet, then legs, then ass goes into the acid. The garage door is practically ripping Philip's arms off. But the noise from the metal door clattering drowns their screams.

"Drop him."

I give the command, and Luigi obliges. There's a sploosh as Duffy lands in the acid, then silence. Philip's dangling and staring at where Duffy just disappeared. The lid slides back into place. I cross my arms and watch my new target.

"Talk, and I'll make your death less painful than being within an inch of your life then slowly swallowed by acid. Give me any shit, and I'll show you what I did to Duff was nothing more than a few love taps."

"Let me down. I can't think straight."

We all laugh. If he's in so much pain already that he can't think straight, this won't take long. Either he'll break and spill it all. Or he'll die.

"You gotta give to get. Tell me something I don't know."

"Duffy was stalking Sinead. He paid me fifteen grand for those listening devices. He wanted the best. But he also took photos of her. Before she met you, he got in her apartment and put in some cameras. He got photos of her naked and when she was with some other guy. He probably jerked off to them."

"I didn't find any cameras."

I'm seething. I look at Luca, and he nods. He'll go to Duffy's to find any photos. He'll destroy them. I know I can trust him simply because he's him. But I also know he loves his wife more than anything in the world, except the baby they're about to have. He won't take any pleasure in seeing them. I don't think Lorenzo would, but I won't doubt Luca. When I glance at Lorenzo, he nods. He gets it. He doesn't take it as an insult, and I'm glad.

"He took them out when I told him I wouldn't do shit to help him if he was going to be that pervy. Fuck. Nixon listened in on people and didn't go to jail. Bugging her place was fine with me. But taking video or photos crossed the line."

"So nice to know you have boundaries. You were going to rape her, but photos were too much. The fuck they were. You didn't want him beating off to the woman you wanted but couldn't have."

He does nothing to deny it. If he was possessive and jealous of Duffy seeing her naked, it makes me wonder if he's done shit that I don't know about to punish Sinead or me for being together. He watches me and grins. He knows what I'm thinking.

"Why'd you hide the dashcam?"

"What dashcam?"

"Sinead already found it."

That makes him falter. Interesting. No one warned him.

"Doesn't matter. She's the defense attorney. She can't just watch it."

"But she can use the mishandling of evidence as grounds for a dismissal. The only reason to hide it is because it exonerates me. If it hinted at my guilt, you would have leaked it to O'Toole to make sure it couldn't disappear."

"There's still enough evidence to convict you. That's why it's going to trial."

"But a smoking gun pointing in another direction outweighs all of it."

I pray that's what the dashcam is.

"What's on the video that you want hidden?"

He clams up. It makes me wonder if he's on it. Interesting. I tilt my head toward the office, and Lorenzo follows me in. I shut the door, but I watch Philip through the two-way mirror. He looks around, sizing up the place. I know he's trying to think if there's a way to escape. There isn't. But I let men think there might be. I give them enough time to formulate a few plans, abandoning each one until they realize there's no way out alive. Their self-created despair is almost as crushing as any beating I could give them.

I look at Lorenzo as he speaks. He's watching Philip too.

"Do you really think he would have assaulted Sinead?"

"I don't know. Maybe. I think he's arrogant enough to believe he could blackmail her into sex and wouldn't have to start forcing her. But I also think his patience could have snapped if she rejected him once too many times or said the wrong thing."

"Do you wish you'd found out about the photos before you put Duffy in the vat?"

"I wish I'd known yesterday. I could have tortured him more for it today, but he was already too far gone to register it."

"Do you need the camera to disappear?"

"I don't know. If Sinead can get this entire shitshow dismissed, then I want the camera. There has to be something on there that incriminates whoever did this. I want it for that. I don't care if it proves I'm innocent if there's no more case to deal with."

"You know Uncle Sal's going to say it's your call. If you want the camera, I can make it happen."

Irony's a bitch sometimes. And at others, it's just funny. The head of the forensics unit has a degree in Computer Science. The guy was from Iowa and didn't know who Lorenzo was when they were in college. They were roommates all four years. It shocked the shit out of them both when the guy came home to their apartment one day just before spring finals. He was all excited to tell Lorenzo that he got a job with the NYPD. He couldn't get why Lorenzo wasn't as enthused as he expected.

The guy started a short internship the next day as a way to train him before he officially started work. That was when he discovered who the Mancinellis are. We were in the middle of a racketeering investigation. Lorenzo made evidence disappear as quickly as this guy could find it.

Fast forward four years, and the guy's brother-in-law was about to go down for a white-collar crime. Lorenzo found out and made evidence disappear without saying anything to his old roommate beforehand. He didn't have to. Lorenzo got a call in the middle of the night from his old friend, promising a favor in return. Lorenzo hasn't cashed in on it yet. He's offering to now.

"Let's see how this plays out a little longer."

The next ten hours feel like ten years. Lorenzo and I take turns working Philip over, but we knew within the first hour that he knew nothing else. We were just punishing him for being involved. I finally ended it with a bullet between his eyes.

I'm clean and on my way to Uncle Massimo and Auntie Nicoletta's. Lorenzo's driving, and I just turned on my phone. Immediately, a text alert pops up.

SINEAD

Good news. Come home ASAP.

I don't know when she sent this. I hit the call button.

"Daddy, you're free."

That's sounds nearly as good as hearing Sinead tell me she loves me.

"Hi, *piccolina*. What happened?"

389

"I got the video from the evidence room, and it shows Morris moving the camera to the other box. But it also shows Tyler watching it with Morris before they put it back in the wrong box. Someone walks in on them, and Morris pulls his gun on the guy. They arrested Tyler, but they can't find Morris."

They will in a few days. We'll make it look like suicide. I know Sinead's hoping I'll fill in the gap in the story where Philip is concerned, but she knows I can't.

"Anyway, Judge Hutchens granted the dismissal. They not only broke the chain of custody, there was clear proof of evidence tampering. I don't know why Tyler agreed to help Morris, but I don't care. It's over."

I glance at Lorenzo, who's paying attention to the road. I don't know if he heard how Sinead started the conversation, but if he did, he's giving nothing away.

"Where are you?"

"At our place. Carmine and Serafina are here. Mario's in the lobby, and some other guys I don't know are outside."

"All right. I'll have Enzo drop me off. I'll be home in an hour."

I pray traffic isn't bad enough for it to take that long. Once I hang up, Lorenzo beats me to it.

"I'll get the camera to you tonight. Stay quiet."

He commands his car to place a call.

"Zack, it's Enzo."

"I already have it. I heard all about it. Where?"

"Leave it in the begonia bush outside the lemon-colored house three streets over from you."

"Are you su—"

"Yes."

"Let me get the dog on the leash. Hang on."

We hear some shuffling around while Lorenzo changes our

route. It only takes a few minutes for me to recognize we're in a neighborhood with about a dozen Cosa Nostra homes. I look at Lorenzo, and he winks. Winks. I don't think he even does that to women. He's enjoying my shock.

I mouth "does he know" as I stare past him and out the driver's side window. We just passed our last *consigliere's* granddaughter's house. She was the first girl I ever slept with. He shakes his head as I sit back. We pass a gas station where I stole my first car because Carmine bet me I couldn't get it started. Lorenzo slows down as his contact speaks again.

"All right. It's there. You could have told me about the neighborhood, Enzo."

"Don't you like it?"

"What's not to like? I'm raising kids surrounded by—"

"Men who will always make sure you're safe."

There's a long pause, and we see him stop walking. He looks around as his dog sits beside his left leg.

"Thank you."

The call ends as we pull up around the corner. It'll be dark in about five minutes. It's already past dusk. We wait fifteen before I slip out of the car. I'm already in dark clothes, so I'm not too noticeable despite my height and size. I flick on my phone's flashlight just long enough to spot it. I pull it out and head back to the car. I wait until we're on the bridge into Manhattan before I turn it on.

"Motherfuckers. I'm going to fucking kill them."

Chapter Twenty-Seven

Sinead

Relieved doesn't even begin to explain how I feel right now. Euphoric might be a closer term. I'm trying not to bounce off the walls as I wait for Gabriele to get home. Neither Serafina nor Carmine expect me to pay much attention to the conversation, and I appreciate it. I know I'm being rude, but I can't help it. All I can think about is Gabriele's going to remain free. This nightmare is over. At least the part with him possibly spending life in prison. I don't want to know how things stand with the Polish Mob. If he could call me, it's because he left that place. I don't think he'd leave *and* call me if it wasn't done.

Duffy and Philip... It didn't surprise me they couldn't find Philip. I paused when I talked to Gabriele in case he wanted to say something. I'm glad he didn't lie. If he had, it would have been because he thought he was protecting me. I'd rather have the silence. I'm certain no one is finding Duffy either. I won't think about how the Mancinellis will handle people asking why both men are gone. I won't make it my business unless I have to defend someone.

I'm out of my seat the moment I see the elevator doors parting. Gabriele practically shoves Lorenzo as his long legs eat up the space between us. I throw myself at him, and he lifts me off my feet. You'd think he'd just been let out of prison the way I cover his face with kisses before we share one that makes my toes curl. When he finally puts me down, he holds onto me as he whispers.

"I love you, *piccolina*. I love coming home to you. I love knowing we're going to curl up together, and being with you is going to make the rest of the world disappear."

"I want to curl up with you and a good book, Daddy. There is no rest of the world. I love you, too."

I feel him sigh, and I know the rest of the world is still here. I gaze up at him and wait.

"I have the dashcam, and I've seen what's on it. I need to meet with my family, and this can't wait. We need to go to Uncle Salvatore's."

It's my turn to sigh. This is one of those times where I—where we —can't come first. The family does. I step away. I expect the three guys and Serafina to head toward the elevator. Lorenzo, Carmine, and Serafina do, but Gabriele doesn't.

"Sinead, you're coming too."

He wraps his arm around my waist and pulls me tight. He keeps his voice low, but I'm sure the others can hear.

"You're my family now, too."

"But we're not—"

"We can be by tomorrow night."

I stare, barely blinking. I don't know if he's serious. He kisses my neck just behind my ear.

"That's not how I'm proposing, *cuore*. But I am proposing soon."

I'm back to grinning like a fool. Lorenzo drives himself along with Carmine and Serafina. Gabriele and I ride in the back of a town car together. A trip to Queens has never been so short. We only have enough time for me to come twice before Gabriele realizes we're pulling into the neighborhood. Three more thrusts, and we're both panting. We're straightening our clothes as we pull into the circular driveway.

It's a veritable mansion-slash-castle. The home is huge. If you didn't know where to look, you would never imagine so many distinguished homes existed in Queens, but they do. And I'm now standing in front of one.

Gabriele slides his hand into mine and leads me to the front door. He punches in a code, and I follow him inside. The first thing I notice is the aroma coming from the kitchen. It's a gastronomic delight before you even taste anything.

We follow the voices into the kitchen, and I can't help but stare. Salvatore, Massimo, Luca, Carmine, Lorenzo, Marco, Matteo, and an older man I don't know are washing and drying dishes.

They have matching gingham aprons on. As if that weren't enough to boggle the mind, it's impossible not to laugh when you realize the aprons would be nearly knee-length on most women but are like micro-minis on them. Good thing they're all wearing pants. I sweep my gaze around the kitchen and spy two little girls standing between Massimo and the man I don't know. I can't hear them, but it looks like they're both giving very strict instructions.

I realize the mouthwatering aromas are coming from the ovens and something simmering on the stove. As I notice this, I hear women's voices to my right.

"Gabriele, they saved the cooking spoons and knives for you. Sinead, come join us."

I recognize Paola's voice. I look up at him, and he's grimacing. I follow his gaze, and my eyes widen. There are at least six butcher's knives, four paring knives, a bread knife, and probably twelve large spoons on the counter beside the sink. It's obvious no one soaked them, and the food is already caked on them. It's going to take some real scrubbing. Marco walks over, an apron dangling from his fingers.

"Be sure to take care of those dishpan hands before you head home, Gabe."

Gabriele shoves Marco. Hard. But the man barely shifts. Instead, he laughs at Gabriele, who mutters something in Italian that I don't understand.

"Gabriele!"

"Yes, Auntie Lotta."

"I heard that."

"Yes, Auntie Lotta."

There's no way she heard anything. Even with supersonic hearing. The woman just knows these guys. When I hear snickering, I find Massimo, Salvatore, and the man I realize must be either Domenico or Cesare laughing at Gabriele. The same voice carries to the kitchen again.

"Mimmo!"

"Yes, Lotta."

"Be nice to him. *Non mettete in imbarazzo il povero ragazzo.*"

I look up at Gabriele, and I think he's blushing. Or maybe it's annoyance because he's scowling as more of the guys laugh. I wait for him to interpret, but he says nothing. Serafina walks up behind me and takes mercy on my confusion.

"She told her husband to not embarrass the poor boy."

"Mimmo?"

I whisper because I don't want to be rude, but I've never heard that name before. Serafina nudges me and gestures toward the living room. I glance up at Gabriele again.

"Go. Dinner will be ready soon."

"They haven't eaten yet? I thought those were leftovers for us or something."

"No. Aunt Sylvia won't serve dinner without the kitchen being clean first. There will be a mountain by the time we're done, and she says she doesn't need an avalanche to clean up. We do the dishes, and she and my aunts cook. We've tried it the other way around, and we realized we'd starve."

I smile and follow Serafina.

"Mimmo is what Auntie Carlotta calls Uncle Domenico. Only she calls him that. The rest of us call him Uncle Domenico or Uncle Dom. Only Carmine calls me Fina, but everyone else calls me Sera. Only Luca calls Olivia Livy."

"And only I call Matteo Matty."

As Maria approaches, I notice she bears a striking resemblance to Luca, Lorenzo, and Marco now that I know the men too. But she's decidedly feminine even though I know she used to be a tomboy. I remember the stories she told me in the hospital. Her smile spells trouble with every letter of the alphabet. A man's voice travels from the kitchen.

"Sinead, don't encourage Bambi. And don't be fooled by how innocent she looks. My wife will lead you to hell and hand you a fan."

"Bambi?"

"Yes. It's short for *bambina*. He used to call me that when we were kids until I beat him at the fifty-yard dash. Once we got together, he went back to calling me that, and I went back to calling him Matty."

I enter the living room with Serafina and Maria, and it's a little overwhelming to see all the women together. I don't know why it intimidates me more than a kitchen filled with linebackers. They all look so friendly and kind, and if they're like

Carlotta, who I remember visiting me in the hospital, I'm sure they are. But it's nerve-wracking.

"We don't bite, Sinead. Promise."

The most elegant woman I've ever seen stands up and offers me her chair. Her Italian accent is as thick as Serafina's. But they're not quite the same. This woman's is a stronger version of Gabriele's diluted one.

Serafina points to people, starting with the woman who offered me a chair.

"This is *Zia* Sylvia. She's my mother's younger sister. She's *Zio* Salvatore's wife, and the mom to those two little generals in the kitchen. She's Carmine's aunt because *Zio* Salvatore is Paola's older brother. You'll probably find it odd that I call them *zio* and *zia* for uncle and aunt, but that's how I've always known them since I grew up in Venice. Now that I'm a Mancinelli, I call the others auntie and uncle. So, this is Auntie Nicoletta. She's Uncle Massimo's wife and Luca, Marco, Lorenzo, and Maria's mom. You met Auntie Carlotta already. She's Uncle Domenico's wife. Her son Matteo married Maria. Auntie Carlotta and Auntie Nicoletta have been best friends since they were children. Uncle Domenico is Uncle Massimo's best friend. Uncle Domenico is Uncle Massimo, *Zio* Salvatore, and Mama's adopted second cousin."

Now I'm so lost. Serafina must see my confusion.

"I call Carmine's mom Mama too. It just feels natural."

Paola walks over to us and kisses Serafina's cheek then mine. I don't think I noticed Serafina called Paola that while we had dinner at Paola's house. Maria grins at me.

"I'll draw you a family tree."

"I might need that."

Serafina walks over to a very pregnant woman and helps her out of the chair.

"This is Olivia, Luca's wife."

"Hello."

I smile at Olivia, and I have a sudden pang of envy. I swallow it down, but Gabriele's words about me having kids with him rings in my ears. I glance at Serafina, then Maria, and wonder if they plan to have kids. I know Maria is my age since she's the same as Gabriele and Carmine. I think Serafina must be close. Olivia looks maybe a year or two younger than us.

I hadn't given serious thought to having kids until now. I turn when I hear two little girls announce dinner's ready. Gabriele has one on each hip. When my gaze meets his, I freeze. He lowers the girls to the floor and whispers something to them that makes them giggle. I move with the crowd until I reach him. He tucks me against his chest.

"What's the matter, *piccolina*?"

"I want that."

"Want what?"

"To see you carrying out kids like that."

The words tumble from my mouth. I'm fucking mad as a hatter.

"I want to see you like Olivia, knowing that we made the baby growing inside you."

"Really?"

"Yes."

I glance around before continuing.

"It's not too soon to talk about this for real?"

"Who says it's too soon? It's the right time for us."

I wrap my arms around his waist and inhale his light cologne. It calms me almost as much as lavender.

"You like my cologne, don't you? You relax when you smell it."

"Almost as much as I do lavender. After the accident, lavender was the only thing that calmed me enough to sleep. I keep it everywhere in my place because it's something I can focus on if I feel a panic attack coming. Before the one you saw, I hadn't had one in years. I don't need it, but I like it."

"Then I'll make sure we have fresh lavender in our homes every day."

"Homes?"

"I have other properties, *piccolina*. I have places in Europe, South America, and Asia."

"Oh."

What else do I say? I let him guide me into the dining room. The food is better than any Michelin star restaurant, and I laugh so hard my cheeks hurt by the end of the meal. But reality crashes over me when the men finish the second round of dishes and head toward a hallway.

"Come on, *piccolina*."

I push back my chair, unsure why Gabriele is holding out his hand. None of the other women are leaving the dining room table, and I didn't think I'd be part of any meeting involving just the other men. I entwine my fingers with his and follow him into an enormous den-cum-office. Matteo's just closed the door when someone knocks. Seeing him in person, I recognize the man from photos at Paola's house.

"Sorry I missed dinner."

Cesare says no more, and I get the feeling no one's going to ask why. I glance at Carmine, but he seems unfazed. I know Cesare and Paola have— an agreement. Maybe it was work that kept him, or maybe he was with someone else. I'm curious, but I'm not nosey enough to ask Gabriele.

I sweep my gaze around the room. There's an enormous old-fashioned wood desk that looks like it belongs in the Oval Office. There are three sofas and four arms chairs scattered around three sides of the desk. Domenico and Cesare sit on one sofa while Lorenzo and Luca share another. Massimo, Carmine, and Matteo take chairs. If I weren't there, I think

Marco would race Gabriele for the last sofa, but he takes the last chair while Gabriele and I sit on the free sofa. The men fill the room, and what felt large a moment ago feels nearly bursting at the seams.

Salvatore holds his hand out as he speaks.

"Gabriele, you watched the video already. Let me connect it for everyone else to see."

Gabriele passes the dashcam to Salvatore. I hadn't realized it was in his pocket, but it's smaller than I'd originally expected. Salvatore connects it to his computer while Massimo turns on a TV. I watch as TV and computer sync, then the video starts.

I lean forward as I watch the car with the camera pull up to where the construction site still stands. The engine turns off, and someone gets out. But I don't hear the door close. Voices are pretty clear, so the car windows must have been open too. The driver walks in front of the car, and some other guy comes from the right. They step near a fence around a loading area and wait underneath a towering spotlight. There's lumber inside the fencing with the construction site on the other side.

Salvatore fast forwards until we see them moving again. The time stamp shows they waited five minutes, then they head back to their cars, and I hear trunks slam. They're carrying boxes to the loading area, and one of them picks the fence's lock. They go inside for fifteen minutes. Again, Salvatore fast forwards, and the time stamp lets me know how long they're in there.

"Asshole's not coming. Let's go."

It was the driver of the dashcam car who speaks. The two guys head back to the vehicle when headlights flash in front of the camera.

"Finally."

I think that was the second guy who came from a different car. It's dark outside, so it's hard to see until the new man walks up to the other two. I think Gabriele is gorgeous, but this guy rivals him. He could be a fucking Armani model. Dark hair that looks black in the dim light. But his blue eyes stand out, and they're a similar color to mine. I had an ex-boyfriend call me the Ice Princess during the fight that broke us up. He said my eyes were the same color as the ice running through my veins.

There are no greetings. The new guy gets straight to the point.

"You know what you're doing, right?"

The accent. It's Russian. I'm certain of it. I glance around, and I can tell all the men in the room knew who this was before he spoke. I twist to see Gabriele.

"Aleksei Kutsenko."

I recognize the last name, but I don't know who this guy is. I keep watching.

"Yeah. We've worked construction for the Mancinellis before. We've seen it done."

"Seen it? That isn't the same as doing it. You told Jacek you've done demolition before."

"We set the fuse and leave."

"No."

The guy twists toward the lumberyard before he looks back at the two men I realize are barely more than teenagers. They're the ones who died in the explosion. The Russian keeps speaking.

"Leave. We aren't doing this. You lied and don't know how to do this. I won't be responsible for you blowing yourselves up. I want Scotto in prison for life, not me on trial for manslaughter. Go."

The owner of the dashcam steps forward, posturing with a lot more bravado than he should have.

"No one's gonna know you had anything to do with this. Just like they aren't gonna know we did, either."

Aleksei shoves the kid, and he falls back against the hood.

"You're useful for now. Don't change my mind."

The second young man interjects, jutting his chin in the air.

"We still gonna get paid?"

"For what? You can't do the job Jacek hired you for. You're lucky I don't make you pay me for lying and wasting my time."

The one who asked about getting paid swings at Aleksei, who grabs his wrist and twists it behind his back as he slams him face down on the hood.

"Come at me again, and I'll break every fucking bone in your body before I dump you in the East River. Drowning is an agonizing death, but with your body shattered into tiny pieces under your skin, you won't be able to swim. Fuck around and find out."

He gives the kid another shove before he steps back.

"I have another job for you. Let's see if you can manage it."

The guy with the dashcam steps between them.

"What is it?"

"There're flammables in barrels just inside the fence." He points. "Pour them everywhere, then get out."

"That's it?"

I can't tell who said that. The guys sound a lot alike, and they're standing too close to the car for the camera to catch their faces. But I can see Aleksei's. Something about it makes my skin crawl.

"Yeah."

"Do you want us to drop a match or something? The place'll light up like the Fourth of July."

"Will it?"

The two young guys laugh, but Aleksei barely cracks a smile. Oh, fuck. I whisper in Gabriele's ear.

"That stuff they carried in were explosives, right?"

"Yeah."

"And Aleksei knows, doesn't he?"

"Yeah."

I turn back to the TV and watch in horror as the two guys break into the lumberyard again. I can't see or hear anything, but Aleksei casually walks toward the open fence. He doesn't get closer to the gate, but he stands in front of it.

Before I can guess what's going to happen, he draws his gun and fires three times. Two go in the same direction. Through the gate and into the guys doing his dirty work. The third bullet hits something metal and causes a spark. I hear the plunk of metal hitting metal, then there's a whoosh as the spark catches whatever they poured all over the lumber and supplies.

"What was that?"

"Micronized copper azole. It's used to treat lumber. But in the state it was in, it was basically tiny copper pieces suspended in water. Along with other chemicals that get mixed in, it's highly flammable. Not what you'd expect for something that goes on wood. It took very little to ignite that place."

I keep watching the video as Aleksei watches the flames spread. He walks away as calm as can be and gets into his Range Rover. He drives away, and you can see his taillights in the distance just before the explosion. A fire ball leaps into the air before it appears to spread to the four corners of the Earth. Really, it spreads across the entire lumberyard and over to the construction site. Both areas go up in a blaze within minutes. Debris lands on the car and shakes the camera, but it keeps recording.

Sirens approach, and we watch firefighters work. Salvatore fast forwards through most of it until there's just some smoldering piles of ash. I recognize Philip Morris when he arrives. He talks to the fire chief and some other people before another firefighter leads him into the crime scene. He looks around then comes back over to his car, which he parked near the one the victim drove. I hear him talking to someone just outside the dashcam's focal range. He asks the first question.

"You know who owns this place?"

"Yeah. Some guy in Connecticut. He owns a bunch of condo communities and was starting a new one here."

"Who worked for him?"

"Mostly Russian and some other Eastern Europeans."

"No Mexicans or Italians?"

"You mean Mancinelli men?"

"Yeah or Diaz."

"Diaz? They're Colombian."

"Whatever. Same difference."

There's a pause as the other officer looks at him. I recognize him. Santiago Ramirez. He's a good guy. I remember talking to him once while waiting to go into court for different cases. His dad's Mexican, and his mom's Puerto Rican. Smooth, Philip.

"No. No Diaz men here that I know of. I don't know about Mancinellis."

"Morris!"

Someone hurries over and stops just beyond the camera.

"We found some two-by-fours the fire missed. They have Scotto stamped on them."

Philip looks constipated, but I know that expression. It's when he's trying not to smile because he knows it's an inappropriate moment. I've seen it too many times.

"He knew all along."

"What?"

Gabriele glances down at me and whispers. I point to the TV.

"That expression. I've seen it before. Morris could be smug as fu— He had a way of forcing himself not to smile when he wanted to laugh at someone he thought he had the upper hand on. I've been on the receiving end of it six times. Each time was right before I impeached him on the stand."

The two cops he was talking to walk away, but Philip stays in range of the dashcam when he pulls out his phone. We watch him tap his screen, then put it to his ear.

"Yeah, it's done, Kutsenko. Entire place is gone. One of my guys found that lumber you dumped after it started. Somehow you got lucky and none of it was touched. The Scotto logo is completely clear."

There's silence for a moment.

"They pulled those two bodies out, or what's left of them. There's not enough to identify them, but I'll make sure to drop breadcrumbs that lead to Scotto. No one will know you were here."

There's silence again.

"I know that's what you pay me to do. I'll get the arrest warrant as fast as I can. But you know he's going to lawyer up."

He turns toward the dashcam and squints.

"I'll fuck with whoever they hire."

He hits speakerphone as he types something into his phone. Aleksei's voice comes through muffled but intelligible.

"You ever heard of Sinead O'Malley?"

"Yeah. She's a defense attorney. Got a pair of tits on her any man would want to fuck."

"Disgusting."

"What? If you saw them, you'd agree."

"I'm married. Move on. What do you know about her? I heard the Mancinellis are asking around about that firm. She's their best attorney."

"She is. Doesn't Massimo handle their legal shit? I'd ask about Gabriele, but he won't be defending himself."

"Massimo won't defend Gabriele on this. The optics

wouldn't be good. They'll get outside counsel for sure. If they hire her, I want everything you know about her."

"I thought you didn't go after women."

"We don't. It doesn't mean we can't be informed."

"I'll get you everything you need."

He ends the call and walks away. Salvatore fast forwards until I recognize the crime scene officer.

"Play this part, please. I know him too."

I watch Ryan approach the car. He's dictating his notes as he goes. When he gets to the camera, he describes the brand and model. He states it was recording at the time that he found it. He checks his watch and says what time he turns it off. Then it goes black.

I sit back as I try to take in everything we just saw. I don't know what the fuck to make of it.

Chapter Twenty-Eight

Gabriele

I watched the video in the car while Lorenzo drove. He heard all of it, but I saw it all. If Philip wasn't already dead, I'd fucking kill him all over again. Aleksei basically gave Philip the go-ahead to spy on Sinead. Maybe he didn't know Philip wanted to fuck Sinead. But he knew the guy was dirty and would do shady shit.

He made Sinead a target. He knew about her before Uncle Salvatore and Uncle Massimo even hired her firm and her. They were already watching her. I'm so far passed enraged I don't know what to call this. If Sinead weren't beside me, I'd be losing my shit. I'm only holding it together to keep from terrifying her. I was furious when I saw it the first time, but I caught things I missed the first time around. Now I want to smash Aleksei's head in. Motherfucker.

"Gabriele?"

I wrap my arm around Sinead's shoulders as she leans against me.

"Can I go home now?"

Not we. I. Does she mean her place?

"If you don't want a driver to take me back to the penthouse, I get it. I know you probably need to stay here and deal with this, but I just want to go home and climb into our bed. This was a lot to see."

What the fuck did I just do? What the fuck did we all just do? I let her watch two men get murdered. I have never been this careless in my life. I let her watch it as my defense attorney to know what really happened. I let her watch it as my girlfriend to reassure her there was legit evidence that proves my innocence. I didn't think about the part where she'd see Aleks shoot two people. Fucking hell.

"Let's go now."

"Don't you need to stay here?"

She darts her gaze over to Uncle Salvatore and Uncle Massimo. They're both watching us. They nod, but Uncle Salvatore looks up at the ceiling.

"I do. We can stay here tonight. I'll be down here talking if you need anything. I'll go up with you and show you our room."

She mouths "our."

I lean to whisper to her.

"No one thinks we're virgins anymore."

Her cheeks flush, and she can't look anywhere but at the floor. It's adorable. I lead her out of the den to a quiet house. The women must have gone to bed. There are enough bedrooms here for everyone to have one. We walk up the stairs in silence, and I let her into the room I use when I spend the night. I have some clothes in here already.

"Are you just going to be talking?"

"Most likely. If I have to go out, I'll wake you and let you know."

"It's a good thing I live with you. You know where to find

your lawyer in the middle of the night."

She tries to jest, and I smile. But I can tell she's exhausted and scared. I point out the bathroom and tell her there are extra toothbrushes in the middle drawer. I open the dresser and pull out one of my t-shirts. When she comes back out, I help her undress before slipping the t-shirt over her head and arms. She squeaks when I carry her bridal style to the bed. She gets under the covers, and I perch on the edge of the bed.

"I won't leave without telling you. If you need me, come back down to the den. If I go out and you need something, Aunt Sylvia and Uncle Salvatore's room is across the landing at the far end. Just knock. Uncle Sal's a light sleeper."

"I won't disturb them in the middle of the night."

She's so aghast you'd think I told her to traipse into a palace and wake a king.

"You can if you need anything. Or you can go to Auntie Paola's room. It's the first one on the right down that hallway."

"Okay."

She sighs and accepts that suggestion.

"Wait. Does that mean if you go do something, Salvatore won't?"

"It's rare any of my uncles to go do something."

I smile at her, and she nods. She won't ask for more, and I appreciate it. She rolls onto her side, and I give her a quick kiss before I return downstairs. Cesare speaks first. He's like a second father to me. He's a good man who married into a family with a bunch of old fuckers who treated him like shit. I can remember both of Carmine's grandfathers. Uncle Salvatore and Uncle Massimo couldn't be less like their father. Same for Cesare and his father. Uncle Salvatore rules with an iron fist, but *all* of his family is everything to him. It's how I didn't get thrown out with the trash years ago.

"Is she all right?"

"Yeah. Tired. I watched that video. I knew what was coming. I shouldn't have let her see it. I can't believe I didn't think about what she'd witness Aleks do."

"We get desensitized to this stuff."

He shrugs. He's right. He may seem like a mild-mannered insurance agent, but he has all the same skills as the rest of us, with plenty of practice. Uncle Salvatore knows his skills are better used elsewhere. He's only been coming to more of our meetings since shit went sideways while Carmine and Serafina were dating.

For all his parents' dysfunction, they were always united about putting Carmine first. He's had to let Carmine make his own mistakes and learn from them, but he's always been there to point out that Carmine has to take responsibility for his actions. Then he'd help Carmine stand back up. Just like Auntie Paola has been a second mom to me, he's been a second dad to me. Right now, his reassurance goes a long way.

I look over when Uncle Salvatore speaks.

"What do you want to do? Your decision."

That's more trust than he's put in me for years. Two years ago, he wouldn't have given me the opportunity to lead even if it were my girlfriend in danger. I've come a long way. I glance at Carmine, and he smiles. We've both come a long way. It helps that our family understands why we did the stupid things we did.

"I want Bartlomiej to lick our boots. His men work exclusively for us. If any work for the Kutsenkos, we ruin all their side hustles. Jacek— he's going to pay us to stay alive. We'll be collecting on that for years."

I look over at the TV, which is now turned off.

"They're going to deny targeting Sinead. They're going to say they were staying informed. They'll say Morris took it upon himself to put those devices in place. They'll say they had nothing to do with O'Toole. They'll fucking deflect. But they knew about her and gave Morris the green light. We all know they'll claim it's nothing like what we did."

I look at Luca and Carmine.

"And it's not. But they've always acted like they're so much better than us. That they would never stoop to involving our women. That's exactly what they did."

I stop to think for a minute. I sit back and grin.

Carmine put his hands up as if to say, "spit it out."

"There's a Yale alumni dinner next week. Laura and Sinead were in the same class. I hadn't planned to attend, but I'll ask Sinead if she wants to go. If she does and Laura's there, I might suggest Sinead strikes up a conversation with Laura. If we go together, it won't be a secret we're involved. I might suggest Sinead mention to Laura how Aleksei told a cop to investigate her. Then that cop got another guy involved who tried to ruin her career and endangered her. I might also have Sinead mention Laura's husband is friends with two men who tried to blow her up. We won't need to do a damn thing after that."

I sit back against the sofa and watch the others laugh. Sinead might be the spark, but Laura is the powder keg. When she detonates, there won't be a Kutsenko brother who doesn't face her wrath.

"You look beautiful, *piccolina*."

I brush the back of my fingers up the outside of her arm, loving how she shivers at my touch. She's wearing an ice-blue cocktail dress that matches her eyes. We picked it out together after I suggested she talk to Laura. She had plenty of idea about things she could say. When we spotted the dress online, she was the one who said it would definitely make Laura think of her husband's eyes. They're the same color as Aleksei's. It would likely make Laura even more pissed, even if it was subconscious.

Now we're riding up the elevator to the floor with the ball-rooms in the hotel that's hosting the alumni dinner. As soon as we step off, we spot Laura and Maksim.

"He's as big as you."

Sinead clearly didn't realize how big Aleksei was in the video because I told her the four Kutsenko brothers could be identical quadruplets. There's less than a year in between each one. Bogdan is the youngest and my age. Nikolai is thirty-two, Aleksei is thirty-three, and Maksim is thirty-four.

"Should we go over now?"

"We can. Are you okay with this, *piccolina*?"

"Yes, Daddy. I feel a little badly that we're dragging Laura into this. She was always nice to me, and we got along. But we aren't friends, and her brother-in-law fucked us over."

We've done nothing to them, letting them think we don't know about their involvement in the shit show at the construction site. I rest my hand at her lower back.

"Do you want me to strike up the conversation?"

"No. You and Maksim can't stand each other. It's better if I start it with Laura."

We're a few feet away, so I wrap my arm around her waist, and we walk directly to them.

"Laura?"

"Sinead? Hi. It's been ages."

Laura gives Sinead a loose hug before she looks at me. Her eyes narrow, and dislike radiates from her. That's fine. I can't fault her for not liking me. Her sister-in-law got hurt because of me. I didn't mean for it to happen, but it did. If she never forgives me, I can't blame her.

"Laura, you know my boyfriend, Gabriele."

"Hello, Laura, Maks."

"Gabe."

Maksim practically spits my name at me. But Sinead shifts the attention back to her and Laura.

"Laura, I heard you left your firm to work with your husband. Congratulations."

"Thank you."

"I also heard you have twins. That's so exciting."

"Konstantin and Mila are almost two and running in different directions. Exciting is one way to put it."

We all laugh, and I admit Maks beams when his wife talks about their kids. But that smile falters when Sinead plunges in.

"It's a small world that you and I should end up with such similar men after going to law school together. I actually thought I saw you, Maks, in a video the other day."

His expression hardens, and I draw Sinead closer to my side. He smirks at me, but it doesn't last.

"Yeah. Turns out it was one of your brothers. Aleks was talking to two guys right before they died in the explosion the cops accused Gabe of setting. It was that explosion that connected me with Gabe. Everything that went along with it was horrible, but I'm glad I met Gabe. It was further into the video that really made me think of you, Laura. It was when Aleks spoke to Detective Morris and mentioned me by name."

She pauses for a moment, her gaze shifting from Laura to Maks and hardening. This is the woman who would have defended me in the courtroom and brought that fuck face Tyler to his knees.

"Gabe swore up and down that your family never targets women. That's why it was so confusing to hear Aleks suggest the detective learn all about me then pass that information on to Aleks and I suppose your husband, too. That detective tampered with evidence that showed your brother-in-law's guilt and Gabe's innocence. Considering Aleks suggested Morris spy on me, it makes me wonder what else your family suggested. Gabe found bugs in my apartment and the hotel room I was supposed to occupy for my safety."

Sinead raises her chin as she looks back at Laura, who opens her mouth, but Sinead continues.

"I know Bartlomiej and Jacek are close acquaintances of yours, Maks. They tried to blow me up. If Gabe hadn't noticed the dome light didn't turn on, we'd both be dead. Just think, Laura. We thought we didn't have that much in common way back when. You pursuing corporate law and me choosing criminal law. But turns out, we aren't so different in our taste in men."

I watch Laura as she watches Sinead. She's biting her tongue when I know she wants to lash out and defend her family. She's reining in her temper, but it's a struggle. The *pièce de résistance* is yet to come. Sinead reaches into her clutch and pulls out a thumb drive, which she holds up.

"After you put the kids to bed, you should curl up and watch this movie. The men in your family are very photogenic. Aleks looks great during his close up."

She offers it to Laura, but she doesn't let go immediately.

"I know what Gabe did. I'll never make excuses for it. Your husband and his brothers can do whatever they have to. But if one of them involves me or any of the women in the Mancinelli family, I will blame you. You and I will be face off, and you and I both know a showdown between us will make anything they've done to each other look like toddlers throwing tantrums."

I confessed everything that happened with Anastasia Kutsenko, Nikolai's wife. I wanted it off my conscience, but I also wanted her prepared when this conversation happened. I didn't want Laura or Maks to say something that would blind-side her. I didn't expect her to issue Laura a threat.

Laura turns more squarely toward Sinead, and it looks like Maks tries to pull her back. She ignores him.

"You're right. You and I know what that will look like. We went up against each other more than once in law school. We're both far more experienced now and with far more to lose. You're about as likely to back down as I am. I'll deal with my family, but you keep *him* under control, and we won't have a problem."

She arches an eyebrow when she talks about me, but she doesn't shift her gaze from Sinead's.

"Agreed."

Sinead thrusts out her hand, and Laura takes it immediately. They stare at each other, and I can tell they're testing each other's strength. Neither lets go, and it goes on way longer than any cock measuring handshake would. I look at Maks, who looks at me. For once, neither of us knows what to do.

"Laura, we should find our seats."

"Sinead, let's grab a drink while the line at the bar is short."

They finally release each other. They plaster fake smiles on their faces as they turn away from each other. Maks and I exchange another glance, unsure what to make of the standoff we just witnessed. We find our seats, and we're at a table that has us facing Maks and Laura at the next table over. Just before dessert, I could swear I see Sinead wink at Laura. I'm certain I saw Laura wink back.

"*Piccolina?*"

I lean to whisper to her as people at our table chat.

"Yes, Daddy?"

"Did you speak to Laura before tonight?"

"No."

"Then why did you just wink at each other?"

"We meant everything we said to each other earlier. Don't doubt that. But we also understand that cooler heads prevail. Neither of us is backing down, but we agree we'll try to get the men in our fam— She'll try to get the men in her family to back off while I ask you to get the men in your family to back off."

"Sinead, you were right the first time. It's our family. You know everyone accepts you and knows we're together for good."

"I know. I just don't want to be too presumptuous."

I brush my thumb along her nape before I kiss her cheek. I lean away as a server puts my dessert in front of me. I know what cream I'd rather have for dessert. I suffer through the final course before we say our goodbyes. As we leave the ballroom, Sinead points down a hallway.

"I'm going to the restroom."

I nod and watch her. When I see her get to the end of the hallway where the fire exit is, I head after her. She watches me separate from the crowd and stalk toward her. She waits until I'm close enough that she's not scared to go into the stairwell alone. When I walk through the door, I hear her heels tapping on the cement steps. I follow her down, taking my time. Every so often, she pauses, and I know she's trying to tell how far behind I am. She doesn't notice I'm watching her over the railing. I see when she stops beside a door leading to hotel rooms. She opens it, and I run down the last flight. I see her running down the hallway, her shoes in her hand. I catch her and wrap my arm around her waist. I fumble in my pocket, but I get the keycard out.

"You're coming with me, little girl."

I can feel her heart pounding. I push open the door before kicking it closed. It doesn't slam, instead quietly clicking closed. I twist us, so she's against the wall beside the door. I press my weight forward, pinning her in place.

"You thought you could run from me, *piccolina*. Don't you

know by now that I'll always come for you?"

I deepen my voice as the end, and she shivers.

"I'll always make you come, Daddy."

"That's right. You'll make me come in your mouth, in your hand, in your cunt, and in your ass. They're all mine."

"Your cum is all mine."

"Yes, it is. One of these days soon, I'm going to fuck you and when I come in your pussy, you're going to keep it all there. And I'm going to keep doing it until I get your pregnant. What do you think of that?"

"I want that, and you know it, Daddy."

"I won't you let you go, Sinead. Not unless you tell me to."

I press harder, but I'm careful not to hurt her.

"Please don't let go. I don't want to go anywhere without you."

"How do you want me to fuck you tonight? I have you now, and I can do whatever the fuck I want. But you can suggest something."

I laugh, and she sighs. I know I'm giving her the fantasy she wants. The more possessive I sound, the more she relaxes into this roleplaying.

"I want to suck you off, Daddy."

"Are you going to swallow?"

"If that's what you want."

"I want to come all over your lips and all over your tits. I want you sloppy with my cum."

I wrap my hand in her hair and tug. I pull up her dress and slide my fingers up her thighs. She's dripping for me, and I'm so fucking hard it's uncomfortable. I slide my fingers into her, and she tries to widen her feet. But she has no space to do it. I've caged her in. My other hand dives under her dress and caresses her ass before gripping the flange of the butt plug I put in her. I twist it until she moans.

"You know what'll happen if I let you open your legs. Then I'll have to spank you."

I put Ben Wa balls into her pussy between the salad and main course. I said I spotted someone to say hi to quickly, and she excused herself to the restroom. I followed her in, ate her out until she came, then stuck the little metal balls in her. We came back to the table from opposite directions, neither of us looking like I just had my tongue in her cunt. She must have had her pussy clenched tight while she ran down the stairs.

"Will you spank me, anyway?"

I step back enough to turn her to face me. My hand rests on her throat as I nip at her earlobe. I rub my cock against her pussy as my free hand grasps her ass and squeezes enough to push her onto her toes, but she doesn't complain.

"I'll do whatever the fuck I want, Sinead. Are you going to stop me?"

I know I'm holding her so tightly against the wall that it must be hard to breathe.

"No. I know I can't."

"Do you want me to stop, *piccolina*?"

"Never."

My mouth captures hers, and it's a brutal kiss that I control. I nip and suck, giving her no chance to pull away. But she doesn't want to. She's as into it as I am. She presses back against me, shifting restlessly, knowing she's driving me to the brink. We finally have to pull apart, or we both risk passing out.

"Daddy, I ache for you. Please, will you touch me?"

"I will, *piccolina*. Do you want to move onto something else, or do you want to keep this going?"

"Whatever you want."

I knew she would say that. At least, I was counting on it. I step away and lead her through the suite to the bedroom. I cover her eyes, and she jumps.

"Shh, *cuore*. Just a moment."

I hit the light switch with my elbow before I step around her. I felt her eyes close when my hands covered them. I let go, and when she opens them, she doesn't know what to look at. She glances down at me, then her eyes dart around the room before she focuses on me again. Her hands cover her mouth, and I smile as I pull her left one down. I laugh when she drops to her knees.

"I'm the one who's supposed to be down on bended knee, *piccolina*."

She just nods. I take both her hands and place them over my heart.

"Sinead, you have amazed me since the moment I met you. I didn't know I would walk into that conference room and meet the woman I'll love for the rest of my life. But I knew as soon as I saw you. You met me at a time when most people would have turned away from me. We've been through a lot in a short amount of time. But we've weathered these challenges together. We've had moments that tested our trust and our faith in each other, but nothing has broken us. It's only made us more determined to share our future. You get me in a way no one else ever has. I want to spend the rest of my days making you happy. I know there will be times when I fail, but I want to be there when you wake the next morning, so I can try all over again. I promise I'll give you everything you need, and I'll do my damnedest to give you everything you want. Will you marry me?"

"Yes!"

She flings her arms around, and if I were any smaller, she would have knocked me over. But I catch her and hold her. It's my turn to relax as we hug. With her, me in her arms, this is where I'm meant to be. I reach into my pocket and pull out a box. She looks down to see what I'm doing. She sits back on her

Sabine Barclay

heels as I open the lid. Her eyes widen, and her fingers cover
her mouth again. For a second time, I pry her left hand away.

"Oh my God, Gabriele. It's exquisite."

I slide the ring on as tears slip down her cheeks. She stares
at it before she presses the softest kiss to my lips. I help her to
her feet, and we strip before climbing into bed. I shift to hover
over her. She runs her hands along my shoulders and abs as she
opens her legs to me. I prop myself up on my right forearm as
my left hand cups her pussy. I slip my fingers into her and
retrieve the Ben Wa balls. I toss them onto our pile of clothes
before easing into her. We move together as though we've been
making love for years not weeks.

"Daddy, that feels so good. More."

I thrust harder and circle my hips. She Kegels, and I almost
come.

"Fuck, Sinead. You're going to get me off too fast."

She giggles.

"Good. I need to come, and I don't want to wait. I want to
make you come now."

I thrust again and again until she tightens around me. Her
arms, her legs, her pussy. She pulls me down so we're chest to
chest, belly to belly. My cocks pulses inside her as she moans. I
rest my forehead against hers as we share soft, short kisses.

"This was absolutely perfect, Gabe. Thank you."

"Anything for you, *cuore*."

I've always believed in soulmates. My parents are definitely
each other's. I've seen other pairs in my family. I just never
imagined I'd meet mine. I guess I figured I was too far past
redemption for God to remember me. But somehow, he saw fit
to bring this angel into my life. And she said yes.

"I love you, Daddy."

"I love you, *piccolina*."

Epilogue

Sinead

"Dad?"

I walk around his chair as my shoulders droop.

"Laney?"

"No, Dad. It's me. Sinead."

"Sinead?"

"Yes, Dad. It's me."

"Ah, my sweet daughter. The good one."

I glance up at Gabriele. I don't know what's hardest. When he doesn't remember me. When he thinks I'm my sister. When he reminds me of how hard it was to love Delaney.

"How're you feeling today?"

"Okay. I saw a rainbow."

I sigh. My smile is a sad one. It's snowing right now.

"Gabriele's here. Will you say hi?"

"Gabriele? Who's that?"

"My husband, Dad."

I cover my swollen belly as I move aside. If I hadn't already

423

loved Gabriele before he met my dad, I would have fallen in love right there and then. The day I introduced him was a rough one. My dad was super upset because he was disoriented and didn't know where he was. It scared him, so he was throwing anything he could reach. The nurses wanted to give him a sedative, and I was crying.

Gabriele walked in, sent the nurses away, sat me in a chair, and approached my dad calmly. He started talking to him about me. Telling him things I'd shared about my childhood. We both knew my dad didn't remember any of it, but he made it sound like he was telling a story. My dad stopped to listen to him. Gabriele helped him put on his coat and fastened the Velcro on his shoes. He helped my dad use his walker to go outside.

"Hi, Dad."

I watch Gabriele lean forward to give him a loose hug.

"Gabe?"

"Yes, Dad. It's me."

"Where's Sinead? Is she coming today?"

"She's right here."

He takes my hand and covers it and my dad's with both of his. I rest my head against my husband's shoulder, and it's like the weight of the world shifted from mine to his much broader ones. He wraps an arm around my waist, and I love the feel of his hand on my hip.

"Sinead?"

"Yeah, Dad. I'm here. Guess what."

"What?"

"We found out what we're having this morning."

"Oh?"

I know he doesn't understand what I mean, but for a moment, he sounds like the man I knew.

"Yeah. We're having a little girl."

"You're having a baby?"

"Yup. In a month."

We waited to find out. We weren't going to, but at the appointment this morning, we caved. For all our kinky talk, we waited a year to start trying, then it took us a year-and-a-half to get pregnant. I started to despair, and I knew Gabriele was upset too. But never once did he make me feel like a life with just the two of us would be anything less than perfect. We want this baby, but we've been happy as just a couple.

"Can you guess what we're going to name her?"

I don't get a response, but I never really expect one to my questions.

"Lily Anne."

"Lily Anne? That's my wife's name."

I fight back the tears.

"I know, Dad. It's such a pretty name."

"Just like my wife. Did you know I have two daughters? They're both as beautiful as their mother."

I close my eyes as the tears slip beneath my lashes. Gabriele holds me tighter, and I listen to him talk.

"I'd like to hear about them. Would you tell me?"

He pulls up a chair for each of us. We spend the next hour listening to my dad jump from story to story. Some actual memories and others made up from who knows where. Through the entire thing, my husband— a man I know plenty fear —a man who does horrible things to horrible people— a man who nearly spent his life in prison for a crime he didn't commit —my husband holds my hand and rubs my belly.

Gabriele. My fallen angel.

Thank you for reading Mafia Angel

Sabine Barclay, a nom de plume also writing Historical Romance as Celeste Barclay, lives near the Southern California coast with her husband and sons. Growing up in the Midwest, Celeste enjoyed spending as much time in and on the water as she could. Now she lives near the beach. She's an avid swimmer, a hopeful future surfer, and a former rower. She loves writing romances that will make your toes curl and your granny blush.

Subscribe to Sabine's bimonthly newsletter to receive exclusive insider perks.

www.sabinebarclay.com

Join the fun and get exclusive insider giveaways, sneak peeks, and new release announcements in
<u>Sabine Barclay's Facebook Dubious Dames Group</u>

Do you also enjoy steamy Historical Romance? Discover Sabine's books written as Celeste Barclay.

The Mancinelli Brotherhood

Mafia Heir

BOOK ONE SNEAK PEEK

LUCA

This asshole is pissing me off. We've been going around in circles for five minutes, and the longer we stand out here, the greater the likelihood someone will spot us. I have a sixth sense about these things. It's why I'm still alive at the ripe old age of thirty-one.

"Espinoza, enough already. Either sell to us or don't, but we set the price. Your tequila is good, but it isn't nectar from the gods."

I'm watching Carlos Espinoza, some lackey for the Mexican Culiacán Cartel, try to maneuver me into paying more than the agreed upon price. I know it's so he can skim off the top.

"It's as close as you're going to get. You've upped the order, so the price per case goes up."

My uncle, Salvatore Mancinelli, is the New York don. He negotiated this deal, and I warned him it was a bad idea. But what do I know as his underboss and heir? I'm not backing down.

"Haven't you ever heard of a bulk discount? The more I order the better the price should be. No one else around here is buying from you. You know we're your only choice in three out of five boroughs. You aren't going to the Bronx because you won't get more than pennies there. You aren't going to Queens because you don't want to run into the Colombians. You aren't going to Manhattan because then you face the bratva along with us. And what are you going to do in Staten Island? Sell to us anyway? We control Staten Island and Brooklyn when it comes to liquor stores, so take the money and go."

"Luca, there are plenty of liquor stores in Brooklyn that aren't owned by Italians. I'll go there."

We aren't friends. He's patronizing me by using my first name. Fuck him and the horse he rode in on. I have other solutions for this shit.

"And I'll just take what I want from them for free. That's not a half bad idea. The deal's over. Take your shit with the worm in it and go."

"Motherfucking racist. Not all tequila has a worm in it."

"You're selling Mezcal. It's known for the fucking worm. I wouldn't start calling me names, you *penche hijo de puta.*" Fucking son of a bitch.

He has twenty-five crates of stolen tequila that he's trying to offload because he knows he can't sell it at his own liquor store.

"What did you call me?"

Carlos takes what he thinks is a menacing step forward, and his two bodyguards do the same. Not smart. Neither of my two bodyguards nor I react, but the three men in each of my cars open their doors. They won't do more than that. It's just a reminder that the Culiacán can try, but the *Cosa Nostra* still run New York City.

"This is the third and final time I say this. Sell or leave."

Every head turns toward the liquor store's back door as it opens. A gorgeous blonde steps out, and I wish I had the time to appreciate her beauty, but she's about to die. Carlos and his men draw their guns and pivot toward her. My men pull their weapons too, but we keep them pointed at the Mexicans. The woman stands like a deer in the headlights for a second before ducking behind the industrial garbage dumpster like a frightened rabbit. Three shots hit the metal almost at the same moment. That's all it takes for my men and me. The two bodyguards standing with me aim for a guard each, and I set my sights on Carlos. We squeeze our triggers, and the men fall.

Screeching tires tell me Carlos's driver takes off. I hear more gunshots as at least one soldier in my cars tries to shoot the escaping vehicle. Glass shatters, but the sedan keeps going. I hear more tires squeal as one of my SUVs takes off and chases the guy. I holster my gun and wave my men to do the same.

I inch forward toward the trash can, but I see the shadow shift. The woman bolts from the other side. She's still the frightened rabbit, but I'm the fox pursuing her. She's fast, I'll give her that. But she has to be at least a foot shorter than me. My legs are a lot longer and cover a lot more ground with each stride.

She weaves among the cars, most likely believing it's harder to hit a moving object. She isn't wrong, but I have no intention of shooting her. I push myself harder and pounce as she darts out and tries to cross the last stretch of parking lot to reach a better lit area near a bus stop. I lunge.

"Stop running, *piccolina*. I won't hurt you."

I wrap my arms around her and pull her back against my chest, but I'm quick to spin her around and put space between us as I grasp her arms. Of course, she fights me.

"If I wanted you dead, I would have shot at you, too."

"It doesn't mean you won't kill me after."

She's breathless as she continues to struggle. I almost let go to take a step back, insulted at what she implied. But I can't blame her. If I were a woman, I'd be terrified of the same thing.

"I'm not going to rape you. I'm going to talk to you."

"Talk? You are not a man who talks if you just killed a guy."

"To keep him and his men from killing you. I told you, if I wanted you dead, I would have shot at you too. And I wouldn't have missed."

She stops struggling against me, but her eyes continue to dart from one place to another, trying to find somewhere to flee. I know I can keep her in place with only one hand, so I release her left arm. I still have a firm hold on her right one, but I haven't held it nearly as tightly as I could.

"I'm Luca. I know you figured out you interrupted something you shouldn't have. Did that man know who you are?"

"Yes."

"What about his driver? Would he know you?"

"Yes."

"Do you have a name?"

"Yes."

"*Piccolina*, we won't get very far if yes is all you can say. Are you willing to answer me with more than one word?"

"No."

I knew that was coming, and I grin. I can't help it. I wasn't wrong about her being gorgeous, but I doubt she wants to know that's what I think. At least, not if I want her to know I won't assault her.

"Fine. I have more than twenty questions I can ask that you can answer with one word. Do you work at the store?"

"Sometimes."

Ah, an improvement.

"Did Carlos know you were still working?"

"No."

"Do you have a car, or do you take the subway or bus?"

She raises her chin and remains silent. Smart but counterproductive.

"The subway or the bus will get you killed. You're too easy to find and follow. Do you have a car?"

"Yes."

"Can you stay with someone instead of going home?"

She refuses to answer.

"If that man knew you and you sometimes work in the store, then he knew where you live. If he found that out, so will someone in his cartel."

"I know. Let me go. The longer I stand here, the more likely someone is to come back for me."

"No one will touch you while I'm here."

"Arrogant. If he shot at me, he would have shot at you."

"And he would have died, anyway. What's your name?"

"Jane."

"Look, I know you won't get in one of my cars and let me drive you somewhere. In most cases, I would say that's a smart move. But you did nothing wrong tonight except for leave work at the wrong time. I know that, and you know that. But the Culiacán won't see it that way, *piccolina*."

She freezes for no more than five seconds before she trembles so much that I can see it. I don't know what drives me next, but it's the same instinct that's made me call her little girl three times. I pull her to my chest and tuck her head against it. I stroke her hair down to her shoulders, rubbing my hand up and down her back. This is the most inopportune moment to notice she isn't wearing a bra. I will my body not to react.

"What does that mean?"

Her voice is barely more than a whisper, but I know what she's asking.

"It means little girl."

"I should be insulted, but the way you say it..."

"It has nothing to do with your height. I know you're not a child."

God, do I know she's not. She feels amazing. Her tits are soft as they press against me, and I can see she has the most delectable ass. I'd love nothing more than to cup it and squeeze until she goes up on her toes and begs for me to wrap her legs around my waist and fuck her. For fuck's sake. Stop, you disgusting asshole. That is not what you need to be thinking about.

"Why didn't you shoot me? Whatever you were talking about, if it was with a Cartel member, then it wasn't completely legal. Carlos didn't want me alive to talk about seeing you together. Why are you letting me live?"

"I told you. You did nothing wrong but try to leave work. He should have checked the building before starting the meeting. That was on him. The only thing I take issue with is you leaving by yourself and walking into a dimly lit parking lot. I suspect you do that often, and that's too dangerous. Jane Doe, I don't hurt women."

Mafia Sinner

Mafia Beauty

Mafia Angel

Mafia Redeemer

Mafia Star

The Ivankov Brotherhood

Bratva Darling

BOOK ONE SNEAK PEEK

LAURA

As I sit across from the four Kutsenko brothers, I press my lips together to keep from drooling. No four men should be so strikingly handsome. Not all from the same family, anyway. I fight a valiant battle against letting my gaze drift toward the eldest, Maksim, whose ice-blue eyes bore into me. After years of negotiating billion-dollar investment contracts while facing countless ruthless businessmen, I've learned to keep my expression studiously blank. But it's a true struggle today. Instead, I focus my attention on the squirrelly lawyer sitting across the conference table. While he's disingenuous with each comment, he's a good negotiator. But I'm better. How cliché am I?

While I feel Maksim watching me, I focus on Dmitry Yakovitch as he continues to argue the merits of the venture capitalist company I represent, RK Capital Group, merging with Kutsenko Partners. What he means is the merits of Kutsenko Partners acquiring RK Capital Group, then stripping it and making it another money-laundering shell corporation. While most people in New York have little awareness of the Russian mafia, I do. The Kutsenko brothers' names appear on no titles or deeds anywhere in New York City, but it wasn't difficult to determine which shell companies likely belong to them. Their assumption that I'm unfamiliar with them is proving beneficial to me as they continue to whisper amongst themselves in Russian. I think they may even believe they're convincing me that they don't speak much English.

The senior partners of RK Capital Group know who I'm negotiating with, though they may not know I'm aware of these Russians' more nefarious operations. They've given me the go-ahead to agree to a merger with an eventual acquisition, but only for the right price. A price to the tune of twenty billion dollars. Considering an investment firm like Goldman Sachs is worth nearly one-hundred-and-twenty billion dollars, my clients' asking price appears reasonable.

"Mr. Yakovitch, I shall stop you now." I raise my left hand, pen caught between my index and middle fingers. When I have his attention, I lean back in my chair and casually twirl the pen over my index finger and thumb. "Fifty billion is my clients' asking price. You know that. Your clients know that. RK doesn't oppose the merger. What they oppose is the insulting offer you've made. It's nearly noon, and I'm hungry, Mr. Yakovitch. I have a delicious ham sandwich waiting for me. I even have three chocolate chip cookies waiting for me. If we aren't going to make any progress, I shall let you go, so I can move onto my eagerly anticipated lunch."

I cant my head just enough for me to appear as though my gaze rests solely on the opposing attorney's face, but I can see each Kutsenko brothers' reaction. My face battles yet again against showing my emotions as I fight not to smirk. Their muted but surprised expressions confirm what I already know.

"Please tell your clients to make a reasonable counteroffer, or I will conclude this meeting and enjoy my ham sandwich and cookies."

Dmitry glares at me before turning to Maksim and his three brothers. In rapid Russian, he doesn't interpret my suggestion. Oh no. There's no need for that. I can't catch every word because his voice is too low. But I catch something along the lines of "The bitch refuses to budge. What now? A fucking ham sandwich. More like a stick up her ass."

Maksim swivels his chair to look at his brothers. In Russian, he says, "Fifty billion is ridiculous. She's not so stupid or naïve not to know that. My guess is they'll settle for twenty billion. We offer fifteen."

"That's barely better than what we already offered," Aleksei, the second-oldest brother, argues. "She'll be eating the fucking sandwich and dipping her cookies in milk before we walk out the door. We need the buildings."

"We offer twenty, Maks," Bogdan, the youngest, insists.

As I watch the brothers discuss, their voices barely lowered, I pull my lunch sack from the black leather satchel by my feet and set it beside my laptop. It's a ridiculously pink floral bag with an embroidered monogram, the L and D overlapping. It's an empty prop, but they don't know that. I watch as five sets of eyes narrow. I offer a smile that would appear innocent in any setting other than this meeting. It's patronizing, and I know it.

Bratva Sweetheart

Bratva Treasure

Bratva Beauty

Bratva Angel

Bratva Jewel

Printed in the USA
CPSIA information can be obtained
at www.ICGtesting.com
JSHW080059281023
50722JS00008B/121

9 781648 395055